John Griffith London (born **John Griffith Chaney**; January 12, 1876 – November 22, 1916) was an American novelist, journalist, and social activist. A pioneer in the world of commercial magazine fiction, he was one of the first writers to become a worldwide celebrity and earn a large fortune from writing. He was also an innovator in the genre that would later become known as science fiction. His most famous works include The Call of the Wild and White Fang, both set in the Klondike Gold Rush, as well as the short stories "To Build a Fire", "An Odyssey of the North", and "Love of Life". He also wrote about the South Pacific in stories such as "The Pearls of Parlay" and "The Heathen". London was part of the radical literary group "The Crowd" in San Francisco and a passionate advocate of unionization, socialism, and the rights of workers. He wrote several powerful works dealing with these topics, such as his dystopian novel The Iron Heel, his non-fiction exposé The People of the Abyss, and The War of the Classes. (Source: Wikipedia)

Literary works:
The Cruise of the Dazzler (1902)
A Daughter of the Snows (1902)
The Call of the Wild (1903)
The Kempton-Wace Letters (1903)
The Sea-Wolf (1904)
The Game (1905)
White Fang (1906)
Before Adam (1907)
The Iron Heel (1908)
Martin Eden (1909)
Burning Daylight (1910)
Adventure (1911)
The Scarlet Plague (1912)
A Son of the Sun (1912)
The Abysmal Brute (1913)
The Valley of the Moon (1913)

THE SON OF
THE WOLF
&
LOST FACE

JACK LONDON

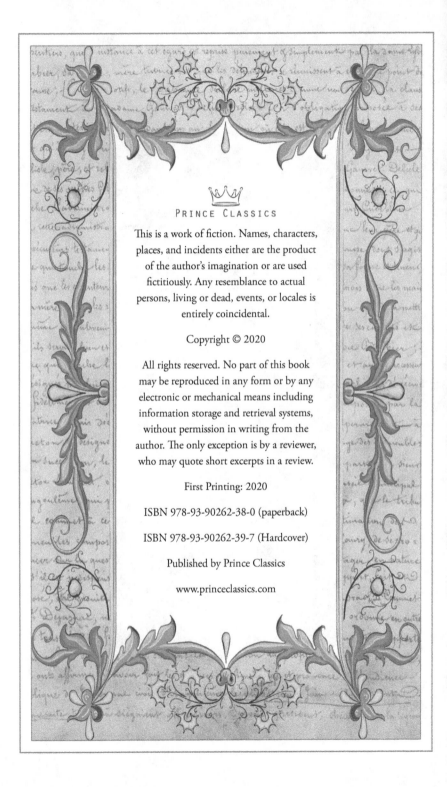

PRINCE CLASSICS

First Printing: 2020

ISBN 978-93-90262-38-0 (paperback)

ISBN 978-93-90262-39-7 (Hardcover)

Published by Prince Classics

www.princeclassics.com

Contents

THE SON OF
THE WOLF
&
LOST FACE

THE SON OF THE WOLF

The White Silence

'Carmen won't last more than a couple of days.' Mason spat out a chunk of ice and surveyed the poor animal ruefully, then put her foot in his mouth and proceeded to bite out the ice which clustered cruelly between the toes.

'I never saw a dog with a highfalutin' name that ever was worth a rap,' he said, as he concluded his task and shoved her aside. 'They just fade away and die under the responsibility. Did ye ever see one go wrong with a sensible name like Cassiar, Siwash, or Husky? No, sir! Take a look at Shookum here, he's—' Snap! The lean brute flashed up, the white teeth just missing Mason's throat.

'Ye will, will ye?' A shrewd clout behind the ear with the butt of the dog whip stretched the animal in the snow, quivering softly, a yellow slaver dripping from its fangs.

'As I was saying, just look at Shookum here—he's got the spirit. Bet ye he eats Carmen before the week's out.' 'I'll bank another proposition against that,' replied Malemute Kid, reversing the frozen bread placed before the fire to thaw. 'We'll eat Shookum before the trip is over. What d'ye say, Ruth?' The Indian woman settled the coffee with a piece of ice, glanced from Malemute Kid to her husband, then at the dogs, but vouchsafed no reply. It was such a palpable truism that none was necessary. Two hundred miles of unbroken trail in prospect, with a scant six days' grub for themselves and none for the dogs, could admit no other alternative. The two men and the woman grouped about the fire and began their meager meal. The dogs lay in their harnesses for it was a midday halt, and watched each mouthful enviously.

'No more lunches after today,' said Malemute Kid. 'And we've got to keep a close eye on the dogs—they're getting vicious. They'd just as soon pull a fellow down as not, if they get a chance.' 'And I was president of an Epworth once, and taught in the Sunday school.' Having irrelevantly delivered himself of this, Mason fell into a dreamy contemplation of his steaming moccasins, but was aroused by Ruth filling his cup.

'Thank God, we've got slathers of tea! I've seen it growing, down in Tennessee. What wouldn't I give for a hot corn pone just now! Never mind, Ruth; you won't starve much longer, nor wear moccasins either.' The woman threw off her gloom at this, and in her eyes welled up a great love for her white lord—the first white man she had ever seen—the first man whom she had known to treat a woman as something better than a mere animal or beast of burden.

'Yes, Ruth,' continued her husband, having recourse to the macaronic jargon in which it was alone possible for them to understand each other; 'wait till we clean up and pull for the Outside. We'll take the White Man's canoe and go to the Salt Water. Yes, bad water, rough water—great mountains dance up and down all the time. And so big, so far, so far away—you travel ten sleep, twenty sleep, forty sleep'—he graphically enumerated the days on his fingers—'all the time water, bad water. Then you come to great village, plenty people, just the same mosquitoes next summer. Wigwams oh, so high—ten, twenty pines.

'Hi-yu skookum!' He paused impotently, cast an appealing glance at Malemute Kid, then laboriously placed the twenty pines, end on end, by sign language. Malemute Kid smiled with cheery cynicism; but Ruth's eyes were wide with wonder, and with pleasure; for she half believed he was joking, and such condescension pleased her poor woman's heart.

'And then you step into a—a box, and pouf! up you go.' He tossed his empty cup in the air by way of illustration and, as he deftly caught it, cried: 'And biff! down you come. Oh, great medicine men! You go Fort Yukon. I go Arctic City—twenty-five sleep—big string, all the time—I catch him string—I say, "Hello, Ruth! How are ye?"—and you say, "Is that my good husband?"—and I say, "Yes"—and you say, "No can bake good bread, no more soda"—then I say, "Look in cache, under flour; good-by." You look and catch plenty soda. All the time you Fort Yukon, me Arctic City. Hi-yu medicine man!' Ruth smiled so ingenuously at the fairy story that both men burst into laughter. A row among the dogs cut short the wonders of the Outside, and by the time the snarling combatants were separated, she had lashed the sleds and all was ready for the trail.—'Mush! Baldy! Hi! Mush on!'

Mason worked his whip smartly and, as the dogs whined low in the traces, broke out the sled with the gee pole. Ruth followed with the second team, leaving Malemute Kid, who had helped her start, to bring up the rear. Strong man, brute that he was, capable of felling an ox at a blow, he could not bear to beat the poor animals, but humored them as a dog driver rarely does—nay, almost wept with them in their misery.

'Come, mush on there, you poor sore-footed brutes!' he murmured, after several ineffectual attempts to start the load. But his patience was at last rewarded, and though whimpering with pain, they hastened to join their fellows.

No more conversation; the toil of the trail will not permit such extravagance.

And of all deadening labors, that of the Northland trail is the worst. Happy is the man who can weather a day's travel at the price of silence, and that on a beaten track. And of all heartbreaking labors, that of breaking trail is the worst. At every step the great webbed shoe sinks till the snow is level with the knee. Then up, straight up, the deviation of a fraction of an inch being a certain precursor of disaster, the snowshoe must be lifted till the surface is cleared; then forward, down, and the other foot is raised perpendicularly for the matter of half a yard. He who tries this for the first time, if haply he avoids bringing his shoes in dangerous propinquity and measures not his length on the treacherous footing, will give up exhausted at the end of a hundred yards; he who can keep out of the way of the dogs for a whole day may well crawl into his sleeping bag with a clear conscience and a pride which passeth all understanding; and he who travels twenty sleeps on the Long Trail is a man whom the gods may envy.

The afternoon wore on, and with the awe, born of the White Silence, the voiceless travelers bent to their work. Nature has many tricks wherewith she convinces man of his finity—the ceaseless flow of the tides, the fury of the storm, the shock of the earthquake, the long roll of heaven's artillery—but the most tremendous, the most stupefying of all, is the passive phase of the White Silence. All movement ceases, the sky clears, the heavens are as brass; the slightest whisper seems sacrilege, and man becomes timid, affrighted at the sound of his own voice. Sole speck of life journeying across the ghostly wastes of a dead world, he trembles at his audacity, realizes that his is a maggot's life, nothing more.

Strange thoughts arise unsummoned, and the mystery of all things strives for utterance.

And the fear of death, of God, of the universe, comes over him—the hope of the Resurrection and the Life, the yearning for immortality, the vain striving of the imprisoned essence—it is then, if ever, man walks alone with God.

So wore the day away. The river took a great bend, and Mason headed his team for the cutoff across the narrow neck of land. But the dogs balked at the high bank. Again and again, though Ruth and Malemute Kid were shoving on the sled, they slipped back. Then came the concerted effort. The miserable creatures, weak from hunger, exerted their last strength. Up—up—the sled poised on the top of the bank; but the leader swung the string of dogs behind him to the right, fouling Mason's snowshoes. The result was grievous.

Mason was whipped off his feet; one of the dogs fell in the traces; and the sled toppled back, dragging everything to the bottom again.

Slash! the whip fell among the dogs savagely, especially upon the one which had fallen.

'Don't,—Mason,' entreated Malemute Kid; 'the poor devil's on its last legs. Wait and we'll put my team on.' Mason deliberately withheld the whip till the last word had fallen, then out flashed the long lash, completely curling about the offending creature's body.

Carmen—for it was Carmen—cowered in the snow, cried piteously, then rolled over on her side.

It was a tragic moment, a pitiful incident of the trail—a dying dog, two comrades in anger.

Ruth glanced solicitously from man to man. But Malemute Kid restrained himself, though there was a world of reproach in his eyes, and, bending over the dog, cut the traces. No word was spoken. The teams were doublespanned and the difficulty overcome; the sleds were under way again, the dying dog dragging herself along in the rear. As long as an animal can travel, it is not shot, and this last chance is accorded it—the crawling into camp, if it can, in the hope of a moose being killed.

Already penitent for his angry action, but too stubborn to make amends, Mason toiled on at the head of the cavalcade, little dreaming that danger hovered in the air. The timber clustered thick in the sheltered bottom, and through this they threaded their way. Fifty feet or more from the trail towered a lofty pine. For generations it had stood there, and for generations destiny had had this one end in view—perhaps the same had been decreed of Mason.

He stooped to fasten the loosened thong of his moccasin. The sleds came to a halt, and the dogs lay down in the snow without a whimper. The stillness was weird; not a breath rustled the frost-encrusted forest; the cold and silence of outer space had chilled the heart and smote the trembling lips of nature. A sigh pulsed through the air—they did not seem to actually hear it, but rather felt it, like the premonition of movement in a motionless void. Then the great tree, burdened with its weight of years and snow, played its last part in the tragedy of life. He heard the warning crash and attempted to spring up but, almost erect, caught the blow squarely on the shoulder.

The sudden danger, the quick death—how often had Malemute Kid faced it! The pine needles were still quivering as he gave his commands and sprang into action. Nor did the Indian girl faint or raise her voice in idle wailing, as might many of her white sisters. At his order, she threw her weight on the end of a quickly extemporized handspike, easing the pressure and listening to her husband's groans, while Malemute Kid attacked the tree with his ax. The steel rang merrily as it bit into the frozen trunk, each stroke being accompanied by a forced, audible respiration, the 'Huh!' 'Huh!' of the woodsman.

At last the Kid laid the pitiable thing that was once a man in the snow. But worse than his comrade's pain was the dumb anguish in the woman's face, the blended look of hopeful, hopeless query. Little was said; those of the Northland are early taught the futility of words and the inestimable value of deeds. With the temperature at sixty-five below zero, a man cannot lie many minutes in the snow and live. So the sled lashings were cut, and the sufferer, rolled in furs, laid on a couch of boughs. Before him roared a fire, built of the very wood which wrought the mishap. Behind and partially over him was stretched the primitive fly—a piece of canvas, which caught the radiating heat and threw it back and down upon him—a trick which men may know who study physics at the fount.

And men who have shared their bed with death know when the call is sounded. Mason was terribly crushed. The most cursory examination revealed it.

His right arm, leg, and back were broken; his limbs were paralyzed from the hips; and the likelihood of internal injuries was large. An occasional moan was his only sign of life.

No hope; nothing to be done. The pitiless night crept slowly by—Ruth's portion, the despairing stoicism of her race, and Malemute Kid adding new lines to his face of bronze.

In fact, Mason suffered least of all, for he spent his time in eastern Tennessee, in the Great Smoky Mountains, living over the scenes of his childhood. And most pathetic was the melody of his long-forgotten Southern vernacular, as he raved of swimming holes and coon hunts and watermelon raids. It was as Greek to Ruth, but the Kid understood and felt—felt as only one can feel who has been shut out for years from all that civilization means.

Morning brought consciousness to the stricken man, and Malemute Kid bent closer to catch his whispers.

'You remember when we foregathered on the Tanana, four years come next ice run? I didn't care so much for her then. It was more like she was pretty, and there was a smack of excitement about it, I think. But d'ye know,

I've come to think a heap of her. She's been a good wife to me, always at my shoulder in the pinch. And when it comes to trading, you know there isn't her equal. D'ye recollect the time she shot the Moosehorn Rapids to pull you and me off that rock, the bullets whipping the water like hailstones?—and the time of the famine at Nuklukyeto?—when she raced the ice run to bring the news?

'Yes, she's been a good wife to me, better'n that other one. Didn't know I'd been there?

'Never told you, eh? Well, I tried it once, down in the States. That's why I'm here. Been raised together, too. I came away to give her a chance for divorce. She got it.

'But that's got nothing to do with Ruth. I had thought of cleaning up and pulling for the Outside next year—her and I—but it's too late. Don't send her back to her people, Kid. It's beastly hard for a woman to go back. Think of it!—nearly four years on our bacon and beans and flour and dried fruit, and then to go back to her fish and caribou. It's not good for her to have tried our ways, to come to know they're better'n her people's, and then return to them. Take care of her, Kid, why don't you—but no, you always fought shy of them—and you never told me why you came to this country. Be kind to her, and send her back to the States as soon as you can. But fix it so she can come back—liable to get homesick, you know.

'And the youngster—it's drawn us closer, Kid. I only hope it is a boy. Think of it!—flesh of my flesh, Kid. He mustn't stop in this country. And if it's a girl, why, she can't. Sell my furs; they'll fetch at least five thousand, and I've got as much more with the company. And handle my interests with yours. I think that bench claim will show up. See that he gets a good schooling; and Kid, above all, don't let him come back. This country was not made for white men.

'I'm a gone man, Kid. Three or four sleeps at the best. You've got to go on. You must go on! Remember, it's my wife, it's my boy—O God! I hope it's a boy! You can't stay by me—and I charge you, a dying man, to pull on.'

19

'Give me three days,' pleaded Malemute Kid. 'You may change for the better; something may turn up.'

'No.'

'Just three days.'

'You must pull on.'

'Two days.'

'It's my wife and my boy, Kid. You would not ask it.'

'One day.'

'No, no! I charge—'

'Only one day. We can shave it through on the grub, and I might knock over a moose.'

'No—all right; one day, but not a minute more. And, Kid, don't—don't leave me to face it alone. Just a shot, one pull on the trigger. You understand. Think of it! Think of it! Flesh of my flesh, and I'll never live to see him!

'Send Ruth here. I want to say good-by and tell her that she must think of the boy and not wait till I'm dead. She might refuse to go with you if I didn't. Goodby, old man; good-by.

'Kid! I say—a—sink a hole above the pup, next to the slide. I panned out forty cents on my shovel there.

'And, Kid!' He stooped lower to catch the last faint words, the dying man's surrender of his pride. 'I'm sorry—for—you know—Carmen.' Leaving the girl crying softly over her man, Malemute Kid slipped into his parka and snowshoes, tucked his rifle under his arm, and crept away into the forest. He was no tyro in the stern sorrows of the Northland, but never had he faced so stiff a problem as this. In the abstract, it was a plain, mathematical proposition—three possible lives as against one doomed one. But now he hesitated. For five years, shoulder to shoulder, on the rivers and trails, in the camps and mines, facing death by field and flood and famine, had they knitted the bonds of their comradeship. So close was the tie that he had often

20

been conscious of a vague jealousy of Ruth, from the first time she had come between. And now it must be severed by his own hand.

Though he prayed for a moose, just one moose, all game seemed to have deserted the land, and nightfall found the exhausted man crawling into camp, lighthanded, heavyhearted. An uproar from the dogs and shrill cries from Ruth hastened him.

Bursting into the camp, he saw the girl in the midst of the snarling pack, laying about her with an ax. The dogs had broken the iron rule of their masters and were rushing the grub.

He joined the issue with his rifle reversed, and the hoary game of natural selection was played out with all the ruthlessness of its primeval environment. Rifle and ax went up and down, hit or missed with monotonous regularity; lithe bodies flashed, with wild eyes and dripping fangs; and man and beast fought for supremacy to the bitterest conclusion. Then the beaten brutes crept to the edge of the firelight, licking their wounds, voicing their misery to the stars.

The whole stock of dried salmon had been devoured, and perhaps five pounds of flour remained to tide them over two hundred miles of wilderness. Ruth returned to her husband, while Malemute Kid cut up the warm body of one of the dogs, the skull of which had been crushed by the ax. Every portion was carefully put away, save the hide and offal, which were cast to his fellows of the moment before.

Morning brought fresh trouble. The animals were turning on each other. Carmen, who still clung to her slender thread of life, was downed by the pack. The lash fell among them unheeded. They cringed and cried under the blows, but refused to scatter till the last wretched bit had disappeared—bones, hide, hair, everything.

Malemute Kid went about his work, listening to Mason, who was back in Tennessee, delivering tangled discourses and wild exhortations to his brethren of other days.

Taking advantage of neighboring pines, he worked rapidly, and Ruth watched him make a cache similar to those sometimes used by hunters to preserve their meat from the wolverines and dogs. One after the other, he bent the tops of two small pines toward each other and nearly to the ground, making them fast with thongs of moosehide. Then he beat the dogs into submission and harnessed them to two of the sleds, loading the same with everything but the furs which enveloped Mason. These he wrapped and lashed tightly about him, fastening either end of the robes to the bent pines. A single stroke of his hunting knife would release them and send the body high in the air.

Ruth had received her husband's last wishes and made no struggle. Poor girl, she had learned the lesson of obedience well. From a child, she had bowed, and seen all women bow, to the lords of creation, and it did not seem in the nature of things for woman to resist. The Kid permitted her one outburst of grief, as she kissed her husband—her own people had no such custom—then led her to the foremost sled and helped her into her snowshoes. Blindly, instinctively, she took the gee pole and whip, and 'mushed' the dogs out on the trail. Then he returned to Mason, who had fallen into a coma, and long after she was out of sight crouched by the fire, waiting, hoping, praying for his comrade to die.

It is not pleasant to be alone with painful thoughts in the White Silence. The silence of gloom is merciful, shrouding one as with protection and breathing a thousand intangible sympathies; but the bright White Silence, clear and cold, under steely skies, is pitiless.

An hour passed—two hours—but the man would not die. At high noon the sun, without raising its rim above the southern horizon, threw a suggestion of fire athwart the heavens, then quickly drew it back. Malemute Kid roused and dragged himself to his comrade's side. He cast one glance about him. The White Silence seemed to sneer, and a great fear came upon him. There was a sharp report; Mason swung into his aerial sepulcher, and Malemute Kid lashed the dogs into a wild gallop as he fled across the snow.

The Son of the Wolf

Man rarely places a proper valuation upon his womankind, at least not until deprived of them. He has no conception of the subtle atmosphere exhaled by the sex feminine, so long as he bathes in it; but let it be withdrawn, and an ever-growing void begins to manifest itself in his existence, and he becomes hungry, in a vague sort of way, for a something so indefinite that he cannot characterize it. If his comrades have no more experience than himself, they will shake their heads dubiously and dose him with strong physic. But the hunger will continue and become stronger; he will lose interest in the things of his everyday life and wax morbid; and one day, when the emptiness has become unbearable, a revelation will dawn upon him.

In the Yukon country, when this comes to pass, the man usually provisions a poling boat, if it is summer, and if winter, harnesses his dogs, and heads for the Southland. A few months later, supposing him to be possessed of a faith in the country, he returns with a wife to share with him in that faith, and incidentally in his hardships. This but serves to show the innate selfishness of man. It also brings us to the trouble of 'Scruff' Mackenzie, which occurred in the old days, before the country was stampeded and staked by a tidal-wave of the che-cha-quas, and when the Klondike's only claim to notice was its salmon fisheries.

'Scruff' Mackenzie bore the earmarks of a frontier birth and a frontier life.

His face was stamped with twenty-five years of incessant struggle with Nature in her wildest moods,—the last two, the wildest and hardest of all, having been spent in groping for the gold which lies in the shadow of the Arctic Circle. When the yearning sickness came upon him, he was not surprised, for he was a practical man and had seen other men thus stricken. But he showed no sign of his malady, save that he worked harder. All summer he fought mosquitoes and washed the sure-thing bars of the Stuart River for a double grubstake. Then he floated a raft of houselogs down the Yukon to

Forty Mile, and put together as comfortable a cabin as any the camp could boast of. In fact, it showed such cozy promise that many men elected to be his partner and to come and live with him. But he crushed their aspirations with rough speech, peculiar for its strength and brevity, and bought a double supply of grub from the trading-post.

As has been noted, 'Scruff' Mackenzie was a practical man. If he wanted a thing he usually got it, but in doing so, went no farther out of his way than was necessary. Though a son of toil and hardship, he was averse to a journey of six hundred miles on the ice, a second of two thousand miles on the ocean, and still a third thousand miles or so to his last stamping-grounds,—all in the mere quest of a wife. Life was too short. So he rounded up his dogs, lashed a curious freight to his sled, and faced across the divide whose westward slopes were drained by the head-reaches of the Tanana.

He was a sturdy traveler, and his wolf-dogs could work harder and travel farther on less grub than any other team in the Yukon. Three weeks later he strode into a hunting-camp of the Upper Tanana Sticks. They marveled at his temerity; for they had a bad name and had been known to kill white men for as trifling a thing as a sharp ax or a broken rifle.

But he went among them single-handed, his bearing being a delicious composite of humility, familiarity, sang-froid, and insolence. It required a deft hand and deep knowledge of the barbaric mind effectually to handle such diverse weapons; but he was a past-master in the art, knowing when to conciliate and when to threaten with Jove-like wrath.

He first made obeisance to the Chief Thling-Tinneh, presenting him with a couple of pounds of black tea and tobacco, and thereby winning his most cordial regard. Then he mingled with the men and maidens, and that night gave a potlach.

The snow was beaten down in the form of an oblong, perhaps a hundred feet in length and quarter as many across. Down the center a long fire was built, while either side was carpeted with spruce boughs. The lodges were forsaken, and the fivescore or so members of the tribe gave tongue to their folk-chants in honor of their guest.

'Scruff' Mackenzie's two years had taught him the not many hundred words of their vocabulary, and he had likewise conquered their deep gutturals, their Japanese idioms, constructions, and honorific and agglutinative particles. So he made oration after their manner, satisfying their instinctive poetry-love with crude flights of eloquence and metaphorical contortions. After Thling-Tinneh and the Shaman had responded in kind, he made trifling presents to the menfolk, joined in their singing, and proved an expert in their fifty-two-stick gambling game.

And they smoked his tobacco and were pleased. But among the younger men there was a defiant attitude, a spirit of braggadocio, easily understood by the raw insinuations of the toothless squaws and the giggling of the maidens. They had known few white men, 'Sons of the Wolf,' but from those few they had learned strange lessons.

Nor had 'Scruff' Mackenzie, for all his seeming carelessness, failed to note these phenomena. In truth, rolled in his sleeping-furs, he thought it all over, thought seriously, and emptied many pipes in mapping out a campaign. One maiden only had caught his fancy,—none other than Zarinska, daughter to the chief. In features, form, and poise, answering more nearly to the white man's type of beauty, she was almost an anomaly among her tribal sisters. He would possess her, make her his wife, and name her—ah, he would name her Gertrude! Having thus decided, he rolled over on his side and dropped off to sleep, a true son of his all-conquering race, a Samson among the Philistines.

It was slow work and a stiff game; but 'Scruff' Mackenzie maneuvered cunningly, with an unconcern which served to puzzle the Sticks. He took great care to impress the men that he was a sure shot and a mighty hunter, and the camp rang with his plaudits when he brought down a moose at six hundred yards. Of a night he visited in Chief Thling-Tinneh's lodge of moose and cariboo skins, talking big and dispensing tobacco with a lavish hand. Nor did he fail to likewise honor the Shaman; for he realized the medicine-man's influence with his people, and was anxious to make of him an ally. But that worthy was high and mighty, refused to be propitiated, and was unerringly marked down as a prospective enemy.

Though no opening presented for an interview with Zarinska, Mackenzie stole many a glance to her, giving fair warning of his intent. And well she knew, yet coquettishly surrounded herself with a ring of women whenever the men were away and he had a chance. But he was in no hurry; besides, he knew she could not help but think of him, and a few days of such thought would only better his suit.

At last, one night, when he deemed the time to be ripe, he abruptly left the chief's smoky dwelling and hastened to a neighboring lodge. As usual, she sat with squaws and maidens about her, all engaged in sewing moccasins and beadwork. They laughed at his entrance, and badinage, which linked Zarinska to him, ran high. But one after the other they were unceremoniously bundled into the outer snow, whence they hurried to spread the tale through all the camp.

His cause was well pleaded, in her tongue, for she did not know his, and at the end of two hours he rose to go.

'So Zarinska will come to the White Man's lodge? Good! I go now to have talk with thy father, for he may not be so minded. And I will give him many tokens; but he must not ask too much. If he say no? Good! Zarinska shall yet come to the White Man's lodge.'

He had already lifted the skin flap to depart, when a low exclamation brought him back to the girl's side. She brought herself to her knees on the bearskin mat, her face aglow with true Eve-light, and shyly unbuckled his heavy belt. He looked down, perplexed, suspicious, his ears alert for the slightest sound without.

But her next move disarmed his doubt, and he smiled with pleasure. She took from her sewing bag a moosehide sheath, brave with bright beadwork, fantastically designed. She drew his great hunting-knife, gazed reverently along the keen edge, half tempted to try it with her thumb, and shot it into place in its new home. Then she slipped the sheath along the belt to its customary resting-place, just above the hip. For all the world, it was like a scene of olden time,—a lady and her knight.

26

Mackenzie drew her up full height and swept her red lips with his moustache, the, to her, foreign caress of the Wolf. It was a meeting of the stone age and the steel; but she was none the less a woman, as her crimson cheeks and the luminous softness of her eyes attested.

There was a thrill of excitement in the air as 'Scruff' Mackenzie, a bulky bundle under his arm, threw open the flap of Thling-Tinneh's tent. Children were running about in the open, dragging dry wood to the scene of the potlach, a babble of women's voices was growing in intensity, the young men were consulting in sullen groups, while from the Shaman's lodge rose the eerie sounds of an incantation.

The chief was alone with his blear-eyed wife, but a glance sufficed to tell Mackenzie that the news was already told. So he plunged at once into the business, shifting the beaded sheath prominently to the fore as advertisement of the betrothal.

'O Thling-Tinneh, mighty chief of the Sticks And the land of the Tanana, ruler of the salmon and the bear, the moose and the cariboo! The White Man is before thee with a great purpose. Many moons has his lodge been empty, and he is lonely. And his heart has eaten itself in silence, and grown hungry for a woman to sit beside him in his lodge, to meet him from the hunt with warm fire and good food. He has heard strange things, the patter of baby moccasins and the sound of children's voices. And one night a vision came upon him, and he beheld the Raven, who is thy father, the great Raven, who is the father of all the Sticks. And the Raven spake to the lonely White Man, saying: "Bind thou thy moccasins upon thee, and gird thy snow-shoes on, and lash thy sled with food for many sleeps and fine tokens for the Chief Thling-Tinneh. For thou shalt turn thy face to where the mid-spring sun is wont to sink below the land and journey to this great chief's hunting-grounds. There thou shalt make big presents, and Thling-Tinneh, who is my son, shall become to thee as a father. In his lodge there is a maiden into whom I breathed the breath of life for thee. This maiden shalt thou take to wife." 'O Chief, thus spake the great Raven; thus do I lay many presents at thy feet; thus am I come to take thy daughter!' The old man drew his furs about him with crude consciousness of royalty, but delayed reply while a youngster crept in, delivered a quick message to appear before the council, and was gone.

27

'O White Man, whom we have named Moose-Killer, also known as the Wolf, and the Son of the Wolf! We know thou comest of a mighty race; we are proud to have thee our potlach-guest; but the king-salmon does not mate with the dogsalmon, nor the Raven with the Wolf.' 'Not so!' cried Mackenzie. 'The daughters of the Raven have I met in the camps of the Wolf,—the squaw of Mortimer, the squaw of Tregidgo, the squaw of Barnaby, who came two ice-runs back, and I have heard of other squaws, though my eyes beheld them not.' 'Son, your words are true; but it were evil mating, like the water with the sand, like the snow-flake with the sun. But met you one Mason and his squaw' No?

He came ten ice-runs ago,—the first of all the Wolves. And with him there was a mighty man, straight as a willow-shoot, and tall; strong as the bald-faced grizzly, with a heart like the full summer moon; his-' 'Oh!' interrupted Mackenzie, recognizing the well-known Northland figure, 'Malemute Kid!' 'The same,—a mighty man. But saw you aught of the squaw? She was full sister to Zarinska.' 'Nay, Chief; but I have heard. Mason—far, far to the north, a spruce-tree, heavy with years, crushed out his life beneath. But his love was great, and he had much gold. With this, and her boy, she journeyed countless sleeps toward the winter's noonday sun, and there she yet lives,—no biting frost, no snow, no summer's midnight sun, no winter's noonday night.'

A second messenger interrupted with imperative summons from the council.

As Mackenzie threw him into the snow, he caught a glimpse of the swaying forms before the council-fire, heard the deep basses of the men in rhythmic chant, and knew the Shaman was fanning the anger of his people. Time pressed. He turned upon the chief.

'Come! I wish thy child. And now, see! Here are tobacco, tea, many cups of sugar, warm blankets, handkerchiefs, both good and large; and here, a true rifle, with many bullets and much powder.' 'Nay,' replied the old man, struggling against the great wealth spread before him. 'Even now are my people come together. They will not have this marriage.'

'But thou art chief.' 'Yet do my young men rage because the Wolves have taken their maidens so that they may not marry.' 'Listen, O Thling-Tinneh! Ere the night has passed into the day, the Wolf shall face his dogs to the Mountains of the East and fare forth to the Country of the Yukon. And Zarinska shall break trail for his dogs.' 'And ere the night has gained its middle, my young men may fling to the dogs the flesh of the Wolf, and his bones be scattered in the snow till the springtime lay them bare.' It was threat and counter-threat. Mackenzie's bronzed face flushed darkly. He raised his voice. The old squaw, who till now had sat an impassive spectator, made to creep by him for the door.

The song of the men broke suddenly and there was a hubbub of many voices as he whirled the old woman roughly to her couch of skins.

'Again I cry—listen, O Thling-Tinneh! The Wolf dies with teeth fast-locked, and with him there shall sleep ten of thy strongest men,—men who are needed, for the hunting is not begun, and the fishing is not many moons away. And again, of what profit should I die? I know the custom of thy people; thy share of my wealth shall be very small. Grant me thy child, and it shall all be thine. And yet again, my brothers will come, and they are many, and their maws are never filled; and the daughters of the Raven shall bear children in the lodges of the Wolf. My people are greater than thy people. It is destiny. Grant, and all this wealth is thine.' Moccasins were crunching the snow without. Mackenzie threw his rifle to cock, and loosened the twin Colts in his belt.

'Grant, O Chief!' 'And yet will my people say no.' 'Grant, and the wealth is thine. Then shall I deal with thy people after.' 'The Wolf will have it so. I will take his tokens,—but I would warn him.' Mackenzie passed over the goods, taking care to clog the rifle's ejector, and capping the bargain with a kaleidoscopic silk kerchief. The Shaman and half a dozen young braves entered, but he shouldered boldly among them and passed out.

'Pack!' was his laconic greeting to Zarinska as he passed her lodge and hurried to harness his dogs. A few minutes later he swept into the council at the head of the team, the woman by his side. He took his place at the upper

29

end of the oblong, by the side of the chief. To his left, a step to the rear, he stationed Zarinska, her proper place. Besides, the time was ripe for mischief, and there was need to guard his back.

On either side, the men crouched to the fire, their voices lifted in a folk-chant out of the forgotten past. Full of strange, halting cadences and haunting recurrences, it was not beautiful. 'Fearful' may inadequately express it. At the lower end, under the eye of the Shaman, danced half a score of women. Stern were his reproofs of those who did not wholly abandon themselves to the ecstasy of the rite. Half hidden in their heavy masses of raven hair, all dishevelled and falling to their waists, they slowly swayed to and fro, their forms rippling to an ever-changing rhythm.

It was a weird scene; an anachronism. To the south, the nineteenth century was reeling off the few years of its last decade; here flourished man primeval, a shade removed from the prehistoric cave-dweller, forgotten fragment of the Elder World. The tawny wolf-dogs sat between their skin-clad masters or fought for room, the firelight cast backward from their red eyes and dripping fangs. The woods, in ghostly shroud, slept on unheeding.

The White Silence, for the moment driven to the rimming forest, seemed ever crushing inward; the stars danced with great leaps, as is their wont in the time of the Great Cold; while the Spirits of the Pole trailed their robes of glory athwart the heavens.

'Scruff' Mackenzie dimly realized the wild grandeur of the setting as his eyes ranged down the fur-fringed sides in quest of missing faces. They rested for a moment on a newborn babe, suckling at its mother's naked breast. It was forty below,—seven and odd degrees of frost. He thought of the tender women of his own race and smiled grimly. Yet from the loins of some such tender woman had he sprung with a kingly inheritance,—an inheritance which gave to him and his dominance over the land and sea, over the animals and the peoples of all the zones. Single-handed against fivescore, girt by the Arctic winter, far from his own, he felt the prompting of his heritage, the desire to possess, the wild danger—love, the thrill of battle, the power to conquer or to die.

The singing and the dancing ceased, and the Shaman flared up in rude eloquence.

Through the sinuosities of their vast mythology, he worked cunningly upon the credulity of his people. The case was strong. Opposing the creative principles as embodied in the Crow and the Raven, he stigmatized Mackenzie as the Wolf, the fighting and the destructive principle. Not only was the combat of these forces spiritual, but men fought, each to his totem. They were the children of Jelchs, the Raven, the Promethean fire-bringer; Mackenzie was the child of the Wolf, or in other words, the Devil. For them to bring a truce to this perpetual warfare, to marry their daughters to the arch-enemy, were treason and blasphemy of the highest order. No phrase was harsh nor figure vile enough in branding Mackenzie as a sneaking interloper and emissary of Satan. There was a subdued, savage roar in the deep chests of his listeners as he took the swing of his peroration.

'Aye, my brothers, Jelchs is all-powerful! Did he not bring heaven-borne fire that we might be warm? Did he not draw the sun, moon, and stars, from their holes that we might see? Did he not teach us that we might fight the Spirits of Famine and of Frost? But now Jelchs is angry with his children, and they are grown to a handful, and he will not help.

'For they have forgotten him, and done evil things, and trod bad trails, and taken his enemies into their lodges to sit by their fires. And the Raven is sorrowful at the wickedness of his children; but when they shall rise up and show they have come back, he will come out of the darkness to aid them. O brothers! the Fire-Bringer has whispered messages to thy Shaman; the same shall ye hear. Let the young men take the young women to their lodges; let them fly at the throat of the Wolf; let them be undying in their enmity! Then shall their women become fruitful and they shall multiply into a mighty people! And the Raven shall lead great tribes of their fathers and their fathers' fathers from out of the North; and they shall beat back the Wolves till they are as last year's campfires; and they shall again come to rule over all the land! 'Tis the message of Jelchs, the Raven.' This foreshadowing of the Messiah's coming brought a hoarse howl from the Sticks as they leaped to their feet. Mackenzie slipped the thumbs of his mittens and waited. There was a clamor for the 'Fox,' not to be stilled till one of the young men stepped forward to speak.

'Brothers! The Shaman has spoken wisely. The Wolves have taken our women, and our men are childless. We are grown to a handful. The Wolves have taken our warm furs and given for them evil spirits which dwell in bottles, and clothes which come not from the beaver or the lynx, but are made from the grass.

And they are not warm, and our men die of strange sicknesses. I, the Fox, have taken no woman to wife; and why? Twice have the maidens which pleased me gone to the camps of the Wolf. Even now have I laid by skins of the beaver, of the moose, of the cariboo, that I might win favor in the eyes of Thling-Tinneh, that I might marry Zarinska, his daughter. Even now are her snow-shoes bound to her feet, ready to break trail for the dogs of the Wolf. Nor do I speak for myself alone.

As I have done, so has the Bear. He, too, had fain been the father of her children, and many skins has he cured thereto. I speak for all the young men who know not wives. The Wolves are ever hungry. Always do they take the choice meat at the killing. To the Ravens are left the leavings.

'There is Gugkla,' he cried, brutally pointing out one of the women, who was a cripple.

'Her legs are bent like the ribs of a birch canoe. She cannot gather wood nor carry the meat of the hunters. Did the Wolves choose her?' 'Ai! ai!' vociferated his tribesmen.

'There is Moyri, whose eyes are crossed by the Evil Spirit. Even the babes are affrighted when they gaze upon her, and it is said the bald-face gives her the trail.

'Was she chosen?' Again the cruel applause rang out.

'And there sits Pischet. She does not hearken to my words. Never has she heard the cry of the chit-chat, the voice of her husband, the babble of her child.

'She lives in the White Silence. Cared the Wolves aught for her? No! Theirs is the choice of the kill; ours is the leavings.

32

'Brothers, it shall not be! No more shall the Wolves slink among our campfires. The time is come.' A great streamer of fire, the aurora borealis, purple, green, and yellow, shot across the zenith, bridging horizon to horizon. With head thrown back and arms extended, he swayed to his climax.

'Behold! The spirits of our fathers have arisen and great deeds are afoot this night!' He stepped back, and another young man somewhat diffidently came forward, pushed on by his comrades. He towered a full head above them, his broad chest defiantly bared to the frost. He swung tentatively from one foot to the other.

Words halted upon his tongue, and he was ill at ease. His face was horrible to look upon, for it had at one time been half torn away by some terrific blow. At last he struck his breast with his clenched fist, drawing sound as from a drum, and his voice rumbled forth as does the surf from an ocean cavern.

'I am the Bear,—the Silver-Tip and the Son of the Silver-Tip! When my voice was yet as a girl's, I slew the lynx, the moose, and the cariboo; when it whistled like the wolverines from under a cache, I crossed the Mountains of the South and slew three of the White Rivers; when it became as the roar of the Chinook, I met the bald-faced grizzly, but gave no trail.' At this he paused, his hand significantly sweeping across his hideous scars.

'I am not as the Fox. My tongue is frozen like the river. I cannot make great talk. My words are few. The Fox says great deeds are afoot this night. Good! Talk flows from his tongue like the freshets of the spring, but he is chary of deeds.

'This night shall I do battle with the Wolf. I shall slay him, and Zarinska shall sit by my fire. The Bear has spoken.' Though pandemonium raged about him, 'Scruff' Mackenzie held his ground.

Aware how useless was the rifle at close quarters, he slipped both holsters to the fore, ready for action, and drew his mittens till his hands were barely shielded by the elbow gauntlets. He knew there was no hope in attack en masse, but true to his boast, was prepared to die with teeth fast-locked. But

33

the Bear restrained his comrades, beating back the more impetuous with his terrible fist. As the tumult began to die away, Mackenzie shot a glance in the direction of Zarinska. It was a superb picture. She was leaning forward on her snow-shoes, lips apart and nostrils quivering, like a tigress about to spring. Her great black eyes were fixed upon her tribesmen, in fear and defiance. So extreme the tension, she had forgotten to breathe. With one hand pressed spasmodically against her breast and the other as tightly gripped about the dog-whip, she was as turned to stone. Even as he looked, relief came to her. Her muscles loosened; with a heavy sigh she settled back, giving him a look of more than love—of worship.

Thling-Tinneh was trying to speak, but his people drowned his voice. Then Mackenzie strode forward. The Fox opened his mouth to a piercing yell, but so savagely did Mackenzie whirl upon him that he shrank back, his larynx all agurgle with suppressed sound. His discomfiture was greeted with roars of laughter, and served to soothe his fellows to a listening mood.

'Brothers! The White Man, whom ye have chosen to call the Wolf, came among you with fair words. He was not like the Innuit; he spoke not lies. He came as a friend, as one who would be a brother. But your men have had their say, and the time for soft words is past.

'First, I will tell you that the Shaman has an evil tongue and is a false prophet, that the messages he spake are not those of the Fire-Bringer. His ears are locked to the voice of the Raven, and out of his own head he weaves cunning fancies, and he has made fools of you. He has no power.

'When the dogs were killed and eaten, and your stomachs were heavy with untanned hide and strips of moccasins; when the old men died, and the old women died, and the babes at the dry dugs of the mothers died; when the land was dark, and ye perished as do the salmon in the fall; aye, when the famine was upon you, did the Shaman bring reward to your hunters? did the Shaman put meat in your bellies? Again I say, the Shaman is without power. Thus I spit upon his face!' Though taken aback by the sacrilege, there was no uproar. Some of the women were even frightened, but among the men there was an uplifting, as though in preparation or anticipation of the miracle. All eyes were turned upon the two central figures. The priest realized the crucial moment, felt his power tottering, opened his mouth in denunciation, but fled backward before the truculent advance, upraised fist, and flashing eyes, of Mackenzie. He sneered and resumed.

'Was I stricken dead? Did the lightning burn me? Did the stars fall from the sky and crush me? Pish! I have done with the dog. Now will I tell you of my people, who are the mightiest of all the peoples, who rule in all the lands. At first we hunt as I hunt, alone.

'After that we hunt in packs; and at last, like the cariboo-run, we sweep across all the land.

'Those whom we take into our lodges live; those who will not come die. Zarinska is a comely maiden, full and strong, fit to become the mother of Wolves. Though I die, such shall she become; for my brothers are many, and they will follow the scent of my dogs.

'Listen to the Law of the Wolf: Whoso taketh the life of one Wolf, the forfeit shall ten of his people pay. In many lands has the price been paid; in many lands shall it yet be paid.

'Now will I deal with the Fox and the Bear. It seems they have cast eyes upon the maiden. So? Behold, I have bought her! Thling-Tinneh leans upon the rifle; the goods of purchase are by his fire. Yet will I be fair to the young men. To the Fox, whose tongue is dry with many words, will I give of tobacco five long plugs.

'Thus will his mouth be wetted that he may make much noise in the council. But to the Bear, of whom I am well proud, will I give of blankets two; of flour, twenty cups; of tobacco, double that of the Fox; and if he fare with me over the Mountains of the East, then will I give him a rifle, mate to Thling-Tinneh's. If not? Good! The Wolf is weary of speech. Yet once again will he say the Law: Whoso taketh the life of one Wolf, the forfeit shall ten of his people pay.'

Mackenzie smiled as he stepped back to his old position, but at heart he was full of trouble. The night was yet dark. The girl came to his side, and he listened closely as she told of the Bear's battle-tricks with the knife.

35

The decision was for war. In a trice, scores of moccasins were widening the space of beaten snow by the fire. There was much chatter about the seeming defeat of the Shaman; some averred he had but withheld his power, while others conned past events and agreed with the Wolf. The Bear came to the center of the battle-ground, a long naked hunting-knife of Russian make in his hand. The Fox called attention to Mackenzie's revolvers; so he stripped his belt, buckling it about Zarinska, into whose hands he also entrusted his rifle. She shook her head that she could not shoot,—small chance had a woman to handle such precious things.

'Then, if danger come by my back, cry aloud, "My husband!" No; thus, "My husband!"'

He laughed as she repeated it, pinched her cheek, and reentered the circle. Not only in reach and stature had the Bear the advantage of him, but his blade was longer by a good two inches. 'Scruff' Mackenzie had looked into the eyes of men before, and he knew it was a man who stood against him; yet he quickened to the glint of light on the steel, to the dominant pulse of his race.

Time and again he was forced to the edge of the fire or the deep snow, and time and again, with the foot tactics of the pugilist, he worked back to the center. Not a voice was lifted in encouragement, while his antagonist was heartened with applause, suggestions, and warnings. But his teeth only shut the tighter as the knives clashed together, and he thrust or eluded with a coolness born of conscious strength. At first he felt compassion for his enemy; but this fled before the primal instinct of life, which in turn gave way to the lust of slaughter. The ten thousand years of culture fell from him, and he was a cave-dweller, doing battle for his female.

Twice he pricked the Bear, getting away unscathed; but the third time caught, and to save himself, free hands closed on fighting hands, and they came together.

Then did he realize the tremendous strength of his opponent. His muscles were knotted in painful lumps, and cords and tendons threatened to snap with the strain; yet nearer and nearer came the Russian steel. He tried to break away, but only weakened himself. The fur-clad circle closed in, certain of and anxious to see the final stroke. But with wrestler's trick, swinging partly to the side, he struck at his adversary with his head. Involuntarily the Bear leaned back, disturbing his center of gravity. Simultaneous with this, Mackenzie tripped properly and threw his whole weight forward, hurling him clear through the circle into the deep snow. The Bear floundered out and came back full tilt.

'O my husband!' Zarinska's voice rang out, vibrant with danger.

To the twang of a bow-string, Mackenzie swept low to the ground, and a bonebarbed arrow passed over him into the breast of the Bear, whose momentum carried him over his crouching foe. The next instant Mackenzie was up and about. The bear lay motionless, but across the fire was the Shaman, drawing a second arrow. Mackenzie's knife leaped short in the air. He caught the heavy blade by the point. There was a flash of light as it spanned the fire. Then the Shaman, the hilt alone appearing without his throat, swayed and pitched forward into the glowing embers.

Click! Click!—the Fox had possessed himself of Thling-Tinneh's rifle and was vainly trying to throw a shell into place. But he dropped it at the sound of Mackenzie's laughter.

'So the Fox has not learned the way of the plaything? He is yet a woman.

'Come! Bring it, that I may show thee!' The Fox hesitated.

'Come, I say!' He slouched forward like a beaten cur.

'Thus, and thus; so the thing is done.' A shell flew into place and the trigger was at cock as Mackenzie brought it to shoulder.

'The Fox has said great deeds were afoot this night, and he spoke true. There have been great deeds, yet least among them were those of the Fox. Is he still intent to take Zarinska to his lodge? Is he minded to tread the trail already broken by the Shaman and the Bear?

'No? Good!'

Mackenzie turned contemptuously and drew his knife from the priest's throat.

'Are any of the young men so minded? If so, the Wolf will take them by two and three till none are left. No? Good! Thling-Tinneh, I now give thee this rifle a second time. If, in the days to come, thou shouldst journey to the Country of the Yukon, know thou that there shall always be a place and much food by the fire of the Wolf. The night is now passing into the day. I go, but I may come again. And for the last time, remember the Law of the Wolf!' He was supernatural in their sight as he rejoined Zarinska. She took her place at the head of the team, and the dogs swung into motion. A few moments later they were swallowed up by the ghostly forest. Till now Mackenzie had waited; he slipped into his snow-shoes to follow.

'Has the Wolf forgotten the five long plugs?' Mackenzie turned upon the Fox angrily; then the humor of it struck him.

'I will give thee one short plug.' 'As the Wolf sees fit,' meekly responded the Fox, stretching out his hand.

The Men of Forty Mile

When Big Jim Belden ventured the apparently innocuous proposition that mush-ice was 'rather pecooliar,' he little dreamed of what it would lead to.

Neither did Lon McFane, when he affirmed that anchor-ice was even more so; nor did Bettles, as he instantly disagreed, declaring the very existence of such a form to be a bugaboo.

'An' ye'd be tellin' me this,' cried Lon, 'after the years ye've spint in the land! An' we atin' out the same pot this many's the day!' 'But the thing's agin reasin,' insisted Bettles.

'Look you, water's warmer than ice—' 'An' little the difference, once ye break through.'

'Still it's warmer, because it ain't froze. An' you say it freezes on the bottom?' 'Only the anchor-ice, David, only the anchor-ice. An' have ye niver drifted along, the water clear as glass, whin suddin, belike a cloud over the sun, the mushy-ice comes bubblin' up an' up till from bank to bank an' bind to bind it's drapin' the river like a first snowfall?' 'Unh, hunh! more'n once when I took a doze at the steering-oar. But it allus come out the nighest side-channel, an' not bubblin' up an' up.' 'But with niver a wink at the helm?'

'No; nor you. It's agin reason. I'll leave it to any man!' Bettles appealed to the circle about the stove, but the fight was on between himself and Lon McFane.

'Reason or no reason, it's the truth I'm tellin' ye. Last fall, a year gone, 'twas Sitka Charley and meself saw the sight, droppin' down the riffle ye'll remember below Fort Reliance. An' regular fall weather it was—the glint o' the sun on the golden larch an' the quakin' aspens; an' the glister of light on ivery ripple; an' beyond, the winter an' the blue haze of the North comin' down hand in hand. It's well ye know the same, with a fringe to the river an' the ice formin' thick in the eddies—an' a snap an' sparkle to the air, an' ye a-feelin' it through all yer blood, a-takin' new lease of life with ivery suck of it. 'Tis then, me boy, the world grows small an' the wandtherlust lays ye by the heels.

'But it's meself as wandthers. As I was sayin', we a-paddlin', with niver a sign of ice, barrin' that by the eddies, when the Injun lifts his paddle an' sings out, "Lon McFane! Look ye below!" So have I heard, but niver thought to see! As ye know, Sitka Charley, like meself, niver drew first breath in the land; so the sight was new. Then we drifted, with a head over ayther side, peerin' down through the sparkly water. For the world like the days I spint with the pearlers, watchin' the coral banks a-growin' the same as so many gardens under the sea. There it was, the anchor-ice, clingin' an' clusterin' to ivery rock, after the manner of the white coral.

'But the best of the sight was to come. Just after clearin' the tail of the riffle, the water turns quick the color of milk, an' the top of it in wee circles, as when the graylin' rise in the spring, or there's a splatter of wet from the sky. 'Twas the anchor-ice comin' up. To the right, to the lift, as far as iver a man cud see, the water was covered with the same.

An' like so much porridge it was, slickin' along the bark of the canoe, stickin' like glue to the paddles. It's many's the time I shot the self-same riffle before, and it's many's the time after, but niver a wink of the same have I seen. 'Twas the sight of a lifetime.' 'Do tell!' dryly commented Bettles. 'D'ye think I'd b'lieve such a yarn? I'd ruther say the glister of light'd gone to your eyes, and the snap of the air to your tongue.' ''Twas me own eyes that beheld it, an' if Sitka Charley was here, he'd be the lad to back me.' 'But facts is facts, an' they ain't no gettin' round 'em. It ain't in the nature of things for the water furtherest away from the air to freeze first.' 'But me own eyes-' 'Don't git het up over it,' admonished Bettles, as the quick Celtic anger began to mount.

'Then yer not after belavin' me?' 'Sence you're so blamed forehanded about it, no; I'd b'lieve nature first, and facts.'

'Is it the lie ye'd be givin' me?' threatened Lon. 'Ye'd better be askin' that Siwash wife of yours. I'll lave it to her, for the truth I spake.' Bettles flared up in sudden wrath. The Irishman had unwittingly wounded him; for his wife was the half-breed daughter of a Russian fur-trader, married to him in the Greek Mission of Nulato, a thousand miles or so down the Yukon, thus being of much higher caste than the common Siwash, or native, wife. It was a mere Northland nuance, which none but the Northland adventurer may understand.

'I reckon you kin take it that way,' was his deliberate affirmation.

The next instant Lon McFane had stretched him on the floor, the circle was broken up, and half a dozen men had stepped between.

Bettles came to his feet, wiping the blood from his mouth. 'It hain't new, this takin' and payin' of blows, and don't you never think but that this will be squared.' 'An' niver in me life did I take the lie from mortal man,' was the retort courteous. 'An' it's an avil day I'll not be to hand, waitin' an' willin' to help ye lift yer debts, barrin' no manner of way.'

'Still got that 38-55?' Lon nodded.

'But you'd better git a more likely caliber. Mine'll rip holes through you the size of walnuts.'

'Niver fear; it's me own slugs smell their way with soft noses, an' they'll spread like flapjacks against the coming out beyand. An' when'll I have the pleasure of waitin' on ye? The waterhole's a strikin' locality.' ''Tain't bad. Jest be there in an hour, and you won't set long on my coming.' Both men mittened and left the Post, their ears closed to the remonstrances of their comrades. It was such a little thing; yet with such men, little things, nourished by quick tempers and stubborn natures, soon blossomed into big things.

Besides, the art of burning to bedrock still lay in the womb of the future, and the men of Forty-Mile, shut in by the long Arctic winter, grew high-stomached with overeating and enforced idleness, and became as irritable as do the bees in the fall of the year when the hives are overstocked with honey.

There was no law in the land. The mounted police was also a thing of the future. Each man measured an offense, and meted out the punishment inasmuch as it affected himself.

Rarely had combined action been necessary, and never in all the dreary history of the camp had the eighth article of the Decalogue been violated.

Big Jim Belden called an impromptu meeting. Scruff Mackenzie was placed as temporary chairman, and a messenger dispatched to solicit Father Roubeau's good offices. Their position was paradoxical, and they knew it. By the right of might could they interfere to prevent the duel; yet such action, while in direct line with their wishes, went counter to their opinions. While their rough-hewn, obsolete ethics recognized the individual prerogative of wiping out blow with blow, they could not bear to think of two good comrades, such as Bettles and McFane, meeting in deadly battle. Deeming the man who would not fight on provocation a dastard, when brought to the test it seemed wrong that he should fight.

But a scurry of moccasins and loud cries, rounded off with a pistol-shot, interrupted the discussion. Then the storm-doors opened and Malemute Kid entered, a smoking Colt's in his hand, and a merry light in his eye.

'I got him.' He replaced the empty shell, and added, 'Your dog, Scruff.' 'Yellow Fang?'

Mackenzie asked.

'No; the lop-eared one.' 'The devil! Nothing the matter with him.' 'Come out and take a look.' 'That's all right after all. Buess he's got 'em, too. Yellow Fang came back this morning and took a chunk out of him, and came near to making a widower of me. Made a rush for Zarinska, but she whisked her skirts in his face and escaped with the loss of the same and a good roll in the snow. Then he took to the woods again. Hope he don't come back. Lost any yourself?' 'One—the best one of the pack—Shookum. Started amuck this morning, but didn't get very far. Ran foul of Sitka Charley's team, and they scattered him all over the street. And now two of them are loose, and raging mad; so you see he got his work in. The dog census will be small in the spring if we don't do something.'

'And the man census, too.' 'How's that? Who's in trouble now?' 'Oh, Bettles and Lon McFane had an argument, and they'll be down by the waterhole in a few minutes to settle it.' The incident was repeated for his benefit, and Malemute Kid, accustomed to an obedience which his fellow men never failed to render, took charge of the affair. His quickly formulated plan was explained, and they promised to follow his lead implicitly.

'So you see,' he concluded, 'we do not actually take away their privilege of fighting; and yet I don't believe they'll fight when they see the beauty of the scheme. Life's a game and men the gamblers. They'll stake their whole pile on the one chance in a thousand.

'Take away that one chance, and—they won't play.' He turned to the man in charge of the Post. 'Storekeeper, weight out three fathoms of your best half-inch manila.

'We'll establish a precedent which will last the men of Forty-Mile to the end of time,' he prophesied. Then he coiled the rope about his arm and led his followers out of doors, just in time to meet the principals.

'What danged right'd he to fetch my wife in?' thundered Bettles to the soothing overtures of a friend. ''Twa'n't called for,' he concluded decisively. ''Twa'n't called for,' he reiterated again and again, pacing up and down and waiting for Lon McFane.

And Lon McFane—his face was hot and tongue rapid as he flaunted insurrection in the face of the Church. 'Then, father,' he cried, 'it's with an aisy heart I'll roll in me flamy blankets, the broad of me back on a bed of coals. Niver shall it be said that Lon McFane took a lie 'twixt the teeth without iver liftin' a hand! An' I'll not ask a blessin'. The years have been wild, but it's the heart was in the right place.' 'But it's not the heart, Lon,' interposed Father Roubeau; 'It's pride that bids you forth to slay your fellow man.' 'Yer Frinch,' Lon replied. And then, turning to leave him, 'An' will ye say a mass if the luck is against me?' But the priest smiled, thrust his moccasined feet to the fore, and went out upon the white breast of the silent river. A packed trail, the width of a sixteen-inch sled, led out to the waterhole. On either side lay the deep, soft snow. The men trod in single file, without conversation; and the black-stoled priest in their midst gave to the function the solemn aspect of a funeral. It was a warm winter's day for Forty-Mile—a day in which the sky, filled with heaviness, drew closer to the earth, and the mercury sought the unwonted level of twenty below. But there was no cheer in the warmth. There was little air in the upper strata, and the clouds hung motionless, giving sullen promise of an early snowfall. And the earth, unresponsive, made no preparation, content in its hibernation.

When the waterhole was reached, Bettles, having evidently reviewed the quarrel during the silent walk, burst out in a final "Twa'n't called for,' while Lon McFane kept grim silence. Indignation so choked him that he could not speak.

Yet deep down, whenever their own wrongs were not uppermost, both men wondered at their comrades. They had expected opposition, and this tacit acquiescence hurt them. It seemed more was due them from the men they had been so close with, and they felt a vague sense of wrong, rebelling at the thought of so many of their brothers coming out, as on a gala occasion, without one word of protest, to see them shoot each other down. It appeared their worth had diminished in the eyes of the community. The proceedings puzzled them.

'Back to back, David. An' will it be fifty paces to the man, or double the quantity?'

'Fifty,' was the sanguinary reply, grunted out, yet sharply cut.

But the new manila, not prominently displayed, but casually coiled about Malemute Kid's arm, caught the quick eye of the Irishman, and thrilled him with a suspicious fear.

'An' what are ye doin' with the rope?' 'Hurry up!' Malemute Kid glanced at his watch.

'I've a batch of bread in the cabin, and I don't want it to fall. Besides, my feet are getting cold.' The rest of the men manifested their impatience in various suggestive ways.

'But the rope, Kid' It's bran' new, an' sure yer bread's not that heavy it needs raisin' with the like of that?' Bettles by this time had faced around.

44

Father Roubeau, the humor of the situation just dawning on him, hid a smile behind his mittened hand.

'No, Lon; this rope was made for a man.' Malemute Kid could be very impressive on occasion.

'What man?' Bettles was becoming aware of a personal interest.

'The other man.' 'An' which is the one ye'd mane by that?' 'Listen, Lon— and you, too, Bettles! We've been talking this little trouble of yours over, and we've come to one conclusion. We know we have no right to stop your fighting-' 'True for ye, me lad!' 'And we're not going to. But this much we can do, and shall do—make this the only duel in the history of Forty-Mile, set an example for every che-cha-qua that comes up or down the Yukon. The man who escapes killing shall be hanged to the nearest tree. Now, go ahead!'

Lon smiled dubiously, then his face lighted up. 'Pace her off, David— fifty paces, wheel, an' niver a cease firin' till a lad's down for good. 'Tis their hearts'll niver let them do the deed, an' it's well ye should know it for a true Yankee bluff.'

He started off with a pleased grin on his face, but Malemute Kid halted him.

'Lon! It's a long while since you first knew me?' 'Many's the day.' 'And you, Bettles?'

'Five year next June high water.' 'And have you once, in all that time, known me to break my word' Or heard of me breaking it?' Both men shook their heads, striving to fathom what lay beyond.

'Well, then, what do you think of a promise made by me?' 'As good as your bond,' from Bettles.

'The thing to safely sling yer hopes of heaven by,' promptly endorsed Lon McFane.

'Listen! I, Malemute Kid, give you my word—and you know what that means that the man who is not shot stretches rope within ten minutes after the shooting.' He stepped back as Pilate might have done after washing his hands.

A pause and a silence came over the men of Forty-Mile. The sky drew still closer, sending down a crystal flight of frost—little geometric designs, perfect, evanescent as a breath, yet destined to exist till the returning sun had covered half its northern journey.

Both men had led forlorn hopes in their time—led with a curse or a jest on their tongues, and in their souls an unswerving faith in the God of Chance. But that merciful deity had been shut out from the present deal. They studied the face of Malemute Kid, but they studied as one might the Sphinx. As the quiet minutes passed, a feeling that speech was incumbent on them began to grow. At last the howl of a wolf-dog cracked the silence from the direction of Forty-Mile. The weird sound swelled with all the pathos of a breaking heart, then died away in a long-drawn sob.

'Well I be danged!' Bettles turned up the collar of his mackinaw jacket and stared about him helplessly.

'It's a gloryus game yer runnin', Kid,' cried Lon McFane. 'All the percentage of the house an' niver a bit to the man that's buckin'. The Devil himself'd niver tackle such a cinch—and damned if I do.' There were chuckles, throttled in gurgling throats, and winks brushed away with the frost which rimed the eyelashes, as the men climbed the ice-notched bank and started across the street to the Post. But the long howl had drawn nearer, invested with a new note of menace. A woman screamed round the corner. There was a cry of, 'Here he comes!' Then an Indian boy, at the head of half a dozen frightened dogs, racing with death, dashed into the crowd. And behind came Yellow Fang, a bristle of hair and a flash of gray. Everybody but the Yankee fled.

The Indian boy had tripped and fallen. Bettles stopped long enough to grip him by the slack of his furs, then headed for a pile of cordwood already occupied by a number of his comrades. Yellow Fang, doubling after one of the dogs, came leaping back. The fleeing animal, free of the rabies, but crazed with fright, whipped Bettles off his feet and flashed on up the street.

Malemute Kid took a flying shot at Yellow Fang. The mad dog whirled a half airspring, came down on his back, then, with a single leap, covered half the distance between himself and Bettles.

But the fatal spring was intercepted. Lon McFane leaped from the woodpile, countering him in midair. Over they rolled, Lon holding him by the throat at arm's length, blinking under the fetid slaver which sprayed his face. Then Bettles, revolver in hand and coolly waiting a chance, settled the combat.

"'Twas a square game, Kid,' Lon remarked, rising to his feet and shaking the snow from out his sleeves; 'with a fair percentage to meself that bucked it.' That night, while Lon McFane sought the forgiving arms of the Church in the direction of Father Roubeau's cabin, Malemute Kid talked long to little purpose.

'But would you,' persisted Mackenzie, 'supposing they had fought?' 'Have I ever broken my word?' 'No; but that isn't the point. Answer the question. Would you?' Malemute Kid straightened up. 'Scruff, I've been asking myself that question ever since, and—'

'Well?'

'Well, as yet, I haven't found the answer.'

In a Far Country

When a man journeys into a far country, he must be prepared to forget many of the things he has learned, and to acquire such customs as are inherent with existence in the new land; he must abandon the old ideals and the old gods, and oftentimes he must reverse the very codes by which his conduct has hitherto been shaped. To those who have the protean faculty of adaptability, the novelty of such change may even be a source of pleasure; but to those who happen to be hardened to the ruts in which they were created, the pressure of the altered environment is unbearable, and they chafe in body and in spirit under the new restrictions which they do not understand. This chafing is bound to act and react, producing divers evils and leading to various misfortunes. It were better for the man who cannot fit himself to the new groove to return to his own country; if he delay too long, he will surely die.

The man who turns his back upon the comforts of an elder civilization, to face the savage youth, the primordial simplicity of the North, may estimate success at an inverse ratio to the quantity and quality of his hopelessly fixed habits. He will soon discover, if he be a fit candidate, that the material habits are the less important. The exchange of such things as a dainty menu for rough fare, of the stiff leather shoe for the soft, shapeless moccasin, of the feather bed for a couch in the snow, is after all a very easy matter. But his pinch will come in learning properly to shape his mind's attitude toward all things, and especially toward his fellow man. For the courtesies of ordinary life, he must substitute unselfishness, forbearance, and tolerance. Thus, and thus only, can he gain that pearl of great price—true comradeship. He must not say 'thank you'; he must mean it without opening his mouth, and prove it by responding in kind. In short, he must substitute the deed for the word, the spirit for the letter.

When the world rang with the tale of Arctic gold, and the lure of the North gripped the heartstrings of men, Carter Weatherbee threw up his snug clerkship, turned the half of his savings over to his wife, and with the remainder bought an outfit. There was no romance in his nature—the bondage of commerce had crushed all that; he was simply tired of the ceaseless grind, and wished to risk great hazards in view of corresponding returns. Like many another fool, disdaining the old trails used by the Northland pioneers for a score of years, he hurried to Edmonton in the spring of the year; and there, unluckily for his soul's welfare, he allied himself with a party of men.

There was nothing unusual about this party, except its plans. Even its goal, like that of all the other parties, was the Klondike. But the route it had mapped out to attain that goal took away the breath of the hardiest native, born and bred to the vicissitudes of the Northwest. Even Jacques Baptiste, born of a Chippewa woman and a renegade voyageur (having raised his first whimpers in a deerskin lodge north of the sixty-fifth parallel, and had the same hushed by blissful sucks of raw tallow), was surprised. Though he sold his services to them and agreed to travel even to the never-opening ice, he shook his head ominously whenever his advice was asked.

Percy Cuthfert's evil star must have been in the ascendant, for he, too, joined this company of argonauts. He was an ordinary man, with a bank account as deep as his culture, which is saying a good deal. He had no reason to embark on such a venture—no reason in the world save that he suffered from an abnormal development of sentimentality. He mistook this for the true spirit of romance and adventure. Many another man has done the like, and made as fatal a mistake.

The first break-up of spring found the party following the ice-run of Elk River. It was an imposing fleet, for the outfit was large, and they were accompanied by a disreputable contingent of half-breed voyageurs with their women and children. Day in and day out, they labored with the bateaux and canoes, fought mosquitoes and other kindred pests, or sweated and swore at the portages. Severe toil like this lays a man naked to the very roots of his soul, and ere Lake Athabasca was lost in the south, each member of the party had hoisted his true colors.

The two shirks and chronic grumblers were Carter Weatherbee and Percy Cuthfert. The whole party complained less of its aches and pains than

49

did either of them. Not once did they volunteer for the thousand and one petty duties of the camp. A bucket of water to be brought, an extra armful of wood to be chopped, the dishes to be washed and wiped, a search to be made through the outfit for some suddenly indispensable article—and these two effete scions of civilization discovered sprains or blisters requiring instant attention.

They were the first to turn in at night, with score of tasks yet undone; the last to turn out in the morning, when the start should be in readiness before the breakfast was begun.

They were the first to fall to at mealtime, the last to have a hand in the cooking; the first to dive for a slim delicacy, the last to discover they had added to their own another man's share. If they toiled at the oars, they slyly cut the water at each stroke and allowed the boat's momentum to float up the blade. They thought nobody noticed; but their comrades swore under their breaths and grew to hate them, while Jacques Baptiste sneered openly and damned them from morning till night. But Jacques Baptiste was no gentleman.

At the Great Slave, Hudson Bay dogs were purchased, and the fleet sank to the guards with its added burden of dried fish and pemican. Then canoe and bateau answered to the swift current of the Mackenzie, and they plunged into the Great Barren Ground. Every likely-looking 'feeder' was prospected, but the elusive 'pay-dirt' danced ever to the north. At the Great Bear, overcome by the common dread of the Unknown Lands, their voyageurs began to desert, and Fort of Good Hope saw the last and bravest bending to the towlines as they bucked the current down which they had so treacherously glided.

Jacques Baptiste alone remained. Had he not sworn to travel even to the never-opening ice? The lying charts, compiled in main from hearsay, were now constantly consulted.

And they felt the need of hurry, for the sun had already passed its northern solstice and was leading the winter south again. Skirting the shores of the bay, where the Mackenzie disembogues into the Arctic Ocean, they entered the mouth of the Little Peel River. Then began the arduous up-stream toil, and the two Incapables fared worse than ever. Towline and pole, paddle and tumpline, rapids and portages—such tortures served to give the one a deep disgust for great hazards, and printed for the other a fiery text on the true romance of adventure. One day they waxed mutinous, and being vilely cursed by Jacques Baptiste, turned, as worms sometimes will. But the half-breed thrashed the twain, and sent them, bruised and bleeding, about their work. It was the first time either had been manhandled.

Abandoning their river craft at the headwaters of the Little Peel, they consumed the rest of the summer in the great portage over the Mackenzie watershed to the West Rat. This little stream fed the Porcupine, which in turn joined the Yukon where that mighty highway of the North countermarches on the Arctic Circle.

But they had lost in the race with winter, and one day they tied their rafts to the thick eddy-ice and hurried their goods ashore. That night the river jammed and broke several times; the following morning it had fallen asleep for good. 'We can't be more'n four hundred miles from the Yukon,' concluded Sloper, multiplying his thumb nails by the scale of the map. The council, in which the two Incapables had whined to excellent disadvantage, was drawing to a close.

'Hudson Bay Post, long time ago. No use um now.' Jacques Baptiste's father had made the trip for the Fur Company in the old days, incidentally marking the trail with a couple of frozen toes.

Sufferin' cracky!' cried another of the party. 'No whites?' 'Nary white,' Sloper sententiously affirmed; 'but it's only five hundred more up the Yukon to Dawson. Call it a rough thousand from here.' Weatherbee and Cuthfert groaned in chorus.

'How long'll that take, Baptiste?' The half-breed figured for a moment. 'Workum like hell, no man play out, ten—twenty—forty—fifty days. Um babies come' (designating the Incapables), 'no can tell. Mebbe when hell freeze over; mebbe not then.' The manufacture of snowshoes and moccasins ceased. Somebody called the name of an absent member, who came out of an ancient cabin at the edge of the campfire and joined them. The cabin was one of the many mysteries which lurk in the vast recesses of the North. Built when and by whom, no man could tell.

Two graves in the open, piled high with stones, perhaps contained the secret of those early wanderers. But whose hand had piled the stones? The moment had come. Jacques Baptiste paused in the fitting of a harness and pinned the struggling dog in the snow. The cook made mute protest for delay, threw a handful of bacon into a noisy pot of beans, then came to attention. Sloper rose to his feet. His body was a ludicrous contrast to the healthy physiques of the Incapables. Yellow and weak, fleeing from a South American fever-hole, he had not broken his flight across the zones, and was still able to toil with men. His weight was probably ninety pounds, with the heavy hunting knife thrown in, and his grizzled hair told of a prime which had ceased to be. The fresh young muscles of either Weatherbee or Cuthfert were equal to ten times the endeavor of his; yet he could walk them into the earth in a day's journey. And all this day he had whipped his stronger comrades into venturing a thousand miles of the stiffest hardship man can conceive. He was the incarnation of the unrest of his race, and the old Teutonic stubbornness, dashed with the quick grasp and action of the Yankee, held the flesh in the bondage of the spirit.

'All those in favor of going on with the dogs as soon as the ice sets, say ay.' 'Ay!' rang out eight voices—voices destined to string a trail of oaths along many a hundred miles of pain.

'Contrary minded?' 'No!' For the first time the Incapables were united without some compromise of personal interests.

'And what are you going to do about it?' Weatherbee added belligerently.

'Majority rule! Majority rule!' clamored the rest of the party.

'I know the expedition is liable to fall through if you don't come,' Sloper replied sweetly; 'but I guess, if we try real hard, we can manage to do without you.

What do you say, boys?' The sentiment was cheered to the echo.

'But I say, you know,' Cuthfert ventured apprehensively; 'what's a chap like me to do?'

52

'Ain't you coming with us.' 'No—o.' 'Then do as you damn well please. We won't have nothing to say.' 'Kind o' calkilate yuh might settle it with that canoodlin' pardner of yourn,' suggested a heavy-going Westerner from the Dakotas, at the same time pointing out Weatherbee. 'He'll be shore to ask yuh what yur a-goin' to do when it comes to cookin' an' gatherin' the wood.' 'Then we'll consider it all arranged,' concluded Sloper.

'We'll pull out tomorrow, if we camp within five miles—just to get everything in running order and remember if we've forgotten anything.' The sleds groaned by on their steel-shod runners, and the dogs strained low in the harnesses in which they were born to die.

Jacques Baptiste paused by the side of Sloper to get a last glimpse of the cabin. The smoke curled up pathetically from the Yukon stovepipe. The two Incapables were watching them from the doorway.

Sloper laid his hand on the other's shoulder.

'Jacques Baptiste, did you ever hear of the Kilkenny cats?' The half-breed shook his head.

'Well, my friend and good comrade, the Kilkenny cats fought till neither hide, nor hair, nor yowl, was left. You understand?—till nothing was left. Very good.

Now, these two men don't like work. They'll be all alone in that cabin all winter—a mighty long, dark winter. Kilkenny cats—well?' The Frenchman in Baptiste shrugged his shoulders, but the Indian in him was silent. Nevertheless, it was an eloquent shrug, pregnant with prophecy. Things prospered in the little cabin at first. The rough badinage of their comrades had made Weatherbee and Cuthfert conscious of the mutual responsibility which had devolved upon them; besides, there was not so much work after all for two healthy men. And the removal of the cruel whiphand, or in other words the bulldozing half-breed, had brought with it a joyous reaction. At first, each strove to outdo the other, and they performed petty tasks with an unction which would have opened the eyes of their comrades who were now wearing out bodies and souls on the Long Trail.

All care was banished. The forest, which shouldered in upon them from three sides, was an inexhaustible woodyard. A few yards from their door slept the Porcupine, and a hole through its winter robe formed a bubbling spring of water, crystal clear and painfully cold. But they soon grew to find fault with even that. The hole would persist in freezing up, and thus gave them many a miserable hour of ice-chopping. The unknown builders of the cabin had extended the sidelogs so as to support a cache at the rear. In this was stored the bulk of the party's provisions.

Food there was, without stint, for three times the men who were fated to live upon it. But the most of it was the kind which built up brawn and sinew, but did not tickle the palate.

True, there was sugar in plenty for two ordinary men; but these two were little else than children. They early discovered the virtues of hot water judiciously saturated with sugar, and they prodigally swam their flapjacks and soaked their crusts in the rich, white syrup.

Then coffee and tea, and especially the dried fruits, made disastrous inroads upon it. The first words they had were over the sugar question. And it is a really serious thing when two men, wholly dependent upon each other for company, begin to quarrel.

Weatherbee loved to discourse blatantly on politics, while Cuthfert, who had been prone to clip his coupons and let the commonwealth jog on as best it might, either ignored the subject or delivered himself of startling epigrams. But the clerk was too obtuse to appreciate the clever shaping of thought, and this waste of ammunition irritated Cuthfert.

He had been used to blinding people by his brilliancy, and it worked him quite a hardship, this loss of an audience. He felt personally aggrieved and unconsciously held his muttonhead companion responsible for it.

Save existence, they had nothing in common—came in touch on no single point.

Weatherbee was a clerk who had known naught but clerking all his life; Cuthfert was a master of arts, a dabbler in oils, and had written not a little. The one was a lower-class man who considered himself a gentleman, and the other was a gentleman who knew himself to be such. From this it may be remarked that a man can be a gentleman without possessing the first instinct of true comradeship. The clerk was as sensuous as the other was aesthetic, and his love adventures, told at great length and chiefly coined from his imagination, affected the supersensitive master of arts in the same way as so many whiffs of sewer gas. He deemed the clerk a filthy, uncultured brute, whose place was in the muck with the swine, and told him so; and he was reciprocally informed that he was a milk-and-water sissy and a cad. Weatherbee could not have defined 'cad' for his life; but it satisfied its purpose, which after all seems the main point in life.

Weatherbee flatted every third note and sang such songs as 'The Boston Burglar' and 'the Handsome Cabin Boy,' for hours at a time, while Cuthfert wept with rage, till he could stand it no longer and fled into the outer cold. But there was no escape. The intense frost could not be endured for long at a time, and the little cabin crowded them—beds, stove, table, and all—into a space of ten by twelve. The very presence of either became a personal affront to the other, and they lapsed into sullen silences which increased in length and strength as the days went by. Occasionally, the flash of an eye or the curl of a lip got the better of them, though they strove to wholly ignore each other during these mute periods.

And a great wonder sprang up in the breast of each, as to how God had ever come to create the other.

With little to do, time became an intolerable burden to them. This naturally made them still lazier. They sank into a physical lethargy which there was no escaping, and which made them rebel at the performance of the smallest chore. One morning when it was his turn to cook the common breakfast, Weatherbee rolled out of his blankets, and to the snoring of his companion, lighted first the slush lamp and then the fire. The kettles were frozen hard, and there was no water in the cabin with which to wash. But he did not mind that. Waiting for it to thaw, he sliced the bacon and plunged into the hateful task of bread-making. Cuthfert had been slyly watching through his half-closed lids.

Consequently there was a scene, in which they fervently blessed each other, and agreed, henceforth, that each do his own cooking. A week later, Cuthfert neglected his morning ablutions, but none the less complacently ate the meal which he had cooked. Weatherbee grinned. After that the foolish custom of washing passed out of their lives.

As the sugar-pile and other little luxuries dwindled, they began to be afraid they were not getting their proper shares, and in order that they might not be robbed, they fell to gorging themselves. The luxuries suffered in this gluttonous contest, as did also the men.

In the absence of fresh vegetables and exercise, their blood became impoverished, and a loathsome, purplish rash crept over their bodies. Yet they refused to heed the warning.

Next, their muscles and joints began to swell, the flesh turning black, while their mouths, gums, and lips took on the color of rich cream. Instead of being drawn together by their misery, each gloated over the other's symptoms as the scurvy took its course.

They lost all regard for personal appearance, and for that matter, common decency. The cabin became a pigpen, and never once were the beds made or fresh pine boughs laid underneath. Yet they could not keep to their blankets, as they would have wished; for the frost was inexorable, and the fire box consumed much fuel. The hair of their heads and faces grew long and shaggy, while their garments would have disgusted a ragpicker. But they did not care. They were sick, and there was no one to see; besides, it was very painful to move about.

To all this was added a new trouble—the Fear of the North. This Fear was the joint child of the Great Cold and the Great Silence, and was born in the darkness of December, when the sun dipped below the horizon for good. It affected them according to their natures.

Weatherbee fell prey to the grosser superstitions, and did his best to resurrect the spirits which slept in the forgotten graves. It was a fascinating thing, and in his dreams they came to him from out of the cold, and snuggled into his blankets, and told him of their toils and troubles ere they died. He shrank away from the clammy contact as they drew closer and twined their frozen limbs about him, and when they whispered in his ear of things to come, the cabin rang with his frightened shrieks. Cuthfert did not understand—for they no longer spoke—and when thus awakened he invariably grabbed for his revolver. Then he would sit up in bed, shivering nervously, with the weapon trained on the unconscious dreamer. Cuthfert deemed the man going mad, and so came to fear for his life.

His own malady assumed a less concrete form. The mysterious artisan who had laid the cabin, log by log, had pegged a wind-vane to the ridgepole. Cuthfert noticed it always pointed south, and one day, irritated by its steadfastness of purpose, he turned it toward the east. He watched eagerly, but never a breath came by to disturb it. Then he turned the vane to the north, swearing never again to touch it till the wind did blow. But the air frightened him with its unearthly calm, and he often rose in the middle of the night to see if the vane had veered—ten degrees would have satisfied him. But no, it poised above him as unchangeable as fate.

His imagination ran riot, till it became to him a fetish. Sometimes he followed the path it pointed across the dismal dominions, and allowed his soul to become saturated with the Fear. He dwelt upon the unseen and the unknown till the burden of eternity appeared to be crushing him. Everything in the Northland had that crushing effect—the absence of life and motion; the darkness; the infinite peace of the brooding land; the ghastly silence, which made the echo of each heartbeat a sacrilege; the solemn forest which seemed to guard an awful, inexpressible something, which neither word nor thought could compass.

The world he had so recently left, with its busy nations and great enterprises, seemed very far away. Recollections occasionally obtruded—recollections of marts and galleries and crowded thoroughfares, of evening dress and social functions, of good men and dear women he had known—but they were dim memories of a life he had lived long centuries agone, on some other planet. This phantasm was the Reality. Standing beneath the wind-vane, his eyes fixed on the polar skies, he could not bring himself to realize that the Southland really existed, that at that very moment it was a-roar with life and action.

There was no Southland, no men being born of women, no giving and taking in marriage.

Beyond his bleak skyline there stretched vast solitudes, and beyond these still vaster solitudes.

There were no lands of sunshine, heavy with the perfume of flowers. Such things were only old dreams of paradise. The sunlands of the West and the spicelands of the East, the smiling Arcadias and blissful Islands of the Blest—ha! ha! His laughter split the void and shocked him with its unwonted sound. There was no sun.

This was the Universe, dead and cold and dark, and he its only citizen. Weatherbee? At such moments Weatherbee did not count. He was a Caliban, a monstrous phantom, fettered to him for untold ages, the penalty of some forgotten crime.

He lived with Death among the dead, emasculated by the sense of his own insignificance, crushed by the passive mastery of the slumbering ages. The magnitude of all things appalled him. Everything partook of the superlative save himself—the perfect cessation of wind and motion, the immensity of the snow-covered wildness, the height of the sky and the depth of the silence. That wind-vane—if it would only move. If a thunderbolt would fall, or the forest flare up in flame.

The rolling up of the heavens as a scroll, the crash of Doom—anything, anything! But no, nothing moved; the Silence crowded in, and the Fear of the North laid icy fingers on his heart.

Once, like another Crusoe, by the edge of the river he came upon a track—the faint tracery of a snowshoe rabbit on the delicate snow-crust. It was a revelation.

There was life in the Northland. He would follow it, look upon it, gloat over it.

He forgot his swollen muscles, plunging through the deep snow in an ecstasy of anticipation. The forest swallowed him up, and the brief midday twilight vanished; but he pursued his quest till exhausted nature asserted itself and laid him helpless in the snow.

There he groaned and cursed his folly, and knew the track to be the fancy of his brain; and late that night he dragged himself into the cabin on hands and knees, his cheeks frozen and a strange numbness about his feet. Weatherbee grinned malevolently, but made no offer to help him. He thrust needles into his toes and thawed them out by the stove. A week later mortification set in.

But the clerk had his own troubles. The dead men came out of their graves more frequently now, and rarely left him, waking or sleeping. He grew to wait and dread their coming, never passing the twin cairns without a shudder. One night they came to him in his sleep and led him forth to an appointed task. Frightened into inarticulate horror, he awoke between the heaps of stones and fled wildly to the cabin. But he had lain there for some time, for his feet and cheeks were also frozen.

Sometimes he became frantic at their insistent presence, and danced about the cabin, cutting the empty air with an axe, and smashing everything within reach.

During these ghostly encounters, Cuthfert huddled into his blankets and followed the madman about with a cocked revolver, ready to shoot him if he came too near.

But, recovering from one of these spells, the clerk noticed the weapon trained upon him.

His suspicions were aroused, and thenceforth he, too, lived in fear of his life. They watched each other closely after that, and faced about in startled fright whenever either passed behind the other's back. The apprehensiveness became a mania which controlled them even in their sleep. Through mutual fear they tacitly let the slush-lamp burn all night, and saw to a plentiful supply of bacon-grease before retiring. The slightest movement on the part of one was sufficient to arouse the other, and many a still watch their gazes countered as they shook beneath their blankets with fingers on the trigger-guards.

What with the Fear of the North, the mental strain, and the ravages of the disease, they lost all semblance of humanity, taking on the appearance of wild beasts, hunted and desperate. Their cheeks and noses, as an aftermath of the freezing, had turned black.

Their frozen toes had begun to drop away at the first and second joints. Every movement brought pain, but the fire box was insatiable, wringing a ransom of torture from their miserable bodies. Day in, day out, it demanded its food—a veritable pound of flesh—and they dragged themselves into the forest to chop wood on their knees. Once, crawling thus in search of dry sticks, unknown to each other they entered a thicket from opposite sides.

Suddenly, without warning, two peering death's-heads confronted each other. Suffering had so transformed them that recognition was impossible. They sprang to their feet, shrieking with terror, and dashed away on their mangled stumps; and falling at the cabin's door, they clawed and scratched like demons till they discovered their mistake.

Occasionally they lapsed normal, and during one of these sane intervals, the chief bone of contention, the sugar, had been divided equally between them. They guarded their separate sacks, stored up in the cache, with jealous eyes; for there were but a few cupfuls left, and they were totally devoid of faith in each other.

But one day Cuthfert made a mistake. Hardly able to move, sick with pain, with his head swimming and eyes blinded, he crept into the cache, sugar canister in hand, and mistook Weatherbee's sack for his own.

January had been born but a few days when this occurred. The sun had some time since passed its lowest southern declination, and at meridian now threw flaunting streaks of yellow light upon the northern sky. On the day following his mistake with the sugar-bag, Cuthfert found himself feeling better, both in body and in spirit. As noontime drew near and the day brightened, he dragged himself outside to feast on the evanescent glow, which was to him an earnest of the sun's future intentions. Weatherbee was also feeling somewhat better, and crawled out beside him. They propped themselves in the snow beneath the moveless wind-vane, and waited.

The stillness of death was about them. In other climes, when nature falls into such moods, there is a subdued air of expectancy, a waiting for some small voice to take up the broken strain. Not so in the North. The two men had lived seeming eons in this ghostly peace.

They could remember no song of the past; they could conjure no song of the future. This unearthly calm had always been—the tranquil silence of eternity.

Their eyes were fixed upon the north. Unseen, behind their backs, behind the towering mountains to the south, the sun swept toward the zenith of another sky than theirs. Sole spectators of the mighty canvas, they watched the false dawn slowly grow. A faint flame began to glow and smoulder. It deepened in intensity, ringing the changes of reddish-yellow, purple, and saffron. So bright did it become that Cuthfert thought the sun must surely be behind it—a miracle, the sun rising in the north! Suddenly, without warning and without fading, the canvas was swept clean. There was no color in the sky. The light had gone out of the day.

They caught their breaths in half-sobs. But lo! the air was aglint with particles of scintillating frost, and there, to the north, the wind-vane lay in vague outline of the snow.

A shadow! A shadow! It was exactly midday. They jerked their heads hurriedly to the south. A golden rim peeped over the mountain's snowy shoulder, smiled upon them an instant, then dipped from sight again.

There were tears in their eyes as they sought each other. A strange softening came over them. They felt irresistibly drawn toward each other. The sun was coming back again. It would be with them tomorrow, and the next day, and the next.

And it would stay longer every visit, and a time would come when it would ride their heaven day and night, never once dropping below the skyline. There would be no night.

The ice-locked winter would be broken; the winds would blow and the forests answer; the land would bathe in the blessed sunshine, and life renew.

Hand in hand, they would quit this horrid dream and journey back to the Southland. They lurched blindly forward, and their hands met—their poor maimed hands, swollen and distorted beneath their mittens.

But the promise was destined to remain unfulfilled. The Northland is the Northland, and men work out their souls by strange rules, which other men, who have not journeyed into far countries, cannot come to understand.

An hour later, Cuthfert put a pan of bread into the oven, and fell to speculating on what the surgeons could do with his feet when he got back. Home did not seem so very far away now. Weatherbee was rummaging in the cache. Of a sudden, he raised a whirlwind of blasphemy, which in turn ceased with startling abruptness. The other man had robbed his sugar-sack. Still, things might have happened differently, had not the two dead men come out from under the stones and hushed the hot words in his throat. They led him quite gently from the cache, which he forgot to close. That consummation was reached; that something they had whispered to him in his dreams was about to happen. They guided him gently, very gently, to the woodpile, where they put the axe in his hands.

Then they helped him shove open the cabin door, and he felt sure they shut it after him—at least he heard it slam and the latch fall sharply into place. And he knew they were waiting just without, waiting for him to do his task.

'Carter! I say, Carter!' Percy Cuthfert was frightened at the look on the clerk's face, and he made haste to put the table between them.

Carter Weatherbee followed, without haste and without enthusiasm. There was neither pity nor passion in his face, but rather the patient, stolid look of one who has certain work to do and goes about it methodically.

'I say, what's the matter?'

The clerk dodged back, cutting off his retreat to the door, but never opening his mouth.

'I say, Carter, I say; let's talk. There's a good chap.' The master of arts was thinking rapidly, now, shaping a skillful flank movement on the bed where his Smith & Wesson lay. Keeping his eyes on the madman, he rolled backward on the bunk, at the same time clutching the pistol.

'Carter!' The powder flashed full in Weatherbee's face, but he swung his weapon and leaped forward. The axe bit deeply at the base of the spine, and Percy Cuthfert felt all consciousness of his lower limbs leave him. Then the clerk fell heavily upon him, clutching him by the throat with feeble fingers. The sharp bite of the axe had caused Cuthfert to drop the pistol, and as his lungs panted for release, he fumbled aimlessly for it among the blankets. Then he remembered. He slid a hand up the clerk's belt to the sheath-knife; and they drew very close to each other in that last clinch.

Percy Cuthfert felt his strength leave him. The lower portion of his body was useless, The inert weight of Weatherbee crushed him—crushed him and pinned him there like a bear under a trap. The cabin became filled with a familiar odor, and he knew the bread to be burning. Yet what did it matter? He would never need it. And there were all of six cupfuls of sugar in the cache—if he had foreseen this he would not have been so saving the last several days. Would the wind-vane ever move? Why not' Had he not seen the sun today? He would go and see. No; it was impossible to move. He had not thought the clerk so heavy a man.

How quickly the cabin cooled! The fire must be out. The cold was forcing in.

It must be below zero already, and the ice creeping up the inside of the door. He could not see it, but his past experience enabled him to gauge its progress by the cabin's temperature. The lower hinge must be white ere now. Would the tale of this ever reach the world? How would his friends take it? They would read it over their coffee, most likely, and talk it over at the clubs. He could see them very clearly, 'Poor Old Cuthfert,' they murmured; 'not such a bad sort of a chap, after all.' He smiled at their eulogies, and passed on in search of a Turkish bath. It was the same old crowd upon the streets.

Strange, they did not notice his moosehide moccasins and tattered German socks! He would take a cab. And after the bath a shave would not be bad. No; he would eat first.

Steak, and potatoes, and green things how fresh it all was! And what was that? Squares of honey, streaming liquid amber! But why did they bring so much? Ha! ha! he could never eat it all.

Shine! Why certainly. He put his foot on the box. The bootblack looked curiously up at him, and he remembered his moosehide moccasins and went away hastily.

Hark! The wind-vane must be surely spinning. No; a mere singing in his ears.

That was all—a mere singing. The ice must have passed the latch by now. More likely the upper hinge was covered. Between the moss-chinked roof-poles, little points of frost began to appear. How slowly they grew! No; not so slowly. There was a new one, and there another. Two—three—four; they were coming too fast to count. There were two growing together. And there, a third had joined them.

Why, there were no more spots. They had run together and formed a sheet.

Well, he would have company. If Gabriel ever broke the silence of the North, they would stand together, hand in hand, before the great White Throne. And God would judge them, God would judge them!

Then Percy Cuthfert closed his eyes and dropped off to sleep.

To the Man on the Trail

'Dump it in!.' 'But I say, Kid, isn't that going it a little too strong? Whisky and alcohol's bad enough; but when it comes to brandy and pepper sauce and-' 'Dump it in. Who's making this punch, anyway?' And Malemute Kid smiled benignantly through the clouds of steam. 'By the time you've been in this country as long as I have, my son, and lived on rabbit tracks and salmon belly, you'll learn that Christmas comes only once per annum.

And a Christmas without punch is sinking a hole to bedrock with nary a pay streak.'

'Stack up on that fer a high cyard,' approved Big Jim Belden, who had come down from his claim on Mazy May to spend Christmas, and who, as everyone knew, had been living the two months past on straight moose meat. 'Hain't fergot the hooch we-uns made on the Tanana, hey yeh?' 'Well, I guess yes. Boys, it would have done your hearts good to see that whole tribe fighting drunk—and all because of a glorious ferment of sugar and sour dough. That was before your time,' Malemute Kid said as he turned to Stanley Prince, a young mining expert who had been in two years. 'No white women in the country then, and Mason wanted to get married. Ruth's father was chief of the Tananas, and objected, like the rest of the tribe. Stiff? Why, I used my last pound of sugar; finest work in that line I ever did in my life. You should have seen the chase, down the river and across the portage.' 'But the squaw?' asked Louis Savoy, the tall French Canadian, becoming interested; for he had heard of this wild deed when at Forty Mile the preceding winter.

Then Malemute Kid, who was a born raconteur, told the unvarnished tale of the Northland Lochinvar. More than one rough adventurer of the North felt his heartstrings draw closer and experienced vague yearnings for the sunnier pastures of the Southland, where life promised something more than a barren struggle with cold and death.

'We struck the Yukon just behind the first ice run,' he concluded, 'and the tribe only a quarter of an hour behind. But that saved us; for the second run broke the jam above and shut them out. When they finally got into Nuklukyeto, the whole post was ready for them.

'And as to the forgathering, ask Father Roubeau here: he performed the ceremony.' The Jesuit took the pipe from his lips but could only express his gratification with patriarchal smiles, while Protestant and Catholic vigorously applauded.

'By gar!' ejaculated Louis Savoy, who seemed overcome by the romance of it. 'La petite squaw: mon Mason brav. By gar!' Then, as the first tin cups of punch went round, Bettles the Unquenchable sprang to his feet and struck up his favorite drinking song: 'There's Henry Ward Beecher And Sunday-school teachers, All drink of the sassafras root; But you bet all the same, If it had its right name, It's the juice of the forbidden fruit.'

'Oh, the juice of the forbidden fruit,' roared out the bacchanalian chorus, 'Oh, the juice of the forbidden fruit; But you bet all the same, If it had its right name, It's the juice of the forbidden fruit.'

Malemute Kid's frightful concoction did its work; the men of the camps and trails unbent in its genial glow, and jest and song and tales of past adventure went round the board.

Aliens from a dozen lands, they toasted each and all. It was the Englishman, Prince, who pledged 'Uncle Sam, the precocious infant of the New World'; the Yankee, Bettles, who drank to 'The Queen, God bless her'; and together, Savoy and Meyers, the German trader, clanged their cups to Alsace and Lorraine.

Then Malemute Kid arose, cup in hand, and glanced at the greased-paper window, where the frost stood full three inches thick. 'A health to the man on trail this night; may his grub hold out; may his dogs keep their legs; may his matches never miss fire.' Crack!

Crack! heard the familiar music of the dog whip, the whining howl of the Malemutes, and the crunch of a sled as it drew up to the cabin. Conversation languished while they waited the issue.

'An old-timer; cares for his dogs and then himself,' whispered Malemute Kid to Prince as they listened to the snapping jaws and the wolfish snarls and yelps of pain which proclaimed to their practiced ears that the stranger was beating back their dogs while he fed his own.

Then came the expected knock, sharp and confident, and the stranger entered.

Dazzled by the light, he hesitated a moment at the door, giving to all a chance for scrutiny. He was a striking personage, and a most picturesque one, in his Arctic dress of wool and fur. Standing six foot two or three, with proportionate breadth of shoulders and depth of chest, his smooth-shaven face nipped by the cold to a gleaming pink, his long lashes and eyebrows white with ice, and the ear and neck flaps of his great wolfskin cap loosely raised, he seemed, of a verity, the Frost King, just stepped in out of the night.

Clasped outside his Mackinaw jacket, a beaded belt held two large Colt's revolvers and a hunting knife, while he carried, in addition to the inevitable dog whip, a smokeless rifle of the largest bore and latest pattern. As he came forward, for all his step was firm and elastic, they could see that fatigue bore heavily upon him.

An awkward silence had fallen, but his hearty 'What cheer, my lads?' put them quickly at ease, and the next instant Malemute Kid and he had gripped hands. Though they had never met, each had heard of the other, and the recognition was mutual. A sweeping introduction and a mug of punch were forced upon him before he could explain his errand.

How long since that basket sled, with three men and eight dogs, passed?' he asked.

'An even two days ahead. Are you after them?' 'Yes; my team. Run them off under my very nose, the cusses. I've gained two days on them already—pick them up on the next run.' 'Reckon they'll show spunk?' asked Belden, in order to keep up the conversation, for Malemute Kid already had the coffeepot on and was busily frying bacon and moose meat.

The stranger significantly tapped his revolvers.

'When'd yeh leave Dawson?' 'Twelve o'clock.' 'Last night?'—as a matter of course.

'Today.' A murmur of surprise passed round the circle. And well it might; for it was just midnight, and seventy-five miles of rough river trail was not to be sneered at for a twelve hours' run.

The talk soon became impersonal, however, harking back to the trails of childhood. As the young stranger ate of the rude fare Malemute Kid attentively studied his face. Nor was he long in deciding that it was fair, honest, and open, and that he liked it. Still youthful, the lines had been firmly traced by toil and hardship.

Though genial in conversation, and mild when at rest, the blue eyes gave promise of the hard steel-glitter which comes when called into action, especially against odds. The heavy jaw and square-cut chin demonstrated rugged pertinacity and indomitability. Nor, though the attributes of the lion were there, was there wanting the certain softness, the hint of womanliness, which bespoke the emotional nature.

'So thet's how me an' the ol' woman got spliced,' said Belden, concluding the exciting tale of his courtship. '"Here we be, Dad," sez she. "An' may yeh be damned," sez he to her, an' then to me, "Jim, yeh—yeh git outen them good duds o' yourn; I want a right peart slice o' thet forty acre plowed 'fore dinner." An' then he sort o' sniffled an' kissed her. An' I was thet happy—but he seen me an' roars out, "Yeh, Jim!" An' yeh bet I dusted fer the barn.' 'Any kids waiting for you back in the States?' asked the stranger.

'Nope; Sal died 'fore any come. Thet's why I'm here.' Belden abstractedly began to light his pipe, which had failed to go out, and then brightened up with, 'How 'bout yerself, stranger—married man?' For reply, he opened his watch, slipped it from the thong which served for a chain, and passed it over. Belden picked up the slush lamp, surveyed the inside of the case critically, and, swearing admiringly to himself, handed it over to Louis Savoy. With numerous 'By gars!' he finally surrendered it to Prince, and they noticed that his hands trembled and his eyes took on a peculiar softness. And so it passed from horny hand to horny hand—the pasted photograph of a woman, the clinging kind that such men fancy, with a babe at the breast. Those who had not yet seen the wonder were keen with curiosity; those who had became silent and retrospective. They could face the pinch of famine, the grip of scurvy, or the quick death by field or flood; but the pictured semblance of a stranger woman and child made women and children of them all.

'Never have seen the youngster yet—he's a boy, she says, and two years old,' said the stranger as he received the treasure back. A lingering moment he gazed upon it, then snapped the case and turned away, but not quick enough to hide the restrained rush of tears. Malemute Kid led him to a bunk and bade him turn in.

'Call me at four sharp. Don't fail me,' were his last words, and a moment later he was breathing in the heaviness of exhausted sleep.

'By Jove! He's a plucky chap,' commented Prince. 'Three hours' sleep after seventy-five miles with the dogs, and then the trail again. Who is he, Kid?' 'Jack Westondale. Been in going on three years, with nothing but the name of working like a horse, and any amount of bad luck to his credit. I never knew him, but Sitka Charley told me about him.' 'It seems hard that a man with a sweet young wife like his should be putting in his years in this Godforsaken hole, where every year counts two on the outside.' 'The trouble with him is clean grit and stubbornness. He's cleaned up twice with a stake, but lost it both times.' Here the conversation was broken off by an uproar from Bettles, for the effect had begun to wear away. And soon the bleak years of monotonous grub and deadening toil were being forgotten in rough merriment. Malemute Kid alone seemed unable to lose himself, and cast many an anxious look at his watch. Once he put on his mittens and beaver-skin cap, and, leaving the cabin, fell to rummaging about in the cache.

Nor could he wait the hour designated; for he was fifteen minutes ahead of time in rousing his guest. The young giant had stiffened badly, and brisk rubbing was necessary to bring him to his feet. He tottered painfully out of the cabin, to find his dogs harnessed and everything ready for the start. The company wished him good luck and a short chase, while Father Roubeau, hurriedly blessing him, led the stampede for the cabin; and small wonder, for it is not good to face seventy-four degrees below zero with naked ears and hands.

Malemute Kid saw him to the main trail, and there, gripping his hand heartily, gave him advice.

'You'll find a hundred pounds of salmon eggs on the sled,' he said. 'The dogs will go as far on that as with one hundred and fifty of fish, and you can't get dog food at Pelly, as you probably expected.' The stranger started, and his eyes flashed, but he did not interrupt. 'You can't get an ounce of food for dog or man till you reach Five Fingers, and that's a stiff two hundred miles. Watch out for open water on the Thirty Mile River, and be sure you take the big cutoff above Le Barge.' 'How did you know it? Surely the news can't be ahead of me already?' 'I don't know it; and what's more, I don't want to know it. But you never owned that team you're chasing. Sitka Charley sold it to them last spring. But he sized you up to me as square once, and I believe him. I've seen your face; I like it. And I've seen—why, damn you, hit the high places for salt water and that wife of yours, and—' Here the Kid unmittened and jerked out his sack.

'No; I don't need it,' and the tears froze on his cheeks as he convulsively gripped Malemute Kid's hand.

'Then don't spare the dogs; cut them out of the traces as fast as they drop; buy them, and think they're cheap at ten dollars a pound. You can get them at Five Fingers, Little Salmon, and Hootalinqua. And watch out for wet feet,' was his parting advice. 'Keep a-traveling up to twenty-five, but if it gets below that, build a fire and change your socks.'

Fifteen minutes had barely elapsed when the jingle of bells announced new arrivals. The door opened, and a mounted policeman of the Northwest Territory entered, followed by two half-breed dog drivers. Like Westondale, they were heavily armed and showed signs of fatigue. The half-breeds had been born to the trail and bore it easily; but the young policeman was badly exhausted. Still, the dogged obstinacy of his race held him to the pace he had set, and would hold him till he dropped in his tracks.

'When did Westondale pull out?' he asked. 'He stopped here, didn't he?' This was supererogatory, for the tracks told their own tale too well.

Malemute Kid had caught Belden's eye, and he, scenting the wind, replied evasively, 'A right peart while back.' 'Come, my man; speak up,' the policeman admonished.

'Yeh seem to want him right smart. Hez he ben gittin' cantankerous down Dawson way?'

'Held up Harry McFarland's for forty thousand; exchanged it at the P.C. store for a check on Seattle; and who's to stop the cashing of it if we don't overtake him? When did he pull out?'

Every eye suppressed its excitement, for Malemute Kid had given the cue, and the young officer encountered wooden faces on every hand.

Striding over to Prince, he put the question to him. Though it hurt him, gazing into the frank, earnest face of his fellow countryman, he replied inconsequentially on the state of the trail.

Then he espied Father Roubeau, who could not lie. 'A quarter of an hour ago,' the priest answered; 'but he had four hours' rest for himself and dogs.' 'Fifteen minutes' start, and he's fresh! My God!' The poor fellow staggered back, half fainting from exhaustion and disappointment, murmuring something about the run from Dawson in ten hours and the dogs being played out.

Malemute Kid forced a mug of punch upon him; then he turned for the door, ordering the dog drivers to follow. But the warmth and promise of rest were too tempting, and they objected strenuously. The Kid was conversant with their French patois, and followed it anxiously.

They swore that the dogs were gone up; that Siwash and Babette would have to be shot before the first mile was covered; that the rest were almost as bad; and that it would be better for all hands to rest up.

'Lend me five dogs?' he asked, turning to Malemute Kid.

But the Kid shook his head.

'I'll sign a check on Captain Constantine for five thousand—here's my papers—I'm authorized to draw at my own discretion.'

Again the silent refusal.

'Then I'll requisition them in the name of the Queen.' Smiling incredulously, the Kid glanced at his well-stocked arsenal, and the Englishman, realizing his impotency, turned for the door. But the dog drivers still objecting, he whirled upon them fiercely, calling them women and curs. The swart face of the older half-breed flushed angrily as he drew himself up and promised in good, round terms that he would travel his leader off his legs, and would then be delighted to plant him in the snow.

The young officer—and it required his whole will—walked steadily to the door, exhibiting a freshness he did not possess. But they all knew and appreciated his proud effort; nor could he veil the twinges of agony that shot across his face. Covered with frost, the dogs were curled up in the snow, and it was almost impossible to get them to their feet. The poor brutes whined under the stinging lash, for the dog drivers were angry and cruel; nor till Babette, the leader, was cut from the traces, could they break out the sled and get under way.

'A dirty scoundrel and a liar!' 'By gar! Him no good!' 'A thief!' 'Worse than an Indian!'

It was evident that they were angry—first at the way they had been deceived; and second at the outraged ethics of the Northland, where honesty, above all, was man's prime jewel.

'An' we gave the cuss a hand, after knowin' what he'd did.' All eyes turned accusingly upon Malemute Kid, who rose from the corner where he had been making Babette comfortable, and silently emptied the bowl for a final round of punch.

'It's a cold night, boys—a bitter cold night,' was the irrelevant commencement of his defense. 'You've all traveled trail, and know what that stands for. Don't jump a dog when he's down. You've only heard one side. A whiter man than Jack Westondale never ate from the same pot nor stretched blanket with you or me.

'Last fall he gave his whole clean-up, forty thousand, to Joe Castrell, to buy in on Dominion. Today he'd be a millionaire. But, while he stayed behind at Circle City, taking care of his partner with the scurvy, what does Castell do? Goes into McFarland's, jumps the limit, and drops the whole sack. Found him dead in the snow the next day. And poor Jack laying his plans to go out this winter to his wife and the boy he's never seen. You'll notice he took exactly what his partner lost—forty thousand. Well, he's gone out; and what are you going to do about it?' The Kid glanced round the circle of his judges, noted the softening of their faces, then raised his mug aloft. 'So a health to the man on trail this night; may his grub hold out; may his dogs keep their legs; may his matches never miss fire.

'God prosper him; good luck go with him; and—' 'Confusion to the Mounted Police!' cried Bettles, to the crash of the empty cups.

The Priestly Prerogative

This is the story of a man who did not appreciate his wife; also, of a woman who did him too great an honor when she gave herself to him. Incidentally, it concerns a Jesuit priest who had never been known to lie. He was an appurtenance, and a very necessary one, to the Yukon country; but the presence of the other two was merely accidental. They were specimens of the many strange waifs which ride the breast of a gold rush or come tailing along behind.

Edwin Bentham and Grace Bentham were waifs; they were also tailing along behind, for the Klondike rush of '97 had long since swept down the great river and subsided into the famine-stricken city of Dawson. When the Yukon shut up shop and went to sleep under a three-foot ice-sheet, this peripatetic couple found themselves at the Five Finger Rapids, with the City of Gold still a journey of many sleeps to the north.

Many cattle had been butchered at this place in the fall of the year, and the offal made a goodly heap. The three fellow-voyagers of Edwin Bentham and wife gazed upon this deposit, did a little mental arithmetic, caught a certain glimpse of a bonanza, and decided to remain. And all winter they sold sacks of bones and frozen hides to the famished dog-teams. It was a modest price they asked, a dollar a pound, just as it came. Six months later, when the sun came back and the Yukon awoke, they buckled on their heavy moneybelts and journeyed back to the Southland, where they yet live and lie mightily about the Klondike they never saw.

But Edwin Bentham—he was an indolent fellow, and had he not been possessed of a wife, would have gladly joined issued in the dog-meat speculation. As it was, she played upon his vanity, told him how great and strong he was, how a man such as he certainly was could overcome all obstacles and of a surety obtain the Golden Fleece. So he squared his jaw, sold his share in the bones and hides for a sled and one dog, and turned his snowshoes to the north. Needless to state, Grace Bentham's snowshoes never allowed his tracks to grow cold. Nay, ere their tribulations had seen three days, it was the man who followed in the rear, and the woman who broke trail in advance. Of course, if anybody hove in sight, the position was instantly reversed. Thus did his manhood remain virgin to the travelers who passed like ghosts on the silent trail. There are such men in this world.

How such a man and such a woman came to take each other for better and for worse is unimportant to this narrative. These things are familiar to us all, and those people who do them, or even question them too closely, are apt to lose a beautiful faith which is known as Eternal Fitness.

Edwin Bentham was a boy, thrust by mischance into a man's body,—a boy who could complacently pluck a butterfly, wing from wing, or cower in abject terror before a lean, nervy fellow, not half his size. He was a selfish cry-baby, hidden behind a man's mustache and stature, and glossed over with a skin-deep veneer of culture and conventionality. Yes; he was a clubman and a society man, the sort that grace social functions and utter inanities with a charm and unction which is indescribable; the sort that talk big, and cry over a toothache; the sort that put more hell into a woman's life by marrying her than can the most graceless libertine that ever browsed in forbidden pastures. We meet these men every day, but we rarely know them for what they are. Second to marrying them, the best way to get this knowledge is to eat out of the same pot and crawl under the same blanket with them for—well, say a week; no greater margin is necessary.

To see Grace Bentham, was to see a slender, girlish creature; to know her, was to know a soul which dwarfed your own, yet retained all the elements of the eternal feminine. This was the woman who urged and encouraged her husband in his Northland quest, who broke trail for him when no one was looking, and cried in secret over her weakling woman's body.

So journeyed this strangely assorted couple down to old Fort Selkirk, then through fivescore miles of dismal wilderness to Stuart River. And when the short day left them, and the man lay down in the snow and blubbered, it was the woman who lashed him to the sled, bit her lips with the pain of her aching limbs, and helped the dog haul him to Malemute Kid's cabin.

Malemute Kid was not at home, but Meyers, the German trader, cooked great moose-steaks and shook up a bed of fresh pine boughs. Lake, Langham, and Parker, were excited, and not unduly so when the cause was taken into account.

'Oh, Sandy! Say, can you tell a porterhouse from a round? Come out and lend us a hand, anyway!' This appeal emanated from the cache, where Langham was vainly struggling with divers quarters of frozen moose.

'Don't you budge from those dishes!' commanded Parker.

'I say, Sandy; there's a good fellow—just run down to the Missouri Camp and borrow some cinnamon,' begged Lake.

'Oh! oh! hurry up! Why don't—' But the crash of meat and boxes, in the cache, abruptly quenched this peremptory summons.

'Come now, Sandy; it won't take a minute to go down to the Missouri—'

'You leave him alone,' interrupted Parker. 'How am I to mix the biscuits if the table isn't cleared off?'

Sandy paused in indecision, till suddenly the fact that he was Langham's 'man' dawned upon him. Then he apologetically threw down the greasy dishcloth, and went to his master's rescue.

These promising scions of wealthy progenitors had come to the Northland in search of laurels, with much money to burn, and a 'man' apiece. Luckily for their souls, the other two men were up the White River in search of a mythical quartz-ledge; so Sandy had to grin under the responsibility of three healthy masters, each of whom was possessed of peculiar cookery ideas. Twice that morning had a disruption of the whole camp been imminent, only averted by immense concessions from one or the other of these knights of the chafing-dish. But at last their mutual creation, a really dainty dinner, was completed.

Then they sat down to a three-cornered game of 'cut-throat,'—a proceeding which did away with all casus belli for future hostilities, and permitted the victor to depart on a most important mission.

This fortune fell to Parker, who parted his hair in the middle, put on his mittens and bearskin cap, and stepped over to Malemute Kid's cabin. And when he returned, it was in the company of Grace Bentham and Malemute Kid,—the former very sorry her husband could not share with her their hospitality, for he had gone up to look at the Henderson Creek mines, and the latter still a trifle stiff from breaking trail down the Stuart River.

Meyers had been asked, but had declined, being deeply engrossed in an experiment of raising bread from hops.

Well, they could do without the husband; but a woman—why they had not seen one all winter, and the presence of this one promised a new era in their lives.

They were college men and gentlemen, these three young fellows, yearning for the flesh-pots they had been so long denied. Probably Grace Bentham suffered from a similar hunger; at least, it meant much to her, the first bright hour in many weeks of darkness.

But that wonderful first course, which claimed the versatile Lake for its parent, had no sooner been served than there came a loud knock at the door.

'Oh! Ah! Won't you come in, Mr. Bentham?' said Parker, who had stepped to see who the newcomer might be.

'Is my wife here?' gruffly responded that worthy.

'Why, yes. We left word with Mr. Meyers.' Parker was exerting his most dulcet tones, inwardly wondering what the deuce it all meant. 'Won't you come in? Expecting you at any moment, we reserved a place. And just in time for the first course, too.' 'Come in, Edwin, dear,' chirped Grace Bentham from her seat at the table.

Parker naturally stood aside.

'I want my wife,' reiterated Bentham hoarsely, the intonation savoring disagreeably of ownership.

Parker gasped, was within an ace of driving his fist into the face of his boorish visitor, but held himself awkwardly in check. Everybody rose. Lake lost his head and caught himself on the verge of saying, 'Must you go?' Then began the farrago of leave-taking. 'So nice of you—' 'I am awfully sorry' 'By Jove! how things did brighten—' 'Really now, you—'

'Thank you ever so much—' 'Nice trip to Dawson—' etc., etc.

In this wise the lamb was helped into her jacket and led to the slaughter. Then the door slammed, and they gazed woefully upon the deserted table.

'Damn!' Langham had suffered disadvantages in his early training, and his oaths were weak and monotonous. 'Damn!' he repeated, vaguely conscious of the incompleteness and vainly struggling for a more virile term. It is a clever woman who can fill out the many weak places in an inefficient man, by her own indomitability, re-enforce his vacillating nature, infuse her ambitious soul into his, and spur him on to great achievements. And it is indeed a very clever and tactful woman who can do all this, and do it so subtly that the man receives all the credit and believes in his inmost heart that everything is due to him and him alone.

This is what Grace Bentham proceeded to do. Arriving in Dawson with a few pounds of flour and several letters of introduction, she at once applied herself to the task of pushing her big baby to the fore. It was she who melted the stony heart and wrung credit from the rude barbarian who presided over the destiny of the P. C. Company; yet it was Edwin Bentham to whom the concession was ostensibly granted. It was she who dragged her baby up and down creeks, over benches and divides, and on a dozen wild stampedes; yet everybody remarked what an energetic fellow that Bentham was. It was she who studied maps, and catechised miners, and hammered geography and locations into his hollow head, till everybody marveled at his broad grasp of the country and knowledge of its conditions. Of course, they said the wife was a brick, and only a few wise ones appreciated and pitied the brave little woman.

She did the work; he got the credit and reward. In the Northwest Territory a married woman cannot stake or record a creek, bench, or quartz claim; so Edwin Bentham went down to the Gold Commissioner and filed on Bench Claim 23, second tier, of French Hill. And when April came they were washing out a thousand dollars a day, with many, many such days in prospect.

At the base of French Hill lay Eldorado Creek, and on a creek claim stood the cabin of Clyde Wharton. At present he was not washing out a diurnal thousand dollars; but his dumps grew, shift by shift, and there would come a time when those dumps would pass through his sluice-boxes, depositing in the riffles, in the course of half a dozen days, several hundred thousand dollars. He often sat in that cabin, smoked his pipe, and dreamed beautiful little dreams,—dreams in which neither the dumps nor the half-ton of dust in the P. C. Company's big safe, played a part.

And Grace Bentham, as she washed tin dishes in her hillside cabin, often glanced down into Eldorado Creek, and dreamed,—not of dumps nor dust, however. They met frequently, as the trail to the one claim crossed the other, and there is much to talk about in the Northland spring; but never once, by the light of an eye nor the slip of a tongue, did they speak their hearts.

This is as it was at first. But one day Edwin Bentham was brutal. All boys are thus; besides, being a French Hill king now, he began to think a great deal of himself and to forget all he owed to his wife. On this day, Wharton heard of it, and waylaid Grace Bentham, and talked wildly. This made her very happy, though she would not listen, and made him promise to not say such things again. Her hour had not come.

But the sun swept back on its northern journey, the black of midnight changed to the steely color of dawn, the snow slipped away, the water dashed again over the glacial drift, and the wash-up began. Day and night the yellow clay and scraped bedrock hurried through the swift sluices, yielding up its ransom to the strong men from the Southland.

And in that time of tumult came Grace Bentham's hour.

To all of us such hours at some time come,—that is, to us who are not too phlegmatic.

Some people are good, not from inherent love of virtue, but from sheer laziness. But those of us who know weak moments may understand.

Edwin Bentham was weighing dust over the bar of the saloon at the Forks—altogether too much of his dust went over that pine board—when his wife came down the hill and slipped into Clyde Wharton's cabin. Wharton was not expecting her, but that did not alter the case. And much subsequent misery and idle waiting might have been avoided, had not Father Roubeau seen this and turned aside from the main creek trail. 'My child,—' 'Hold on, Father Roubeau! Though I'm not of your faith, I respect you; but you can't come in between this woman and me!' 'You know what you are doing?' 'Know! Were you God Almighty, ready to fling me into eternal fire, I'd bank my will against yours in this matter.' Wharton had placed Grace on a stool and stood belligerently before her.

'You sit down on that chair and keep quiet,' he continued, addressing the Jesuit. 'I'll take my innings now. You can have yours after.'

Father Roubeau bowed courteously and obeyed. He was an easy-going man and had learned to bide his time. Wharton pulled a stool alongside the woman's, smothering her hand in his.

'Then you do care for me, and will take me away?' Her face seemed to reflect the peace of this man, against whom she might draw close for shelter.

'Dear, don't you remember what I said before? Of course I-' 'But how can you?—the wash-up?' 'Do you think that worries? Anyway, I'll give the job to Father Roubeau, here.

'I can trust him to safely bank the dust with the company.' 'To think of it!—I'll never see him again.' 'A blessing!' 'And to go—O, Clyde, I can't! I can't!' 'There, there; of course you can, just let me plan it.—You see, as soon as we get a few traps together, we'll start, and-' 'Suppose he comes back?' 'I'll break every-' 'No, no! No fighting, Clyde! Promise me that.' 'All right! I'll just tell the men to throw him off the claim. They've seen how he's treated you, and haven't much love for him.'

'You mustn't do that. You mustn't hurt him.' 'What then? Let him come right in here and take you away before my eyes?' 'No-o,' she half whispered, stroking his hand softly.

'Then let me run it, and don't worry. I'll see he doesn't get hurt. Precious lot he cared whether you got hurt or not! We won't go back to Dawson. I'll send word down for a couple of the boys to outfit and pole a boat up the Yukon. We'll cross the divide and raft down the Indian River to meet them. Then—' 'And then?' Her head was on his shoulder.

Their voices sank to softer cadences, each word a caress. The Jesuit fidgeted nervously.

'And then?' she repeated.

'Why we'll pole up, and up, and up, and portage the White Horse Rapids and the Box Canon.' 'Yes?' 'And the Sixty-Mile River; then the lakes, Chilcoot, Dyea, and Salt Water.' 'But, dear, I can't pole a boat.' 'You little goose! I'll get Sitka Charley; he knows all the good water and best camps, and he is the best traveler I ever met, if he is an Indian. All you'll have to do, is to sit in the middle of the boat, and sing songs, and play Cleopatra, and fight—no, we're in luck; too early for mosquitoes.'

'And then, O my Antony?' 'And then a steamer, San Francisco, and the world! Never to come back to this cursed hole again. Think of it! The world, and ours to choose from! I'll sell out. Why, we're rich! The Waldworth Syndicate will give me half a million for what's left in the ground, and I've got twice as much in the dumps and with the P. C. Company. We'll go to the Fair in Paris in 1900. We'll go to Jerusalem, if you say so.

'We'll buy an Italian palace, and you can play Cleopatra to your heart's content. No, you shall be Lucretia, Acte, or anybody your little heart sees fit to become. But you mustn't, you really mustn't-' 'The wife of Caesar shall be above reproach.' 'Of course, but—' 'But I won't be your wife, will I, dear?' 'I didn't mean that.' 'But you'll love me just as much, and never even think— oh! I know you'll be like other men; you'll grow tired, and—and-'

'How can you? I—' 'Promise me.' 'Yes, yes; I do promise.' 'You say it so easily, dear; but how do you know?—or I know? I have so little to give, yet it is so much, and all I have. O, Clyde! promise me you won't?'

'There, there! You mustn't begin to doubt already. Till death do us part, you know.'

'Think! I once said that to—to him, and now?' 'And now, little sweetheart, you're not to bother about such things any more.

Of course, I never, never will, and—' And for the first time, lips trembled against lips.

Father Roubeau had been watching the main trail through the window, but could stand the strain no longer.

He cleared his throat and turned around.

'Your turn now, Father!' Wharton's face was flushed with the fire of his first embrace.

There was an exultant ring to his voice as he abdicated in the other's favor. He had no doubt as to the result. Neither had Grace, for a smile played about her mouth as she faced the priest.

'My child,' he began, 'my heart bleeds for you. It is a pretty dream, but it cannot be.'

'And why, Father? I have said yes.' 'You knew not what you did. You did not think of the oath you took, before your God, to that man who is your husband. It remains for me to make you realize the sanctity of such a pledge.' 'And if I do realize, and yet refuse?'

'Then God'

'Which God? My husband has a God which I care not to worship. There must be many such.' 'Child! unsay those words! Ah! you do not mean them. I understand. I, too, have had such moments.' For an instant he was back in his native France, and a wistful, sad-eyed face came as a mist between him and the woman before him.

'Then, Father, has my God forsaken me? I am not wicked above women. My misery with him has been great. Why should it be greater? Why shall I

82

not grasp at happiness? I cannot, will not, go back to him!' 'Rather is your God forsaken. Return. Throw your burden upon Him, and the darkness shall be lifted. O my child,—' 'No; it is useless; I have made my bed and so shall I lie. I will go on. And if God punishes me, I shall bear it somehow. You do not understand. You are not a woman.' 'My mother was a woman.'

'But—' 'And Christ was born of a woman.' She did not answer. A silence fell. Wharton pulled his mustache impatiently and kept an eye on the trail. Grace leaned her elbow on the table, her face set with resolve. The smile had died away. Father Roubeau shifted his ground.

'You have children?'

'At one time I wished—but now—no. And I am thankful.' 'And a mother?' 'Yes.' 'She loves you?' 'Yes.' Her replies were whispers.

'And a brother?—no matter, he is a man. But a sister?' Her head drooped a quavering 'Yes.' 'Younger? Very much?' 'Seven years.' 'And you have thought well about this matter? About them? About your mother? And your sister? She stands on the threshold of her woman's life, and this wildness of yours may mean much to her. Could you go before her, look upon her fresh young face, hold her hand in yours, or touch your cheek to hers?'

To his words, her brain formed vivid images, till she cried out, 'Don't! don't!' and shrank away as do the wolf-dogs from the lash.

'But you must face all this; and better it is to do it now.' In his eyes, which she could not see, there was a great compassion, but his face, tense and quivering, showed no relenting.

She raised her head from the table, forced back the tears, struggled for control.

'I shall go away. They will never see me, and come to forget me. I shall be to them as dead. And—and I will go with Clyde—today.' It seemed final. Wharton stepped forward, but the priest waved him back.

'You have wished for children?' A silent 'Yes.' 'And prayed for them?' 'Often.' 'And have you thought, if you should have children?' Father Roubeau's eyes rested for a moment on the man by the window.

A quick light shot across her face. Then the full import dawned upon her. She raised her hand appealingly, but he went on.

'Can you picture an innocent babe in your arms? A boy? The world is not so hard upon a girl. Why, your very breast would turn to gall! And you could be proud and happy of your boy, as you looked on other children?—' 'O, have pity! Hush!' 'A scapegoat—'

'Don't! don't! I will go back!' She was at his feet.

'A child to grow up with no thought of evil, and one day the world to fling a tender name in his face. A child to look back and curse you from whose loins he sprang!'

'O my God! my God!' She groveled on the floor. The priest sighed and raised her to her feet.

Wharton pressed forward, but she motioned him away.

'Don't come near me, Clyde! I am going back!' The tears were coursing pitifully down her face, but she made no effort to wipe them away.

'After all this? You cannot! I will not let you!' 'Don't touch me!' She shivered and drew back.

'I will! You are mine! Do you hear? You are mine!' Then he whirled upon the priest. 'O what a fool I was to ever let you wag your silly tongue! Thank your God you are not a common man, for I'd—but the priestly prerogative must be exercised, eh? Well, you have exercised it. Now get out of my house, or I'll forget who and what you are!' Father Roubeau bowed, took her hand, and started for the door. But Wharton cut them off.

'Grace! You said you loved me?' 'I did.' 'And you do now?' 'I do.' 'Say it again.'

'I do love you, Clyde; I do.' 'There, you priest!' he cried. 'You have heard it, and with those words on her lips you would send her back to live a lie and a hell with that man?'

84

But Father Roubeau whisked the woman into the inner room and closed the door. 'No words!' he whispered to Wharton, as he struck a casual posture on a stool. 'Remember, for her sake,' he added.

The room echoed to a rough knock at the door; the latch raised and Edwin Bentham stepped in.

'Seen anything of my wife?' he asked as soon as salutations had been exchanged.

Two heads nodded negatively.

'I saw her tracks down from the cabin,' he continued tentatively, 'and they broke off, just opposite here, on the main trail.' His listeners looked bored.

'And I—I thought—'

'She was here!' thundered Wharton.

The priest silenced him with a look. 'Did you see her tracks leading up to this cabin, my son?' Wily Father Roubeau—he had taken good care to obliterate them as he came up the same path an hour before.

'I didn't stop to look, I—' His eyes rested suspiciously on the door to the other room, then interrogated the priest. The latter shook his head; but the doubt seemed to linger.

Father Roubeau breathed a swift, silent prayer, and rose to his feet. 'If you doubt me, why—' He made as though to open the door.

A priest could not lie. Edwin Bentham had heard this often, and believed it.

'Of course not, Father,' he interposed hurriedly. 'I was only wondering where my wife had gone, and thought maybe—I guess she's up at Mrs. Stanton's on French Gulch. Nice weather, isn't it? Heard the news? Flour's gone down to forty dollars a hundred, and they say the che-cha-quas are flocking down the river in droves.

'But I must be going; so good-by.' The door slammed, and from the window they watched him take his guest up French Gulch. A few weeks later, just after the June high-water, two men shot a canoe into mid-stream and made fast to a derelict pine. This tightened the painter and jerked the frail craft along as would a tow-boat. Father Roubeau had been directed to leave the Upper Country and return to his swarthy children at Minook. The white men had come among them, and they were devoting too little time to fishing, and too much to a certain deity whose transient habitat was in countless black bottles.

Malemute Kid also had business in the Lower Country, so they journeyed together.

But one, in all the Northland, knew the man Paul Roubeau, and that man was Malemute Kid. Before him alone did the priest cast off the sacerdotal garb and stand naked. And why not? These two men knew each other. Had they not shared the last morsel of fish, the last pinch of tobacco, the last and inmost thought, on the barren stretches of Bering Sea, in the heartbreaking mazes of the Great Delta, on the terrible winter journey from Point Barrow to the Porcupine? Father Roubeau puffed heavily at his trail-worn pipe, and gazed on the reddisked sun, poised somberly on the edge of the northern horizon.

Malemute Kid wound up his watch. It was midnight.

'Cheer up, old man!' The Kid was evidently gathering up a broken thread.

'God surely will forgive such a lie. Let me give you the word of a man who strikes a true note: If She have spoken a word, remember thy lips are sealed, And the brand of the Dog is upon him by whom is the secret revealed.

If there be trouble to Herward, and a lie of the blackest can clear, Lie, while thy lips can move or a man is alive to hear.'

Father Roubeau removed his pipe and reflected. 'The man speaks true, but my soul is not vexed with that. The lie and the penance stand with God; but—but—'

'What then? Your hands are clean.' 'Not so. Kid, I have thought much, and yet the thing remains. I knew, and made her go back.' The clear note of a robin rang out from the wooden bank, a partridge drummed the call in the distance, a moose lunged noisily in the eddy; but the twain smoked on in silence.

The Wisdom of the Trail

Sitka Charley had achieved the impossible. Other Indians might have known as much of the wisdom of the trail as he did; but he alone knew the white man's wisdom, the honor of the trail, and the law. But these things had not come to him in a day. The aboriginal mind is slow to generalize, and many facts, repeated often, are required to compass an understanding. Sitka Charley, from boyhood, had been thrown continually with white men, and as a man he had elected to cast his fortunes with them, expatriating himself, once and for all, from his own people. Even then, respecting, almost venerating their power, and pondering over it, he had yet to divine its secret essence—the honor and the law. And it was only by the cumulative evidence of years that he had finally come to understand. Being an alien, when he did know, he knew it better than the white man himself; being an Indian, he had achieved the impossible.

And of these things had been bred a certain contempt for his own people—a contempt which he had made it a custom to conceal, but which now burst forth in a polyglot whirlwind of curses upon the heads of Kah-Chucte and Gowhee. They cringed before him like a brace of snarling wolf dogs, too cowardly to spring, too wolfish to cover their fangs. They were not handsome creatures. Neither was Sitka Charley. All three were frightful-looking. There was no flesh to their faces; their cheekbones were massed with hideous scabs which had cracked and frozen alternately under the intense frost; while their eyes burned luridly with the light which is born of desperation and hunger. Men so situated, beyond the pale of the honor and the law, are not to be trusted. Sitka Charley knew this; and this was why he had forced them to abandon their rifles with the rest of the camp outfit ten days before. His rifle and Captain Eppingwell's were the only ones that remained.

'Come, get a fire started,' he commanded, drawing out the precious matchbox with its attendant strips of dry birchbark.

The two Indians fell sullenly to the task of gathering dead branches and underwood. They were weak and paused often, catching themselves, in the act of stooping, with giddy motions, or staggering to the center of operations with their knees shaking like castanets.

After each trip they rested for a moment, as though sick and deadly weary. At times their eyes took on the patient stoicism of dumb suffering; and again the ego seemed almost burst forth with its wild cry, 'I, I, I want to exist!'—the dominant note of the whole living universe.

A light breath of air blew from the south, nipping the exposed portions of their bodies and driving the frost, in needles of fire, through fur and flesh to the bones. So, when the fire had grown lusty and thawed a damp circle in the snow about it, Sitka Charley forced his reluctant comrades to lend a hand in pitching a fly. It was a primitive affair, merely a blanket stretched parallel with the fire and to windward of it, at an angle of perhaps forty-five degrees. This shut out the chill wind and threw the heat backward and down upon those who were to huddle in its shelter. Then a layer of green spruce boughs were spread, that their bodies might not come in contact with the snow. When this task was completed, Kah-Chucte and Gowhee proceeded to take care of their feet. Their icebound moccasins were sadly worn by much travel, and the sharp ice of the river jams had cut them to rags.

Their Siwash socks were similarly conditioned, and when these had been thawed and removed, the dead-white tips of the toes, in the various stages of mortification, told their simple tale of the trail.

Leaving the two to the drying of their footgear, Sitka Charley turned back over the course he had come. He, too, had a mighty longing to sit by the fire and tend his complaining flesh, but the honor and the law forbade. He toiled painfully over the frozen field, each step a protest, every muscle in revolt. Several times, where the open water between the jams had recently crusted, he was forced to miserably accelerate his movements as the fragile footing swayed and threatened beneath him. In such places death was quick and easy; but it was not his desire to endure no more.

89

His deepening anxiety vanished as two Indians dragged into view round a bend in the river. They staggered and panted like men under heavy burdens; yet the packs on their backs were a matter of but a few pounds. He questioned them eagerly, and their replies seemed to relieve him. He hurried on. Next came two white men, supporting between them a woman. They also behaved as though drunken, and their limbs shook with weakness. But the woman leaned lightly upon them, choosing to carry herself forward with her own strength. At the sight of her a flash of joy cast its fleeting light across Sitka Charley's face. He cherished a very great regard for Mrs. Eppingwell. He had seen many white women, but this was the first to travel the trail with him. When Captain Eppingwell proposed the hazardous undertaking and made him an offer for his services, he had shaken his head gravely; for it was an unknown journey through the dismal vastnesses of the Northland, and he knew it to be of the kind that try to the uttermost the souls of men.

But when he learned that the captain's wife was to accompany them, he had refused flatly to have anything further to do with it. Had it been a woman of his own race he would have harbored no objections; but these women of the Southland—no, no, they were too soft, too tender, for such enterprises.

Sitka Charley did not know this kind of woman. Five minutes before, he did not even dream of taking charge of the expedition; but when she came to him with her wonderful smile and her straight clean English, and talked to the point, without pleading or persuading, he had incontinently yielded. Had there been a softness and appeal to mercy in the eyes, a tremble to the voice, a taking advantage of sex, he would have stiffened to steel; instead her clear-searching eyes and clear-ringing voice, her utter frankness and tacit assumption of equality, had robbed him of his reason. He felt, then, that this was a new breed of woman; and ere they had been trail mates for many days he knew why the sons of such women mastered the land and the sea, and why the sons of his own womankind could not prevail against them. Tender and soft! Day after day he watched her, muscle-weary, exhausted, indomitable, and the words beat in upon him in a perennial refrain. Tender and soft! He knew her feet had been born to easy paths and sunny lands, strangers to the moccasined pain of the North, unkissed by the chill lips of the frost, and he watched and marveled at them twinkling ever through the weary day.

She had always a smile and a word of cheer, from which not even the meanest packer was excluded. As the way grew darker she seemed to stiffen and gather greater strength, and when Kah-Chucte and Gowhee, who had bragged that they knew every landmark of the way as a child did the skin bails of the tepee, acknowledged that they knew not where they were, it was she who raised a forgiving voice amid the curses of the men. She had sung to them that night till they felt the weariness fall from them and were ready to face the future with fresh hope. And when the food failed and each scant stint was measured jealously, she it was who rebelled against the machinations of her husband and Sitka Charley, and demanded and received a share neither greater nor less than that of the others.

Sitka Charley was proud to know this woman. A new richness, a greater breadth, had come into his life with her presence. Hitherto he had been his own mentor, had turned to right or left at no man's beck; he had moulded himself according to his own dictates, nourished his manhood regardless of all save his own opinion. For the first time he had felt a call from without for the best that was in him, just a glance of appreciation from the clear-searching eyes, a word of thanks from the clear-ringing voice, just a slight wreathing of the lips in the wonderful smile, and he walked with the gods for hours to come. It was a new stimulant to his manhood; for the first time he thrilled with a conscious pride in his wisdom of the trail; and between the twain they ever lifted the sinking hearts of their comrades. The faces of the two men and the woman brightened as they saw him, for after all he was the staff they leaned upon. But Sitka Charley, rigid as was his wont, concealing pain and pleasure impartially beneath an iron exterior, asked them the welfare of the rest, told the distance to the fire, and continued on the back-trip.

Next he met a single Indian, unburdened, limping, lips compressed, and eyes set with the pain of a foot in which the quick fought a losing battle with the dead. All possible care had been taken of him, but in the last extremity the weak and unfortunate must perish, and Sitka Charley deemed his days to be few. The man could not keep up for long, so he gave him rough cheering words. After that came two more Indians, to whom he had allotted the task of helping along Joe, the third white man of the party. They had deserted him.

91

Sitka Charley saw at a glance the lurking spring in their bodies, and knew they had at last cast off his mastery. So he was not taken unawares when he ordered them back in quest of their abandoned charge, and saw the gleam of the hunting knives that they drew from the sheaths. A pitiful spectacle, three weak men lifting their puny strength in the face of the mighty vastness; but the two recoiled under the fierce rifle blows of the one and returned like beaten dogs to the leash. Two hours later, with Joe reeling between them and Sitka Charley bringing up the rear, they came to the fire, where the remainder of the expedition crouched in the shelter of the fly.

'A few words, my comrades, before we sleep,' Sitka Charley said after they had devoured their slim rations of unleavened bread. He was speaking to the Indians in their own tongue, having already given the import to the whites. 'A few words, my comrades, for your own good, that ye may yet perchance live. I shall give you the law; on his own head by the death of him that breaks it. We have passed the Hills of Silence, and we now travel the head reaches of the Stuart. It may be one sleep, it may be several, it may be many sleeps, but in time we shall come among the men of the Yukon, who have much grub. It were well that we look to the law. Today Kah-Chucte and Gowhee, whom I commanded to break trail, forgot they were men, and like frightened children ran away.

'True, they forgot; so let us forget. But hereafter, let them remember. If it should happen they do not...' He touched his rifle carelessly, grimly. 'Tomorrow they shall carry the flour and see that the white man Joe lies not down by the trail. The cups of flour are counted; should so much as an ounce be wanting at nightfall... Do ye understand? Today there were others that forgot. Moose Head and Three Salmon left the white man Joe to lie in the snow. Let them forget no more. With the light of day shall they go forth and break trail. Ye have heard the law. Look well, lest ye break it.' Sitka Charley found it beyond him to keep the line close up. From Moose Head and Three Salmon, who broke trail in advance, to Kah-Chucte, Gowhee, and Joe, it straggled out over a mile. Each staggered, fell or rested as he saw fit.

The line of march was a progression through a chain of irregular halts. Each drew upon the last remnant of his strength and stumbled onward till it was expended, but in some miraculous way there was always another last remnant. Each time a man fell it was with the firm belief that he would rise no more; yet he did rise, and again and again. The flesh yielded, the will conquered; but each triumph was a tragedy. The Indian with the frozen foot, no longer erect, crawled forward on hand and knee. He rarely rested, for he knew the penalty exacted by the frost.

Even Mrs. Eppingwell's lips were at last set in a stony smile, and her eyes, seeing, saw not. Often she stopped, pressing a mittened hand to her heart, gasping and dizzy.

Joe, the white man, had passed beyond the stage of suffering. He no longer begged to be let alone, prayed to die; but was soothed and content under the anodyne of delirium. Kah-Chucte and Gowhee dragged him on roughly, venting upon him many a savage glance or blow. To them it was the acme of injustice.

Their hearts were bitter with hate, heavy with fear. Why should they cumber their strength with his weakness? To do so meant death; not to do so—and they remembered the law of Sitka Charley, and the rifle.

Joe fell with greater frequency as the daylight waned, and so hard was he to raise that they dropped farther and farther behind. Sometimes all three pitched into the snow, so weak had the Indians become. Yet on their backs was life, and strength, and warmth.

Within the flour sacks were all the potentialities of existence. They could not but think of this, and it was not strange, that which came to pass. They had fallen by the side of a great timber jam where a thousand cords of firewood waited the match. Near by was an air hole through the ice. Kah-Chucte looked on the wood and the water, as did Gowhee; then they looked at each other.

Never a word was spoken. Gowhee struck a fire; Kah-Chucte filled a tin cup with water and heated it; Joe babbled of things in another land, in a tongue they did not understand.

They mixed flour with the warm water till it was a thin paste, and of this they drank many cups. They did not offer any to Joe; but he did not mind. He did not mind anything, not even his moccasins, which scorched and smoked among the coals.

A crystal mist of snow fell about them, softly, caressingly, wrapping them in clinging robes of white. And their feet would have yet trod many trails had not destiny brushed the clouds aside and cleared the air. Nay, ten minutes' delay would have been salvation.

Sitka Charley, looking back, saw the pillared smoke of their fire, and guessed. And he looked ahead at those who were faithful, and at Mrs. Eppingwell. 'So, my good comrades, ye have again forgotten that you were men? Good! Very good. There will be fewer bellies to feed.' Sitka Charley retied the flour as he spoke, strapping the pack to the one on his own back. He kicked Joe till the pain broke through the poor devil's bliss and brought him doddering to his feet. Then he shoved him out upon the trail and started him on his way. The two Indians attempted to slip off.

'Hold, Gowhee! And thou, too, Kah-Chucte! Hath the flour given such strength to thy legs that they may outrun the swift-winged lead? Think not to cheat the law. Be men for the last time, and be content that ye die full-stomached.

Come, step up, back to the timber, shoulder to shoulder. Come!' The two men obeyed, quietly, without fear; for it is the future which pressed upon the man, not the present.

'Thou, Gowhee, hast a wife and children and a deerskin lodge in the Chipewyan. What is thy will in the matter?' 'Give thou her of the goods which are mine by the word of the captain—the blankets, the beads, the tobacco, the box which makes strange sounds after the manner of the white men. Say that I did die on the trail, but say not how.' 'And thou, Kah-Chucte, who hast nor wife nor child?' 'Mine is a sister, the wife of the factor at Koshim. He beats her, and she is not happy. Give thou her the goods which are mine by the contract, and tell her it were well she go back to her own people. Shouldst thou meet the man, and be so minded, it were a good deed that he should die. He beats her, and she is afraid.' 'Are ye content to die by the law?' 'We are.' 'Then good-bye, my good comrades. May ye sit by the well-filled pot, in warm lodges, ere the day is done.' As he spoke he raised his rifle, and many echoes broke the silence. Hardly had they died away when other rifles spoke in the distance. Sitka Charley started.

There had been more than one shot, yet there was but one other rifle in the party.

He gave a fleeting glance at the men who lay so quietly, smiled viciously at the wisdom of the trail, and hurried on to meet the men of the Yukon.

The Wife of a King

Once when the northland was very young, the social and civic virtues were remarkably alike for their paucity and their simplicity. When the burden of domestic duties grew grievous, and the fireside mood expanded to a constant protest against its bleak loneliness, the adventurers from the Southland, in lieu of better, paid the stipulated prices and took unto themselves native wives. It was a foretaste of Paradise to the women, for it must be confessed that the white rovers gave far better care and treatment of them than did their Indian copartners. Of course, the white men themselves were satisfied with such deals, as were also the Indian men for that matter. Having sold their daughters and sisters for cotton blankets and obsolete rifles and traded their warm furs for flimsy calico and bad whisky, the sons of the soil promptly and cheerfully succumbed to quick consumption and other swift diseases correlated with the blessings of a superior civilization.

It was in these days of Arcadian simplicity that Cal Galbraith journeyed through the land and fell sick on the Lower River. It was a refreshing advent in the lives of the good Sisters of the Holy Cross, who gave him shelter and medicine; though they little dreamed of the hot elixir infused into his veins by the touch of their soft hands and their gentle ministrations. Cal Galbraith, became troubled with strange thoughts which clamored for attention till he laid eyes on the Mission girl, Madeline. Yet he gave no sign, biding his time patiently. He strengthened with the coming spring, and when the sun rode the heavens in a golden circle, and the joy and throb of life was in all the land, he gathered his still weak body together and departed.

Now, Madeline, the Mission girl, was an orphan. Her white father had failed to give a bald-faced grizzly the trail one day, and had died quickly. Then her Indian mother, having no man to fill the winter cache, had tried the hazardous experiment of waiting till the salmon-run on fifty pounds of flour and half as many of bacon. After that, the baby, Chook-ra, went to live with the good Sisters, and to be thenceforth known by another name.

But Madeline still had kinsfolk, the nearest being a dissolute uncle who outraged his vitals with inordinate quantities of the white man's whisky. He strove daily to walk with the gods, and incidentally, his feet sought shorter trails to the grave. When sober he suffered exquisite torture. He had no conscience. To this ancient vagabond Cal Galbraith duly presented himself, and they consumed many words and much tobacco in the conversation that followed. Promises were also made; and in the end the old heathen took a few pounds of dried salmon and his birch-bark canoe, and paddled away to the Mission of the Holy Cross.

It is not given the world to know what promises he made and what lies he told—the Sisters never gossip; but when he returned, upon his swarthy chest there was a brass crucifix, and in his canoe his niece Madeline. That night there was a grand wedding and a potlach; so that for two days to follow there was no fishing done by the village. But in the morning Madeline shook the dust of the Lower River from her moccasins, and with her husband, in a poling-boat, went to live on the Upper River in a place known as the Lower Country. And in the years which followed she was a good wife, sharing her husband's hardships and cooking his food. And she kept him in straight trails, till he learned to save his dust and to work mightily. In the end, he struck it rich and built a cabin in Circle City; and his happiness was such that men who came to visit him in his home-circle became restless at the sight of it and envied him greatly.

But the Northland began to mature and social amenities to make their appearance.

Hitherto, the Southland had sent forth its sons; but it now belched forth a new exodus—this time of its daughters. Sisters and wives they were not; but they did not fail to put new ideas in the heads of the men, and to elevate the tone of things in ways peculiarly their own. No more did the squaws gather at the dances, go roaring down the center in the good, old Virginia reels, or make merry with jolly 'Dan Tucker.' They fell back on their natural stoicism and uncomplainingly watched the rule of their white sisters from their cabins.

Then another exodus came over the mountains from the prolific Southland.

This time it was of women that became mighty in the land. Their word was law; their law was steel. They frowned upon the Indian wives, while the other women became mild and walked humbly. There were cowards who became ashamed of their ancient covenants with the daughters of the soil, who looked with a new distaste upon their dark-skinned children; but there were also others—men—who remained true and proud of their aboriginal vows. When it became the fashion to divorce the native wives. Cal Galbraith retained his manhood, and in so doing felt the heavy hand of the women who had come last, knew least, but who ruled the land.

One day, the Upper Country, which lies far above Circle City, was pronounced rich. Dog-teams carried the news to Salt Water; golden argosies freighted the lure across the North Pacific; wires and cables sang with the tidings; and the world heard for the first time of the Klondike River and the Yukon Country. Cal Galbraith had lived the years quietly. He had been a good husband to Madeline, and she had blessed him. But somehow discontent fell upon him; he felt vague yearnings for his own kind, for the life he had been shut out from—a general sort of desire, which men sometimes feel, to break out and taste the prime of living. Besides, there drifted down the river wild rumors of the wonderful El Dorado, glowing descriptions of the city of logs and tents, and ludicrous accounts of the che-cha-quas who had rushed in and were stampeding the whole country.

Circle City was dead. The world had moved on up river and become a new and most marvelous world.

Cal Galbraith grew restless on the edge of things, and wished to see with his own eyes.

So, after the wash-up, he weighed in a couple of hundred pounds of dust on the Company's big scales, and took a draft for the same on Dawson. Then he put Tom Dixon in charge of his mines, kissed Madeline good-by, promised to be back before the first mush-ice ran, and took passage on an up-river steamer.

Madeline waited, waited through all the three months of daylight. She fed the dogs, gave much of her time to Young Cal, watched the short summer fade away and the sun begin its long journey to the south. And she prayed much in the manner of the Sisters of the Holy Cross. The fall came, and with it there was mush-ice on the Yukon, and Circle City kings returning to the winter's work at their mines, but no Cal Galbraith. Tom Dixon received a letter, however, for his men sledded up her winter's supply of dry pine. The Company received a letter for its dogteams filled her cache with their best provisions, and she was told that her credit was limitless.

Through all the ages man has been held the chief instigator of the woes of woman; but in this case the men held their tongues and swore harshly at one of their number who was away, while the women failed utterly to emulate them. So, without needless delay, Madeline heard strange tales of Cal Galbraith's doings; also, of a certain Greek dancer who played with men as children did with bubbles. Now Madeline was an Indian woman, and further, she had no woman friend to whom to go for wise counsel. She prayed and planned by turns, and that night, being quick of resolve and action, she harnessed the dogs, and with Young Cal securely lashed to the sled, stole away.

Though the Yukon still ran free, the eddy-ice was growing, and each day saw the river dwindling to a slushy thread. Save him who has done the like, no man may know what she endured in traveling a hundred miles on the rim-ice; nor may they understand the toil and hardship of breaking the two hundred miles of packed ice which remained after the river froze for good. But Madeline was an Indian woman, so she did these things, and one night there came a knock at Malemute Kid's door. Thereat he fed a team of starving dogs, put a healthy youngster to bed, and turned his attention to an exhausted woman. He removed her icebound moccasins while he listened to her tale, and stuck the point of his knife into her feet that he might see how far they were frozen.

Despite his tremendous virility, Malemute Kid was possessed of a softer, womanly element, which could win the confidence of a snarling wolf-dog or draw confessions from the most wintry heart. Nor did he seek them. Hearts opened to him as spontaneously as flowers to the sun. Even the priest, Father Roubeau, had been known to confess to him, while the men and women of the Northland were ever knocking at his door—a door from which the latch-string hung always out. To Madeline, he could do no wrong, make no mistake. She had known him from the time she first cast her lot among the people of her father's race; and to her half-barbaric mind it seemed that in him was centered the wisdom of the ages, that between his vision and the future there could be no intervening veil.

There were false ideals in the land. The social strictures of Dawson were not synonymous with those of the previous era, and the swift maturity of the Northland involved much wrong. Malemute Kid was aware of this, and he had Cal Galbraith's measure accurately.

He knew a hasty word was the father of much evil; besides, he was minded to teach a great lesson and bring shame upon the man. So Stanley Prince, the young mining expert, was called into the conference the following night as was also Lucky Jack Harrington and his violin. That same night, Bettles, who owed a great debt to Malemute Kid, harnessed up Cal Galbraith's dogs, lashed Cal Galbraith, Junior, to the sled, and slipped away in the dark for Stuart River.

II

'So; one—two—three, one—two—three. Now reverse! No, no! Start up again, Jack. See—this way.' Prince executed the movement as one should who has led the cotillion.

'Now; one—two—three, one—two—three. Reverse! Ah! that's better. Try it again. I say, you know, you mustn't look at your feet. One—two—three, one—two—three. Shorter steps! You are not hanging to the gee-pole just now. Try it over.

'There! that's the way. One—two—three, one—two—three.' Round and round went Prince and Madeline in an interminable waltz. The table and stools had been shoved over against the wall to increase the room. Malemute Kid sat on the bunk, chin to knees, greatly interested. Jack Harrington sat beside him, scraping away on his violin and following the dancers.

It was a unique situation, the undertaking of these three men with the woman.

The most pathetic part, perhaps, was the businesslike way in which they went about it.

No athlete was ever trained more rigidly for a coming contest, nor wolf-dog for the harness, than was she. But they had good material, for Madeline, unlike most women of her race, in her childhood had escaped the carrying of heavy burdens and the toil of the trail. Besides, she was a clean-limbed, willowy creature, possessed of much grace which had not hitherto been realized. It was this grace which the men strove to bring out and knock into shape.

'Trouble with her she learned to dance all wrong,' Prince remarked to the bunk after having deposited his breathless pupil on the table. 'She's quick at picking up; yet I could do better had she never danced a step. But say, Kid, I can't understand this.' Prince imitated a peculiar movement of the shoulders and head—a weakness Madeline suffered from in walking.

'Lucky for her she was raised in the Mission,' Malemute Kid answered. 'Packing, you know,—the head-strap. Other Indian women have it bad, but she didn't do any packing till after she married, and then only at first. Saw hard lines with that husband of hers. They went through the Forty-Mile famine together.' 'But can we break it?' 'Don't know.

'Perhaps long walks with her trainers will make the riffle. Anyway, they'll take it out some, won't they, Madeline?' The girl nodded assent. If Malemute Kid, who knew all things, said so, why it was so. That was all there was about it.

She had come over to them, anxious to begin again. Harrington surveyed her in quest of her points much in the same manner men usually do horses. It certainly was not disappointing, for he asked with sudden interest, 'What did that beggarly uncle of yours get anyway?' 'One rifle, one blanket, twenty bottles of hooch. Rifle broke.' She said this last scornfully, as though disgusted at how low her maiden-value had been rated.

She spoke fair English, with many peculiarities of her husband's speech, but there was still perceptible the Indian accent, the traditional groping after strange gutturals. Even this her instructors had taken in hand, and with no small success, too.

At the next intermission, Prince discovered a new predicament.

'I say, Kid,' he said, 'we're wrong, all wrong. She can't learn in moccasins.

'Put her feet into slippers, and then onto that waxed floor—phew!' Madeline raised a foot and regarded her shapeless house-moccasins dubiously. In previous winters, both at Circle City and Forty-Mile, she had danced many a night away with similar footgear, and there had been nothing the matter.

But now—well, if there was anything wrong it was for Malemute Kid to know, not her.

But Malemute Kid did know, and he had a good eye for measures; so he put on his cap and mittens and went down the hill to pay Mrs. Eppingwell a call. Her husband, Clove Eppingwell, was prominent in the community as one of the great Government officials.

The Kid had noted her slender little foot one night, at the Governor's Ball. And as he also knew her to be as sensible as she was pretty, it was no task to ask of her a certain small favor.

On his return, Madeline withdrew for a moment to the inner room. When she reappeared Prince was startled.

'By Jove!' he gasped. 'Who'd a' thought it! The little witch! Why my sister—' 'Is an English girl,' interrupted Malemute Kid, 'with an English foot. This girl comes of a small-footed race. Moccasins just broadened her feet healthily, while she did not misshape them by running with the dogs in her childhood.' But this explanation failed utterly to allay Prince's admiration. Harrington's commercial instinct was touched, and as he looked upon the exquisitely turned foot and ankle, there ran through his mind the sordid list—'One rifle, one blanket, twenty bottles of hooch.' Madeline was the wife of a king, a king whose yellow treasure could buy outright a score of fashion's puppets; yet in all her life her feet had known no gear save red-tanned moosehide. At first she had looked in awe at the tiny white-satin slippers; but she had quickly understood the admiration which shone, manlike, in the eyes of the men. Her face flushed with pride. For the moment she was drunken with her woman's loveliness; then she murmured, with increased scorn, 'And one rifle, broke!' So the training went on. Every day Malemute Kid led the girl out on long walks devoted to the correction of her carriage and the shortening of her stride.

There was little likelihood of her identity being discovered, for Cal Galbraith and the rest of the Old-Timers were like lost children among the many strangers who had rushed into the land. Besides, the frost of the North has a bitter tongue, and the tender women of the South, to shield their cheeks from its biting caresses, were prone to the use of canvas masks. With faces obscured and bodies lost in squirrel-skin parkas, a mother and daughter, meeting on trail, would pass as strangers.

The coaching progressed rapidly. At first it had been slow, but later a sudden acceleration had manifested itself. This began from the moment Madeline tried on the white-satin slippers, and in so doing found herself. The pride of her renegade father, apart from any natural self-esteem she might possess, at that instant received its birth. Hitherto, she had deemed herself a woman of an alien breed, of inferior stock, purchased by her lord's favor. Her husband had seemed to her a god, who had lifted her, through no essential virtues on her part, to his own godlike level. But she had never forgotten, even when Young Cal was born, that she was not of his people. As he had been a god, so had his womenkind been goddesses. She might have contrasted herself with them, but she had never compared.

It might have been that familiarity bred contempt; however, be that as it may, she had ultimately come to understand these roving white men, and to weigh them.

True, her mind was dark to deliberate analysis, but she yet possessed her woman's clarity of vision in such matters. On the night of the slippers she had measured the bold, open admiration of her three man-friends; and for the first time comparison had suggested itself. It was only a foot and an ankle, but—but comparison could not, in the nature of things, cease at that point. She judged herself by their standards till the divinity of her white sisters was shattered. After all, they were only women, and why should she not exalt herself to their midst? In doing these things she learned where she lacked and with the knowledge of her weakness came her strength. And so mightily did she strive that her three trainers often marveled late into the night over the eternal mystery of woman.

In this way Thanksgiving Night drew near. At irregular intervals Bettles sent word down from Stuart River regarding the welfare of Young Cal. The time of their return was approaching. More than once a casual caller, hearing dance-music and the rhythmic pulse of feet, entered, only to find Harrington scraping away and the other two beating time or arguing noisily over a mooted step. Madeline was never in evidence, having precipitately fled to the inner room.

On one of these nights Cal Galbraith dropped in. Encouraging news had just come down from Stuart River, and Madeline had surpassed herself—not in walk alone, and carriage and grace, but in womanly roguishness. They had indulged in sharp repartee and she had defended herself brilliantly; and then, yielding to the intoxication of the moment, and of her own power, she had bullied, and mastered, and wheedled, and patronized them with most astonishing success. And instinctively, involuntarily, they had bowed, not to her beauty, her wisdom, her wit, but to that indefinable something in woman to which man yields yet cannot name.

The room was dizzy with sheer delight as she and Prince whirled through the last dance of the evening. Harrington was throwing in inconceivable flourishes, while Malemute Kid, utterly abandoned, had seized the broom and was executing mad gyrations on his own account.

At this instant the door shook with a heavy rap-rap, and their quick glances noted the lifting of the latch. But they had survived similar situations before. Harrington never broke a note. Madeline shot through the waiting door to the inner room. The broom went hurtling under the bunk, and by the time Cal Galbraith and Louis Savoy got their heads in, Malemute Kid and Prince were in each other's arms, wildly schottisching down the room.

As a rule, Indian women do not make a practice of fainting on provocation, but Madeline came as near to it as she ever had in her life. For an hour she crouched on the floor, listening to the heavy voices of the men rumbling up and down in mimic thunder. Like familiar chords of childhood melodies, every intonation, every trick of her husband's voice swept in upon her, fluttering her heart and weakening her knees till she lay half-fainting against the door. It was well she could neither see nor hear when he took his departure.

'When do you expect to go back to Circle City?' Malemute Kid asked simply.

'Haven't thought much about it,' he replied. 'Don't think till after the ice breaks.' 'And Madeline?'

He flushed at the question, and there was a quick droop to his eyes. Malemute Kid could have despised him for that, had he known men less. As it was, his gorge rose against the wives and daughters who had come into the land, and not satisfied with usurping the place of the native women, had put unclean thoughts in the heads of the men and made them ashamed.

'I guess she's all right,' the Circle City King answered hastily, and in an apologetic manner. 'Tom Dixon's got charge of my interests, you know, and he sees to it that she has everything she wants.' Malemute Kid laid hand upon his arm and hushed him suddenly. They had stepped without. Overhead, the aurora, a gorgeous wanton, flaunted miracles of color; beneath lay the sleeping town. Far below, a solitary dog gave tongue.

The King again began to speak, but the Kid pressed his hand for silence. The sound multiplied. Dog after dog took up the strain till the full-throated chorus swayed the night.

To him who hears for the first time this weird song, is told the first and greatest secret of the Northland; to him who has heard it often, it is the solemn knell of lost endeavor. It is the plaint of tortured souls, for in it is invested the heritage of the North, the suffering of countless generations—the warning and the requiem to the world's estrays.

Cal Galbraith shivered slightly as it died away in half-caught sobs. The Kid read his thoughts openly, and wandered back with him through all the weary days of famine and disease; and with him was also the patient Madeline, sharing his pains and perils, never doubting, never complaining. His mind's retina vibrated to a score of pictures, stern, clear-cut, and the hand of the past drew back with heavy fingers on his heart. It was the psychological moment. Malemute Kid was half-tempted to play his reserve card and win the game; but the lesson was too mild as yet, and he let it pass. The next instant they had gripped hands, and the King's beaded moccasins were drawing protests from the outraged snow as he crunched down the hill.

Madeline in collapse was another woman to the mischievous creature of an hour before, whose laughter had been so infectious and whose heightened color and flashing eyes had made her teachers for the while forget. Weak and nerveless, she sat in the chair just as she had been dropped there by Prince and Harrington.

Malemute Kid frowned. This would never do. When the time of meeting her husband came to hand, she must carry things off with high-handed imperiousness. It was very necessary she should do it after the manner of white women, else the victory would be no victory at all. So he talked to her, sternly, without mincing of words, and initiated her into the weaknesses of his own sex, till she came to understand what simpletons men were after all, and why the word of their women was law.

A few days before Thanksgiving Night, Malemute Kid made another call on Mrs. Eppingwell. She promptly overhauled her feminine fripperies, paid a protracted visit to the dry-goods department of the P. C. Company, and returned with the Kid to make Madeline's acquaintance. After that came a period such as the cabin had never seen before, and what with cutting, and fitting, and basting, and stitching, and numerous other wonderful and unknowable things, the male conspirators were more often banished the premises than not. At such times the Opera House opened its double storm-doors to them.

So often did they put their heads together, and so deeply did they drink to curious toasts, that the loungers scented unknown creeks of incalculable richness, and it is known that several checca-quas and at least one Old-Timer kept their stampeding packs stored behind the bar, ready to hit the trail at a moment's notice.

Mrs. Eppingwell was a woman of capacity; so, when she turned Madeline over to her trainers on Thanksgiving Night she was so transformed that they were almost afraid of her. Prince wrapped a Hudson Bay blanket about her with a mock reverence more real than feigned, while Malemute Kid, whose arm she had taken, found it a severe trial to resume his wonted mentorship. Harrington, with the list of purchases still running through his head, dragged along in the rear, nor opened his mouth once all the way down into the town. When they came to the back door of the Opera House they took the blanket from Madeline's shoulders and spread it on the snow. Slipping out of Prince's moccasins, she stepped upon it in new satin slippers. The masquerade was at its height. She hesitated, but they jerked open the door and shoved her in. Then they ran around to come in by the front entrance.

III

'Where is Freda?' the Old-Timers questioned, while the che-cha-quas were equally energetic in asking who Freda was. The ballroom buzzed with her name.

It was on everybody's lips. Grizzled 'sour-dough boys,' day-laborers at the mines but proud of their degree, either patronized the spruce-looking tenderfeet and lied eloquently—the 'sour-dough boys' being specially created to toy with truth—or gave them savage looks of indignation because of their ignorance. Perhaps forty kings of the Upper and Lower Countries were on the floor, each deeming himself hot on the trail and sturdily backing his judgment with the yellow dust of the realm. An assistant was sent to the man at the scales, upon whom had fallen the burden of weighing up the sacks, while several of the gamblers, with the rules of chance at their finger-ends, made up alluring books on the field and favorites.

Which was Freda? Time and again the 'Greek Dancer' was thought to have been discovered, but each discovery brought panic to the betting ring and a frantic registering of new wagers by those who wished to hedge. Malemute Kid took an interest in the hunt, his advent being hailed uproariously by the revelers, who knew him to a man. The Kid had a good eye for the trick of a step, and ear for the lilt of a voice, and his private choice was a marvelous creature who scintillated as the 'Aurora Borealis.' But the Greek dancer was too subtle for even his penetration. The majority of the gold-hunters seemed to have centered their verdict on the 'Russian Princess,' who was the most graceful in the room, and hence could be no other than Freda Moloof.

During a quadrille a roar of satisfaction went up. She was discovered. At previous balls, in the figure, 'all hands round,' Freda had displayed an inimitable step and variation peculiarly her own. As the figure was called, the 'Russian Princess' gave the unique rhythm to limb and body. A chorus of I-told-you-so's shook the squared roof-beams, when lo! it was noticed that 'Aurora Borealis' and another masque, the 'Spirit of the Pole,' were performing the same trick equally well. And when two twin 'Sun-Dogs' and a 'Frost Queen' followed suit, a second assistant was dispatched to the aid of the man at the scales.

Bettles came off trail in the midst of the excitement, descending upon them in a hurricane of frost. His rimed brows turned to cataracts as he whirled about; his mustache, still frozen, seemed gemmed with diamonds and turned the light in varicolored rays; while the flying feet slipped on the chunks of ice which rattled from his moccasins and German socks. A Northland dance is quite an informal affair, the men of the creeks and trails having lost whatever fastidiousness they might have at one time possessed; and only in the high official circles are conventions at all observed. Here, caste carried no significance. Millionaires and paupers, dog-drivers and mounted policemen joined hands with 'ladies in the center,' and swept around the circle performing most remarkable capers. Primitive in their pleasure, boisterous and rough, they displayed no rudeness, but rather a crude chivalry more genuine than the most polished courtesy.

108

In his quest for the 'Greek Dancer,' Cal Galbraith managed to get into the same set with the 'Russian Princess,' toward whom popular suspicion had turned.

But by the time he had guided her through one dance, he was willing not only to stake his millions that she was not Freda, but that he had had his arm about her waist before. When or where he could not tell, but the puzzling sense of familiarity so wrought upon him that he turned his attention to the discovery of her identity. Malemute Kid might have aided him instead of occasionally taking the Princess for a few turns and talking earnestly to her in low tones. But it was Jack Harrington who paid the 'Russian Princess' the most assiduous court. Once he drew Cal Galbraith aside and hazarded wild guesses as to who she was, and explained to him that he was going in to win. That rankled the Circle City King, for man is not by nature monogamic, and he forgot both Madeline and Freda in the new quest.

It was soon noised about that the 'Russian Princess' was not Freda Moloof. Interest deepened. Here was a fresh enigma. They knew Freda though they could not find her, but here was somebody they had found and did not know. Even the women could not place her, and they knew every good dancer in the camp. Many took her for one of the official clique, indulging in a silly escapade. Not a few asserted she would disappear before the unmasking. Others were equally positive that she was the woman-reporter of the Kansas City Star, come to write them up at ninety dollars per column. And the men at the scales worked busily.

At one o'clock every couple took to the floor. The unmasking began amid laughter and delight, like that of carefree children. There was no end of Oh's and Ah's as mask after mask was lifted. The scintillating 'Aurora Borealis' became the brawny negress whose income from washing the community's clothes ran at about five hundred a month. The twin 'Sun-Dogs' discovered mustaches on their upper lips, and were recognized as brother Fraction-Kings of El Dorado. In one of the most prominent sets, and the slowest in uncovering, was Cal Galbraith with the 'Spirit of the Pole.' Opposite him was Jack Harrington and the 'Russian Princess.' The rest had discovered themselves, yet the 'Greek Dancer' was still missing. All eyes were upon the group. Cal Galbraith, in response to their cries, lifted his partner's mask. Freda's wonderful face and brilliant eyes flashed out upon them. A roar went up, to be squelched suddenly in the new and absorbing mystery of the 'Russian Princess.' Her face was still hidden, and Jack Harrington was struggling with her. The dancers tittered on the tiptoes of expectancy. He crushed her dainty costume roughly, and then—and then the revelers exploded. The joke was on them. They had danced all night with a tabooed native woman.

But those that knew, and they were many, ceased abruptly, and a hush fell upon the room.

Cal Galbraith crossed over with great strides, angrily, and spoke to Madeline in polyglot Chinook. But she retained her composure, apparently oblivious to the fact that she was the cynosure of all eyes, and answered him in English. She showed neither fright nor anger, and Malemute Kid chuckled at her well-bred equanimity. The King felt baffled, defeated; his common Siwash wife had passed beyond him.

'Come!' he said finally. 'Come home.' 'I beg pardon,' she replied; 'I have agreed to go to supper with Mr. Harrington. Besides, there's no end of dances promised.'

Harrington extended his arm to lead her away. He evinced not the slightest disinclination toward showing his back, but Malemute Kid had by this time edged in closer. The Circle City King was stunned. Twice his hand dropped to his belt, and twice the Kid gathered himself to spring; but the retreating couple passed through the supper-room door where canned oysters were spread at five dollars the plate.

The crowd sighed audibly, broke up into couples, and followed them. Freda pouted and went in with Cal Galbraith; but she had a good heart and a sure tongue, and she spoiled his oysters for him. What she said is of no importance, but his face went red and white at intervals, and he swore repeatedly and savagely at himself.

The supper-room was filled with a pandemonium of voices, which ceased suddenly as Cal Galbraith stepped over to his wife's table. Since the unmasking considerable weights of dust had been placed as to the outcome. Everybody watched with breathless interest.

110

Harrington's blue eyes were steady, but under the overhanging tablecloth a Smith & Wesson balanced on his knee. Madeline looked up, casually, with little interest.

'May—may I have the next round dance with you?' the King stuttered.

The wife of the King glanced at her card and inclined her head.

An Odyssey of the North

The sleds were singing their eternal lament to the creaking of the harness and the tinkling bells of the leaders; but the men and dogs were tired and made no sound. The trail was heavy with new-fallen snow, and they had come far, and the runners, burdened with flint-like quarters of frozen moose, clung tenaciously to the unpacked surface and held back with a stubbornness almost human.

Darkness was coming on, but there was no camp to pitch that night. The snow fell gently through the pulseless air, not in flakes, but in tiny frost crystals of delicate design. It was very warm—barely ten below zero—and the men did not mind. Meyers and Bettles had raised their ear flaps, while Malemute Kid had even taken off his mittens.

The dogs had been fagged out early in the after noon, but they now began to show new vigor. Among the more astute there was a certain restlessness—an impatience at the restraint of the traces, an indecisive quickness of movement, a sniffing of snouts and pricking of ears. These became incensed at their more phlegmatic brothers, urging them on with numerous sly nips on their hinder quarters. Those, thus chidden, also contracted and helped spread the contagion. At last the leader of the foremost sled uttered a sharp whine of satisfaction, crouching lower in the snow and throwing himself against the collar. The rest followed suit.

There was an ingathering of back hands, a tightening of traces; the sleds leaped forward, and the men clung to the gee poles, violently accelerating the uplift of their feet that they might escape going under the runners. The weariness of the day fell from them, and they whooped encouragement to the dogs. The animals responded with joyous yelps. They were swinging through the gathering darkness at a rattling gallop.

'Gee! Gee!' the men cried, each in turn, as their sleds abruptly left the main trail, heeling over on single runners like luggers on the wind.

Then came a hundred yards' dash to the lighted parchment window, which told its own story of the home cabin, the roaring Yukon stove, and the steaming pots of tea. But the home cabin had been invaded. Threescore huskies chorused defiance, and as many furry forms precipitated themselves upon the dogs which drew the first sled. The door was flung open, and a man, clad in the scarlet tunic of the Northwest Police, waded knee-deep among the furious brutes, calmly and impartially dispensing soothing justice with the butt end of a dog whip. After that the men shook hands; and in this wise was Malemute Kid welcomed to his own cabin by a stranger.

Stanley Prince, who should have welcomed him, and who was responsible for the Yukon stove and hot tea aforementioned, was busy with his guests. There were a dozen or so of them, as nondescript a crowd as ever served the Queen in the enforcement of her laws or the delivery of her mails. They were of many breeds, but their common life had formed of them a certain type—a lean and wiry type, with trail-hardened muscles, and sun-browned faces, and untroubled souls which gazed frankly forth, clear-eyed and steady.

They drove the dogs of the Queen, wrought fear in the hearts of her enemies, ate of her meager fare, and were happy. They had seen life, and done deeds, and lived romances; but they did not know it.

And they were very much at home. Two of them were sprawled upon Malemute Kid's bunk, singing chansons which their French forebears sang in the days when first they entered the Northwest land and mated with its Indian women. Bettles' bunk had suffered a similar invasion, and three or four lusty voyageurs worked their toes among its blankets as they listened to the tale of one who had served on the boat brigade with Wolseley when he fought his way to Khartoum.

And when he tired, a cowboy told of courts and kings and lords and ladies he had seen when Buffalo Bill toured the capitals of Europe. In a corner two half-breeds, ancient comrades in a lost campaign, mended harnesses and talked of the days when the Northwest flamed with insurrection and Louis Riel was king.

Rough jests and rougher jokes went up and down, and great hazards by trail and river were spoken of in the light of commonplaces, only to be recalled by virtue of some grain of humor or ludicrous happening. Prince was led away by these uncrowned heroes who had seen history made, who regarded the great and the romantic as but the ordinary and the incidental in the routine of life. He passed his precious tobacco among them with lavish disregard, and rusty chains of reminiscence were loosened, and forgotten odysseys resurrected for his especial benefit.

When conversation dropped and the travelers filled the last pipes and lashed their tight-rolled sleeping furs. Prince fell back upon his comrade for further information.

'Well, you know what the cowboy is,' Malemute Kid answered, beginning to unlace his moccasins; 'and it's not hard to guess the British blood in his bed partner. As for the rest, they're all children of the coureurs du bois, mingled with God knows how many other bloods. The two turning in by the door are the regulation 'breeds' or Boisbrules. That lad with the worsted breech scarf—notice his eyebrows and the turn of his jaw—shows a Scotchman wept in his mother's smoky tepee. And that handsome looking fellow putting the capote under his head is a French half-breed—you heard him talking; he doesn't like the two Indians turning in next to him. You see, when the 'breeds' rose under the Riel the full-bloods kept the peace, and they've not lost much love for one another since.' 'But I say, what's that glum-looking fellow by the stove? I'll swear he can't talk English. He hasn't opened his mouth all night.' 'You're wrong. He knows English well enough. Did you follow his eyes when he listened? I did. But he's neither kith nor kin to the others. When they talked their own patois you could see he didn't understand. I've been wondering myself what he is. Let's find out.' 'Fire a couple of sticks into the stove!'

Malemute Kid commanded, raising his voice and looking squarely at the man in question.

He obeyed at once.

114

'Had discipline knocked into him somewhere.' Prince commented in a low tone.

Malemute Kid nodded, took off his socks, and picked his way among recumbent men to the stove. There he hung his damp footgear among a score or so of mates.

'When do you expect to get to Dawson?' he asked tentatively.

The man studied him a moment before replying. 'They say seventy-five mile. So? Maybe two days.' The very slightest accent was perceptible, while there was no awkward hesitancy or groping for words.

'Been in the country before?' 'No.' 'Northwest Territory?' 'Yes.' 'Born there?' 'No.'

'Well, where the devil were you born? You're none of these.' Malemute Kid swept his hand over the dog drivers, even including the two policemen who had turned into Prince's bunk. 'Where did you come from? I've seen faces like yours before, though I can't remember just where.' 'I know you,' he irrelevantly replied, at once turning the drift of Malemute Kid's questions.

'Where? Ever see me?' 'No; your partner, him priest, Pastilik, long time ago. Him ask me if I see you, Malemute Kid. Him give me grub. I no stop long. You hear him speak 'bout me?' 'Oh! you're the fellow that traded the otter skins for the dogs?' The man nodded, knocked out his pipe, and signified his disinclination for conversation by rolling up in his furs. Malemute Kid blew out the slush lamp and crawled under the blankets with Prince.

'Well, what is he?' 'Don't know—turned me off, somehow, and then shut up like a clam.

'But he's a fellow to whet your curiosity. I've heard of him. All the coast wondered about him eight years ago. Sort of mysterious, you know. He came down out of the North in the dead of winter, many a thousand miles from here, skirting Bering Sea and traveling as though the devil were after him. No one ever learned where he came from, but he must have come far. He was badly travel-worn when he got food from the Swedish missionary on

Golovin Bay and asked the way south. We heard of all this afterward. Then he abandoned the shore line, heading right across Norton Sound. Terrible weather, snowstorms and high winds, but he pulled through where a thousand other men would have died, missing St. Michaels and making the land at Pastilik. He'd lost all but two dogs, and was nearly gone with starvation.

'He was so anxious to go on that Father Roubeau fitted him out with grub; but he couldn't let him have any dogs, for he was only waiting my arrival, to go on a trip himself. Mr. Ulysses knew too much to start on without animals, and fretted around for several days. He had on his sled a bunch of beautifully cured otter skins, sea otters, you know, worth their weight in gold. There was also at Pastilik an old Shylock of a Russian trader, who had dogs to kill. Well, they didn't dicker very long, but when the Strange One headed south again, it was in the rear of a spanking dog team. Mr. Shylock, by the way, had the otter skins. I saw them, and they were magnificent. We figured it up and found the dogs brought him at least five hundred apiece. And it wasn't as if the Strange One didn't know the value of sea otter; he was an Indian of some sort, and what little he talked showed he'd been among white men.

'After the ice passed out of the sea, word came up from Nunivak Island that he'd gone in there for grub. Then he dropped from sight, and this is the first heard of him in eight years. Now where did he come from? and what was he doing there? and why did he come from there? He's Indian, he's been nobody knows where, and he's had discipline, which is unusual for an Indian. Another mystery of the North for you to solve, Prince.' 'Thanks awfully, but I've got too many on hand as it is,' he replied.

Malemute Kid was already breathing heavily; but the young mining engineer gazed straight up through the thick darkness, waiting for the strange orgasm which stirred his blood to die away. And when he did sleep, his brain worked on, and for the nonce he, too, wandered through the white unknown, struggled with the dogs on endless trails, and saw men live, and toil, and die like men. The next morning, hours before daylight, the dog drivers and policemen pulled out for Dawson. But the powers that saw to Her Majesty's interests and ruled the destinies of her lesser creatures gave the mailmen little rest, for a week later they appeared at Stuart River, heavily burdened with letters for Salt Water.

However, their dogs had been replaced by fresh ones; but, then, they were dogs.

The men had expected some sort of a layover in which to rest up; besides, this Klondike was a new section of the Northland, and they had wished to see a little something of the Golden City where dust flowed like water and dance halls rang with never-ending revelry. But they dried their socks and smoked their evening pipes with much the same gusto as on their former visit, though one or two bold spirits speculated on desertion and the possibility of crossing the unexplored Rockies to the east, and thence, by the Mackenzie Valley, of gaining their old stamping grounds in the Chippewyan country.

Two or three even decided to return to their homes by that route when their terms of service had expired, and they began to lay plans forthwith, looking forward to the hazardous undertaking in much the same way a city-bred man would to a day's holiday in the woods.

He of the Otter Skins seemed very restless, though he took little interest in the discussion, and at last he drew Malemute Kid to one side and talked for some time in low tones.

Prince cast curious eyes in their direction, and the mystery deepened when they put on caps and mittens and went outside. When they returned, Malemute Kid placed his gold scales on the table, weighed out the matter of sixty ounces, and transferred them to the Strange One's sack. Then the chief of the dog drivers joined the conclave, and certain business was transacted with him.

The next day the gang went on upriver, but He of the Otter Skins took several pounds of grub and turned his steps back toward Dawson.

'Didn't know what to make of it,' said Malemute Kid in response to Prince's queries; 'but the poor beggar wanted to be quit of the service for some reason or other—at least it seemed a most important one to him, though he wouldn't let on what. You see, it's just like the army: he signed for two years, and the only way to get free was to buy himself out. He couldn't desert and then stay here, and he was just wild to remain in the country.

'Made up his mind when he got to Dawson, he said; but no one knew him, hadn't a cent, and I was the only one he'd spoken two words with. So he talked it over with the lieutenant-governor, and made arrangements in case he could get the money from me—loan, you know. Said he'd pay back in the year, and, if I wanted, would put me onto something rich. Never'd seen it, but he knew it was rich.

'And talk! why, when he got me outside he was ready to weep. Begged and pleaded; got down in the snow to me till I hauled him out of it. Palavered around like a crazy man.

'Swore he's worked to this very end for years and years, and couldn't bear to be disappointed now. Asked him what end, but he wouldn't say.

'Said they might keep him on the other half of the trail and he wouldn't get to Dawson in two years, and then it would be too late. Never saw a man take on so in my life. And when I said I'd let him have it, had to yank him out of the snow again. Told him to consider it in the light of a grubstake. Think he'd have it? No sir! Swore he'd give me all he found, make me rich beyond the dreams of avarice, and all such stuff. Now a man who puts his life and time against a grubstake ordinarily finds it hard enough to turn over half of what he finds. Something behind all this, Prince; just you make a note of it. We'll hear of him if he stays in the country—' 'And if he doesn't?' 'Then my good nature gets a shock, and I'm sixty some odd ounces out.' The cold weather had come on with the long nights, and the sun had begun to play his ancient game of peekaboo along the southern snow line ere aught was heard of Malemute Kid's grubstake. And then, one bleak morning in early January, a heavily laden dog train pulled into his cabin below Stuart River. He of the Otter Skins was there, and with him walked a man such as the gods have almost forgotten how to fashion. Men never talked of luck and pluck and five-hundred-dollar dirt without bringing in the name of Axel Gunderson; nor could tales of nerve or strength or daring pass up and down the campfire without the summoning of his presence. And when the conversation flagged, it blazed anew at mention of the woman who shared his fortunes.

118

As has been noted, in the making of Axel Gunderson the gods had remembered their old-time cunning and cast him after the manner of men who were born when the world was young. Full seven feet he towered in his picturesque costume which marked a king of Eldorado. His chest, neck, and limbs were those of a giant. To bear his three hundred pounds of bone and muscle, his snowshoes were greater by a generous yard than those of other men. Rough-hewn, with rugged brow and massive jaw and unflinching eyes of palest blue, his face told the tale of one who knew but the law of might. Of the yellow of ripe corn silk, his frost-incrusted hair swept like day across the night and fell far down his coat of bearskin.

A vague tradition of the sea seemed to cling about him as he swung down the narrow trail in advance of the dogs; and he brought the butt of his dog whip against Malemute Kid's door as a Norse sea rover, on southern foray, might thunder for admittance at the castle gate.

Prince bared his womanly arms and kneaded sour-dough bread, casting, as he did so, many a glance at the three guests—three guests the like of which might never come under a man's roof in a lifetime. The Strange One, whom Malemute Kid had surnamed Ulysses, still fascinated him; but his interest chiefly gravitated between Axel Gunderson and Axel Gunderson's wife. She felt the day's journey, for she had softened in comfortable cabins during the many days since her husband mastered the wealth of frozen pay streaks, and she was tired. She rested against his great breast like a slender flower against a wall, replying lazily to Malemute Kid's good-natured banter, and stirring Prince's blood strangely with an occasional sweep of her deep, dark eyes. For Prince was a man, and healthy, and had seen few women in many months. And she was older than he, and an Indian besides. But she was different from all native wives he had met: she had traveled—had been in his country among others, he gathered from the conversation; and she knew most of the things the women of his own race knew, and much more that it was not in the nature of things for them to know. She could make a meal of sun-dried fish or a bed in the snow; yet she teased them with tantalizing details of many-course dinners, and caused strange internal dissensions to arise at the mention of various quondam dishes which they had well-nigh

119

forgotten. She knew the ways of the moose, the bear, and the little blue fox, and of the wild amphibians of the Northern seas; she was skilled in the lore of the woods, and the streams, and the tale writ by man and bird and beast upon the delicate snow crust was to her an open book; yet Prince caught the appreciative twinkle in her eye as she read the Rules of the Camp. These rules had been fathered by the Unquenchable Bettles at a time when his blood ran high, and were remarkable for the terse simplicity of their humor.

Prince always turned them to the wall before the arrival of ladies; but who could suspect that this native wife—Well, it was too late now.

This, then, was the wife of Axel Gunderson, a woman whose name and fame had traveled with her husband's, hand in hand, through all the Northland. At table, Malemute Kid baited her with the assurance of an old friend, and Prince shook off the shyness of first acquaintance and joined in. But she held her own in the unequal contest, while her husband, slower in wit, ventured naught but applause. And he was very proud of her; his every look and action revealed the magnitude of the place she occupied in his life. He of the Otter Skins ate in silence, forgotten in the merry battle; and long ere the others were done he pushed back from the table and went out among the dogs. Yet all too soon his fellow travelers drew on their mittens and parkas and followed him.

There had been no snow for many days, and the sleds slipped along the hardpacked Yukon trail as easily as if it had been glare ice. Ulysses led the first sled; with the second came Prince and Axel Gunderson's wife; while Malemute Kid and the yellow-haired giant brought up the third.

'It's only a hunch, Kid,' he said, 'but I think it's straight. He's never been there, but he tells a good story, and shows a map I heard of when I was in the Kootenay country years ago. I'd like to have you go along; but he's a strange one, and swore point-blank to throw it up if anyone was brought in. But when I come back you'll get first tip, and I'll stake you next to me, and give you a half share in the town site besides.' 'No! no!' he cried, as the other strove to interrupt. 'I'm running this, and before I'm done it'll need two heads.

'If it's all right, why, it'll be a second Cripple Creek, man; do you hear?—a second Cripple Creek! It's quartz, you know, not placer; and if we work it right we'll corral the whole thing—millions upon millions. I've heard of the place before, and so have you. We'll build a town—thousands of workmen—good waterways—steamship lines—big carrying trade—light-draught steamers for head reaches—survey a railroad, perhaps—sawmills—electric-light plant— do our own banking—commercial company—syndicate—Say! Just you hold your hush till I get back!' The sleds came to a halt where the trail crossed the mouth of Stuart River. An unbroken sea of frost, its wide expanse stretched away into the unknown east.

The snowshoes were withdrawn from the lashings of the sleds. Axel Gunderson shook hands and stepped to the fore, his great webbed shoes sinking a fair half yard into the feathery surface and packing the snow so the dogs should not wallow. His wife fell in behind the last sled, betraying long practice in the art of handling the awkward footgear. The stillness was broken with cheery farewells; the dogs whined; and He of the Otter Skins talked with his whip to a recalcitrant wheeler.

An hour later the train had taken on the likeness of a black pencil crawling in a long, straight line across a mighty sheet of foolscap.

II

One night, many weeks later, Malemute Kid and Prince fell to solving chess problems from the torn page of an ancient magazine. The Kid had just returned from his Bonanza properties and was resting up preparatory to a long moose hunt.

Prince, too, had been on creek and trail nearly all winter, and had grown hungry for a blissful week of cabin life.

'Interpose the black knight, and force the king. No, that won't do. See, the next move-'

'Why advance the pawn two squares? Bound to take it in transit, and with the bishop out of the way-' 'But hold on! That leaves a hole, and-' 'No; it's protected. Go ahead! You'll see it works.' It was very interesting. Somebody knocked at the door a second time before Malemute Kid said, 'Come in.' The door swung open. Something staggered in.

Prince caught one square look and sprang to his feet. The horror in his eyes caused Malemute Kid to whirl about; and he, too, was startled, though he had seen bad things before. The thing tottered blindly toward them. Prince edged away till he reached the nail from which hung his Smith & Wesson.

'My God! what is it?' he whispered to Malemute Kid.

'Don't know. Looks like a case of freezing and no grub,' replied the Kid, sliding away in the opposite direction. 'Watch out! It may be mad,' he warned, coming back from closing the door.

The thing advanced to the table. The bright flame of the slush lamp caught its eye. It was amused, and gave voice to eldritch cackles which betokened mirth.

Then, suddenly, he—for it was a man—swayed back, with a hitch to his skin trousers, and began to sing a chantey, such as men lift when they swing around the capstan circle and the sea snorts in their ears: Yan-kee ship come down de ri-ib-er, Pull! my bully boys! Pull! D'yeh want—to know de captain ru-uns her? Pull! my bully boys! Pull! Jon-a-than Jones ob South Caho-li-in-a, Pull! my bully. He broke off abruptly, tottered with a wolfish snarl to the meat shelf, and before they could intercept was tearing with his teeth at a chunk of raw bacon. The struggle was fierce between him and Malemute Kid; but his mad strength left him as suddenly as it had come, and he weakly surrendered the spoil. Between them they got him upon a stool, where he sprawled with half his body across the table.

A small dose of whiskey strengthened him, so that he could dip a spoon into the sugar caddy which Malemute Kid placed before him. After his appetite had been somewhat cloyed, Prince, shuddering as he did so, passed him a mug of weak beef tea.

The creature's eyes were alight with a somber frenzy, which blazed and waned with every mouthful. There was very little skin to the face. The face, for that matter, sunken and emaciated, bore little likeness to human countenance.

Frost after frost had bitten deeply, each depositing its stratum of scab upon the half-healed scar that went before. This dry, hard surface was of a bloody-black color, serrated by grievous cracks wherein the raw red flesh peeped forth. His skin garments were dirty and in tatters, and the fur of one side was singed and burned away, showing where he had lain upon his fire.

Malemute Kid pointed to where the sun-tanned hide had been cut away, strip by strip—the grim signature of famine.

'Who—are—you?' slowly and distinctly enunciated the Kid.

The man paid no heed.

'Where do you come from?' 'Yan-kee ship come down de ri-ib-er,' was the quavering response.

'Don't doubt the beggar came down the river,' the Kid said, shaking him in an endeavor to start a more lucid flow of talk.

But the man shrieked at the contact, clapping a hand to his side in evident pain. He rose slowly to his feet, half leaning on the table.

'She laughed at me—so—with the hate in her eye; and she—would—not—come.' His voice died away, and he was sinking back when Malemute Kid gripped him by the wrist and shouted, 'Who? Who would not come?' 'She, Unga. She laughed, and struck at me, so, and so. And then-' 'Yes?'

'And then—' 'And then what?' 'And then he lay very still in the snow a long time. He is-still in—the—snow.' The two men looked at each other helplessly.

'Who is in the snow?' 'She, Unga. She looked at me with the hate in her eye, and then—'

'Yes, yes.' 'And then she took the knife, so; and once, twice—she was weak. I traveled very slow. And there is much gold in that place, very much gold.' 'Where is Unga?' For all Malemute Kid knew, she might be dying a mile away. He shook the man savagely, repeating again and again, 'Where is Unga? Who is Unga?' 'She—is—in—the—snow.' 'Go on!' The Kid was pressing his wrist cruelly.

'So—I—would—be—in—the snow—but—I—had—a—debt—to—pay. It—was—heavy—I—had—a-debt—to—pay—a—debt—to—pay I—had-' The faltering monosyllables ceased as he fumbled in his pouch and drew forth a buckskin sack. 'A—debt—to—pay—five—pounds—of—gold-grub— stake—Mal—e—mute—Kid—I—y—' The exhausted head dropped upon the table; nor could Malemute Kid rouse it again.

'It's Ulysses,' he said quietly, tossing the bag of dust on the table. 'Guess it's all day with Axel Gunderson and the woman. Come on, let's get him between the blankets. He's Indian; he'll pull through and tell a tale besides.' As they cut his garments from him, near his right breast could be seen two unhealed, hard-lipped knife thrusts.

III

'I will talk of the things which were in my own way; but you will understand. I will begin at the beginning, and tell of myself and the woman, and, after that, of the man.' He of the Otter Skins drew over to the stove as do men who have been deprived of fire and are afraid the Promethean gift may vanish at any moment. Malemute Kid picked up the slush lamp and placed it so its light might fall upon the face of the narrator. Prince slid his body over the edge of the bunk and joined them.

'I am Naass, a chief, and the son of a chief, born between a sunset and a rising, on the dark seas, in my father's oomiak. All of a night the men toiled at the paddles, and the women cast out the waves which threw in upon us, and we fought with the storm. The salt spray froze upon my mother's breast till her breath passed with the passing of the tide. But I—I raised my voice with the wind and the storm, and lived.

124

'We dwelt in Akatan—' 'Where?' asked Malemute Kid.

'Akatan, which is in the Aleutians; Akatan, beyond Chignik, beyond Kardalak, beyond Unimak. As I say, we dwelt in Akatan, which lies in the midst of the sea on the edge of the world. We farmed the salt seas for the fish, the seal, and the otter; and our homes shouldered about one another on the rocky strip between the rim of the forest and the yellow beach where our kayaks lay. We were not many, and the world was very small. There were strange lands to the east—islands like Akatan; so we thought all the world was islands and did not mind.

'I was different from my people. In the sands of the beach were the crooked timbers and wave-warped planks of a boat such as my people never built; and I remember on the point of the island which overlooked the ocean three ways there stood a pine tree which never grew there, smooth and straight and tall. It is said the two men came to that spot, turn about, through many days, and watched with the passing of the light. These two men came from out of the sea in the boat which lay in pieces on the beach. And they were white like you, and weak as the little children when the seal have gone away and the hunters come home empty. I know of these things from the old men and the old women, who got them from their fathers and mothers before them. These strange white men did not take kindly to our ways at first, but they grew strong, what of the fish and the oil, and fierce. And they built them each his own house, and took the pick of our women, and in time children came. Thus he was born who was to become the father of my father's father.

'As I said, I was different from my people, for I carried the strong, strange blood of this white man who came out of the sea. It is said we had other laws in the days before these men; but they were fierce and quarrelsome, and fought with our men till there were no more left who dared to fight. Then they made themselves chiefs, and took away our old laws, and gave us new ones, insomuch that the man was the son of his father, and not his mother, as our way had been. They also ruled that the son, first-born, should have all things which were his father's before him, and that the brothers and sisters should shift for themselves. And they gave us other laws. They showed us new ways in the catching of fish and the killing of bear which were thick in the woods; and they taught us to lay by bigger stores for the time of famine. And these things were good.

'But when they had become chiefs, and there were no more men to face their anger, they fought, these strange white men, each with the other. And the one whose blood I carry drove his seal spear the length of an arm through the other's body. Their children took up the fight, and their children's children; and there was great hatred between them, and black doings, even to my time, so that in each family but one lived to pass down the blood of them that went before. Of my blood I was alone; of the other man's there was but a girl. Unga, who lived with her mother. Her father and my father did not come back from the fishing one night; but afterward they washed up to the beach on the big tides, and they held very close to each other.

'The people wondered, because of the hatred between the houses, and the old men shook their heads and said the fight would go on when children were born to her and children to me. They told me this as a boy, till I came to believe, and to look upon Unga as a foe, who was to be the mother of children which were to fight with mine. I thought of these things day by day, and when I grew to a stripling I came to ask why this should be so.

'And they answered, "We do not know, but that in such way your fathers did." And I marveled that those which were to come should fight the battles of those that were gone, and in it I could see no right. But the people said it must be, and I was only a stripling.

'And they said I must hurry, that my blood might be the older and grow strong before hers. This was easy, for I was head man, and the people looked up to me because of the deeds and the laws of my fathers, and the wealth which was mine. Any maiden would come to me, but I found none to my liking. And the old men and the mothers of maidens told me to hurry, for even then were the hunters bidding high to the mother of Unga; and should her children grow strong before mine, mine would surely die.

'Nor did I find a maiden till one night coming back from the fishing. The sunlight was lying, so, low and full in the eyes, the wind free, and the kayacks racing with the white seas. Of a sudden the kayak of Unga came driving past me, and she looked upon me, so, with her black hair flying like a cloud of night and the spray wet on her cheek. As I say, the sunlight was full in the eyes, and I was a stripling; but somehow it was all clear, and I knew it to be the call of kind to kind.

'As she whipped ahead she looked back within the space of two strokes—looked as only the woman Unga could look—and again I knew it as the call of kind. The people shouted as we ripped past the lazy oomiaks and left them far behind. But she was quick at the paddle, and my heart was like the belly of a sail, and I did not gain. The wind freshened, the sea whitened, and, leaping like the seals on the windward breech, we roared down the golden pathway of the sun.' Naass was crouched half out of his stool, in the attitude of one driving a paddle, as he ran the race anew. Somewhere across the stove he beheld the tossing kayak and the flying hair of Unga. The voice of the wind was in his ears, and its salt beat fresh upon his nostrils.

'But she made the shore, and ran up the sand, laughing, to the house of her mother. And a great thought came to me that night—a thought worthy of him that was chief over all the people of Akatan. So, when the moon was up, I went down to the house of her mother, and looked upon the goods of Yash-Noosh, which were piled by the door—the goods of Yash-Noosh, a strong hunter who had it in mind to be the father of the children of Unga. Other young men had piled their goods there and taken them away again; and each young man had made a pile greater than the one before.

'And I laughed to the moon and the stars, and went to my own house where my wealth was stored. And many trips I made, till my pile was greater by the fingers of one hand than the pile of Yash-Noosh. There were fish, dried in the sun and smoked; and forty hides of the hair seal, and half as many of the fur, and each hide was tied at the mouth and big bellied with oil; and ten skins of bear which I killed in the woods when they came out in the spring. And there were beads and blankets and scarlet cloths, such as I got in trade from the people who lived to the east, and who got them in trade from the people who lived still beyond in the east.

'And I looked upon the pile of Yash-Noosh and laughed, for I was head man in Akatan, and my wealth was greater than the wealth of all my young men, and my fathers had done deeds, and given laws, and put their names for all time in the mouths of the people.

'So, when the morning came, I went down to the beach, casting out of the corner of my eye at the house of the mother of Unga. My offer yet stood untouched.

'And the women smiled, and said sly things one to the other. I wondered, for never had such a price been offered; and that night I added more to the pile, and put beside it a kayak of well-tanned skins which never yet had swam in the sea. But in the day it was yet there, open to the laughter of all men. The mother of Unga was crafty, and I grew angry at the shame in which I stood before my people. So that night I added till it became a great pile, and I hauled up my oomiak, which was of the value of twenty kayaks. And in the morning there was no pile.

'Then made I preparation for the wedding, and the people that lived even to the east came for the food of the feast and the potlatch token. Unga was older than I by the age of four suns in the way we reckoned the years. I was only a stripling; but then I was a chief, and the son of a chief, and it did not matter.

'But a ship shoved her sails above the floor of the ocean, and grew larger with the breath of the wind. From her scuppers she ran clear water, and the men were in haste and worked hard at the pumps. On the bow stood a mighty man, watching the depth of the water and giving commands with a voice of thunder. His eyes were of the pale blue of the deep waters, and his head was maned like that of a sea lion. And his hair was yellow, like the straw of a southern harvest or the manila rope yarns which sailormen plait.

'Of late years we had seen ships from afar, but this was the first to come to the beach of Akatan. The feast was broken, and the women and children fled to the houses, while we men strung our bows and waited with spears in hand. But when the ship's forefoot smelled the beach the strange men took no notice of us, being busy with their own work. With the falling of the tide they careened the schooner and patched a great hole in her bottom. So the women crept back, and the feast went on.

128

'When the tide rose, the sea wanderers kedged the schooner to deep water and then came among us. They bore presents and were friendly; so I made room for them, and out of the largeness of my heart gave them tokens such as I gave all the guests, for it was my wedding day, and I was head man in Akatan. And he with the mane of the sea lion was there, so tall and strong that one looked to see the earth shake with the fall of his feet. He looked much and straight at Unga, with his arms folded, so, and stayed till the sun went away and the stars came out. Then he went down to his ship. After that I took Unga by the hand and led her to my own house. And there was singing and great laughter, and the women said sly things, after the manner of women at such times. But we did not care. Then the people left us alone and went home.

'The last noise had not died away when the chief of the sea wanderers came in by the door. And he had with him black bottles, from which we drank and made merry. You see, I was only a stripling, and had lived all my days on the edge of the world. So my blood became as fire, and my heart as light as the froth that flies from the surf to the cliff. Unga sat silent among the skins in the corner, her eyes wide, for she seemed to fear. And he with the mane of the sea lion looked upon her straight and long. Then his men came in with bundles of goods, and he piled before me wealth such as was not in all Akatan. There were guns, both large and small, and powder and shot and shell, and bright axes and knives of steel, and cunning tools, and strange things the like of which I had never seen. When he showed me by sign that it was all mine, I thought him a great man to be so free; but he showed me also that Unga was to go away with him in his ship.

'Do you understand?—that Unga was to go away with him in his ship. The blood of my fathers flamed hot on the sudden, and I made to drive him through with my spear. But the spirit of the bottles had stolen the life from my arm, and he took me by the neck, so, and knocked my head against the wall of the house. And I was made weak like a newborn child, and my legs would no more stand under me.

'Unga screamed, and she laid hold of the things of the house with her hands, till they fell all about us as he dragged her to the door. Then he took her in his great arms, and when she tore at his yellow hair laughed with a sound like that of the big bull seal in the rut.

'I crawled to the beach and called upon my people, but they were afraid. Only Yash-Noosh was a man, and they struck him on the head with an oar, till he lay with his face in the sand and did not move. And they raised the sails to the sound of their songs, and the ship went away on the wind.

'The people said it was good, for there would be no more war of the bloods in Akatan; but I said never a word, waiting till the time of the full moon, when I put fish and oil in my kayak and went away to the east. I saw many islands and many people, and I, who had lived on the edge, saw that the world was very large. I talked by signs; but they had not seen a schooner nor a man with the mane of a sea lion, and they pointed always to the east. And I slept in queer places, and ate odd things, and met strange faces. Many laughed, for they thought me light of head; but sometimes old men turned my face to the light and blessed me, and the eyes of the young women grew soft as they asked me of the strange ship, and Unga, and the men of the sea.

'And in this manner, through rough seas and great storms, I came to Unalaska. There were two schooners there, but neither was the one I sought. So I passed on to the east, with the world growing ever larger, and in the island of Unamok there was no word of the ship, nor in Kadiak, nor in Atognak. And so I came one day to a rocky land, where men dug great holes in the mountain. And there was a schooner, but not my schooner, and men loaded upon it the rocks which they dug. This I thought childish, for all the world was made of rocks; but they gave me food and set me to work. When the schooner was deep in the water, the captain gave me money and told me to go; but I asked which way he went, and he pointed south. I made signs that I would go with him, and he laughed at first, but then, being short of men, took me to help work the ship. So I came to talk after their manner, and to heave on ropes, and to reef the stiff sails in sudden squalls, and to take my turn at the wheel. But it was not strange, for the blood of my fathers was the blood of the men of the sea.

'I had thought it an easy task to find him I sought, once I got among his own people; and when we raised the land one day, and passed between a gateway of the sea to a port, I looked for perhaps as many schooners as there were fingers to my hands. But the ships lay against the wharves for miles, packed like so many little fish; and when I went among them to ask for a man with the mane of a sea lion, they laughed, and answered me in the tongues of many peoples. And I found that they hailed from the uttermost parts of the earth.

'And I went into the city to look upon the face of every man. But they were like the cod when they run thick on the banks, and I could not count them. And the noise smote upon me till I could not hear, and my head was dizzy with much movement. So I went on and on, through the lands which sang in the warm sunshine; where the harvests lay rich on the plains; and where great cities were fat with men that lived like women, with false words in their mouths and their hearts black with the lust of gold. And all the while my people of Akatan hunted and fished, and were happy in the thought that the world was small.

'But the look in the eyes of Unga coming home from the fishing was with me always, and I knew I would find her when the time was met. She walked down quiet lanes in the dusk of the evening, or led me chases across the thick fields wet with the morning dew, and there was a promise in her eyes such as only the woman Unga could give.

'So I wandered through a thousand cities. Some were gentle and gave me food, and others laughed, and still others cursed; but I kept my tongue between my teeth, and went strange ways and saw strange sights. Sometimes I, who was a chief and the son of a chief, toiled for men—men rough of speech and hard as iron, who wrung gold from the sweat and sorrow of their fellow men. Yet no word did I get of my quest till I came back to the sea like a homing seal to the rookeries.

'But this was at another port, in another country which lay to the north. And there I heard dim tales of the yellow-haired sea wanderer, and I learned that he was a hunter of seals, and that even then he was abroad on the ocean.

131

'So I shipped on a seal schooner with the lazy Siwashes, and followed his trackless trail to the north where the hunt was then warm. And we were away weary months, and spoke many of the fleet, and heard much of the wild doings of him I sought; but never once did we raise him above the sea. We went north, even to the Pribilofs, and killed the seals in herds on the beach, and brought their warm bodies aboard till our scuppers ran grease and blood and no man could stand upon the deck. Then were we chased by a ship of slow steam, which fired upon us with great guns. But we put sail till the sea was over our decks and washed them clean, and lost ourselves in a fog.

'It is said, at this time, while we fled with fear at our hearts, that the yellow-haired sea wanderer put in to the Pribilofs, right to the factory, and while the part of his men held the servants of the company, the rest loaded ten thousand green skins from the salt houses. I say it is said, but I believe; for in the voyages I made on the coast with never a meeting the northern seas rang with his wildness and daring, till the three nations which have lands there sought him with their ships.

'And I heard of Unga, for the captains sang loud in her praise, and she was always with him. She had learned the ways of his people, they said, and was happy. But I knew better—knew that her heart harked back to her own people by the yellow beach of Akatan.

'So, after a long time, I went back to the port which is by a gateway of the sea, and there I learned that he had gone across the girth of the great ocean to hunt for the seal to the east of the warm land which runs south from the Russian seas.

'And I, who was become a sailorman, shipped with men of his own race, and went after him in the hunt of the seal. And there were few ships off that new land; but we hung on the flank of the seal pack and harried it north through all the spring of the year. And when the cows were heavy with pup and crossed the Russian line, our men grumbled and were afraid. For there was much fog, and every day men were lost in the boats. They would not work, so the captain turned the ship back toward the way it came. But I knew the yellow-haired sea wanderer was unafraid, and would hang by the pack, even to the Russian Isles, where few men go. So I took a boat, in the black of night, when the lookout dozed on the fo'c'slehead, and went alone to the warm, long land. And I journeyed south to meet the men by Yeddo Bay, who are wild and unafraid. And the Yoshiwara girls were small, and bright like steel, and good to look upon; but I could not stop, for I knew that Unga rolled on the tossing floor by the rookeries of the north.

'The men by Yeddo Bay had met from the ends of the earth, and had neither gods nor homes, sailing under the flag of the Japanese. And with them I went to the rich beaches of Copper Island, where our salt piles became high with skins.

'And in that silent sea we saw no man till we were ready to come away. Then one day the fog lifted on the edge of a heavy wind, and there jammed down upon us a schooner, with close in her wake the cloudy funnels of a Russian man-of-war. We fled away on the beam of the wind, with the schooner jamming still closer and plunging ahead three feet to our two. And upon her poop was the man with the mane of the sea lion, pressing the rails under with the canvas and laughing in his strength of life. And Unga was there—I knew her on the moment—but he sent her below when the cannons began to talk across the sea.

As I say, with three feet to our two, till we saw the rudder lift green at every jump—and I swinging on to the wheel and cursing, with my back to the Russian shot. For we knew he had it in mind to run before us, that he might get away while we were caught. And they knocked our masts out of us till we dragged into the wind like a wounded gull; but he went on over the edge of the sky line—he and Unga.

'What could we? The fresh hides spoke for themselves. So they took us to a Russian port, and after that to a lone country, where they set us to work in the mines to dig salt. And some died, and—and some did not die.' Naass swept the blanket from his shoulders, disclosing the gnarled and twisted flesh, marked with the unmistakable striations of the knout. Prince hastily covered him, for it was not nice to look upon.

133

'We were there a weary time and sometimes men got away to the south, but they always came back. So, when we who hailed from Yeddo Bay rose in the night and took the guns from the guards, we went to the north. And the land was very large, with plains, soggy with water, and great forests. And the cold came, with much snow on the ground, and no man knew the way. Weary months we journeyed through the endless forest—I do not remember, now, for there was little food and often we lay down to die. But at last we came to the cold sea, and but three were left to look upon it. One had shipped from Yeddo as captain, and he knew in his head the lay of the great lands, and of the place where men may cross from one to the other on the ice. And he led us—I do not know, it was so long—till there were but two. When we came to that place we found five of the strange people which live in that country, and they had dogs and skins, and we were very poor. We fought in the snow till they died, and the captain died, and the dogs and skins were mine. Then I crossed on the ice, which was broken, and once I drifted till a gale from the west put me upon the shore. And after that, Golovin Bay, Pastilik, and the priest. Then south, south, to the warm sunlands where first I wandered.

'But the sea was no longer fruitful, and those who went upon it after the seal went to little profit and great risk. The fleets scattered, and the captains and the men had no word of those I sought. So I turned away from the ocean which never rests, and went among the lands, where the trees, the houses, and the mountains sit always in one place and do not move. I journeyed far, and came to learn many things, even to the way of reading and writing from books. It was well I should do this, for it came upon me that Unga must know these things, and that someday, when the time was met—we—you understand, when the time was met.

'So I drifted, like those little fish which raise a sail to the wind but cannot steer. But my eyes and my ears were open always, and I went among men who traveled much, for I knew they had but to see those I sought to remember. At last there came a man, fresh from the mountains, with pieces of rock in which the free gold stood to the size of peas, and he had heard, he had met, he knew them. They were rich, he said, and lived in the place where they drew the gold from the ground.

'It was in a wild country, and very far away; but in time I came to the camp, hidden between the mountains, where men worked night and day, out of the sight of the sun. Yet the time was not come. I listened to the talk of the people. He had gone away—they had gone away—to England, it was said, in the matter of bringing men with much money together to form companies. I saw the house they had lived in; more like a palace, such as one sees in the old countries. In the nighttime I crept in through a window that I might see in what manner he treated her. I went from room to room, and in such way thought kings and queens must live, it was all so very good. And they all said he treated her like a queen, and many marveled as to what breed of woman she was for there was other blood in her veins, and she was different from the women of Akatan, and no one knew her for what she was. Aye, she was a queen; but I was a chief, and the son of a chief, and I had paid for her an untold price of skin and boat and bead.

'But why so many words? I was a sailorman, and knew the way of the ships on the seas. I followed to England, and then to other countries. Sometimes I heard of them by word of mouth, sometimes I read of them in the papers; yet never once could I come by them, for they had much money, and traveled fast, while I was a poor man. Then came trouble upon them, and their wealth slipped away one day like a curl of smoke. The papers were full of it at the time; but after that nothing was said, and I knew they had gone back where more gold could be got from the ground.

'They had dropped out of the world, being now poor, and so I wandered from camp to camp, even north to the Kootenay country, where I picked up the cold scent. They had come and gone, some said this way, and some that, and still others that they had gone to the country of the Yukon. And I went this way, and I went that, ever journeying from place to place, till it seemed I must grow weary of the world which was so large. But in the Kootenay I traveled a bad trail, and a long trail, with a breed of the Northwest, who saw fit to die when the famine pinched. He had been to the Yukon by an unknown way over the mountains, and when he knew his time was near gave me the map and the secret of a place where he swore by his gods there was much gold.

135

'After that all the world began to flock into the north. I was a poor man; I sold myself to be a driver of dogs. The rest you know. I met him and her in Dawson.

'She did not know me, for I was only a stripling, and her life had been large, so she had no time to remember the one who had paid for her an untold price.

'So? You bought me from my term of service. I went back to bring things about in my own way, for I had waited long, and now that I had my hand upon him was in no hurry.

'As I say, I had it in mind to do my own way, for I read back in my life, through all I had seen and suffered, and remembered the cold and hunger of the endless forest by the Russian seas. As you know, I led him into the east—him and Unga—into the east where many have gone and few returned. I led them to the spot where the bones and the curses of men lie with the gold which they may not have.

'The way was long and the trail unpacked. Our dogs were many and ate much; nor could our sleds carry till the break of spring. We must come back before the river ran free. So here and there we cached grub, that our sleds might be lightened and there be no chance of famine on the back trip. At the McQuestion there were three men, and near them we built a cache, as also did we at the Mayo, where was a hunting camp of a dozen Pellys which had crossed the divide from the south.

'After that, as we went on into the east, we saw no men; only the sleeping river, the moveless forest, and the White Silence of the North. As I say, the way was long and the trail unpacked. Sometimes, in a day's toil, we made no more than eight miles, or ten, and at night we slept like dead men. And never once did they dream that I was Naass, head man of Akatan, the righter of wrongs.

'We now made smaller caches, and in the nighttime it was a small matter to go back on the trail we had broken and change them in such way that one might deem the wolverines the thieves. Again there be places where there is a fall to the river, and the water is unruly, and the ice makes above and is eaten away beneath.

'In such a spot the sled I drove broke through, and the dogs; and to him and Unga it was ill luck, but no more. And there was much grub on that sled, and the dogs the strongest.

'But he laughed, for he was strong of life, and gave the dogs that were left little grub till we cut them from the harnesses one by one and fed them to their mates. We would go home light, he said, traveling and eating from cache to cache, with neither dogs nor sleds; which was true, for our grub was very short, and the last dog died in the traces the night we came to the gold and the bones and the curses of men.

'To reach that place—and the map spoke true—in the heart of the great mountains, we cut ice steps against the wall of a divide. One looked for a valley beyond, but there was no valley; the snow spread away, level as the great harvest plains, and here and there about us mighty mountains shoved their white heads among the stars. And midway on that strange plain which should have been a valley the earth and the snow fell away, straight down toward the heart of the world.

'Had we not been sailormen our heads would have swung round with the sight, but we stood on the dizzy edge that we might see a way to get down. And on one side, and one side only, the wall had fallen away till it was like the slope of the decks in a topsail breeze. I do not know why this thing should be so, but it was so. "It is the mouth of hell," he said; "let us go down." And we went down.

'And on the bottom there was a cabin, built by some man, of logs which he had cast down from above. It was a very old cabin, for men had died there alone at different times, and on pieces of birch bark which were there we read their last words and their curses.

'One had died of scurvy; another's partner had robbed him of his last grub and powder and stolen away; a third had been mauled by a baldface grizzly; a fourth had hunted for game and starved—and so it went, and they had been loath to leave the gold, and had died by the side of it in one way or another. And the worthless gold they had gathered yellowed the floor of the cabin like in a dream.

'But his soul was steady, and his head clear, this man I had led thus far. "We have nothing to eat," he said, "and we will only look upon this gold, and see whence it comes and how much there be. Then we will go away quick, before it gets into our eyes and steals away our judgment. And in this way we may return in the end, with more grub, and possess it all." So we looked upon the great vein, which cut the wall of the pit as a true vein should, and we measured it, and traced it from above and below, and drove the stakes of the claims and blazed the trees in token of our rights. Then, our knees shaking with lack of food, and a sickness in our bellies, and our hearts chugging close to our mouths, we climbed the mighty wall for the last time and turned our faces to the back trip.

'The last stretch we dragged Unga between us, and we fell often, but in the end we made the cache. And lo, there was no grub. It was well done, for he thought it the wolverines, and damned them and his gods in one breath. But Unga was brave, and smiled, and put her hand in his, till I turned away that I might hold myself. "We will rest by the fire," she said, "till morning, and we will gather strength from our moccasins." So we cut the tops of our moccasins in strips, and boiled them half of the night, that we might chew them and swallow them. And in the morning we talked of our chance. The next cache was five days' journey; we could not make it. We must find game.

'"We will go forth and hunt," he said.

'"Yes," said I, "we will go forth and hunt." 'And he ruled that Unga stay by the fire and save her strength. And we went forth, he in quest of the moose and I to the cache I had changed. But I ate little, so they might not see in me much strength. And in the night he fell many times as he drew into camp. And I, too, made to suffer great weakness, stumbling over my snowshoes as though each step might be my last. And we gathered strength from our moccasins.

138

'He was a great man. His soul lifted his body to the last; nor did he cry aloud, save for the sake of Unga. On the second day I followed him, that I might not miss the end. And he lay down to rest often. That night he was near gone; but in the morning he swore weakly and went forth again. He was like a drunken man, and I looked many times for him to give up, but his was the strength of the strong, and his soul the soul of a giant, for he lifted his body through all the weary day. And he shot two ptarmigan, but would not eat them. He needed no fire; they meant life; but his thought was for Unga, and he turned toward camp.

'He no longer walked, but crawled on hand and knee through the snow. I came to him, and read death in his eyes. Even then it was not too late to eat of the ptarmigan. He cast away his rifle and carried the birds in his mouth like a dog. I walked by his side, upright. And he looked at me during the moments he rested, and wondered that I was so strong. I could see it, though he no longer spoke; and when his lips moved, they moved without sound.

'As I say, he was a great man, and my heart spoke for softness; but I read back in my life, and remembered the cold and hunger of the endless forest by the Russian seas. Besides, Unga was mine, and I had paid for her an untold price of skin and boat and bead.

'And in this manner we came through the white forest, with the silence heavy upon us like a damp sea mist. And the ghosts of the past were in the air and all about us; and I saw the yellow beach of Akatan, and the kayaks racing home from the fishing, and the houses on the rim of the forest. And the men who had made themselves chiefs were there, the lawgivers whose blood I bore and whose blood I had wedded in Unga. Aye, and Yash-Noosh walked with me, the wet sand in his hair, and his war spear, broken as he fell upon it, still in his hand. And I knew the time was meet, and saw in the eyes of Unga the promise.

'As I say, we came thus through the forest, till the smell of the camp smoke was in our nostrils. And I bent above him, and tore the ptarmigan from his teeth.

139

'He turned on his side and rested, the wonder mounting in his eyes, and the hand which was under slipping slow toward the knife at his hip. But I took it from him, smiling close in his face. Even then he did not understand. So I made to drink from black bottles, and to build high upon the snow a pile—of goods, and to live again the things which had happened on the night of my marriage. I spoke no word, but he understood. Yet was he unafraid. There was a sneer to his lips, and cold anger, and he gathered new strength with the knowledge. It was not far, but the snow was deep, and he dragged himself very slow.

'Once he lay so long I turned him over and gazed into his eyes. And sometimes he looked forth, and sometimes death. And when I loosed him he struggled on again. In this way we came to the fire. Unga was at his side on the instant. His lips moved without sound; then he pointed at me, that Unga might understand. And after that he lay in the snow, very still, for a long while. Even now is he there in the snow.

'I said no word till I had cooked the ptarmigan. Then I spoke to her, in her own tongue, which she had not heard in many years. She straightened herself, so, and her eyes were wonder-wide, and she asked who I was, and where I had learned that speech.

'"I am Naass," I said.

'"You?" she said. "You?" And she crept close that she might look upon me.

'"Yes," I answered; "I am Naass, head man of Akatan, the last of the blood, as you are the last of the blood." 'And she laughed. By all the things I have seen and the deeds I have done may I never hear such a laugh again. It put the chill to my soul, sitting there in the White Silence, alone with death and this woman who laughed.

'"Come!" I said, for I thought she wandered. "Eat of the food and let us be gone. It is a far fetch from here to Akatan." 'But she shoved her face in his yellow mane, and laughed till it seemed the heavens must fall about our ears. I had thought she would be overjoyed at the sight of me, and eager to go back to the memory of old times, but this seemed a strange form to take.

140

'"Come!" I cried, taking her strong by the hand. "The way is long and dark. Let us hurry!" "Where?" she asked, sitting up, and ceasing from her strange mirth.

'"To Akatan," I answered, intent on the light to grow on her face at the thought. But it became like his, with a sneer to the lips, and cold anger.

'"Yes," she said; "we will go, hand in hand, to Akatan, you and I. And we will live in the dirty huts, and eat of the fish and oil, and bring forth a spawn—a spawn to be proud of all the days of our life. We will forget the world and be happy, very happy. It is good, most good. Come! Let us hurry. Let us go back to Akatan." And she ran her hand through his yellow hair, and smiled in a way which was not good. And there was no promise in her eyes.

'I sat silent, and marveled at the strangeness of woman. I went back to the night when he dragged her from me and she screamed and tore at his hair—at his hair which now she played with and would not leave. Then I remembered the price and the long years of waiting; and I gripped her close, and dragged her away as he had done. And she held back, even as on that night, and fought like a she-cat for its whelp. And when the fire was between us and the man. I loosed her, and she sat and listened. And I told her of all that lay between, of all that had happened to me on strange seas, of all that I had done in strange lands; of my weary quest, and the hungry years, and the promise which had been mine from the first. Aye, I told all, even to what had passed that day between the man and me, and in the days yet young. And as I spoke I saw the promise grow in her eyes, full and large like the break of dawn. And I read pity there, the tenderness of woman, the love, the heart and the soul of Unga. And I was a stripling again, for the look was the look of Unga as she ran up the beach, laughing, to the home of her mother. The stern unrest was gone, and the hunger, and the weary waiting.

'The time was met. I felt the call of her breast, and it seemed there I must pillow my head and forget. She opened her arms to me, and I came against her. Then, sudden, the hate flamed in her eye, her hand was at my hip. And once, twice, she passed the knife.

'"Dog!" she sneered, as she flung me into the snow. "Swine!" And then she laughed till the silence cracked, and went back to her dead.

'As I say, once she passed the knife, and twice; but she was weak with hunger, and it was not meant that I should die. Yet was I minded to stay in that place, and to close my eyes in the last long sleep with those whose lives had crossed with mine and led my feet on unknown trails. But there lay a debt upon me which would not let me rest.

'And the way was long, the cold bitter, and there was little grub. The Pellys had found no moose, and had robbed my cache. And so had the three white men, but they lay thin and dead in their cabins as I passed. After that I do not remember, till I came here, and found food and fire—much fire.' As he finished, he crouched closely, even jealously, over the stove. For a long while the slush-lamp shadows played tragedies upon the wall.

'But Unga!' cried Prince, the vision still strong upon him.

'Unga? She would not eat of the ptarmigan. She lay with her arms about his neck, her face deep in his yellow hair. I drew the fire close, that she might not feel the frost, but she crept to the other side. And I built a fire there; yet it was little good, for she would not eat. And in this manner they still lie up there in the snow.'

'And you?' asked Malemute Kid.

'I do not know; but Akatan is small, and I have little wish to go back and live on the edge of the world. Yet is there small use in life. I can go to Constantine, and he will put irons upon me, and one day they will tie a piece of rope, so, and I will sleep good. Yet—no; I do not know.' 'But, Kid,' protested Prince, 'this is murder!' 'Hush!' commanded Malemute Kid. 'There be things greater than our wisdom, beyond our justice. The right and the wrong of this we cannot say, and it is not for us to judge.' Naass drew yet closer to the fire. There was a great silence, and in each man's eyes many pictures came and went.

The End

142

LOST FACE

LOST FACE

It was the end. Subienkow had travelled a long trail of bitterness and horror, homing like a dove for the capitals of Europe, and here, farther away than ever, in Russian America, the trail ceased. He sat in the snow, arms tied behind him, waiting the torture. He stared curiously before him at a huge Cossack, prone in the snow, moaning in his pain. The men had finished handling the giant and turned him over to the women. That they exceeded the fiendishness of the men, the man's cries attested.

Subienkow looked on, and shuddered. He was not afraid to die. He had carried his life too long in his hands, on that weary trail from Warsaw to Nulato, to shudder at mere dying. But he objected to the torture. It offended his soul. And this offence, in turn, was not due to the mere pain he must endure, but to the sorry spectacle the pain would make of him. He knew that he would pray, and beg, and entreat, even as Big Ivan and the others that had gone before. This would not be nice. To pass out bravely and cleanly, with a smile and a jest—ah! that would have been the way. But to lose control, to have his soul upset by the pangs of the flesh, to screech and gibber like an ape, to become the veriest beast—ah, that was what was so terrible.

There had been no chance to escape. From the beginning, when he dreamed the fiery dream of Poland's independence, he had become a puppet in the hands of Fate. From the beginning, at Warsaw, at St. Petersburg, in the Siberian mines, in Kamtchatka, on the crazy boats of the fur-thieves, Fate had been driving him to this end. Without doubt, in the foundations of the world was graved this end for him—for him, who was so fine and sensitive, whose nerves scarcely sheltered under his skin, who was a dreamer, and a poet, and an artist. Before he was dreamed of, it had been determined that the quivering bundle of sensitiveness that constituted him should be doomed to live in raw and howling savagery, and to die in this far land of night, in this dark place beyond the last boundaries of the world.

He sighed. So that thing before him was Big Ivan—Big Ivan the giant, the man without nerves, the man of iron, the Cossack turned freebooter of the seas, who was as phlegmatic as an ox, with a nervous system so low that what was pain to ordinary men was scarcely a tickle to him. Well, well, trust these Nulato Indians to find Big Ivan's nerves and trace them to the roots of his quivering soul. They were certainly doing it. It was inconceivable that a man could suffer so much and yet live. Big Ivan was paying for his low order of nerves. Already he had lasted twice as long as any of the others.

Subienkow felt that he could not stand the Cossack's sufferings much longer. Why didn't Ivan die? He would go mad if that screaming did not cease. But when it did cease, his turn would come. And there was Yakaga awaiting him, too, grinning at him even now in anticipation—Yakaga, whom only last week he had kicked out of the fort, and upon whose face he had laid the lash of his dog-whip. Yakaga would attend to him. Doubtlessly Yakaga was saving for him more refined tortures, more exquisite nerve-racking. Ah! that must have been a good one, from the way Ivan screamed. The squaws bending over him stepped back with laughter and clapping of hands. Subienkow saw the monstrous thing that had been perpetrated, and began to laugh hysterically. The Indians looked at him in wonderment that he should laugh. But Subienkow could not stop.

This would never do. He controlled himself, the spasmodic twitchings slowly dying away. He strove to think of other things, and began reading back in his own life. He remembered his mother and his father, and the little spotted pony, and the French tutor who had taught him dancing and sneaked him an old worn copy of Voltaire. Once more he saw Paris, and dreary London, and gay Vienna, and Rome. And once more he saw that wild group of youths who had dreamed, even as he, the dream of an independent Poland with a king of Poland on the throne at Warsaw. Ah, there it was that the long trail began. Well, he had lasted longest. One by one, beginning with the two executed at St. Petersburg, he took up the count of the passing of those brave spirits. Here one had been beaten to death by a jailer, and there, on that bloodstained highway of the exiles, where they had marched for endless months, beaten and maltreated by their Cossack guards, another had dropped by the way. Always it had been savagery—brutal, bestial savagery. They had died—of fever, in the mines, under the knout. The last two had died after the escape, in the battle with the Cossacks, and he alone had won to Kamtchatka with the stolen papers and the money of a traveller he had left lying in the snow.

It had been nothing but savagery. All the years, with his heart in studios, and theatres, and courts, he had been hemmed in by savagery. He had purchased his life with blood. Everybody had killed. He had killed that traveller for his passports. He had proved that he was a man of parts by duelling with two Russian officers on a single day. He had had to prove himself in order to win to a place among the fur-thieves. He had had to win to that place. Behind him lay the thousand-years-long road across all Siberia and Russia. He could not escape that way. The only way was ahead, across the dark and icy sea of Bering to Alaska. The way had led from savagery to deeper savagery. On the scurvy-rotten ships of the fur-thieves, out of food and out of water, buffeted by the interminable storms of that stormy sea, men had become animals. Thrice he had sailed east from Kamtchatka. And thrice, after all manner of hardship and suffering, the survivors had come back to Kamtchatka. There had been no outlet for escape, and he could not go back the way he had come, for the mines and the knout awaited him.

Again, the fourth and last time, he had sailed east. He had been with those who first found the fabled Seal Islands; but he had not returned with them to share the wealth of furs in the mad orgies of Kamtchatka. He had sworn never to go back. He knew that to win to those dear capitals of Europe he must go on. So he had changed ships and remained in the dark new land. His comrades were Slavonian hunters and Russian adventurers, Mongols and Tartars and Siberian aborigines; and through the savages of the new world they had cut a path of blood. They had massacred whole villages that refused to furnish the fur-tribute; and they, in turn, had been massacred by ships' companies. He, with one Finn, had been the sole survivor of such a company. They had spent a winter of solitude and starvation on a lonely Aleutian isle, and their rescue in the spring by another fur-ship had been one chance in a thousand.

But always the terrible savagery had hemmed him in. Passing from ship to ship, and ever refusing to return, he had come to the ship that explored south. All down the Alaska coast they had encountered nothing but hosts of savages. Every anchorage among the beetling islands or under the frowning cliffs of the mainland had meant a battle or a storm. Either the gales blew, threatening destruction, or the war canoes came off, manned by howling natives with the war-paint on their faces, who came to learn the bloody virtues of the sea-rovers' gunpowder. South, south they had coasted, clear to the myth-land of California. Here, it was said, were Spanish adventurers who had fought their way up from Mexico. He had had hopes of those Spanish adventurers. Escaping to them, the rest would have been easy—a year or two, what did it matter more or less—and he would win to Mexico, then a ship, and Europe would be his. But they had met no Spaniards. Only had they encountered the same impregnable wall of savagery. The denizens of the confines of the world, painted for war, had driven them back from the shores. At last, when one boat was cut off and every man killed, the commander had abandoned the quest and sailed back to the north.

The years had passed. He had served under Tebenkoff when Michaelovski Redoubt was built. He had spent two years in the Kuskokwim country. Two summers, in the month of June, he had managed to be at the head of Kotzebue Sound. Here, at this time, the tribes assembled for barter; here were to be found spotted deerskins from Siberia, ivory from the Diomedes, walrus skins from the shores of the Arctic, strange stone lamps, passing in trade from tribe to tribe, no one knew whence, and, once, a hunting-knife of English make; and here, Subienkow knew, was the school in which to learn geography. For he met Eskimos from Norton Sound, from King Island and St. Lawrence Island, from Cape Prince of Wales, and Point Barrow. Such places had other names, and their distances were measured in days.

It was a vast region these trading savages came from, and a vaster region from which, by repeated trade, their stone lamps and that steel knife had come. Subienkow bullied, and cajoled, and bribed. Every far-journeyer or strange tribesman was brought before him. Perils unaccountable and unthinkable were mentioned, as well as wild beasts, hostile tribes, impenetrable forests, and mighty mountain ranges; but always from beyond came the rumour and the tale of white-skinned men, blue of eye and fair of hair, who fought like devils and who sought always for furs. They were to the east—far, far to the east. No one had seen them. It was the word that had been passed along.

It was a hard school. One could not learn geography very well through the medium of strange dialects, from dark minds that mingled fact and fable and that measured distances by "sleeps" that varied according to the difficulty of the going. But at last came the whisper that gave Subienkow courage. In the east lay a great river where were these blue-eyed men. The river was called the Yukon. South of Michaelovski Redoubt emptied another great river which the Russians knew as the Kwikpak. These two rivers were one, ran the whisper.

Subienkow returned to Michaelovski. For a year he urged an expedition up the Kwikpak. Then arose Malakoff, the Russian half-breed, to lead the wildest and most ferocious of the hell's broth of mongrel adventurers who had crossed from Kamtchatka. Subienkow was his lieutenant. They threaded the mazes of the great delta of the Kwikpak, picked up the first low hills on the northern bank, and for half a thousand miles, in skin canoes loaded to the gunwales with trade-goods and ammunition, fought their way against the five-knot current of a river that ran from two to ten miles wide in a channel many fathoms deep. Malakoff decided to build the fort at Nulato. Subienkow urged to go farther. But he quickly reconciled himself to Nulato. The long winter was coming on. It would be better to wait. Early the following summer, when the ice was gone, he would disappear up the Kwikpak and work his way to the Hudson Bay Company's posts. Malakoff had never heard the whisper that the Kwikpak was the Yukon, and Subienkow did not tell him.

Came the building of the fort. It was enforced labour. The tiered walls of logs arose to the sighs and groans of the Nulato Indians. The lash was laid upon their backs, and it was the iron hand of the freebooters of the sea that laid on the lash. There were Indians that ran away, and when they were caught they were brought back and spread-eagled before the fort, where they and their tribe learned the efficacy of the knout. Two died under it; others were injured for life; and the rest took the lesson to heart and ran away no more. The snow was flying ere the fort was finished, and then it was the time for furs. A heavy tribute was laid upon the tribe. Blows and lashings continued, and that the tribute should be paid, the women and children were held as hostages and treated with the barbarity that only the fur-thieves knew.

Well, it had been a sowing of blood, and now was come the harvest. The fort was gone. In the light of its burning, half the fur-thieves had been cut down. The other half had passed under the torture. Only Subienkow remained, or Subienkow and Big Ivan, if that whimpering, moaning thing in the snow could be called Big Ivan. Subienkow caught Yakaga grinning at him. There was no gainsaying Yakaga. The mark of the lash was still on his face. After all, Subienkow could not blame him, but he disliked the thought of what Yakaga would do to him. He thought of appealing to Makamuk, the head-chief; but his judgment told him that such appeal was useless. Then, too, he thought of bursting his bonds and dying fighting. Such an end would be quick. But he could not break his bonds. Caribou thongs were stronger than he. Still devising, another thought came to him. He signed for Makamuk, and that an interpreter who knew the coast dialect should be brought.

"Oh, Makamuk," he said, "I am not minded to die. I am a great man, and it were foolishness for me to die. In truth, I shall not die. I am not like these other carrion."

He looked at the moaning thing that had once been Big Ivan, and stirred it contemptuously with his toe.

"I am too wise to die. Behold, I have a great medicine. I alone know this medicine. Since I am not going to die, I shall exchange this medicine with you."

"What is this medicine?" Makamuk demanded.

"It is a strange medicine."

Subienkow debated with himself for a moment, as if loth to part with the secret.

"I will tell you. A little bit of this medicine rubbed on the skin makes the skin hard like a rock, hard like iron, so that no cutting weapon can cut

152

it. The strongest blow of a cutting weapon is a vain thing against it. A bone knife becomes like a piece of mud; and it will turn the edge of the iron knives we have brought among you. What will you give me for the secret of the medicine?"

"I will give you your life," Makamuk made answer through the interpreter.

Subienkow laughed scornfully.

"And you shall be a slave in my house until you die."

The Pole laughed more scornfully.

"Untie my hands and feet and let us talk," he said.

The chief made the sign; and when he was loosed Subienkow rolled a cigarette and lighted it.

"This is foolish talk," said Makamuk. "There is no such medicine. It cannot be. A cutting edge is stronger than any medicine."

The chief was incredulous, and yet he wavered. He had seen too many deviltries of fur-thieves that worked. He could not wholly doubt.

"I will give you your life; but you shall not be a slave," he announced.

"More than that."

Subienkow played his game as coolly as if he were bartering for a foxskin.

"It is a very great medicine. It has saved my life many times. I want a sled and dogs, and six of your hunters to travel with me down the river and give me safety to one day's sleep from Michaelovski Redoubt."

"You must live here, and teach us all of your deviltries," was the reply.

Subienkow shrugged his shoulders and remained silent. He blew cigarette smoke out on the icy air, and curiously regarded what remained of the big Cossack.

"That scar!" Makamuk said suddenly, pointing to the Pole's neck, where a livid mark advertised the slash of a knife in a Kamtchatkan brawl. "The medicine is not good. The cutting edge was stronger than the medicine."

"It was a strong man that drove the stroke." (Subienkow considered.) "Stronger than you, stronger than your strongest hunter, stronger than he."

Again, with the toe of his moccasin, he touched the Cossack—a grisly spectacle, no longer conscious—yet in whose dismembered body the pain-racked life clung and was loth to go.

"Also, the medicine was weak. For at that place there were no berries of a certain kind, of which I see you have plenty in this country. The medicine here will be strong."

"I will let you go down river," said Makamuk; "and the sled and the dogs and the six hunters to give you safety shall be yours."

"You are slow," was the cool rejoinder. "You have committed an offence against my medicine in that you did not at once accept my terms. Behold, I now demand more. I want one hundred beaver skins." (Makamuk sneered.)

"I want one hundred pounds of dried fish." (Makamuk nodded, for fish were plentiful and cheap.) "I want two sleds—one for me and one for my furs and fish. And my rifle must be returned to me. If you do not like the price, in a little while the price will grow."

Yakaga whispered to the chief.

"But how can I know your medicine is true medicine?" Makamuk asked.

"It is very easy. First, I shall go into the woods—"

Again Yakaga whispered to Makamuk, who made a suspicious dissent.

"You can send twenty hunters with me," Subienkow went on. "You see, I must get the berries and the roots with which to make the medicine. Then, when you have brought the two sleds and loaded on them the fish and the beaver skins and the rifle, and when you have told off the six hunters who will go with me—then, when all is ready, I will rub the medicine on my neck, so, and lay my neck there on that log. Then can your strongest hunter take the axe and strike three times on my neck. You yourself can strike the three times."

Makamuk stood with gaping mouth, drinking in this latest and most wonderful magic of the fur-thieves.

"But first," the Pole added hastily, "between each blow I must put on fresh medicine. The axe is heavy and sharp, and I want no mistakes."

"All that you have asked shall be yours," Makamuk cried in a rush of acceptance. "Proceed to make your medicine."

Subienkow concealed his elation. He was playing a desperate game, and there must be no slips. He spoke arrogantly.

"You have been slow. My medicine is offended. To make the offence clean you must give me your daughter."

He pointed to the girl, an unwholesome creature, with a cast in one eye and a bristling wolf-tooth. Makamuk was angry, but the Pole remained imperturbable, rolling and lighting another cigarette.

"Make haste," he threatened. "If you are not quick, I shall demand yet more."

In the silence that followed, the dreary northland scene faded before him, and he saw once more his native land, and France, and, once, as he glanced at the wolf-toothed girl, he remembered another girl, a singer and a dancer, whom he had known when first as a youth he came to Paris.

"What do you want with the girl?" Makamuk asked.

"To go down the river with me." Subienkow glanced over her critically. "She will make a good wife, and it is an honour worthy of my medicine to be married to your blood."

Again he remembered the singer and dancer and hummed aloud a song she had taught him. He lived the old life over, but in a detached, impersonal sort of way, looking at the memory-pictures of his own life as if they were

155

pictures in a book of anybody's life. The chief's voice, abruptly breaking the silence, startled him

"It shall be done," said Makamuk. "The girl shall go down the river with you. But be it understood that I myself strike the three blows with the axe on your neck."

"But each time I shall put on the medicine," Subienkow answered, with a show of ill-concealed anxiety.

"You shall put the medicine on between each blow. Here are the hunters who shall see you do not escape. Go into the forest and gather your medicine."

Makamuk had been convinced of the worth of the medicine by the Pole's rapacity. Surely nothing less than the greatest of medicines could enable a man in the shadow of death to stand up and drive an old-woman's bargain.

"Besides," whispered Yakaga, when the Pole, with his guard, had disappeared among the spruce trees, "when you have learned the medicine you can easily destroy him."

"But how can I destroy him?" Makamuk argued. "His medicine will not let me destroy him."

"There will be some part where he has not rubbed the medicine," was Yakaga's reply. "We will destroy him through that part. It may be his ears. Very well; we will thrust a spear in one ear and out the other. Or it may be his eyes. Surely the medicine will be much too strong to rub on his eyes."

The chief nodded. "You are wise, Yakaga. If he possesses no other devil-things, we will then destroy him."

Subienkow did not waste time in gathering the ingredients for his medicine, he selected whatsoever came to hand such as spruce needles, the inner bark of the willow, a strip of birch bark, and a quantity of moss-berries, which he made the hunters dig up for him from beneath the snow. A few frozen roots completed his supply, and he led the way back to camp.

Makamuk and Yakaga crouched beside him, noting the quantities and kinds of the ingredients he dropped into the pot of boiling water.

"You must be careful that the moss-berries go in first," he explained.

"And—oh, yes, one other thing—the finger of a man. Here, Yakaga, let me cut off your finger."

But Yakaga put his hands behind him and scowled.

"Just a small finger," Subienkow pleaded.

"Yakaga, give him your finger," Makamuk commanded.

"There be plenty of fingers lying around," Yakaga grunted, indicating the human wreckage in the snow of the score of persons who had been tortured to death.

"It must be the finger of a live man," the Pole objected.

"Then shall you have the finger of a live man." Yakaga strode over to the Cossack and sliced off a finger.

"He is not yet dead," he announced, flinging the bloody trophy in the snow at the Pole's feet. "Also, it is a good finger, because it is large."

Subienkow dropped it into the fire under the pot and began to sing. It was a French love-song that with great solemnity he sang into the brew.

"Without these words I utter into it, the medicine is worthless," he explained. "The words are the chiefest strength of it. Behold, it is ready."

"Name the words slowly, that I may know them," Makamuk commanded.

"Not until after the test. When the axe flies back three times from my neck, then will I give you the secret of the words."

"But if the medicine is not good medicine?" Makamuk queried anxiously.

Subienkow turned upon him wrathfully.

"My medicine is always good. However, if it is not good, then do by me as you have done to the others. Cut me up a bit at a time, even as you have cut him up." He pointed to the Cossack. "The medicine is now cool. Thus, I rub it on my neck, saying this further medicine."

With great gravity he slowly intoned a line of the "Marseillaise," at the same time rubbing the villainous brew thoroughly into his neck.

An outcry interrupted his play-acting. The giant Cossack, with a last resurgence of his tremendous vitality, had arisen to his knees. Laughter and cries of surprise and applause arose from the Nulatos, as Big Ivan began flinging himself about in the snow with mighty spasms.

Subienkow was made sick by the sight, but he mastered his qualms and made believe to be angry.

"This will not do," he said. "Finish him, and then we will make the test. Here, you, Yakaga, see that his noise ceases."

While this was being done, Subienkow turned to Makamuk.

"And remember, you are to strike hard. This is not baby-work. Here, take the axe and strike the log, so that I can see you strike like a man."

Makamuk obeyed, striking twice, precisely and with vigour, cutting out a large chip.

"It is well." Subienkow looked about him at the circle of savage faces that somehow seemed to symbolize the wall of savagery that had hemmed him about ever since the Czar's police had first arrested him in Warsaw. "Take your axe, Makamuk, and stand so. I shall lie down. When I raise my hand, strike, and strike with all your might. And be careful that no one stands behind you. The medicine is good, and the axe may bounce from off my neck and right out of your hands."

He looked at the two sleds, with the dogs in harness, loaded with furs and fish. His rifle lay on top of the beaver skins. The six hunters who were to act as his guard stood by the sleds.

"Where is the girl?" the Pole demanded. "Bring her up to the sleds before the test goes on."

When this had been carried out, Subienkow lay down in the snow, resting his head on the log like a tired child about to sleep. He had lived so many dreary years that he was indeed tired.

"I laugh at you and your strength, O Makamuk," he said. "Strike, and strike hard."

He lifted his hand. Makamuk swung the axe, a broadaxe for the squaring of logs. The bright steel flashed through the frosty air, poised for a perceptible instant above Makamuk's head, then descended upon Subienkow's bare neck. Clear through flesh and bone it cut its way, biting deeply into the log beneath. The amazed savages saw the head bounce a yard away from the blood-spouting trunk.

There was a great bewilderment and silence, while slowly it began to dawn in their minds that there had been no medicine. The fur-thief had outwitted them. Alone, of all their prisoners, he had escaped the torture. That had been the stake for which he played. A great roar of laughter went up. Makamuk bowed his head in shame. The fur-thief had fooled him. He had lost face before all his people. Still they continued to roar out their laughter. Makamuk turned, and with bowed head stalked away. He knew that thenceforth he would be no longer known as Makamuk. He would be Lost Face; the record of his shame would be with him until he died; and whenever the tribes gathered in the spring for the salmon, or in the summer for the trading, the story would pass back and forth across the camp-fires of how the fur-thief died peaceably, at a single stroke, by the hand of Lost Face.

"Who was Lost Face?" he could hear, in anticipation, some insolent young buck demand, "Oh, Lost Face," would be the answer, "he who once was Makamuk in the days before he cut off the fur-thief's head."

TRUST

All lines had been cast off, and the *Seattle No. 4* was pulling slowly out from the shore. Her decks were piled high with freight and baggage, and swarmed with a heterogeneous company of Indians, dogs, and dog-mushers, prospectors, traders, and homeward-bound gold-seekers. A goodly portion of Dawson was lined up on the bank, saying good-bye. As the gang-plank came in and the steamer nosed into the stream, the clamour of farewell became deafening. Also, in that eleventh moment, everybody began to remember final farewell messages and to shout them back and forth across the widening stretch of water. Louis Bondell, curling his yellow moustache with one hand and languidly waving the other hand to his friends on shore, suddenly remembered something and sprang to the rail.

"Oh, Fred!" he bawled. "Oh, Fred!"

The "Fred" desired thrust a strapping pair of shoulders through the forefront of the crowd on the bank and tried to catch Louis Bondell's message. The latter grew red in the face with vain vociferation. Still the water widened between steamboat and shore.

"Hey, you, Captain Scott!" he yelled at the pilot-house. "Stop the boat!"

The gongs clanged, and the big stern wheel reversed, then stopped. All hands on steamboat and on bank took advantage of this respite to exchange final, new, and imperative farewells. More futile than ever was Louis Bondell's effort to make himself heard. The *Seattle No.* 4 lost way and drifted downstream, and Captain Scott had to go ahead and reverse a second time. His head disappeared inside the pilot-house, coming into view a moment later behind a big megaphone.

Now Captain Scott had a remarkable voice, and the "Shut up!" he launched at the crowd on deck and on shore could have been heard at the top of Moosehide Mountain and as far as Klondike City. This official remonstrance from the pilot-house spread a film of silence over the tumult.

"Now, what do you want to say?" Captain Scott demanded.

"Tell Fred Churchill—he's on the bank there—tell him to go to Macdonald. It's in his safe—a small gripsack of mine. Tell him to get it and bring it out when he comes."

In the silence Captain Scott bellowed the message ashore through the megaphone:—

"You, Fred Churchill, go to Macdonald—in his safe—small gripsack— belongs to Louis Bondell—important! Bring it out when you come! Got it!"

Churchill waved his hand in token that he had got it. In truth, had Macdonald, half a mile away, opened his window, he'd have got it, too. The tumult of farewell rose again, the gongs clanged, and the *Seattle No.* 4 went ahead, swung out into the stream, turned on her heel, and headed down the Yukon, Bondell and Churchill waving farewell and mutual affection to the last.

That was in midsummer. In the fall of the year, the *W. H. Willis* started up the Yukon with two hundred homeward-bound pilgrims on board. Among them was Churchill. In his state-room, in the middle of a clothes-bag, was Louis Bondell's grip. It was a small, stout leather affair, and its weight of forty pounds always made Churchill nervous when he wandered too far from it. The man in the adjoining state-room had a treasure of gold-dust hidden similarly in a clothes-bag, and the pair of them ultimately arranged to stand watch and watch. While one went down to eat, the other kept an eye on the two state-room doors. When Churchill wanted to take a hand at whist, the other man mounted guard, and when the other man wanted to relax his soul, Churchill read four-months' old newspapers on a camp stool between the two doors.

There were signs of an early winter, and the question that was discussed from dawn till dark, and far into the dark, was whether they would get out before the freeze-up or be compelled to abandon the steamboat and tramp out over the ice. There were irritating delays. Twice the engines broke down and had to be tinkered up, and each time there were snow flurries to warn them of the imminence of winter. Nine times the *W. H. Willis* essayed to ascend the Five-Finger Rapids with her impaired machinery, and when she succeeded, she was four days behind her very liberal schedule. The question that then arose was whether or not the steamboat *Flora* would wait for her above the Box Cañon. The stretch of water between the head of the Box Cañon and the foot of the White Horse Rapids was unnavigable for steamboats, and passengers were transhipped at that point, walking around the rapids from one steamboat to the other. There were no telephones in the country, hence no way of informing the waiting *Flora* that the *Willis* was four days late, but coming.

When the *W. H. Willis* pulled into White Horse, it was learned that the *Flora* had waited three days over the limit, and had departed only a few hours before. Also, it was learned that she would tie up at Tagish Post till nine o'clock, Sunday morning. It was then four o'clock, Saturday afternoon. The pilgrims called a meeting. On board was a large Peterborough canoe, consigned to the police post at the head of Lake Bennett. They agreed to be responsible for it and to deliver it. Next, they called for volunteers. Two men were needed to make a race for the *Flora*. A score of men volunteered on the instant. Among them was Churchill, such being his nature that he volunteered before he thought of Bondell's gripsack. When this thought came to him, he began to hope that he would not be selected; but a man who had made a name as captain of a college football eleven, as a president of an athletic club, as a dog-musher and a stampeder in the Yukon, and, moreover, who possessed such shoulders as he, had no right to avoid the honour. It was thrust upon him and upon a gigantic German, Nick Antonsen.

While a crowd of the pilgrims, the canoe on their shoulders, started on a trot over the portage, Churchill ran to his state-room. He turned the contents of the clothes-bag on the floor and caught up the grip, with the intention of entrusting it to the man next door. Then the thought smote him that it was not his grip, and that he had no right to let it out of his possession. So he dashed ashore with it and ran up the portage changing it often from one hand to the other, and wondering if it really did not weigh more than forty pounds.

162

It was half-past four in the afternoon when the two men started. The current of the Thirty Mile River was so strong that rarely could they use the paddles. It was out on one bank with a tow-line over the shoulders, stumbling over the rocks, forcing a way through the underbrush, slipping at times and falling into the water, wading often up to the knees and waist; and then, when an insurmountable bluff was encountered, it was into the canoe, out paddles, and a wild and losing dash across the current to the other bank, in paddles, over the side, and out tow-line again. It was exhausting work. Antonsen toiled like the giant he was, uncomplaining, persistent, but driven to his utmost by the powerful body and indomitable brain of Churchill. They never paused for rest. It was go, go, and keep on going. A crisp wind blew down the river, freezing their hands and making it imperative, from time to time, to beat the blood back into the numbed fingers.

As night came on, they were compelled to trust to luck. They fell repeatedly on the untravelled banks and tore their clothing to shreds in the underbrush they could not see. Both men were badly scratched and bleeding. A dozen times, in their wild dashes from bank to bank, they struck snags and were capsized. The first time this happened, Churchill dived and groped in three feet of water for the gripsack. He lost half an hour in recovering it, and after that it was carried securely lashed to the canoe. As long as the canoe floated it was safe. Antonsen jeered at the grip, and toward morning began to curse it; but Churchill vouchsafed no explanations.

Their delays and mischances were endless. On one swift bend, around which poured a healthy young rapid, they lost two hours, making a score of attempts and capsizing twice. At this point, on both banks, were precipitous bluffs, rising out of deep water, and along which they could neither tow nor pole, while they could not gain with the paddles against the current. At each attempt they strained to the utmost with the paddles, and each time, with heads nigh to bursting from the effort, they were played out and swept back. They succeeded finally by an accident. In the swiftest current, near the end of another failure, a freak of the current sheered the canoe out of Churchill's control and flung it against the bluff. Churchill made a blind leap at the bluff and landed in a crevice. Holding on with one hand, he held the swamped canoe with the other till Antonsen dragged himself out of the water. Then they pulled the canoe out and rested. A fresh start at this crucial point took them by. They landed on the bank above and plunged immediately ashore and into the brush with the tow-line.

Daylight found them far below Tagish Post. At nine o'clock Sunday morning they could hear the *Flora* whistling her departure. And when, at ten o'clock, they dragged themselves in to the Post, they could barely see the *Flora*'s smoke far to the southward. It was a pair of worn-out tatterdemalions that Captain Jones of the Mounted Police welcomed and fed, and he afterward averred that they possessed two of the most tremendous appetites he had ever observed. They lay down and slept in their wet rags by the stove. At the end of two hours Churchill got up, carried Bondell's grip, which he had used for a pillow, down to the canoe, kicked Antonsen awake, and started in pursuit of the Flora.

"There's no telling what might happen—machinery break down, or something," was his reply to Captain Jones's expostulations. "I'm going to catch that steamer and send her back for the boys."

Tagish Lake was white with a fall gale that blew in their teeth. Big, swinging seas rushed upon the canoe, compelling one man to bale and leaving one man to paddle. Headway could not be made. They ran along the shallow shore and went overboard, one man ahead on the tow-line, the other shoving on the canoe. They fought the gale up to their waists in the icy water, often up to their necks, often over their heads and buried by the big, crested waves. There was no rest, never a moment's pause from the cheerless, heart-breaking battle. That night, at the head of Tagish Lake, in the thick of a driving snow-squall, they overhauled the *Flora*. Antonsen fell on board, lay where he had fallen, and snored. Churchill looked like a wild man. His clothes barely clung to him. His face was iced up and swollen from the protracted effort of twenty-four hours, while his hands were so swollen that he could not close the fingers. As for his feet, it was an agony to stand upon them.

The captain of the *Flora* was loth to go back to White Horse. Churchill was persistent and imperative; the captain was stubborn. He pointed out finally that nothing was to be gained by going back, because the only ocean steamer at Dyea, the *Athenian*, was to sail on Tuesday morning, and that he could not make the back trip to White Horse and bring up the stranded pilgrims in time to make the connection.

"What time does the *Athenian* sail?" Churchill demanded.

"Seven o'clock, Tuesday morning."

"All right," Churchill said, at the same time kicking a tattoo on the ribs of the snoring Antonsen. "You go back to White Home. We'll go ahead and hold the *Athenian*."

Antonsen, stupid with sleep, not yet clothed in his waking mind, was bundled into the canoe, and did not realize what had happened till he was drenched with the icy spray of a big sea, and heard Churchill snarling at him through the darkness:—

"Paddle, can't you! Do you want to be swamped?"

Daylight found them at Caribou Crossing, the wind dying down, and Antonsen too far gone to dip a paddle. Churchill grounded the canoe on a quiet beach, where they slept. He took the precaution of twisting his arm under the weight of his head. Every few minutes the pain of the pent circulation aroused him, whereupon he would look at his watch and twist the other arm under his head. At the end of two hours he fought with Antonsen to rouse him. Then they started. Lake Bennett, thirty miles in length, was like a millpond; but, half way across, a gale from the south smote them and turned the water white. Hour after hour they repeated the struggle on Tagish, over the side, pulling and shoving on the canoe, up to their waists and necks, and over their heads, in the icy water; toward the last the good-natured giant played completely out. Churchill drove him mercilessly; but when he pitched forward and bade fair to drown in three feet of water, the other dragged him into the canoe. After that, Churchill fought on alone, arriving at the police post at the head of Bennett in the early afternoon. He tried to help Antonsen out of the canoe, but failed. He listened to the exhausted man's heavy breathing, and envied him when he thought of what he himself had yet to undergo. Antonsen could lie there and sleep; but he, behind time, must go on over mighty Chilcoot and down to the sea. The real struggle lay before him, and he almost regretted the strength that resided in his frame because of the torment it could inflict upon that frame.

Churchill pulled the canoe up on the beach, seized Bondell's grip, and started on a limping dog-trot for the police post.

"There's a canoe down there, consigned to you from Dawson," he hurled at the officer who answered his knock. "And there's a man in it pretty near dead. Nothing serious; only played out. Take care of him. I've got to rush. Good-bye. Want to catch the *Athenian*."

A mile portage connected Lake Bennett and Lake Linderman, and his last words he flung back after him as he resumed the trot. It was a very painful trot, but he clenched his teeth and kept on, forgetting his pain most of the time in the fervent heat with which he regarded the gripsack. It was a severe handicap. He swung it from one hand to the other, and back again. He tucked it under his arm. He threw one hand over the opposite shoulder, and the bag bumped and pounded on his back as he ran along. He could scarcely hold it in his bruised and swollen fingers, and several times he dropped it. Once, in changing from one hand to the other, it escaped his clutch and fell in front of him, tripped him up, and threw him violently to the ground.

At the far end of the portage he bought an old set of pack-straps for a dollar, and in them he swung the grip. Also, he chartered a launch to run him the six miles to the upper end of Lake Linderman, where he arrived at four in the afternoon. The *Athenian* was to sail from Dyea next morning at seven. Dyea was twenty-eight miles away, and between towered Chilcoot. He sat down to adjust his foot-gear for the long climb, and woke up. He had dozed the instant he sat down, though he had not slept thirty seconds. He was afraid his next doze might be longer, so he finished fixing his foot-gear standing up. Even then he was overpowered for a fleeting moment. He experienced the flash of unconsciousness; becoming aware of it, in mid-air, as his relaxed body was sinking to the ground and as he caught himself together, he stiffened his muscles with a spasmodic wrench, and escaped the fall. The

166

sudden jerk back to consciousness left him sick and trembling. He beat his head with the heel of his hand, knocking wakefulness into the numbed brain.

Jack Burns's pack-train was starting back light for Crater Lake, and Churchill was invited to a mule. Burns wanted to put the gripsack on another animal, but Churchill held on to it, carrying it on his saddle-pommel. But he dozed, and the grip persisted in dropping off the pommel, one side or the other, each time wakening him with a sickening start. Then, in the early darkness, Churchill's mule brushed him against a projecting branch that laid his cheek open. To cap it, the mule blundered off the trail and fell, throwing rider and gripsack out upon the rocks. After that, Churchill walked, or stumbled rather, over the apology for a trail, leading the mule. Stray and awful odours, drifting from each side of the trail, told of the horses that had died in the rush for gold. But he did not mind. He was too sleepy. By the time Long Lake was reached, however, he had recovered from his sleepiness; and at Deep Lake he resigned the gripsack to Burns. But thereafter, by the light of the dim stars, he kept his eyes on Burns. There were not going to be any accidents with that bag.

At Crater Lake, the pack-train went into camp, and Churchill, slinging the grip on his back, started the steep climb for the summit. For the first time, on that precipitous wall, he realized how tired he was. He crept and crawled like a crab, burdened by the weight of his limbs. A distinct and painful effort of will was required each time he lifted a foot. An hallucination came to him that he was shod with lead, like a deep-sea diver, and it was all he could do to resist the desire to reach down and feel the lead. As for Bondell's gripsack, it was inconceivable that forty pounds could weigh so much. It pressed him down like a mountain, and he looked back with unbelief to the year before, when he had climbed that same pass with a hundred and fifty pounds on his back. If those loads had weighed a hundred and fifty pounds, then Bondell's grip weighed five hundred.

The first rise of the divide from Crater Lake was across a small glacier. Here was a well-defined trail. But above the glacier, which was also above timber-line, was naught but a chaos of naked rock and enormous boulders. There was no way of seeing the trail in the darkness, and he blundered on,

167

paying thrice the ordinary exertion for all that he accomplished. He won the summit in the thick of howling wind and driving snow, providentially stumbling upon a small, deserted tent, into which he crawled. There he found and bolted some ancient fried potatoes and half a dozen raw eggs.

When the snow ceased and the wind eased down, he began the almost impossible descent. There was no trail, and he stumbled and blundered, often finding himself, at the last moment, on the edge of rocky walls and steep slopes the depth of which he had no way of judging. Part way down, the stars clouded over again, and in the consequent obscurity he slipped and rolled and slid for a hundred feet, landing bruised and bleeding on the bottom of a large shallow hole. From all about him arose the stench of dead horses. The hole was handy to the trail, and the packers had made a practice of tumbling into it their broken and dying animals. The stench overpowered him, making him deadly sick, and as in a nightmare he scrambled out. Half-way up, he recollected Bondell's gripsack. It had fallen into the hole with him; the pack-strap had evidently broken, and he had forgotten it. Back he went into the pestilential charnel-pit, where he crawled around on hands and knees and groped for half an hour. Altogether he encountered and counted seventeen dead horses (and one horse still alive that he shot with his revolver) before he found Bondell's grip. Looking back upon a life that had not been without valour and achievement, he unhesitatingly declared to himself that this return after the grip was the most heroic act he had ever performed. So heroic was it that he was twice on the verge of fainting before he crawled out of the hole.

By the time he had descended to the Scales, the steep pitch of Chilcoot was past, and the way became easier. Not that it was an easy way, however, in the best of places; but it became a really possible trail, along which he could have made good time if he had not been worn out, if he had had light with which to pick his steps, and if it had not been for Bondell's gripsack. To him, in his exhausted condition, it was the last straw. Having barely strength to carry himself along, the additional weight of the grip was sufficient to throw him nearly every time he tripped or stumbled. And when he escaped tripping, branches reached out in the darkness, hooked the grip between his shoulders, and held him back.

His mind was made up that if he missed the *Athenian* it would be the fault of the gripsack. In fact, only two things remained in his consciousness— Bondell's grip and the steamer. He knew only those two things, and they became identified, in a way, with some stern mission upon which he had journeyed and toiled for centuries. He walked and struggled on as in a dream. As part of the dream was his arrival at Sheep Camp. He stumbled into a saloon, slid his shoulders out of the straps, and started to deposit the grip at his feet. But it slipped from his fingers and struck the floor with a heavy thud that was not unnoticed by two men who were just leaving. Churchill drank a glass of whisky, told the barkeeper to call him in ten minutes, and sat down, his feet on the grip, his head on his knees.

So badly did his misused body stiffen, that when he was called it required another ten minutes and a second glass of whisky to unbend his joints and limber up the muscles.

"Hey not that way!" the barkeeper shouted, and then went after him and started him through the darkness toward Canyon City. Some little husk of inner consciousness told Churchill that the direction was right, and, still as in a dream, he took the cañon trail. He did not know what warned him, but after what seemed several centuries of travelling, he sensed danger and drew his revolver. Still in the dream, he saw two men step out and heard them halt him. His revolver went off four times, and he saw the flashes and heard the explosions of their revolvers. Also, he was aware that he had been hit in the thigh. He saw one man go down, and, as the other came for him, he smashed him a straight blow with the heavy revolver full in the face. Then he turned and ran. He came from the dream shortly afterward, to find himself plunging down the trail at a limping lope. His first thought was for the gripsack. It was still on his back. He was convinced that what had happened was a dream till he felt for his revolver and found it gone. Next he became aware of a sharp stinging of his thigh, and after investigating, he found his hand warm with blood. It was a superficial wound, but it was incontestable. He became wider awake, and kept up the lumbering run to Canyon City.

He found a man, with a team of horses and a wagon, who got out of bed and harnessed up for twenty dollars. Churchill crawled in on the wagon-bed and slept, the gripsack still on his back. It was a rough ride, over water-washed boulders down the Dyea Valley; but he roused only when the wagon hit the highest places. Any altitude of his body above the wagon-bed of less than a foot did not faze him. The last mile was smooth going, and he slept soundly.

He came to in the grey dawn, the driver shaking him savagely and howling into his ear that the *Athenian* was gone. Churchill looked blankly at the deserted harbour.

"There's a smoke over at Skaguay," the man said.

Churchill's eyes were too swollen to see that far, but he said: "It's she. Get me a boat."

The driver was obliging and found a skiff, and a man to row it for ten dollars, payment in advance. Churchill paid, and was helped into the skiff. It was beyond him to get in by himself. It was six miles to Skaguay, and he had a blissful thought of sleeping those six miles. But the man did not know how to row, and Churchill took the oars and toiled for a few more centuries. He never knew six longer and more excruciating miles. A snappy little breeze blew up the inlet and held him back. He had a gone feeling at the pit of the stomach, and suffered from faintness and numbness. At his command, the man took the baler and threw salt water into his face.

The *Athenian's* anchor was up-and-down when they came alongside, and Churchill was at the end of his last remnant of strength.

"Stop her! Stop her!" he shouted hoarsely.

"Important message! Stop her!"

Then he dropped his chin on his chest and slept. When half a dozen men started to carry him up the gang-plank, he awoke, reached for the grip, and clung to it like a drowning man.

On deck he became a centre of horror and curiosity. The clothing in which he had left White Horse was represented by a few rags, and he was as frayed as his clothing. He had travelled for fifty-five hours at the top notch of endurance. He had slept six hours in that time, and he was twenty pounds lighter than when he started. Face and hands and body were scratched and bruised, and he could scarcely see. He tried to stand up, but failed, sprawling out on the deck, hanging on to the gripsack, and delivering his message.

"Now, put me to bed," he finished; "I'll eat when I wake up."

They did him honour, carrying him down in his rags and dirt and depositing him and Bondell's grip in the bridal chamber, which was the biggest and most luxurious state-room in the ship. Twice he slept the clock around, and he had bathed and shaved and eaten and was leaning over the rail smoking a cigar when the two hundred pilgrims from White Horse came alongside.

By the time the *Athenian* arrived in Seattle, Churchill had fully recuperated, and he went ashore with Bondell's grip in his hand. He felt proud of that grip. To him it stood for achievement and integrity and trust. "I've delivered the goods," was the way he expressed these various high terms to himself. It was early in the evening, and he went straight to Bondell's home. Louis Bondell was glad to see him, shaking hands with both hands at the same time and dragging him into the house.

"Oh, thanks, old man; it was good of you to bring it out," Bondell said when he received the gripsack.

He tossed it carelessly upon a couch, and Churchill noted with an appreciative eye the rebound of its weight from the springs. Bondell was volleying him with questions.

"How did you make out? How're the boys? What became of Bill Smithers? Is Del Bishop still with Pierce? Did he sell my dogs? How did Sulphur Bottom show up? You're looking fine. What steamer did you come out on?"

To all of which Churchill gave answer, till half an hour had gone by and the first lull in the conversation had arrived.

"Hadn't you better take a look at it?" he suggested, nodding his head at the gripsack.

"Oh, it's all right," Bondell answered. "Did Mitchell's dump turn out as much as he expected?"

"I think you'd better look at it," Churchill insisted. "When I deliver a thing, I want to be satisfied that it's all right. There's always the chance that somebody might have got into it when I was asleep, or something."

"It's nothing important, old man," Bondell answered, with a laugh.

"Nothing important," Churchill echoed in a faint, small voice. Then he spoke with decision: "Louis, what's in that bag? I want to know."

Louis looked at him curiously, then left the room and returned with a bunch of keys. He inserted his hand and drew out a heavy Colt's revolver. Next came out a few boxes of ammunition for the revolver and several boxes of Winchester cartridges.

Churchill took the gripsack and looked into it. Then he turned it upside down and shook it gently.

"The gun's all rusted," Bondell said. "Must have been out in the rain."

"Yes," Churchill answered. "Too bad it got wet. I guess I was a bit careless."

He got up and went outside. Ten minutes later Louis Bondell went out and found him on the steps, sitting down, elbows on knees and chin on hands, gazing steadfastly out into the darkness.

TO BUILD A FIRE

Day had broken cold and grey, exceedingly cold and grey, when the man turned aside from the main Yukon trail and climbed the high earth-bank, where a dim and little-travelled trail led eastward through the fat spruce timberland. It was a steep bank, and he paused for breath at the top, excusing the act to himself by looking at his watch. It was nine o'clock. There was no sun nor hint of sun, though there was not a cloud in the sky. It was a clear day, and yet there seemed an intangible pall over the face of things, a subtle gloom that made the day dark, and that was due to the absence of sun. This fact did not worry the man. He was used to the lack of sun. It had been days since he had seen the sun, and he knew that a few more days must pass before that cheerful orb, due south, would just peep above the sky-line and dip immediately from view.

The man flung a look back along the way he had come. The Yukon lay a mile wide and hidden under three feet of ice. On top of this ice were as many feet of snow. It was all pure white, rolling in gentle undulations where the ice-jams of the freeze-up had formed. North and south, as far as his eye could see, it was unbroken white, save for a dark hair-line that curved and twisted from around the spruce-covered island to the south, and that curved and twisted away into the north, where it disappeared behind another spruce-covered island. This dark hair-line was the trail—the main trail—that led south five hundred miles to the Chilcoot Pass, Dyea, and salt water; and that led north seventy miles to Dawson, and still on to the north a thousand miles to Nulato, and finally to St. Michael on Bering Sea, a thousand miles and half a thousand more.

But all this—the mysterious, far-reaching hairline trail, the absence of sun from the sky, the tremendous cold, and the strangeness and weirdness of it all—made no impression on the man. It was not because he was long used to it. He was a new-comer in the land, a *chechaquo*, and this was his first winter. The trouble with him was that he was without imagination. He was quick and alert in the things of life, but only in the things, and not in the significances. Fifty degrees below zero meant eighty odd degrees of frost. Such fact impressed him as being cold and uncomfortable, and that was all. It did not lead him to meditate upon his frailty as a creature of temperature, and upon man's frailty in general, able only to live within certain narrow limits of heat and cold; and from there on it did not lead him to the conjectural field of immortality and man's place in the universe. Fifty degrees below zero stood for a bite of frost that hurt and that must be guarded against by the use of mittens, ear-flaps, warm moccasins, and thick socks. Fifty degrees below zero was to him just precisely fifty degrees below zero. That there should be anything more to it than that was a thought that never entered his head.

As he turned to go on, he spat speculatively. There was a sharp, explosive crackle that startled him. He spat again. And again, in the air, before it could fall to the snow, the spittle crackled. He knew that at fifty below spittle crackled on the snow, but this spittle had crackled in the air. Undoubtedly it was colder than fifty below—how much colder he did not know. But the temperature did not matter. He was bound for the old claim on the left fork of Henderson Creek, where the boys were already. They had come over across the divide from the Indian Creek country, while he had come the roundabout way to take a look at the possibilities of getting out logs in the spring from the islands in the Yukon. He would be in to camp by six o'clock; a bit after dark, it was true, but the boys would be there, a fire would be going, and a hot supper would be ready. As for lunch, he pressed his hand against the protruding bundle under his jacket. It was also under his shirt, wrapped up in a handkerchief and lying against the naked skin. It was the only way to keep the biscuits from freezing. He smiled agreeably to himself as he thought of those biscuits, each cut open and sopped in bacon grease, and each enclosing a generous slice of fried bacon.

He plunged in among the big spruce trees. The trail was faint. A foot of snow had fallen since the last sled had passed over, and he was glad he was without a sled, travelling light. In fact, he carried nothing but the lunch wrapped in the handkerchief. He was surprised, however, at the cold. It certainly was cold, he concluded, as he rubbed his numbed nose and cheek-bones with his mittened hand. He was a warm-whiskered man, but the hair on his face did not protect the high cheek-bones and the eager nose that thrust itself aggressively into the frosty air.

At the man's heels trotted a dog, a big native husky, the proper wolf-dog, grey-coated and without any visible or temperamental difference from its brother, the wild wolf. The animal was depressed by the tremendous cold. It knew that it was no time for travelling. Its instinct told it a truer tale than was told to the man by the man's judgment. In reality, it was not merely colder than fifty below zero; it was colder than sixty below, than seventy below. It was seventy-five below zero. Since the freezing-point is thirty-two above zero, it meant that one hundred and seven degrees of frost obtained. The dog did not know anything about thermometers. Possibly in its brain there was no sharp consciousness of a condition of very cold such as was in the man's brain. But the brute had its instinct. It experienced a vague but menacing apprehension that subdued it and made it slink along at the man's heels, and that made it question eagerly every unwonted movement of the man as if expecting him to go into camp or to seek shelter somewhere and build a fire. The dog had learned fire, and it wanted fire, or else to burrow under the snow and cuddle its warmth away from the air.

The frozen moisture of its breathing had settled on its fur in a fine powder of frost, and especially were its jowls, muzzle, and eyelashes whitened by its crystalled breath. The man's red beard and moustache were likewise frosted, but more solidly, the deposit taking the form of ice and increasing with every warm, moist breath he exhaled. Also, the man was chewing tobacco, and the muzzle of ice held his lips so rigidly that he was unable to clear his chin when he expelled the juice. The result was that a crystal beard of the colour and solidity of amber was increasing its length on his chin. If he fell down it would shatter itself, like glass, into brittle fragments. But he did not mind the appendage. It was the penalty all tobacco-chewers paid in that country, and he had been out before in two cold snaps. They had not been so cold as this, he knew, but by the spirit thermometer at Sixty Mile he knew they had been registered at fifty below and at fifty-five.

175

He held on through the level stretch of woods for several miles, crossed a wide flat of nigger-heads, and dropped down a bank to the frozen bed of a small stream. This was Henderson Creek, and he knew he was ten miles from the forks. He *looked* at his watch. It was ten o'clock. He was making four miles an hour, and he calculated that he would arrive at the forks at half-past twelve. He decided to celebrate that event by eating his lunch there.

The dog dropped in again at his heels, with a tail drooping discouragement, as the man swung along the creek-bed. The furrow of the old sled-trail was plainly visible, but a dozen inches of snow covered the marks of the last runners. In a month no man had come up or down that silent creek. The man held steadily on. He was not much given to thinking, and just then particularly he had nothing to think about save that he would eat lunch at the forks and that at six o'clock he would be in camp with the boys. There was nobody to talk to and, had there been, speech would have been impossible because of the ice-muzzle on his mouth. So he continued monotonously to chew tobacco and to increase the length of his amber beard.

Once in a while the thought reiterated itself that it was very cold and that he had never experienced such cold. As he walked along he rubbed his cheek-bones and nose with the back of his mittened hand. He did this automatically, now and again changing hands. But rub as he would, the instant he stopped his cheek-bones went numb, and the following instant the end of his nose went numb. He was sure to frost his cheeks; he knew that, and experienced a pang of regret that he had not devised a nose-strap of the sort Bud wore in cold snaps. Such a strap passed across the cheeks, as well, and saved them. But it didn't matter much, after all. What were frosted cheeks? A bit painful, that was all; they were never serious.

Empty as the man's mind was of thoughts, he was keenly observant, and he noticed the changes in the creek, the curves and bends and timber-jams, and always he sharply noted where he placed his feet. Once, coming around a bend, he shied abruptly, like a startled horse, curved away from the place where he had been walking, and retreated several paces back along the trail. The creek he knew was frozen clear to the bottom—no creek could contain water in that arctic winter—but he knew also that there were springs that

176

bubbled out from the hillsides and ran along under the snow and on top the ice of the creek. He knew that the coldest snaps never froze these springs, and he knew likewise their danger. They were traps. They hid pools of water under the snow that might be three inches deep, or three feet. Sometimes a skin of ice half an inch thick covered them, and in turn was covered by the snow. Sometimes there were alternate layers of water and ice-skin, so that when one broke through he kept on breaking through for a while, sometimes wetting himself to the waist.

That was why he had shied in such panic. He had felt the give under his feet and heard the crackle of a snow-hidden ice-skin. And to get his feet wet in such a temperature meant trouble and danger. At the very least it meant delay, for he would be forced to stop and build a fire, and under its protection to bare his feet while he dried his socks and moccasins. He stood and studied the creek-bed and its banks, and decided that the flow of water came from the right. He reflected awhile, rubbing his nose and cheeks, then skirted to the left, stepping gingerly and testing the footing for each step. Once clear of the danger, he took a fresh chew of tobacco and swung along at his four-mile gait.

In the course of the next two hours he came upon several similar traps. Usually the snow above the hidden pools had a sunken, candied appearance that advertised the danger. Once again, however, he had a close call; and once, suspecting danger, he compelled the dog to go on in front. The dog did not want to go. It hung back until the man shoved it forward, and then it went quickly across the white, unbroken surface. Suddenly it broke through, floundered to one side, and got away to firmer footing. It had wet its forefeet and legs, and almost immediately the water that clung to it turned to ice. It made quick efforts to lick the ice off its legs, then dropped down in the snow and began to bite out the ice that had formed between the toes. This was a matter of instinct. To permit the ice to remain would mean sore feet. It did not know this. It merely obeyed the mysterious prompting that arose from the deep crypts of its being. But the man knew, having achieved a judgment on the subject, and he removed the mitten from his right hand and helped tear out the ice-particles. He did not expose his fingers more than a minute, and was astonished at the swift numbness that smote them. It certainly was cold. He pulled on the mitten hastily, and beat the hand savagely across his chest.

At twelve o'clock the day was at its brightest. Yet the sun was too far south on its winter journey to clear the horizon. The bulge of the earth intervened between it and Henderson Creek, where the man walked under a clear sky at noon and cast no shadow. At half-past twelve, to the minute, he arrived at the forks of the creek. He was pleased at the speed he had made. If he kept it up, he would certainly be with the boys by six. He unbuttoned his jacket and shirt and drew forth his lunch. The action consumed no more than a quarter of a minute, yet in that brief moment the numbness laid hold of the exposed fingers. He did not put the mitten on, but, instead, struck the fingers a dozen sharp smashes against his leg. Then he sat down on a snow-covered log to eat. The sting that followed upon the striking of his fingers against his leg ceased so quickly that he was startled, he had had no chance to take a bite of biscuit. He struck the fingers repeatedly and returned them to the mitten, baring the other hand for the purpose of eating. He tried to take a mouthful, but the ice-muzzle prevented. He had forgotten to build a fire and thaw out. He chuckled at his foolishness, and as he chuckled he noted the numbness creeping into the exposed fingers. Also, he noted that the stinging which had first come to his toes when he sat down was already passing away. He wondered whether the toes were warm or numbed. He moved them inside the moccasins and decided that they were numbed.

He pulled the mitten on hurriedly and stood up. He was a bit frightened. He stamped up and down until the stinging returned into the feet. It certainly was cold, was his thought. That man from Sulphur Creek had spoken the truth when telling how cold it sometimes got in the country. And he had laughed at him at the time! That showed one must not be too sure of things. There was no mistake about it, it was cold. He strode up and down, stamping his feet and threshing his arms, until reassured by the returning warmth. Then he got out matches and proceeded to make a fire. From the undergrowth, where high water of the previous spring had lodged a supply of seasoned twigs, he got his firewood. Working carefully from a small beginning, he soon had a roaring fire, over which he thawed the ice from his face and in the protection of which he ate his biscuits. For the moment the cold of space was outwitted. The dog took satisfaction in the fire, stretching out close enough for warmth and far enough away to escape being singed.

When the man had finished, he filled his pipe and took his comfortable time over a smoke. Then he pulled on his mittens, settled the ear-flaps of his cap firmly about his ears, and took the creek trail up the left fork. The dog was disappointed and yearned back toward the fire. This man did not know cold. Possibly all the generations of his ancestry had been ignorant of cold, of real cold, of cold one hundred and seven degrees below freezing-point. But the dog knew; all its ancestry knew, and it had inherited the knowledge. And it knew that it was not good to walk abroad in such fearful cold. It was the time to lie snug in a hole in the snow and wait for a curtain of cloud to be drawn across the face of outer space whence this cold came. On the other hand, there was keen intimacy between the dog and the man. The one was the toil-slave of the other, and the only caresses it had ever received were the caresses of the whip-lash and of harsh and menacing throat-sounds that threatened the whip-lash. So the dog made no effort to communicate its apprehension to the man. It was not concerned in the welfare of the man; it was for its own sake that it yearned back toward the fire. But the man whistled, and spoke to it with the sound of whip-lashes, and the dog swung in at the man's heels and followed after.

The man took a chew of tobacco and proceeded to start a new amber beard. Also, his moist breath quickly powdered with white his moustache, eyebrows, and lashes. There did not seem to be so many springs on the left fork of the Henderson, and for half an hour the man saw no signs of any. And then it happened. At a place where there were no signs, where the soft, unbroken snow seemed to advertise solidity beneath, the man broke through. It was not deep. He wetted himself half-way to the knees before he floundered out to the firm crust.

He was angry, and cursed his luck aloud. He had hoped to get into camp with the boys at six o'clock, and this would delay him an hour, for he would have to build a fire and dry out his foot-gear. This was imperative at that low temperature—he knew that much; and he turned aside to the bank, which he climbed. On top, tangled in the underbrush about the trunks of several small spruce trees, was a high-water deposit of dry firewood—sticks and twigs principally, but also larger portions of seasoned branches and fine, dry, last-year's grasses. He threw down several large pieces on top of the snow. This served for a foundation and prevented the young flame from drowning itself in the snow it otherwise would melt. The flame he got by touching a match to a small shred of birch-bark that he took from his pocket. This burned even more readily than paper. Placing it on the foundation, he fed the young flame with wisps of dry grass and with the tiniest dry twigs.

He worked slowly and carefully, keenly aware of his danger. Gradually, as the flame grew stronger, he increased the size of the twigs with which he fed it. He squatted in the snow, pulling the twigs out from their entanglement in the brush and feeding directly to the flame. He knew there must be no failure. When it is seventy-five below zero, a man must not fail in his first attempt to build a fire—that is, if his feet are wet. If his feet are dry, and he fails, he can run along the trail for half a mile and restore his circulation. But the circulation of wet and freezing feet cannot be restored by running when it is seventy-five below. No matter how fast he runs, the wet feet will freeze the harder.

All this the man knew. The old-timer on Sulphur Creek had told him about it the previous fall, and now he was appreciating the advice. Already all sensation had gone out of his feet. To build the fire he had been forced to remove his mittens, and the fingers had quickly gone numb. His pace of four miles an hour had kept his heart pumping blood to the surface of his body and to all the extremities. But the instant he stopped, the action of the pump eased down. The cold of space smote the unprotected tip of the planet, and he, being on that unprotected tip, received the full force of the blow. The blood of his body recoiled before it. The blood was alive, like the dog, and like the dog it wanted to hide away and cover itself up from the fearful cold. So long as he walked four miles an hour, he pumped that blood, willy-nilly, to the surface; but now it ebbed away and sank down into the recesses of his body. The extremities were the first to feel its absence. His wet feet froze the faster, and his exposed fingers numbed the faster, though they had not yet begun to freeze. Nose and cheeks were already freezing, while the skin of all his body chilled as it lost its blood.

But he was safe. Toes and nose and cheeks would be only touched by the frost, for the fire was beginning to burn with strength. He was feeding it with twigs the size of his finger. In another minute he would be able to feed it with branches the size of his wrist, and then he could remove his wet foot-gear, and, while it dried, he could keep his naked feet warm by the fire, rubbing them at first, of course, with snow. The fire was a success. He was safe. He remembered the advice of the old-timer on Sulphur Creek, and smiled. The old-timer had been very serious in laying down the law that no man must travel alone in the Klondike after fifty below. Well, here he was; he had had the accident; he was alone; and he had saved himself. Those old-timers were rather womanish, some of them, he thought. All a man had to do was to keep his head, and he was all right. Any man who was a man could travel alone. But it was surprising, the rapidity with which his cheeks and nose were freezing. And he had not thought his fingers could go lifeless in so short a time. Lifeless they were, for he could scarcely make them move together to grip a twig, and they seemed remote from his body and from him. When he touched a twig, he had to look and see whether or not he had hold of it. The wires were pretty well down between him and his finger-ends.

All of which counted for little. There was the fire, snapping and crackling and promising life with every dancing flame. He started to untie his moccasins. They were coated with ice; the thick German socks were like sheaths of iron half-way to the knees; and the mocassin strings were like rods of steel all twisted and knotted as by some conflagration. For a moment he tugged with his numbed fingers, then, realizing the folly of it, he drew his sheath-knife.

But before he could cut the strings, it happened. It was his own fault or, rather, his mistake. He should not have built the fire under the spruce tree. He should have built it in the open. But it had been easier to pull the twigs from the brush and drop them directly on the fire. Now the tree under which he had done this carried a weight of snow on its boughs. No wind had blown for weeks, and each bough was fully freighted. Each time he had pulled a twig he had communicated a slight agitation to the tree—an imperceptible agitation, so far as he was concerned, but an agitation sufficient to bring about the disaster. High up in the tree one bough capsized its load of snow. This fell on the boughs beneath, capsizing them. This process continued, spreading out and involving the whole tree. It grew like an avalanche, and it descended without warning upon the man and the fire, and the fire was blotted out! Where it had burned was a mantle of fresh and disordered snow.

The man was shocked. It was as though he had just heard his own sentence of death. For a moment he sat and stared at the spot where the fire had been. Then he grew very calm. Perhaps the old-timer on Sulphur Creek was right. If he had only had a trail-mate he would have been in no danger now. The trail-mate could have built the fire. Well, it was up to him to build the fire over again, and this second time there must be no failure. Even if he succeeded, he would most likely lose some toes. His feet must be badly frozen by now, and there would be some time before the second fire was ready.

Such were his thoughts, but he did not sit and think them. He was busy all the time they were passing through his mind, he made a new foundation for a fire, this time in the open; where no treacherous tree could blot it out. Next, he gathered dry grasses and tiny twigs from the high-water flotsam. He could not bring his fingers together to pull them out, but he was able to gather them by the handful. In this way he got many rotten twigs and bits of green moss that were undesirable, but it was the best he could do. He worked methodically, even collecting an armful of the larger branches to be used later when the fire gathered strength. And all the while the dog sat and watched him, a certain yearning wistfulness in its eyes, for it looked upon him as the fire-provider, and the fire was slow in coming.

When all was ready, the man reached in his pocket for a second piece of birch-bark. He knew the bark was there, and, though he could not feel it with his fingers, he could hear its crisp rustling as he fumbled for it. Try as he would, he could not clutch hold of it. And all the time, in his consciousness, was the knowledge that each instant his feet were freezing. This thought tended to put him in a panic, but he fought against it and kept calm. He pulled on his mittens with his teeth, and threshed his arms back and forth, beating his hands with all his might against his sides. He did this sitting down, and he stood up to do it; and all the while the dog sat in the snow, its wolf-brush of a tail curled around warmly over its forefeet, its sharp wolf-ears pricked forward intently as it watched the man. And the man as he beat and threshed with his arms and hands, felt a great surge of envy as he regarded the creature that was warm and secure in its natural covering.

After a time he was aware of the first far-away signals of sensation in his beaten fingers. The faint tingling grew stronger till it evolved into a stinging ache that was excruciating, but which the man hailed with satisfaction. He stripped the mitten from his right hand and fetched forth the birch-bark. The exposed fingers were quickly going numb again. Next he brought out his bunch of sulphur matches. But the tremendous cold had already driven the life out of his fingers. In his effort to separate one match from the others, the whole bunch fell in the snow. He tried to pick it out of the snow, but failed. The dead fingers could neither touch nor clutch. He was very careful. He drove the thought of his freezing feet; and nose, and cheeks, out of his mind, devoting his whole soul to the matches. He watched, using the sense of vision in place of that of touch, and when he saw his fingers on each side the bunch, he closed them—that is, he willed to close them, for the wires were drawn, and the fingers did not obey. He pulled the mitten on the right hand, and beat it fiercely against his knee. Then, with both mittened hands, he scooped the bunch of matches, along with much snow, into his lap. Yet he was no better off.

After some manipulation he managed to get the bunch between the heels of his mittened hands. In this fashion he carried it to his mouth. The ice crackled and snapped when by a violent effort he opened his mouth. He drew the lower jaw in, curled the upper lip out of the way, and scraped the bunch with his upper teeth in order to separate a match. He succeeded in getting one, which he dropped on his lap. He was no better off. He could not pick it up. Then he devised a way. He picked it up in his teeth and scratched it on his leg. Twenty times he scratched before he succeeded in lighting it. As it flamed he held it with his teeth to the birch-bark. But the burning brimstone went up his nostrils and into his lungs, causing him to cough spasmodically. The match fell into the snow and went out.

The old-timer on Sulphur Creek was right, he thought in the moment of controlled despair that ensued: after fifty below, a man should travel with a partner. He beat his hands, but failed in exciting any sensation. Suddenly he bared both hands, removing the mittens with his teeth. He caught the whole bunch between the heels of his hands. His arm-muscles not being frozen enabled him to press the hand-heels tightly against the matches. Then he scratched the bunch along his leg. It flared into flame, seventy sulphur matches at once! There was no wind to blow them out. He kept his head to one side to escape the strangling fumes, and held the blazing bunch to the birch-bark. As he so held it, he became aware of sensation in his hand. His flesh was burning. He could smell it. Deep down below the surface he could feel it. The sensation developed into pain that grew acute. And still he endured it, holding the flame of the matches clumsily to the bark that would not light readily because his own burning hands were in the way, absorbing most of the flame.

At last, when he could endure no more, he jerked his hands apart. The blazing matches fell sizzling into the snow, but the birch-bark was alight. He began laying dry grasses and the tiniest twigs on the flame. He could not pick and choose, for he had to lift the fuel between the heels of his hands. Small pieces of rotten wood and green moss clung to the twigs, and he bit them off as well as he could with his teeth. He cherished the flame carefully and awkwardly. It meant life, and it must not perish. The withdrawal of blood from the surface of his body now made him begin to shiver, and he grew more awkward. A large piece of green moss fell squarely on the little fire. He tried to poke it out with his fingers, but his shivering frame made him poke too far, and he disrupted the nucleus of the little fire, the burning grasses and tiny twigs separating and scattering. He tried to poke them together again, but in spite of the tenseness of the effort, his shivering got away with him, and the twigs were hopelessly scattered. Each twig gushed a puff of smoke and went out. The fire-provider had failed. As he looked apathetically about him, his eyes chanced on the dog, sitting across the ruins of the fire from him, in the snow, making restless, hunching movements, slightly lifting one forefoot and then the other, shifting its weight back and forth on them with wistful eagerness.

184

The sight of the dog put a wild idea into his head. He remembered the tale of the man, caught in a blizzard, who killed a steer and crawled inside the carcass, and so was saved. He would kill the dog and bury his hands in the warm body until the numbness went out of them. Then he could build another fire. He spoke to the dog, calling it to him; but in his voice was a strange note of fear that frightened the animal, who had never known the man to speak in such way before. Something was the matter, and its suspicious nature sensed danger,—it knew not what danger but somewhere, somehow, in its brain arose an apprehension of the man. It flattened its ears down at the sound of the man's voice, and its restless, hunching movements and the liftings and shiftings of its forefeet became more pronounced but it would not come to the man. He got on his hands and knees and crawled toward the dog. This unusual posture again excited suspicion, and the animal sidled mincingly away.

The man sat up in the snow for a moment and struggled for calmness. Then he pulled on his mittens, by means of his teeth, and got upon his feet. He glanced down at first in order to assure himself that he was really standing up, for the absence of sensation in his feet left him unrelated to the earth. His erect position in itself started to drive the webs of suspicion from the dog's mind; and when he spoke peremptorily, with the sound of whip-lashes in his voice, the dog rendered its customary allegiance and came to him. As it came within reaching distance, the man lost his control. His arms flashed out to the dog, and he experienced genuine surprise when he discovered that his hands could not clutch, that there was neither bend nor feeling in the lingers. He had forgotten for the moment that they were frozen and that they were freezing more and more. All this happened quickly, and before the animal could get away, he encircled its body with his arms. He sat down in the snow, and in this fashion held the dog, while it snarled and whined and struggled.

But it was all he could do, hold its body encircled in his arms and sit there. He realized that he could not kill the dog. There was no way to do it. With his helpless hands he could neither draw nor hold his sheath-knife nor throttle the animal. He released it, and it plunged wildly away, with tail between its legs, and still snarling. It halted forty feet away and surveyed him

185

curiously, with ears sharply pricked forward. The man looked down at his hands in order to locate them, and found them hanging on the ends of his arms. It struck him as curious that one should have to use his eyes in order to find out where his hands were. He began threshing his arms back and forth, beating the mittened hands against his sides. He did this for five minutes, violently, and his heart pumped enough blood up to the surface to put a stop to his shivering. But no sensation was aroused in the hands. He had an impression that they hung like weights on the ends of his arms, but when he tried to run the impression down, he could not find it.

A certain fear of death, dull and oppressive, came to him. This fear quickly became poignant as he realized that it was no longer a mere matter of freezing his fingers and toes, or of losing his hands and feet, but that it was a matter of life and death with the chances against him. This threw him into a panic, and he turned and ran up the creek-bed along the old, dim trail. The dog joined in behind and kept up with him. He ran blindly, without intention, in fear such as he had never known in his life. Slowly, as he ploughed and floundered through the snow, he began to see things again— the banks of the creek, the old timber-jams, the leafless aspens, and the sky. The running made him feel better. He did not shiver. Maybe, if he ran on, his feet would thaw out; and, anyway, if he ran far enough, he would reach camp and the boys. Without doubt he would lose some fingers and toes and some of his face; but the boys would take care of him, and save the rest of him when he got there. And at the same time there was another thought in his mind that said he would never get to the camp and the boys; that it was too many miles away, that the freezing had too great a start on him, and that he would soon be stiff and dead. This thought he kept in the background and refused to consider. Sometimes it pushed itself forward and demanded to be heard, but he thrust it back and strove to think of other things.

It struck him as curious that he could run at all on feet so frozen that he could not feel them when they struck the earth and took the weight of his body. He seemed to himself to skim along above the surface and to have no connection with the earth. Somewhere he had once seen a winged Mercury, and he wondered if Mercury felt as he felt when skimming over the earth.

186

His theory of running until he reached camp and the boys had one flaw in it: he lacked the endurance. Several times he stumbled, and finally he tottered, crumpled up, and fell. When he tried to rise, he failed. He must sit and rest, he decided, and next time he would merely walk and keep on going. As he sat and regained his breath, he noted that he was feeling quite warm and comfortable. He was not shivering, and it even seemed that a warm glow had come to his chest and trunk. And yet, when he touched his nose or cheeks, there was no sensation. Running would not thaw them out. Nor would it thaw out his hands and feet. Then the thought came to him that the frozen portions of his body must be extending. He tried to keep this thought down, to forget it, to think of something else; he was aware of the panicky feeling that it caused, and he was afraid of the panic. But the thought asserted itself, and persisted, until it produced a vision of his body totally frozen. This was too much, and he made another wild run along the trail. Once he slowed down to a walk, but the thought of the freezing extending itself made him run again.

And all the time the dog ran with him, at his heels. When he fell down a second time, it curled its tail over its forefeet and sat in front of him facing him curiously eager and intent. The warmth and security of the animal angered him, and he cursed it till it flattened down its ears appeasingly. This time the shivering came more quickly upon the man. He was losing in his battle with the frost. It was creeping into his body from all sides. The thought of it drove him on, but he ran no more than a hundred feet, when he staggered and pitched headlong. It was his last panic. When he had recovered his breath and control, he sat up and entertained in his mind the conception of meeting death with dignity. However, the conception did not come to him in such terms. His idea of it was that he had been making a fool of himself, running around like a chicken with its head cut off—such was the simile that occurred to him. Well, he was bound to freeze anyway, and he might as well take it decently. With this new-found peace of mind came the first glimmerings of drowsiness. A good idea, he thought, to sleep off to death. It was like taking an anæsthetic. Freezing was not so bad as people thought. There were lots worse ways to die.

He pictured the boys finding his body next day. Suddenly he found himself with them, coming along the trail and looking for himself. And, still with them, he came around a turn in the trail and found himself lying in the snow. He did not belong with himself any more, for even then he was out of himself, standing with the boys and looking at himself in the snow. It certainly was cold, was his thought. When he got back to the States he could tell the folks what real cold was. He drifted on from this to a vision of the old-timer on Sulphur Creek. He could see him quite clearly, warm and comfortable, and smoking a pipe.

"You were right, old hoss; you were right," the man mumbled to the old-timer of Sulphur Creek.

Then the man drowsed off into what seemed to him the most comfortable and satisfying sleep he had ever known. The dog sat facing him and waiting. The brief day drew to a close in a long, slow twilight. There were no signs of a fire to be made, and, besides, never in the dog's experience had it known a man to sit like that in the snow and make no fire. As the twilight drew on, its eager yearning for the fire mastered it, and with a great lifting and shifting of forefeet, it whined softly, then flattened its ears down in anticipation of being chidden by the man. But the man remained silent. Later, the dog whined loudly. And still later it crept close to the man and caught the scent of death. This made the animal bristle and back away. A little longer it delayed, howling under the stars that leaped and danced and shone brightly in the cold sky. Then it turned and trotted up the trail in the direction of the camp it knew, where were the other food-providers and fire-providers.

THAT SPOT

I don't think much of Stephen Mackaye any more, though I used to swear by him. I know that in those days I loved him more than my own brother. If ever I meet Stephen Mackaye again, I shall not be responsible for my actions. It passes beyond me that a man with whom I shared food and blanket, and with whom I mushed over the Chilcoot Trail, should turn out the way he did. I always sized Steve up as a square man, a kindly comrade, without an iota of anything vindictive or malicious in his nature. I shall never trust my judgment in men again. Why, I nursed that man through typhoid fever; we starved together on the headwaters of the Stewart; and he saved my life on the Little Salmon. And now, after the years we were together, all I can say of Stephen Mackaye is that he is the meanest man I ever knew.

We started for the Klondike in the fall rush of 1897, and we started too late to get over Chilcoot Pass before the freeze-up. We packed our outfit on our backs part way over, when the snow began to fly, and then we had to buy dogs in order to sled it the rest of the way. That was how we came to get that Spot. Dogs were high, and we paid one hundred and ten dollars for him. He looked worth it. I say looked, because he was one of the finest-appearing dogs I ever saw. He weighed sixty pounds, and he had all the lines of a good sled animal. We never could make out his breed. He wasn't husky, nor Malemute, nor Hudson Bay; he looked like all of them and he didn't look like any of them; and on top of it all he had some of the white man's dog in him, for on one side, in the thick of the mixed yellow-brown-red-and-dirty-white that was his prevailing colour, there was a spot of coal-black as big as a water-bucket. That was why we called him Spot.

He was a good looker all right. When he was in condition his muscles stood out in bunches all over him. And he was the strongest-looking brute I ever saw in Alaska, also the most intelligent-looking. To run your eyes over him, you'd think he could outpull three dogs of his own weight. Maybe he could, but I never saw it. His intelligence didn't run that way. He could steal and forage to perfection; he had an instinct that was positively gruesome for divining when work was to be done and for making a sneak accordingly; and for getting lost and not staying lost he was nothing short of inspired. But when it came to work, the way that intelligence dribbled out of him and left him a mere clot of wobbling, stupid jelly would make your heart bleed.

There are times when I think it wasn't stupidity. Maybe, like some men I know, he was too wise to work. I shouldn't wonder if he put it all over us with that intelligence of his. Maybe he figured it all out and decided that a licking now and again and no work was a whole lot better than work all the time and no licking. He was intelligent enough for such a computation. I tell you, I've sat and looked into that dog's eyes till the shivers ran up and down my spine and the marrow crawled like yeast, what of the intelligence I saw shining out. I can't express myself about that intelligence. It is beyond mere words. I saw it, that's all. At times it was like gazing into a human soul, to look into his eyes; and what I saw there frightened me and started all sorts of ideas in my own mind of reincarnation and all the rest. I tell you I sensed something big in that brute's eyes; there was a message there, but I wasn't big enough myself to catch it. Whatever it was (I know I'm making a fool of myself)—whatever it was, it baffled me. I can't give an inkling of what I saw in that brute's eyes; it wasn't light, it wasn't colour; it was something that moved, away back, when the eyes themselves weren't moving. And I guess I didn't see it move either; I only sensed that it moved. It was an expression—that's what it was—and I got an impression of it. No; it was different from a mere expression; it was more than that. I don't know what it was, but it gave me a feeling of kinship just the same. Oh, no, not sentimental kinship. It was, rather, a kinship of equality. Those eyes never pleaded like a deer's eyes. They challenged. No, it wasn't defiance. It was just a calm assumption of equality. And I don't think it was deliberate. My belief is that it was unconscious on his part. It was there because it was there, and it couldn't help shining out. No, I don't mean shine. It didn't shine; it *moved*. I know I'm talking rot, but if you'd looked into that animal's eyes the way I have, you'd understand. Steve was affected the same way I was. Why, I tried to kill that Spot once—he was no good for anything; and I fell down on it. I led him out into the brush, and he came along slow and unwilling. He knew what was going on. I stopped in a likely place, put my foot on the rope, and pulled my big Colt's. And that dog sat down and looked at me. I tell you he didn't plead. He just looked. And I saw all kinds of incomprehensible things moving, yes, moving, in those eyes of his. I didn't really see them move; I thought I saw them, for, as I said before, I guess I only sensed them. And I want to tell you right now that it got beyond me. It was like killing a man, a conscious, brave man, who looked calmly into your gun as much as to say, "Who's afraid?"

Then, too, the message seemed so near that, instead of pulling the trigger quick, I stopped to see if I could catch the message. There it was, right before me, glimmering all around in those eyes of his. And then it was too late. I got scared. I was trembly all over, and my stomach generated a nervous palpitation that made me seasick. I just sat down and looked at the dog, and he looked at me, till I thought I was going crazy. Do you want to know what I did? I threw down the gun and ran back to camp with the fear of God in my heart. Steve laughed at me. But I notice that Steve led Spot into the woods, a week later, for the same purpose, and that Steve came back alone, and a little later Spot drifted back, too.

At any rate, Spot wouldn't work. We paid a hundred and ten dollars for him from the bottom of our sack, and he wouldn't work. He wouldn't even tighten the traces. Steve spoke to him the first time we put him in harness, and he sort of shivered, that was all. Not an ounce on the traces. He just stood still and wobbled, like so much jelly. Steve touched him with the whip. He yelped, but not an ounce. Steve touched him again, a bit harder, and he howled—the regular long wolf howl. Then Steve got mad and gave him half a dozen, and I came on the run from the tent.

I told Steve he was brutal with the animal, and we had some words—the first we'd ever had. He threw the whip down in the snow and walked away mad. I picked it up and went to it. That Spot trembled and wobbled and cowered before ever I swung the lash, and with the first bite of it he howled like a lost soul. Next he lay down in the snow. I started the rest of the dogs, and they dragged him along while I threw the whip into him. He rolled over on his back and bumped along, his four legs waving in the air, himself howling as though he was going through a sausage machine. Steve came back and laughed at me, and I apologized for what I'd said.

191

There was no getting any work out of that Spot; and to make up for it, he was the biggest pig-glutton of a dog I ever saw. On top of that, he was the cleverest thief. There was no circumventing him. Many a breakfast we went without our bacon because Spot had been there first. And it was because of him that we nearly starved to death up the Stewart. He figured out the way to break into our meat-cache, and what he didn't eat, the rest of the team did. But he was impartial. He stole from everybody. He was a restless dog, always very busy snooping around or going somewhere. And there was never a camp within five miles that he didn't raid. The worst of it was that they always came back on us to pay his board bill, which was just, being the law of the land; but it was mighty hard on us, especially that first winter on the Chilcoot, when we were busted, paying for whole hams and sides of bacon that we never ate. He could fight, too, that Spot. He could do everything but work. He never pulled a pound, but he was the boss of the whole team. The way he made those dogs stand around was an education. He bullied them, and there was always one or more of them fresh-marked with his fangs. But he was more than a bully. He wasn't afraid of anything that walked on four legs; and I've seen him march, single-handed, into a strange team, without any provocation whatever, and put the *kibosh* on the whole outfit. Did I say he could eat? I caught him eating the whip once. That's straight. He started in at the lash, and when I caught him he was down to the handle, and still going.

But he was a good looker. At the end of the first week we sold him for seventy-five dollars to the Mounted Police. They had experienced dog-drivers, and we knew that by the time he'd covered the six hundred miles to Dawson he'd be a good sled-dog. I say we *knew*, for we were just getting acquainted with that Spot. A little later we were not brash enough to know anything where he was concerned. A week later we woke up in the morning to the dangdest dog-fight we'd ever heard. It was that Spot come back and knocking the team into shape. We ate a pretty depressing breakfast, I can tell you; but cheered up two hours afterward when we sold him to an official courier, bound in to Dawson with government despatches. That Spot was only three days in coming back, and, as usual, celebrated his arrival with a rough house.

We spent the winter and spring, after our own outfit was across the pass, freighting other people's outfits; and we made a fat stake. Also, we made money out of Spot. If we sold him once, we sold him twenty times. He always came back, and no one asked for their money. We didn't want the money. We'd have paid handsomely for any one to take him off our hands for keeps'. We had to get rid of him, and we couldn't give him away, for that would have been suspicious. But he was such a fine looker that we never had any difficulty in selling him. "Unbroke," we'd say, and they'd pay any old price for him. We sold him as low as twenty-five dollars, and once we got a hundred and fifty for him. That particular party returned him in person, refused to take his money back, and the way he abused us was something awful. He said it was cheap at the price to tell us what he thought of us; and we felt he was so justified that we never talked back. But to this day I've never quite regained all the old self-respect that was mine before that man talked to me.

When the ice cleared out of the lakes and river, we put our outfit in a Lake Bennett boat and started for Dawson. We had a good team of dogs, and of course we piled them on top the outfit. That Spot was along—there was no losing him; and a dozen times, the first day, he knocked one or another of the dogs overboard in the course of fighting with them. It was close quarters, and he didn't like being crowded.

"What that dog needs is space," Steve said the second day. "Let's maroon him."

We did, running the boat in at Caribou Crossing for him to jump ashore. Two of the other dogs, good dogs, followed him; and we lost two whole days trying to find them. We never saw those two dogs again; but the quietness and relief we enjoyed made us decide, like the man who refused his hundred and fifty, that it was cheap at the price. For the first time in months Steve and I laughed and whistled and sang. We were as happy as clams. The dark days were over. The nightmare had been lifted. That Spot was gone.

Three weeks later, one morning, Steve and I were standing on the river-bank at Dawson. A small boat was just arriving from Lake Bennett. I saw

Steve give a start, and heard him say something that was not nice and that was not under his breath. Then I looked; and there, in the bow of the boat, with ears pricked up, sat Spot. Steve and I sneaked immediately, like beaten curs, like cowards, like absconders from justice. It was this last that the lieutenant of police thought when he saw us sneaking. He surmised that there were law-officers in the boat who were after us. He didn't wait to find out, but kept us in sight, and in the M. & M. saloon got us in a corner. We had a merry time explaining, for we refused to go back to the boat and meet Spot; and finally he held us under guard of another policeman while he went to the boat. After we got clear of him, we started for the cabin, and when we arrived, there was that Spot sitting on the stoop waiting for us. Now how did he know we lived there? There were forty thousand people in Dawson that summer, and how did he *savve* our cabin out of all the cabins? How did he know we were in Dawson, anyway? I leave it to you. But don't forget what I said about his intelligence and that immortal something I have seen glimmering in his eyes.

There was no getting rid of him any more. There were too many people in Dawson who had bought him up on Chilcoot, and the story got around. Half a dozen times we put him on board steamboats going down the Yukon; but he merely went ashore at the first landing and trotted back up the bank. We couldn't sell him, we couldn't kill him (both Steve and I had tried), and nobody else was able to kill him. He bore a charmed life. I've seen him go down in a dogfight on the main street with fifty dogs on top of him, and when they were separated, he'd appear on all his four legs, unharmed, while two of the dogs that had been on top of him would be lying dead.

I saw him steal a chunk of moose-meat from Major Dinwiddie's cache so heavy that he could just keep one jump ahead of Mrs. Dinwiddie's squaw cook, who was after him with an axe. As he went up the hill, after the squaw gave up, Major Dinwiddie himself came out and pumped his Winchester into the landscape. He emptied his magazine twice, and never touched that Spot. Then a policeman came along and arrested him for discharging firearms inside the city limits. Major Dinwiddie paid his fine, and Steve and I paid him for the moose-meat at the rate of a dollar a pound, bones and all. That was what he paid for it. Meat was high that year.

I am only telling what I saw with my own eyes. And now I'll tell you something also. I saw that Spot fall through a water-hole. The ice was three and a half feet thick, and the current sucked him under like a straw. Three hundred yards below was the big water-hole used by the hospital. Spot crawled out of the hospital water-hole, licked off the water, bit out the ice that had formed between his toes, trotted up the bank, and whipped a big Newfoundland belonging to the Gold Commissioner.

In the fall of 1898, Steve and I poled up the Yukon on the last water, bound for Stewart River. We took the dogs along, all except Spot. We figured we'd been feeding him long enough. He'd cost us more time and trouble and money and grub than we'd got by selling him on the Chilcoot—especially grub. So Steve and I tied him down in the cabin and pulled our freight. We camped that night at the mouth of Indian River, and Steve and I were pretty facetious over having shaken him. Steve was a funny cuss, and I was just sitting up in the blankets and laughing when a tornado hit camp. The way that Spot walked into those dogs and gave them what-for was hair-raising. Now how did he get loose? It's up to you. I haven't any theory. And how did he get across the Klondike River? That's another facer. And anyway, how did he know we had gone up the Yukon? You see, we went by water, and he couldn't smell our tracks. Steve and I began to get superstitious about that dog. He got on our nerves, too; and, between you and me, we were just a mite afraid of him.

The freeze-up came on when we were at the mouth of Henderson Creek, and we traded him off for two sacks of flour to an outfit that was bound up White River after copper. Now that whole outfit was lost. Never trace nor hide nor hair of men, dogs, sleds, or anything was ever found. They dropped clean out of sight. It became one of the mysteries of the country. Steve and I plugged away up the Stewart, and six weeks afterward that Spot crawled into camp. He was a perambulating skeleton, and could just drag along; but he got there. And what I want to know is, who told him we were up the Stewart? We could have gone to a thousand other places. How did he know? You tell me, and I'll tell you.

No losing him. At the Mayo he started a row with an Indian dog. The buck who owned the dog took a swing at Spot with an axe, missed him, and killed his own dog. Talk about magic and turning bullets aside—I, for one, consider it a blamed sight harder to turn an axe aside with a big buck at the other end of it. And I saw him do it with my own eyes. That buck didn't want to kill his own dog. You've got to show me.

I told you about Spot breaking into our meat cache. It was nearly the death of us. There wasn't any more meat to be killed, and meat was all we had to live on. The moose had gone back several hundred miles and the Indians with them. There we were. Spring was on, and we had to wait for the river to break. We got pretty thin before we decided to eat the dogs, and we decided to eat Spot first. Do you know what that dog did? He sneaked. Now how did he know our minds were made up to eat him? We sat up nights laying for him, but he never came back, and we ate the other dogs. We ate the whole team.

And now for the sequel. You know what it is when a big river breaks up and a few billion tons of ice go out, jamming and milling and grinding. Just in the thick of it, when the Stewart went out, rumbling and roaring, we sighted Spot out in the middle. He'd got caught as he was trying to cross up above somewhere. Steve and I yelled and shouted and ran up and down the bank, tossing our hats in the air. Sometimes we'd stop and hug each other, we were that boisterous, for we saw Spot's finish. He didn't have a chance in a million. He didn't have any chance at all. After the ice-run, we got into a canoe and paddled down to the Yukon, and down the Yukon to Dawson, stopping to feed up for a week at the cabins at the mouth of Henderson Creek. And as we came in to the bank at Dawson, there sat that Spot, waiting for us, his ears pricked up, his tail wagging, his mouth smiling, extending a hearty welcome to us. Now how did he get out of that ice? How did he know we were coming to Dawson, to the very hour and minute, to be out there on the bank waiting for us?

The more I think of that Spot, the more I am convinced that there are things in this world that go beyond science. On no scientific grounds can that Spot be explained. It's psychic phenomena, or mysticism, or something of

196

that sort, I guess, with a lot of Theosophy thrown in. The Klondike is a good country. I might have been there yet, and become a millionaire, if it hadn't been for Spot. He got on my nerves. I stood him for two years altogether, and then I guess my stamina broke. It was the summer of 1899 when I pulled out. I didn't say anything to Steve. I just sneaked. But I fixed it up all right. I wrote Steve a note, and enclosed a package of "rough-on-rats," telling him what to do with it. I was worn down to skin and bone by that Spot, and I was that nervous that I'd jump and look around when there wasn't anybody within hailing distance. But it was astonishing the way I recuperated when I got quit of him. I got back twenty pounds before I arrived in San Francisco, and by the time I'd crossed the ferry to Oakland I was my old self again, so that even my wife looked in vain for any change in me.

Steve wrote to me once, and his letter seemed irritated. He took it kind of hard because I'd left him with Spot. Also, he said he'd used the "rough-on-rats," per directions, and that there was nothing doing. A year went by. I was back in the office and prospering in all ways—even getting a bit fat. And then Steve arrived. He didn't look me up. I read his name in the steamer list, and wondered why. But I didn't wonder long. I got up one morning and found that Spot chained to the gate-post and holding up the milkman. Steve went north to Seattle, I learned, that very morning. I didn't put on any more weight. My wife made me buy him a collar and tag, and within an hour he showed his gratitude by killing her pet Persian cat. There is no getting rid of that Spot. He will be with me until I die, for he'll never die. My appetite is not so good since he arrived, and my wife says I am looking peaked. Last night that Spot got into Mr. Harvey's hen-house (Harvey is my next-door neighbour) and killed nineteen of his fancy-bred chickens. I shall have to pay for them. My neighbours on the other side quarrelled with my wife and then moved out. Spot was the cause of it. And that is why I am disappointed in Stephen Mackaye. I had no idea he was so mean a man.

FLUSH OF GOLD

Lon McFane was a bit grumpy, what of losing his tobacco pouch, or else he might have told me, before we got to it, something about the cabin at Surprise Lake. All day, turn and turn about, we had spelled each other at going to the fore and breaking trail for the dogs. It was heavy snowshoe work, and did not tend to make a man voluble, yet Lon McFane might have found breath enough at noon, when we stopped to boil coffee, with which to tell me. But he didn't. Surprise Lake?—it was Surprise Cabin to me. I had never heard of it before. I confess I was a bit tired. I had been looking for Lon to stop and make camp any time for an hour; but I had too much pride to suggest making camp or to ask him his intentions; and yet he was my man, lured at a handsome wage to mush my dogs for me and to obey my commands. I guess I was a bit grumpy myself. He said nothing, and I was resolved to ask nothing, even if we tramped on all night.

We came upon the cabin abruptly. For a week of trail we had met no one, and, in my mind, there had been little likelihood of meeting any one for a week to come. And yet there it was, right before my eyes, a cabin, with a dim light in the window and smoke curling up from the chimney.

"Why didn't you tell me—" I began, but was interrupted by Lon, who muttered—

"Surprise Lake—it lies up a small feeder half a mile on. It's only a pond."

"Yes, but the cabin—who lives in it?"

"A woman," was the answer, and the next moment Lon had rapped on the door, and a woman's voice bade him enter.

"Have you seen Dave recently?" she asked.

"Nope," Lon answered carelessly. "I've been in the other direction, down Circle City way. Dave's up Dawson way, ain't he?"

The woman nodded, and Lon fell to unharnessing the dogs, while I unlashed the sled and carried the camp outfit into the cabin. The cabin was a large, one-room affair, and the woman was evidently alone in it. She pointed to the stove, where water was already boiling, and Lon set about the preparation of supper, while I opened the fish-bag and fed the dogs. I looked for Lon to introduce us, and was vexed that he did not, for they were evidently old friends.

"You are Lon McFane, aren't you?" I heard her ask him. "Why, I remember you now. The last time I saw you it was on a steamboat, wasn't it? I remember . . . "

Her speech seemed suddenly to be frozen by the spectacle of dread which, I knew, from the tenor I saw mounting in her eyes, must be on her inner vision. To my astonishment, Lon was affected by her words and manner. His face showed desperate, for all his voice sounded hearty and genial, as he said—

"The last time we met was at Dawson, Queen's Jubilee, or Birthday, or something—don't you remember?—the canoe races in the river, and the obstacle races down the main street?"

The terror faded out of her eyes and her whole body relaxed. "Oh, yes, I do remember," she said. "And you won one of the canoe races."

"How's Dave been makin' it lately? Strikin' it as rich as ever, I suppose?" Lon asked, with apparent irrelevance.

She smiled and nodded, and then, noticing that I had unlashed the bed roll, she indicated the end of the cabin where I might spread it. Her own bunk, I noticed, was made up at the opposite end.

"I thought it was Dave coming when I heard your dogs," she said.

After that she said nothing, contenting herself with watching Lon's cooking operations, and listening the while as for the sound of dogs along the trail. I lay back on the blankets and smoked and watched. Here was mystery; I could make that much out, but no more could I make out. Why in the deuce hadn't Lon given me the tip before we arrived? I looked at her face, unnoticed by her, and the longer I looked the harder it was to take my eyes away. It was a wonderfully beautiful face, unearthly, I may say, with a light in it or an expression or something "that was never on land or sea." Fear and terror had completely vanished, and it was a placidly beautiful face—if by "placid" one can characterize that intangible and occult something that I cannot say was a radiance or a light any more than I can say it was an expression.

Abruptly, as if for the first time, she became aware of my presence.

"Have you seen Dave recently?" she asked me. It was on the tip of my tongue to say "Dave who?" when Lon coughed in the smoke that arose from the sizzling bacon. The bacon might have caused that cough, but I took it as a hint and left my question unasked. "No, I haven't," I answered. "I'm new in this part of the country—"

"But you don't mean to say," she interrupted, "that you've never heard of Dave—of Big Dave Walsh?"

"You see," I apologised, "I'm new in the country. I've put in most of my time in the Lower Country, down Nome way."

"Tell him about Dave," she said to Lon.

Lon seemed put out, but he began in that hearty, genial manner that I had noticed before. It seemed a shade too hearty and genial, and it irritated me.

"Oh, Dave is a fine man," he said. "He's a man, every inch of him, and he stands six feet four in his socks. His word is as good as his bond. The man lies who ever says Dave told a lie, and that man will have to fight with me, too, as well—if there's anything left of him when Dave gets done with him. For Dave is a fighter. Oh, yes, he's a scrapper from way back. He got a grizzly with a '38 popgun. He got clawed some, but he knew what he was doin'. He went into the cave on purpose to get that grizzly. 'Fraid of nothing. Free an' easy with his money, or his last shirt an' match when out of money. Why, he drained Surprise Lake here in three weeks an' took out ninety thousand,

200

didn't he?" She flushed and nodded her head proudly. Through his recital she had followed every word with keenest interest. "An' I must say," Lon went on, "that I was disappointed sore on not meeting Dave here to-night."

Lon served supper at one end of the table of whip-sawed spruce, and we fell to eating. A howling of the dogs took the woman to the door. She opened it an inch and listened.

"Where is Dave Walsh?" I asked, in an undertone.

"Dead," Lon answered. "In hell, maybe. I don't know. Shut up."

"But you just said that you expected to meet him here to-night," I challenged.

"Oh, shut up, can't you," was Lon's reply, in the same cautious undertone.

The woman had closed the door and was returning, and I sat and meditated upon the fact that this man who told me to shut up received from me a salary of two hundred and fifty dollars a month and his board.

Lon washed the dishes, while I smoked and watched the woman. She seemed more beautiful than ever—strangely and weirdly beautiful, it is true. After looking at her steadfastly for five minutes, I was compelled to come back to the real world and to glance at Lon McFane. This enabled me to know, without discussion, that the woman, too, was real. At first I had taken her for the wife of Dave Walsh; but if Dave Walsh were dead, as Lon had said, then she could be only his widow.

It was early to bed, for we faced a long day on the morrow; and as Lon crawled in beside me under the blankets, I ventured a question.

"That woman's crazy, isn't she?"

"Crazy as a loon," he answered.

And before I could formulate my next question, Lon McFane, I swear, was off to sleep. He always went to sleep that way—just crawled into the blankets, closed his eyes, and was off, a demure little heavy breathing rising on the air. Lon never snored.

And in the morning it was quick breakfast, feed the dogs, load the sled, and hit the trail. We said good-bye as we pulled out, and the woman stood in the doorway and watched us off. I carried the vision of her unearthly beauty away with me, just under my eyelids, and all I had to do, any time, was to close them and see her again. The way was unbroken, Surprise Lake being far off the travelled trails, and Lon and I took turn about at beating down the feathery snow with our big, webbed shoes so that the dogs could travel. "But you said you expected to meet Dave Walsh at the cabin," trembled on the tip of my tongue a score of times. I did not utter it. I could wait until we knocked off in the middle of the day. And when the middle of the day came, we went right on, for, as Lon explained, there was a camp of moose hunters at the forks of the Teelee, and we could make there by dark. But we didn't make there by dark, for Bright, the lead-dog, broke his shoulder-blade, and we lost an hour over him before we shot him. Then, crossing a timber jam on the frozen bed of the Teelee, the sled suffered a wrenching capsize, and it was a case of make camp and repair the runner. I cooked supper and fed the dogs while Lon made the repairs, and together we got in the night's supply of ice and firewood. Then we sat on our blankets, our moccasins steaming on upended sticks before the fire, and had our evening smoke.

"You didn't know her?" Lon queried suddenly. I shook my head.

"You noticed the colour of her hair and eyes and her complexion, well, that's where she got her name—she was like the first warm glow of a golden sunrise. She was called Flush of Gold. Ever heard of her?"

Somewhere I had a confused and misty remembrance of having heard the name, yet it meant nothing to me. "Flush of Gold," I repeated; "sounds like the name of a dance-house girl." Lon shook his head. "No, she was a good woman, at least in that sense, though she sinned greatly just the same."

"But why do you speak always of her in the past tense, as though she were dead?"

"Because of the darkness on her soul that is the same as the darkness of death. The Flush of Gold that I knew, that Dawson knew, and that Forty Mile knew before that, is dead. That dumb, lunatic creature we saw last night was not Flush of Gold."

202

"And Dave?" I queried.

"He built that cabin," Lon answered, "He built it for her . . . and for himself. He is dead. She is waiting for him there. She half believes he is not dead. But who can know the whim of a crazed mind? Maybe she wholly believes he is not dead. At any rate, she waits for him there in the cabin he built. Who would rouse the dead? Then who would rouse the living that are dead? Not I, and that is why I let on to expect to meet Dave Walsh there last night. I'll bet a stack that I'd a been more surprised than she if I *had* met him there last night."

"I do not understand," I said. "Begin at the beginning, as a white man should, and tell me the whole tale."

And Lon began. "Victor Chauvet was an old Frenchman—born in the south of France. He came to California in the days of gold. He was a pioneer. He found no gold, but, instead, became a maker of bottled sunshine—in short, a grape-grower and wine-maker. Also, he followed gold excitements. That is what brought him to Alaska in the early days, and over the Chilcoot and down the Yukon long before the Carmack strike. The old town site of Ten Mile was Chauvet's. He carried the first mail into Arctic City. He staked those coal-mines on the Porcupine a dozen years ago. He grubstaked Loftus into the Nippennuck Country. Now it happened that Victor Chauvet was a good Catholic, loving two things in this world, wine and woman. Wine of all kinds he loved, but of woman, only one, and she was the mother of Marie Chauvet."

Here I groaned aloud, having meditated beyond self-control over the fact that I paid this man two hundred and fifty dollars a month.

"What's the matter now?" he demanded.

"Matter?" I complained. "I thought you were telling the story of Flush of Gold. I don't want a biography of your old French wine-bibber."

Lon calmly lighted his pipe, took one good puff, then put the pipe aside. "And you asked me to begin at the beginning," he said.

"Yes," said I; "the beginning."

"And the beginning of Flush of Gold is the old French wine-bibber, for he was the father of Marie Chauvet, and Marie Chauvet was the Flush of Gold. What more do you want? Victor Chauvet never had much luck to speak of. He managed to live, and to get along, and to take good care of Marie, who resembled the one woman he had loved. He took very good care of her. Flush of Gold was the pet name he gave her. Flush of Gold Creek was named after her—Flush of Gold town site, too. The old man was great on town sites, only he never landed them.

"Now, honestly," Lon said, with one of his lightning changes, "you've seen her, what do you think of her—of her looks, I mean? How does she strike your beauty sense?"

"She is remarkably beautiful," I said. "I never saw anything like her in my life. In spite of the fact, last night, that I guessed she was mad, I could not keep my eyes off of her. It wasn't curiosity. It was wonder, sheer wonder, she was so strangely beautiful."

"She was more strangely beautiful before the darkness fell upon her," Lon said softly. "She was truly the Flush of Gold. She turned all men's hearts . . . and heads. She recalls, with an effort, that I once won a canoe race at Dawson—I, who once loved her, and was told by her of her love for me. It was her beauty that made all men love her. She'd 'a' got the apple from Paris, on application, and there wouldn't have been any Trojan War, and to top it off she'd have thrown Paris down. And now she lives in darkness, and she who was always fickle, for the first time is constant—and constant to a shade, to a dead man she does not realize is dead.

"And this is the way it was. You remember what I said last night of Dave Walsh—Big Dave Walsh? He was all that I said, and more, many times more. He came into this country in the late eighties—that's a pioneer for you. He was twenty years old then. He was a young bull. When he was twenty-five he could lift clear of the ground thirteen fifty-pound sacks of flour. At first, each fall of the year, famine drove him out. It was a lone land in those days. No river steamboats, no grub, nothing but salmon bellies and rabbit tracks.

But after famine chased him out three years, he said he'd had enough of being chased; and the next year he stayed. He lived on straight meat when he was lucky enough to get it; he ate eleven dogs that winter; but he stayed. And the next winter he stayed, and the next. He never did leave the country again. He was a bull, a great bull. He could kill the strongest man in the country with hard work. He could outpack a Chilcat Indian, he could outpaddle a Stick, and he could travel all day with wet feet when the thermometer registered fifty below zero, and that's going some, I tell you, for vitality. You'd freeze your feet at twenty-five below if you wet them and tried to keep on.

"Dave Walsh was a bull for strength. And yet he was soft and easy-natured. Anybody could do him, the latest short-horn in camp could lie his last dollar out of him. 'But it doesn't worry me,' he had a way of laughing off his softness; 'it doesn't keep me awake nights.' Now don't get the idea that he had no backbone. You remember about the bear he went after with the popgun. When it came to fighting Dave was the blamedest ever. He was the limit, if by that I may describe his unlimitedness when he got into action, he was easy and kind with the weak, but the strong had to give trail when he went by. And he was a man that men liked, which is the finest word of all, a man's man.

"Dave never took part in the big stampede to Dawson when Carmack made the Bonanza strike. You see, Dave was just then over on Mammon Creek strikin' it himself. He discovered Mammon Creek. Cleaned eighty-four thousand up that winter, and opened up the claim so that it promised a couple of hundred thousand for the next winter. Then, summer bein' on and the ground sloshy, he took a trip up the Yukon to Dawson to see what Carmack's strike looked like. And there he saw Flush of Gold. I remember the night. I shall always remember. It was something sudden, and it makes one shiver to think of a strong man with all the strength withered out of him by one glance from the soft eyes of a weak, blond, female creature like Flush of Gold. It was at her dad's cabin, old Victor Chauvet's. Some friend had brought Dave along to talk over town sites on Mammon Creek. But little talking did he do, and what he did was mostly gibberish. I tell you the sight of Flush of Gold had sent Dave clean daffy. Old Victor Chauvet insisted after

Dave left that he had been drunk. And so he had. He was drunk, but Flush of Gold was the strong drink that made him so.

"That settled it, that first glimpse he caught of her. He did not start back down the Yukon in a week, as he had intended. He lingered on a month, two months, all summer. And we who had suffered understood, and wondered what the outcome would be. Undoubtedly, in our minds, it seemed that Flush of Gold had met her master. And why not? There was romance sprinkled all over Dave Walsh. He was a Mammon King, he had made the Mammon Creek strike; he was an old sour dough, one of the oldest pioneers in the land—men turned to look at him when he went by, and said to one another in awed undertones, 'There goes Dave Walsh.' And why not? He stood six feet four; he had yellow hair himself that curled on his neck; and he was a bull—a yellow-maned bull just turned thirty-one.

"And Flush of Gold loved him, and, having danced him through a whole summer's courtship, at the end their engagement was made known. The fall of the year was at hand, Dave had to be back for the winter's work on Mammon Creek, and Flush of Gold refused to be married right away. Dave put Dusky Burns in charge of the Mammon Creek claim, and himself lingered on in Dawson. Little use. She wanted her freedom a while longer; she must have it, and she would not marry until next year. And so, on the first ice, Dave Walsh went alone down the Yukon behind his dogs, with the understanding that the marriage would take place when he arrived on the first steamboat of the next year.

"Now Dave was as true as the Pole Star, and she was as false as a magnetic needle in a cargo of loadstone. Dave was as steady and solid as she was fickle and fly-away, and in some way Dave, who never doubted anybody, doubted her. It was the jealousy of his love, perhaps, and maybe it was the message ticked off from her soul to his; but at any rate Dave was worried by fear of her inconstancy. He was afraid to trust her till the next year, he had so to trust her, and he was pretty well beside himself. Some of it I got from old Victor Chauvet afterwards, and from all that I have pieced together I conclude that there was something of a scene before Dave pulled north with his dogs. He stood up before the old Frenchman, with Flush of Gold beside him, and

206

announced that they were plighted to each other. He was very dramatic, with fire in his eyes, old Victor said. He talked something about 'until death do us part'; and old Victor especially remembered that at one place Dave took her by the shoulder with his great paw and almost shook her as he said: 'Even unto death are you mine, and I would rise from the grave to claim you.' Old Victor distinctly remembered those words 'Even unto death are you mine, and I would rise from the grave to claim you.' And he told me afterwards that Flush of Gold was pretty badly frightened, and that he afterwards took Dave to one side privately and told him that that wasn't the way to hold Flush of Gold—that he must humour her and gentle her if he wanted to keep her.

"There is no discussion in my mind but that Flush of Gold was frightened. She was a savage herself in her treatment of men, while men had always treated her as a soft and tender and too utterly-utter something that must not be hurt. She didn't know what harshness was . . . until Dave Walsh, standing his six feet four, a big bull, gripped her and pawed her and assured her that she was his until death, and then some. And besides, in Dawson, that winter, was a music-player—one of those macaroni-eating, greasy-tenor-Eyetalian-dago propositions—and Flush of Gold lost her heart to him. Maybe it was only fascination—I don't know. Sometimes it seems to me that she really did love Dave Walsh. Perhaps it was because he had frightened her with that even-unto-death, rise-from-the-grave stunt of his that she in the end inclined to the dago music-player. But it is all guesswork, and the facts are, sufficient. He wasn't a dago; he was a Russian count—this was straight; and he wasn't a professional piano-player or anything of the sort. He played the violin and the piano, and he sang—sang well—but it was for his own pleasure and for the pleasure of those he sang for. He had money, too—and right here let me say that Flush of Gold never cared a rap for money. She was fickle, but she was never sordid.

"But to be getting along. She was plighted to Dave, and Dave was coming up on the first steamboat to get her—that was the summer of '98, and the first steamboat was to be expected the middle of June. And Flush of Gold was afraid to throw Dave down and face him afterwards. It was all planned suddenly. The Russian music-player, the Count, was her obedient

slave. She planned it, I know. I learned as much from old Victor afterwards.
The Count took his orders from her, and caught that first steamboat down.
It was the *Golden Rocket*. And so did Flush of Gold catch it. And so did I. I
was going to Circle City, and I was flabbergasted when I found Flush of Gold
on board. I didn't see her name down on the passenger list. She was with the
Count fellow all the time, happy and smiling, and I noticed that the Count
fellow was down on the list as having his wife along. There it was, state-
room, number, and all. The first I knew that he was married, only I didn't see
anything of the wife . . . unless Flush of Gold was so counted. I wondered
if they'd got married ashore before starting. There'd been talk about them in
Dawson, you see, and bets had been laid that the Count fellow had cut Dave
out.

"I talked with the purser. He didn't know anything more about it than
I did; he didn't know Flush of Gold, anyway, and besides, he was almost
rushed to death. You know what a Yukon steamboat is, but you can't guess
what the *Golden Rocket* was when it left Dawson that June of 1898. She was
a hummer. Being the first steamer out, she carried all the scurvy patients and
hospital wrecks. Then she must have carried a couple of millions of Klondike
dust and nuggets, to say nothing of a packed and jammed passenger list, deck
passengers galore, and bucks and squaws and dogs without end. And she was
loaded down to the guards with freight and baggage. There was a mountain
of the same on the fore-lower-deck, and each little stop along the way added
to it. I saw the box come aboard at Teelee Portage, and I knew it for what
it was, though I little guessed the joker that was in it. And they piled it on
top of everything else on the fore-lower-deck, and they didn't pile it any too
securely either. The mate expected to come back to it again, and then forgot
about it. I thought at the time that there was something familiar about the
big husky dog that climbed over the baggage and freight and lay down next
to the box. And then we passed the *Glendale*, bound up for Dawson. As she
saluted us, I thought of Dave on board of her and hurrying to Dawson to
Flush of Gold. I turned and looked at her where she stood by the rail. Her
eyes were bright, but she looked a bit frightened by the sight of the other
steamer, and she was leaning closely to the Count fellow as for protection.
She needn't have leaned so safely against him, and I needn't have been so sure

of a disappointed Dave Walsh arriving at Dawson. For Dave Walsh wasn't on the *Glendale*. There were a lot of things I didn't know, but was soon to know—for instance, that the pair were not yet married. Inside half an hour preparations for the marriage took place. What of the sick men in the main cabin, and of the crowded condition of the *Golden Rocket*, the likeliest place for the ceremony was found forward, on the lower deck, in an open space next to the rail and gang-plank and shaded by the mountain of freight with the big box on top and the sleeping dog beside it. There was a missionary on board, getting off at Eagle City, which was the next step, so they had to use him quick. That's what they'd planned to do, get married on the boat.

"But I've run ahead of the facts. The reason Dave Walsh wasn't on the *Glendale* was because he was on the *Golden Rocket*. It was this way. After loiterin' in Dawson on account of Flush of Gold, he went down to Mammon Creek on the ice. And there he found Dusky Burns doing so well with the claim, there was no need for him to be around. So he put some grub on the sled, harnessed the dogs, took an Indian along, and pulled out for Surprise Lake. He always had a liking for that section. Maybe you don't know how the creek turned out to be a four-flusher; but the prospects were good at the time, and Dave proceeded to build his cabin and hers. That's the cabin we slept in. After he finished it, he went off on a moose hunt to the forks of the Teelee, takin' the Indian along.

"And this is what happened. Came on a cold snap. The juice went down forty, fifty, sixty below zero. I remember that snap—I was at Forty Mile; and I remember the very day. At eleven o'clock in the morning the spirit thermometer at the N. A. T. & T. Company's store went down to seventy-five below zero. And that morning, near the forks of the Teelee, Dave Walsh was out after moose with that blessed Indian of his. I got it all from the Indian afterwards—we made a trip over the ice together to Dyea. That morning Mr. Indian broke through the ice and wet himself to the waist. Of course he began to freeze right away. The proper thing was to build a fire. But Dave Walsh was a bull. It was only half a mile to camp, where a fire was already burning. What was the good of building another? He threw Mr. Indian over his shoulder—and ran with him—half a mile—with the thermometer at seventy-five below. You know what that means. Suicide. There's no other name for it. Why, that buck Indian weighed over two hundred himself, and Dave ran half a mile with him. Of course he froze his lungs. Must have frozen them near solid. It was a tomfool trick for any man to do. And anyway, after lingering horribly for several weeks, Dave Walsh died.

"The Indian didn't know what to do with the corpse. Ordinarily he'd have buried him and let it go at that. But he knew that Dave Walsh was a big man, worth lots of money, a *hi-yu skookum* chief. Likewise he'd seen the bodies of other *hi-yu skookums* carted around the country like they were worth something. So he decided to take Dave's body to Forty Mile, which was Dave's headquarters. You know how the ice is on the grass roots in this country—well, the Indian planted Dave under a foot of soil—in short, he put Dave on ice. Dave could have stayed there a thousand years and still been the same old Dave. You understand—just the same as a refrigerator. Then the Indian brings over a whipsaw from the cabin at Surprise Lake and makes lumber enough for the box. Also, waiting for the thaw, he goes out and shoots about ten thousand pounds of moose. This he keeps on ice, too. Came the thaw. The Teelee broke. He built a raft and loaded it with the meat, the big box with Dave inside, and Dave's team of dogs, and away they went down the Teelee.

"The raft got caught on a timber jam and hung up two days. It was scorching hot weather, and Mr. Indian nearly lost his moose meat. So when he got to Teelee Portage he figured a steamboat would get to Forty Mile quicker than his raft. He transferred his cargo, and there you are, fore-lower deck of the *Golden Rocket*, Flush of Gold being married, and Dave Walsh in his big box casting the shade for her. And there's one thing I clean forgot. No wonder I thought the husky dog that came aboard at Teelee Portage was familiar. It was Pee-lat, Dave Walsh's lead-dog and favourite—a terrible fighter, too. He was lying down beside the box.

"Flush of Gold caught sight of me, called me over, shook hands with me, and introduced me to the Count. She was beautiful. I was as mad for her then as ever. She smiled into my eyes and said I must sign as one of the witnesses. And there was no refusing her. She was ever a child, cruel as children are cruel. Also, she told me she was in possession of the only two bottles of champagne in Dawson—or that had been in Dawson the night before; and before I knew it I was scheduled to drink her and the Count's health. Everybody crowded round, the captain of the steamboat, very prominent, trying to ring in on the wine, I guess. It was a funny wedding. On the upper deck the hospital wrecks, with various feet in the grave, gathered and looked down to see. There were Indians all jammed in the circle, too, big bucks, and their squaws and kids, to say nothing of about twenty-five snarling wolf-dogs. The missionary lined the two of them up and started in with the service. And just then a dog-fight started, high up on the pile of freight—Pee-lat lying beside the big box, and a white-haired brute belonging to one of the Indians. The fight wasn't explosive at all. The brutes just snarled at each other from a distance—tapping at each other long-distance, you know, saying dast and dassent, dast and dassent. The noise was rather disturbing, but you could hear the missionary's voice above it.

"There was no particularly easy way of getting at the two dogs, except from the other side of the pile. But nobody was on that side—everybody watching the ceremony, you see. Even then everything might have been all right if the captain hadn't thrown a club at the dogs. That was what precipitated everything. As I say, if the captain hadn't thrown that club, nothing might have happened.

"The missionary had just reached the point where he was saying 'In sickness and in health,' and 'Till death us do part.' And just then the captain threw the club. I saw the whole thing. It landed on Pee-lat, and at that instant the white brute jumped him. The club caused it. Their two bodies struck the box, and it began to slide, its lower end tilting down. It was a long oblong box, and it slid down slowly until it reached the perpendicular, when it came down on the run. The onlookers on that side the circle had time to get out from under. Flush of Gold and the Count, on the opposite side of the circle, were facing the box; the missionary had his back to it. The box must have fallen ten feet straight up and down, and it hit end on.

"Now mind you, not one of us knew that Dave Walsh was dead. We thought he was on the *Glendale*, bound for Dawson. The missionary had edged off to one side, and so Flush of Gold faced the box when it struck. It was like in a play. It couldn't have been better planned. It struck on end, and on the right end; the whole front of the box came off; and out swept Dave Walsh on his feet, partly wrapped in a blanket, his yellow hair flying and showing bright in the sun. Right out of the box, on his feet, he swept upon Flush of Gold. She didn't know he was dead, but it was unmistakable, after hanging up two days on a timber jam, that he was rising all right from the dead to claim her. Possibly that is what she thought. At any rate, the sight froze her. She couldn't move. She just sort of wilted and watched Dave Walsh coming for her! And he got her. It looked almost as though he threw his arms around her, but whether or not this happened, down to the deck they went together. We had to drag Dave Walsh's body clear before we could get hold of her. She was in a faint, but it would have been just as well if she had never come out of that faint; for when she did, she fell to screaming the way insane people do. She kept it up for hours, till she was exhausted. Oh, yes, she recovered. You saw her last night, and know how much recovered she is. She is not violent, it is true, but she lives in darkness. She believes that she is waiting for Dave Walsh, and so she waits in the cabin he built for her. She is no longer fickle. It is nine years now that she has been faithful to Dave Walsh, and the outlook is that she'll be faithful to him to the end."

Lon McFane pulled down the top of the blankets and prepared to crawl in.

"We have her grub hauled to her each year," he added, "and in general keep an eye on her. Last night was the first time she ever recognized me, though."

"Who are we?" I asked.

"Oh," was the answer, "the Count and old Victor Chauvet and me. Do you know, I think the Count is the one to be really sorry for. Dave Walsh never did know that she was false to him. And she does not suffer. Her darkness is merciful to her."

I lay silently under the blankets for the space of a minute.

212

"Is the Count still in the country?" I asked.

But there was a gentle sound of heavy breathing, and I knew Lon McFane was asleep.

THE PASSING OF MARCUS O'BRIEN

"It is the judgment of this court that you vamose the camp . . . in the customary way, sir, in the customary way."

Judge Marcus O'Brien was absent-minded, and Mucluc Charley nudged him in the ribs. Marcus O'Brien cleared his throat and went on—

"Weighing the gravity of the offence, sir, and the extenuating circumstances, it is the opinion of this court, and its verdict, that you be outfitted with three days' grub. That will do, I think."

Arizona Jack cast a bleak glance out over the Yukon. It was a swollen, chocolate flood, running a mile wide and nobody knew how deep. The earth-bank on which he stood was ordinarily a dozen feet above the water, but the river was now growling at the top of the bank, devouring, instant by instant, tiny portions of the top-standing soil. These portions went into the gaping mouths of the endless army of brown swirls and vanished away. Several inches more, and Red Cow would be flooded.

"It won't do," Arizona Jack said bitterly. "Three days' grub ain't enough."

"There was Manchester," Marcus O'Brien replied gravely. "He didn't get any grub."

"And they found his remains grounded on the Lower River an' half eaten by huskies," was Arizona Jack's retort. "And his killin' was without provocation. Joe Deeves never did nothin', never warbled once, an' jes' because his stomach was out of order, Manchester ups an' plugs him. You ain't givin' me a square deal, O'Brien, I tell you that straight. Give me a week's grub, and I play even to win out. Three days' grub, an' I cash in."

"What for did you kill Ferguson?" O'Brien demanded. "I haven't any patience for these unprovoked killings. And they've got to stop. Red Cow's none so populous. It's a good camp, and there never used to be any killings. Now they're epidemic. I'm sorry for you, Jack, but you've got to be made an example of. Ferguson didn't provoke enough for a killing."

"Provoke!" Arizona Jack snorted. "I tell you, O'Brien, you don't savve. You ain't got no artistic sensibilities. What for did I kill Ferguson? What for did Ferguson sing 'Then I wisht I was a little bird'? That's what I want to know. Answer me that. What for did he sing 'little bird, little bird'? One little bird was enough. I could a-stood one little bird. But no, he must sing two little birds. I gave 'm a chanst. I went to him almighty polite and requested him kindly to discard one little bird. I pleaded with him. There was witnesses that testified to that.

"An' Ferguson was no jay-throated songster," some one spoke up from the crowd.

O'Brien betrayed indecision.

"Ain't a man got a right to his artistic feelin's?" Arizona Jack demanded. "I gave Ferguson warnin'. It was violatin' my own nature to go on listening to his little birds. Why, there's music sharps that fine-strung an' keyed-up they'd kill for heaps less'n I did. I'm willin' to pay for havin' artistic feelin's. I can take my medicine an' lick the spoon, but three days' grub is drawin' it a shade fine, that's all, an' I hereby register my kick. Go on with the funeral."

O'Brien was still wavering. He glanced inquiringly at Mucluc Charley.

"I should say, Judge, that three days' grub was a mite severe," the latter suggested; "but you're runnin' the show. When we elected you judge of this here trial court, we agreed to abide by your decisions, an' we've done it, too, b'gosh, an' we're goin' to keep on doin' it."

"Mebbe I've been a trifle harsh, Jack," O'Brien said apologetically—"I'm that worked up over those killings; an' I'm willing to make it a week's grub." He cleared his throat magisterially and looked briskly about him. "And now we might as well get along and finish up the business. The boat's ready. You go and get the grub, Leclaire. We'll settle for it afterward."

Arizona Jack looked grateful, and, muttering something about "damned little birds," stepped aboard the open boat that rubbed restlessly against the bank. It was a large skiff, built of rough pine planks that had been sawed by hand from the standing timber of Lake Linderman, a few hundred miles above, at the foot of Chilcoot. In the boat were a pair of oars and Arizona Jack's blankets. Leclaire brought the grub, tied up in a flour-sack, and put it on board. As he did so, he whispered—"I gave you good measure, Jack. You done it with provocation."

"Cast her off!" Arizona Jack cried.

Somebody untied the painter and threw it in. The current gripped the boat and whirled it away. The murderer did not bother with the oars, contenting himself with sitting in the stern-sheets and rolling a cigarette. Completing it, he struck a match and lighted up. Those that watched on the bank could see the tiny puffs of smoke. They remained on the bank till the boat swung out of sight around the bend half a mile below. Justice had been done.

The denizens of Red Cow imposed the law and executed sentences without the delays that mark the softness of civilization. There was no law on the Yukon save what they made for themselves. They were compelled to make it for themselves. It was in an early day that Red Cow flourished on the Yukon—1887—and the Klondike and its populous stampedes lay in the unguessed future. The men of Red Cow did not even know whether their camp was situated in Alaska or in the North-west Territory, whether they drew breath under the stars and stripes or under the British flag. No surveyor had ever happened along to give them their latitude and longitude. Red Cow was situated somewhere along the Yukon, and that was sufficient for them. So far as flags were concerned, they were beyond all jurisdiction. So far as the law was concerned, they were in No-Man's land.

They made their own law, and it was very simple. The Yukon executed their decrees. Some two thousand miles below Red Cow the Yukon flowed into Bering Sea through a delta a hundred miles wide. Every mile of those two thousand miles was savage wilderness. It was true, where the Porcupine flowed into the Yukon inside the Arctic Circle there was a Hudson Bay Company trading post. But that was many hundreds of miles away. Also, it was rumoured that many hundreds of miles farther on there were missions. This last, however, was merely rumour; the men of Red Cow had never been

216

there. They had entered the lone land by way of Chilcoot and the head-waters of the Yukon.

The men of Red Cow ignored all minor offences. To be drunk and disorderly and to use vulgar language were looked upon as natural and inalienable rights. The men of Red Cow were individualists, and recognized as sacred but two things, property and life. There were no women present to complicate their simple morality. There were only three log-cabins in Red Cow—the majority of the population of forty men living in tents or brush shacks; and there was no jail in which to confine malefactors, while the inhabitants were too busy digging gold or seeking gold to take a day off and build a jail. Besides, the paramount question of grub negatived such a procedure. Wherefore, when a man violated the rights of property or life, he was thrown into an open boat and started down the Yukon. The quantity of grub he received was proportioned to the gravity of the offence. Thus, a common thief might get as much as two weeks' grub; an uncommon thief might get no more than half of that. A murderer got no grub at all. A man found guilty of manslaughter would receive grub for from three days to a week. And Marcus O'Brien had been elected judge, and it was he who apportioned the grub. A man who broke the law took his chances. The Yukon swept him away, and he might or might not win to Bering Sea. A few days' grub gave him a fighting chance. No grub meant practically capital punishment, though there was a slim chance, all depending on the season of the year.

Having disposed of Arizona Jack and watched him out of sight, the population turned from the bank and went to work on its claims—all except Curly Jim, who ran the one faro layout in all the Northland and who speculated in prospect-holes on the sides. Two things happened that day that were momentous. In the late morning Marcus O'Brien struck it. He washed out a dollar, a dollar and a half, and two dollars, from three successive pans. He had found the streak. Curly Jim looked into the hole, washed a few pans himself, and offered O'Brien ten thousand dollars for all rights—five thousand in dust, and, in lieu of the other five thousand, a half interest in his faro layout. O'Brien refused the offer. He was there to make money out of the earth, he declared with heat, and not out of his fellow-men. And anyway, he didn't like faro. Besides, he appraised his strike at a whole lot more than ten thousand.

The second event of moment occurred in the afternoon, when Siskiyou Pearly ran his boat into the bank and tied up. He was fresh from the Outside, and had in his possession a four-months-old newspaper. Furthermore, he had half a dozen barrels of whisky, all consigned to Curly Jim. The men of Red Cow quit work. They sampled the whisky—at a dollar a drink, weighed out on Curly's scales; and they discussed the news. And all would have been well, had not Curly Jim conceived a nefarious scheme, which was, namely, first to get Marcus O'Brien drunk, and next, to buy his mine from him.

The first half of the scheme worked beautifully. It began in the early evening, and by nine o'clock O'Brien had reached the singing stage. He clung with one arm around Curly Jim's neck, and even essayed the late lamented Ferguson's song about the little birds. He considered he was quite safe in this, what of the fact that the only man in camp with artistic feelings was even then speeding down the Yukon on the breast of a five-mile current.

But the second half of the scheme failed to connect. No matter how much whisky was poured down his neck, O'Brien could not be brought to realize that it was his bounden and friendly duty to sell his claim. He hesitated, it is true, and trembled now and again on the verge of giving in. Inside his muddled head, however, he was chuckling to himself. He was up to Curly Jim's game, and liked the hands that were being dealt him. The whisky was good. It came out of one special barrel, and was about a dozen times better than that in the other five barrels.

Siskiyou Pearly was dispensing drinks in the bar-room to the remainder of the population of Red Cow, while O'Brien and Curly had out their business orgy in the kitchen. But there was nothing small about O'Brien. He went into the bar-room and returned with Mucluc Charley and Percy Leclaire.

"Business 'sociates of mine, business 'sociates," he announced, with a broad wink to them and a guileless grin to Curly. "Always trust their judgment, always trust 'em. They're all right. Give 'em some fire-water, Curly, an' le's talk it over."

218

This was ringing in; but Curly Jim, making a swift revaluation of the claim, and remembering that the last pan he washed had turned out seven dollars, decided that it was worth the extra whisky, even if it was selling in the other room at a dollar a drink.

"I'm not likely to consider," O'Brien was hiccoughing to his two friends in the course of explaining to them the question at issue. "Who? Me?—sell for ten thousand dollars! No indeed. I'll dig the gold myself, an' then I'm goin' down to God's country—Southern California—that's the place for me to end my declinin' days—an' then I'll start . . . as I said before, then I'll start . . . what did I say I was goin' to start?"

"Ostrich farm," Mucluc Charley volunteered.

"Sure, just what I'm goin' to start." O'Brien abruptly steadied himself and looked with awe at Mucluc Charley. "How did you know? Never said so. Jes' thought I said so. You're a min' reader, Charley. Le's have another."

Curly Jim filled the glasses and had the pleasure of seeing four dollars' worth of whisky disappear, one dollar's worth of which he punished himself—O'Brien insisted that he should drink as frequently as his guests.

"Better take the money now," Leclaire argued. "Take you two years to dig it out the hole, an' all that time you might be hatchin' teeny little baby ostriches an' pulling feathers out the big ones."

O'Brien considered the proposition and nodded approval. Curly Jim looked gratefully at Leclaire and refilled the glasses.

"Hold on there!" spluttered Mucluc Charley, whose tongue was beginning to wag loosely and trip over itself. "As your father confessor—there I go—as your brother—O hell!" He paused and collected himself for another start. "As your frien'—business frien', I should say, I would suggest, rather—I would take the liberty, as it was, to mention—I mean, suggest, that there may be more ostriches . . . O hell!" He downed another glass, and went on more carefully. "What I'm drivin' at is . . . what am I drivin' at?" He smote the side of his head sharply half a dozen times with the heel of his palm to shake up his ideas. "I got it!" he cried jubilantly. "Supposen there's slathers more'n ten thousand dollars in that hole!"

O'Brien, who apparently was all ready to close the bargain, switched about.

"Great!" he cried. "Splen'd idea. Never thought of it all by myself." He took Mucluc Charley warmly by the hand. "Good frien'! Good 's'ciate!" He turned belligerently on Curly Jim. "Maybe hundred thousand dollars in that hole. You wouldn't rob your old frien', would you, Curly? Course you wouldn't. I know you—better'n yourself, better'n yourself. Le's have another: We're good frien's, all of us, I say, all of us."

And so it went, and so went the whisky, and so went Curly Jim's hopes up and down. Now Leclaire argued in favour of immediate sale, and almost won the reluctant O'Brien over, only to lose him to the more brilliant counter-argument of Mucluc Charley. And again, it was Mucluc Charley who presented convincing reasons for the sale and Percy Leclaire who held stubbornly back. A little later it was O'Brien himself who insisted on selling, while both friends, with tears and curses, strove to dissuade him. The more whiskey they downed, the more fertile of imagination they became. For one sober pro or con they found a score of drunken ones; and they convinced one another so readily that they were perpetually changing sides in the argument.

The time came when both Mucluc Charley and Leclaire were firmly set upon the sale, and they gleefully obliterated O'Brien's objections as fast as he entered them. O'Brien grew desperate. He exhausted his last argument and sat speechless. He looked pleadingly at the friends who had deserted him. He kicked Mucluc Charley's shins under the table, but that graceless hero immediately unfolded a new and most logical reason for the sale. Curly Jim got pen and ink and paper and wrote out the bill of sale. O'Brien sat with pen poised in hand.

"Le's have one more," he pleaded. "One more before I sign away a hundred thousan' dollars."

Curly Jim filled the glasses triumphantly. O'Brien downed his drink and bent forward with wobbling pen to affix his signature. Before he had made more than a blot, he suddenly started up, impelled by the impact of an idea colliding with his consciousness. He stood upon his feet and swayed back and forth before them, reflecting in his startled eyes the thought process that was taking place behind. Then he reached his conclusion. A benevolent radiance suffused his countenance. He turned to the faro dealer, took his hand, and spoke solemnly.

"Curly, you're my frien'. There's my han'. Shake. Ol' man, I won't do it. Won't sell. Won't rob a frien'. No son-of-a-gun will ever have chance to say Marcus O'Brien robbed frien' cause frien' was drunk. You're drunk, Curly, an' I won't rob you. Jes' had thought—never thought it before—don't know what the matter 'ith me, but never thought it before. Suppose, jes' suppose, Curly, my ol' frien', jes' suppose there ain't ten thousan' in whole damn claim. You'd be robbed. No, sir; won't do it. Marcus O'Brien makes money out of the groun', not out of his frien's."

Percy Leclaire and Mucluc Charley drowned the faro dealer's objections in applause for so noble a sentiment. They fell upon O'Brien from either side, their arms lovingly about his neck, their mouths so full of words they could not hear Curly's offer to insert a clause in the document to the effect that if there weren't ten thousand in the claim he would be given back the difference between yield and purchase price. The longer they talked the more maudlin and the more noble the discussion became. All sordid motives were banished. They were a trio of philanthropists striving to save Curly Jim from himself and his own philanthropy. They insisted that he was a philanthropist. They refused to accept for a moment that there could be found one ignoble thought in all the world. They crawled and climbed and scrambled over high ethical plateaux and ranges, or drowned themselves in metaphysical seas of sentimentality.

Curly Jim sweated and fumed and poured out the whisky. He found himself with a score of arguments on his hands, not one of which had anything to do with the gold-mine he wanted to buy. The longer they talked the farther away they got from that gold-mine, and at two in the morning Curly Jim acknowledged himself beaten. One by one he led his helpless guests across the kitchen floor and thrust them outside. O'Brien came last, and the three, with arms locked for mutual aid, titubated gravely on the stoop.

"Good business man, Curly," O'Brien was saying. "Must say like your style—fine an' generous, free-handed hospital . . . hospital . . . hospitality. Credit to you. Nothin' base 'n graspin' in your make-up. As I was sayin'—"

But just then the faro dealer slammed the door.

The three laughed happily on the stoop. They laughed for a long time. Then Mucluc Charley essayed speech.

"Funny—laughed so hard—ain't what I want to say. My idea is . . . what wash it? Oh, got it! Funny how ideas slip. Elusive idea—chasin' elusive idea—great sport. Ever chase rabbits, Percy, my frien'? I had dog—great rabbit dog. Whash 'is name? Don't know name—never had no name—forget name—elusive name—chasin' elusive name—no, idea—elusive idea, but got it—what I want to say was—O hell!"

Thereafter there was silence for a long time. O'Brien slipped from their arms to a sitting posture on the stoop, where he slept gently. Mucluc Charley chased the elusive idea through all the nooks and crannies of his drowning consciousness. Leclaire hung fascinated upon the delayed utterance. Suddenly the other's hand smote him on the back.

"Got it!" Mucluc Charley cried in stentorian tones.

The shock of the jolt broke the continuity of Leclaire's mental process.

"How much to the pan?" he demanded.

"Pan nothin'!" Mucluc Charley was angry. "Idea—got it—got leg-hold—ran it down."

Leclaire's face took on a rapt, admiring expression, and again he hung upon the other's lips.

" . . . O hell!" said Mucluc Charley.

At this moment the kitchen door opened for an instant, and Curly Jim shouted, "Go home!"

"Funny," said Mucluc Charley. "Shame idea—very shame as mine. Le's go home."

222

They gathered O'Brien up between them and started. Mucluc Charley began aloud the pursuit of another idea. Leclaire followed the pursuit with enthusiasm. But O'Brien did not follow it. He neither heard, nor saw, nor knew anything. He was a mere wobbling automaton, supported affectionately and precariously by his two business associates.

They took the path down by the bank of the Yukon. Home did not lie that way, but the elusive idea did. Mucluc Charley giggled over the idea that he could not catch for the edification of Leclaire. They came to where Siskiyou Pearly's boat lay moored to the bank. The rope with which it was tied ran across the path to a pine stump. They tripped over it and went down, O'Brien underneath. A faint flash of consciousness lighted his brain. He felt the impact of bodies upon his and struck out madly for a moment with his fists. Then he went to sleep again. His gentle snore arose on the air, and Mucluc Charley began to giggle.

"New idea," he volunteered, "brand new idea. Jes' caught it—no trouble at all. Came right up an' I patted it on the head. It's mine. 'Brien's drunk—beashly drunk. Shame—damn shame—learn'm lesshon. Trash Pearly's boat. Put 'Brien in Pearly's boat. Casht off—let her go down Yukon. 'Brien wake up in mornin'. Current too strong—can't row boat 'gainst current—mush walk back. Come back madder 'n hatter. You an' me headin' for tall timber. Learn 'm lesshon jes' shame, learn 'm lesshon."

Siskiyou Pearly's boat was empty, save for a pair of oars. Its gunwale rubbed against the bank alongside of O'Brien. They rolled him over into it. Mucluc Charley cast off the painter, and Leclaire shoved the boat out into the current. Then, exhausted by their labours, they lay down on the bank and slept.

Next morning all Red Cow knew of the joke that had been played on Marcus O'Brien. There were some tall bets as to what would happen to the two perpetrators when the victim arrived back. In the afternoon a lookout was set, so that they would know when he was sighted. Everybody wanted to see him come in. But he didn't come, though they sat up till midnight. Nor did he come next day, nor the next. Red Cow never saw Marcus O'Brien again, and though many conjectures were entertained, no certain clue was ever gained to dispel the mystery of his passing.

* * * * *

Only Marcus O'Brien knew, and he never came back to tell. He awoke next morning in torment. His stomach had been calcined by the inordinate quantity of whisky he had drunk, and was a dry and raging furnace. His head ached all over, inside and out; and, worse than that, was the pain in his face. For six hours countless thousands of mosquitoes had fed upon him, and their ungrateful poison had swollen his face tremendously. It was only by a severe exertion of will he was able to open narrow slits in his face through which he could peer. He happened to move his hands, and they hurt. He squinted at them, but failed to recognize them, so puffed were they by the mosquito virus. He was lost, or rather, his identity was lost to him. There was nothing familiar about him, which, by association of ideas, would cause to rise in his consciousness the continuity of his existence. He was divorced utterly from his past, for there was nothing about him to resurrect in his consciousness a memory of that past. Besides, he was so sick and miserable that he lacked energy and inclination to seek after who and what he was.

It was not until he discovered a crook in a little finger, caused by an unset breakage of years before, that he knew himself to be Marcus O'Brien. On the instant his past rushed into his consciousness. When he discovered a blood-blister under a thumb-nail, which he had received the previous week, his self-identification became doubly sure, and he knew that those unfamiliar hands belonged to Marcus O'Brien, or, just as much to the point, that Marcus O'Brien belonged to the hands. His first thought was that he was ill—that he had had river fever. It hurt him so much to open his eyes that he kept them closed. A small floating branch struck the boat a sharp rap. He thought it was some one knocking on the cabin door, and said, "Come in." He waited for a while, and then said testily, "Stay out, then, damn you." But just the same he wished they would come in and tell him about his illness.

But as he lay there, the past night began to reconstruct itself in his brain. He hadn't been sick at all, was his thought; he had merely been drunk, and

224

it was time for him to get up and go to work. Work suggested his mine, and he remembered that he had refused ten thousand dollars for it. He sat up abruptly and squeezed open his eyes. He saw himself in a boat, floating on the swollen brown flood of the Yukon. The spruce-covered shores and islands were unfamiliar. He was stunned for a time. He couldn't make it out. He could remember the last night's orgy, but there was no connection between that and his present situation.

He closed his eyes and held his aching head in his hands. What had happened? Slowly the dreadful thought arose in his mind. He fought against it, strove to drive it away, but it persisted: he had killed somebody. That alone could explain why he was in an open boat drifting down the Yukon. The law of Red Cow that he had so long administered had now been administered to him. He had killed some one and been set adrift. But whom? He racked his aching brain for the answer, but all that came was a vague memory of bodies falling upon him and of striking out at them. Who were they? Maybe he had killed more than one. He reached to his belt. The knife was missing from its sheath. He had done it with that undoubtedly. But there must have been some reason for the killing. He opened his eyes and in a panic began to search about the boat. There was no grub, not an ounce of grub. He sat down with a groan. He had killed without provocation. The extreme rigour of the law had been visited upon him.

For half an hour he remained motionless, holding his aching head and trying to think. Then he cooled his stomach with a drink of water from overside and felt better. He stood up, and alone on the wide-stretching Yukon, with naught but the primeval wilderness to hear, he cursed strong drink. After that he tied up to a huge floating pine that was deeper sunk in the current than the boat and that consequently drifted faster. He washed his face and hands, sat down in the stern-sheets, and did some more thinking. It was late in June. It was two thousand miles to Bering Sea. The boat was averaging five miles an hour. There was no darkness in such high latitudes at that time of the year, and he could run the river every hour of the twenty-four. This would mean, daily, a hundred and twenty miles. Strike out the twenty for accidents, and there remained a hundred miles a day. In twenty

225

days he would reach Bering Sea. And this would involve no expenditure of energy; the river did the work. He could lie down in the bottom of the boat and husband his strength.

For two days he ate nothing. Then, drifting into the Yukon Flats, he went ashore on the low-lying islands and gathered the eggs of wild geese and ducks. He had no matches, and ate the eggs raw. They were strong, but they kept him going. When he crossed the Arctic Circle, he found the Hudson Bay Company's post. The brigade had not yet arrived from the Mackenzie, and the post was completely out of grub. He was offered wild-duck eggs, but he informed them that he had a bushel of the same on the boat. He was also offered a drink of whisky, which he refused with an exhibition of violent repugnance. He got matches, however, and after that he cooked his eggs. Toward the mouth of the river head-winds delayed him, and he was twenty-four days on the egg diet. Unfortunately, while asleep he had drifted by both the missions of St. Paul and Holy Cross. And he could sincerely say, as he afterward did, that talk about missions on the Yukon was all humbug. There weren't any missions, and he was the man to know.

Once on Bering Sea he exchanged the egg diet for seal diet, and he never could make up his mind which he liked least. In the fall of the year he was rescued by a United States revenue cutter, and the following winter he made quite a hit in San Francisco as a temperance lecturer. In this field he found his vocation. "Avoid the bottle" is his slogan and battle-cry. He manages subtly to convey the impression that in his own life a great disaster was wrought by the bottle. He has even mentioned the loss of a fortune that was caused by that hell-bait of the devil, but behind that incident his listeners feel the loom of some terrible and unguessed evil for which the bottle is responsible. He has made a success in his vocation, and has grown grey and respected in the crusade against strong drink. But on the Yukon the passing of Marcus O'Brien remains tradition. It is a mystery that ranks at par with the disappearance of Sir John Franklin.

226

THE WIT OF PORPORTUK

El-Soo had been a Mission girl. Her mother had died when she was very small, and Sister Alberta had plucked El-Soo as a brand from the burning, one summer day, and carried her away to Holy Cross Mission and dedicated her to God. El-Soo was a full-blooded Indian, yet she exceeded all the half-breed and quarter-breed girls. Never had the good sisters dealt with a girl so adaptable and at the same time so spirited.

El-Soo was quick, and deft, and intelligent; but above all she was fire, the living flame of life, a blaze of personality that was compounded of will, sweetness, and daring. Her father was a chief, and his blood ran in her veins. Obedience, on the part of El-Soo, was a matter of terms and arrangement. She had a passion for equity, and perhaps it was because of this that she excelled in mathematics.

But she excelled in other things. She learned to read and write English as no girl had ever learned in the Mission. She led the girls in singing, and into song she carried her sense of equity. She was an artist, and the fire of her flowed toward creation. Had she from birth enjoyed a more favourable environment, she would have made literature or music.

Instead, she was El-Soo, daughter of Klakee-Nah, a chief, and she lived in the Holy Cross Mission where were no artists, but only pure-souled Sisters who were interested in cleanliness and righteousness and the welfare of the spirit in the land of immortality that lay beyond the skies.

The years passed. She was eight years old when she entered the Mission; she was sixteen, and the Sisters were corresponding with their superiors in the Order concerning the sending of El-Soo to the United States to complete her education, when a man of her own tribe arrived at Holy Cross and had talk with her. El-Soo was somewhat appalled by him. He was dirty. He was a Caliban-like creature, primitively ugly, with a mop of hair that had never been combed. He looked at her disapprovingly and refused to sit down.

"Thy brother is dead," he said shortly.

El-Soo was not particularly shocked. She remembered little of her brother. "Thy father is an old man, and alone," the messenger went on. "His house is large and empty, and he would hear thy voice and look upon thee."

Him she remembered—Klakee-Nah, the headman of the village, the friend of the missionaries and the traders, a large man thewed like a giant, with kindly eyes and masterful ways, and striding with a consciousness of crude royalty in his carriage.

"Tell him that I will come," was El-Soo's answer.

Much to the despair of the Sisters, the brand plucked from the burning went back to the burning. All pleading with El-Soo was vain. There was much argument, expostulation, and weeping. Sister Alberta even revealed to her the project of sending her to the United States. El-Soo stared wide-eyed into the golden vista thus opened up to her, and shook her head. In her eyes persisted another vista. It was the mighty curve of the Yukon at Tana-naw Station. With the St. George Mission on one side, and the trading post on the other, and midway between the Indian village and a certain large log house where lived an old man tended upon by slaves.

All dwellers on the Yukon bank for twice a thousand miles knew the large log house, the old man and the tending slaves; and well did the Sisters know the house, its unending revelry, its feasting and its fun. So there was weeping at Holy Cross when El-Soo departed.

There was a great cleaning up in the large house when El-Soo arrived. Klakee-Nah, himself masterful, protested at this masterful conduct of his young daughter; but in the end, dreaming barbarically of magnificence, he went forth and borrowed a thousand dollars from old Porportuk, than whom there was no richer Indian on the Yukon. Also, Klakee-Nah ran up a heavy bill at the trading post. El-Soo re-created the large house. She invested it with new splendour, while Klakee-Nah maintained its ancient traditions of hospitality and revelry.

All this was unusual for a Yukon Indian, but Klakee-Nah was an unusual Indian. Not alone did he like to render inordinate hospitality, but, what of being a chief and of acquiring much money, he was able to do it. In the primitive trading days he had been a power over his people, and he had dealt profitably with the white trading companies. Later on, with Porportuk, he had made a gold-strike on the *Koyokuk* River. Klakee-Nah was by training and nature an aristocrat. Porportuk was bourgeois, and Porportuk bought him out of the gold-mine. Porportuk was content to plod and accumulate. Klakee-Nah went back to his large house and proceeded to spend. Porportuk was known as the richest Indian in Alaska. Klakee-Nah was known as the whitest. Porportuk was a money-lender and a usurer. Klakee-Nah was an anachronism—a mediæval ruin, a fighter and a feaster, happy with wine and song.

El-Soo adapted herself to the large house and its ways as readily as she had adapted herself to Holy Cross Mission and its ways. She did not try to reform her father and direct his footsteps toward God. It is true, she reproved him when he drank overmuch and profoundly, but that was for the sake of his health and the direction of his footsteps on solid earth.

The latchstring to the large house was always out. What with the coming and the going, it was never still. The rafters of the great living-room shook with the roar of wassail and of song. At table sat men from all the world and chiefs from distant tribes—Englishmen and Colonials, lean Yankee traders and rotund officials of the great companies, cowboys from the Western ranges, sailors from the sea, hunters and dog-mushers of a score of nationalities.

El-Soo drew breath in a cosmopolitan atmosphere. She could speak English as well as she could her native tongue, and she sang English songs and ballads. The passing Indian ceremonials she knew, and the perishing traditions. The tribal dress of the daughter of a chief she knew how to wear upon occasion. But for the most part she dressed as white women dress. Not for nothing was her needlework at the Mission and her innate artistry. She carried her clothes like a white woman, and she made clothes that could be so carried.

In her way she was as unusual as her father, and the position she occupied was as unique as his. She was the one Indian woman who was the social equal with the several white women at Tana-naw Station. She was the one Indian woman to whom white men honourably made proposals of marriage. And she was the one Indian woman whom no white man ever insulted.

For El-Soo was beautiful—not as white women are beautiful, not as Indian women are beautiful. It was the flame of her, that did not depend upon feature, that was her beauty. So far as mere line and feature went, she was the classic Indian type. The black hair and the fine bronze were hers, and the black eyes, brilliant and bold, keen as sword-light, proud; and hers the delicate eagle nose with the thin, quivering nostrils, the high cheek-bones that were not broad apart, and the thin lips that were not too thin. But over all and through all poured the flame of her—the unanalysable something that was fire and that was the soul of her, that lay mellow-warm or blazed in her eyes, that sprayed the cheeks of her, that distended the nostrils, that curled the lips, or, when the lip was in repose, that was still there in the lip, the lip palpitant with its presence.

And El-Soo had wit—rarely sharp to hurt, yet quick to search out forgivable weakness. The laughter of her mind played like lambent flame over all about her, and from all about her arose answering laughter. Yet she was never the centre of things. This she would not permit. The large house, and all of which it was significant, was her father's; and through it, to the last, moved his heroic figure—host, master of the revels, and giver of the law. It is true, as the strength oozed from him, that she caught up responsibilities from his failing hands. But in appearance he still ruled, dozing, ofttimes at the board, a bacchanalian ruin, yet in all seeming the ruler of the feast.

And through the large house moved the figure of Porportuk, ominous, with shaking head, coldly disapproving, paying for it all. Not that he really paid, for he compounded interest in weird ways, and year by year absorbed the properties of Klakee-Nah. Porportuk once took it upon himself to chide El-Soo upon the wasteful way of life in the large house—it was when he had about absorbed the last of Klakee-Nah's wealth—but he never ventured so to chide again. El-Soo, like her father, was an aristocrat, as disdainful of money as he, and with an equal sense of honour as finely strung.

230

Porportuk continued grudgingly to advance money, and ever the money flowed in golden foam away. Upon one thing El-Soo was resolved—her father should die as he had lived. There should be for him no passing from high to low, no diminution of the revels, no lessening of the lavish hospitality. When there was famine, as of old, the Indians came groaning to the large house and went away content. When there was famine and no money, money was borrowed from Porportuk, and the Indians still went away content. El-Soo might well have repeated, after the aristocrats of another time and place, that after her came the deluge. In her case the deluge was old Porportuk. With every advance of money, he looked upon her with a more possessive eye, and felt bourgeoning within him ancient fires.

But El-Soo had no eyes for him. Nor had she eyes for the white men who wanted to marry her at the Mission with ring and priest and book. For at Tana-naw Station was a young man, Akoon, of her own blood, and tribe, and village. He was strong and beautiful to her eyes, a great hunter, and, in that he had wandered far and much, very poor; he had been to all the unknown wastes and places; he had journeyed to Sitka and to the United States; he had crossed the continent to Hudson Bay and back again, and as seal-hunter on a ship he had sailed to Siberia and for Japan.

When he returned from the gold-strike in Klondike he came, as was his wont, to the large house to make report to old Klakee-Nah of all the world that he had seen; and there he first saw El-Soo, three years back from the Mission. Thereat, Akoon wandered no more. He refused a wage of twenty dollars a day as pilot on the big steamboats. He hunted some and fished some, but never far from Tana-naw Station, and he was at the large house often and long. And El-Soo measured him against many men and found him good. He sang songs to her, and was ardent and glowed until all Tana-naw Station knew he loved her. And Porportuk but grinned and advanced more money for the upkeep of the large house.

Then came the death table of Klakee-Nah.

He sat at feast, with death in his throat, that he could not drown with wine. And laughter and joke and song went around, and Akoon told a story

231

that made the rafters echo. There were no tears or sighs at that table. It was no more than fit that Klakee-Nah should die as he had lived, and none knew this better than El-Soo, with her artist sympathy. The old roystering crowd was there, and, as of old, three frost-bitten sailors were there, fresh from the long traverse from the Arctic, survivors of a ship's company of seventy-four. At Klakee-Nah's back were four old men, all that were left him of the slaves of his youth. With rheumy eyes they saw to his needs, with palsied hands filling his glass or striking him on the back between the shoulders when death stirred and he coughed and gasped.

It was a wild night, and as the hours passed and the fun laughed and roared along, death stirred more restlessly in Klakee-Nah's throat. Then it was that he sent for Porportuk. And Porportuk came in from the outside frost to look with disapproving eyes upon the meat and wine on the table for which he had paid. But as he looked down the length of flushed faces to the far end and saw the face of El-Soo, the light in his eyes flared up, and for a moment the disapproval vanished.

Place was made for him at Klakee-Nah's side, and a glass placed before him. Klakee-Nah, with his own hands, filled the glass with fervent spirits. "Drink!" he cried. "Is it not good?"

And Porportuk's eyes watered as he nodded his head and smacked his lips.

"When, in your own house, have you had such drink?" Klakee-Nah demanded.

"I will not deny that the drink is good to this old throat of mine," Porportuk made answer, and hesitated for the speech to complete the thought.

"But it costs overmuch," Klakee-Nah roared, completing it for him.

Porportuk winced at the laughter that went down the table. His eyes burned malevolently. "We were boys together, of the same age," he said. "In your throat is death. I am still alive and strong."

232

An ominous murmur arose from the company. Klakee-Nah coughed and strangled, and the old slaves smote him between the shoulders. He emerged gasping, and waved his hand to still the threatening rumble.

"You have grudged the very fire in your house because the wood cost overmuch!" he cried. "You have grudged life. To live cost overmuch, and you have refused to pay the price. Your life has been like a cabin where the fire is out and there are no blankets on the floor." He signalled to a slave to fill his glass, which he held aloft. "But I have lived. And I have been warm with life as you have never been warm. It is true, you shall live long. But the longest nights are the cold nights when a man shivers and lies awake. My nights have been short, but I have slept warm."

He drained the glass. The shaking hand of a slave failed to catch it as it crashed to the floor. Klakee-Nah sank back, panting, watching the upturned glasses at the lips of the drinkers, his own lips slightly smiling to the applause. At a sign, two slaves attempted to help him sit upright again. But they were weak, his frame was mighty, and the four old men tottered and shook as they helped him forward.

"But manner of life is neither here nor there," he went on. "We have other business, Porportuk, you and I, to-night. Debts are mischances, and I am in mischance with you. What of my debt, and how great is it?"

Porportuk searched in his pouch and brought forth a memorandum. He sipped at his glass and began. "There is the note of August, 1889, for three hundred dollars. The interest has never been paid. And the note of the next year for five hundred dollars. This note was included in the note of two months later for a thousand dollars. Then there is the note—"

"Never mind the many notes!" Klakee-Nah cried out impatiently. "They make my head go around and all the things inside my head. The whole! The round whole! How much is it?"

Porportuk referred to his memorandum. "Fifteen thousand nine hundred and sixty-seven dollars and seventy-five cents," he read with careful precision.

"Make it sixteen thousand, make it sixteen thousand," Klakee-Nah said grandly. "Odd numbers were ever a worry. And now—and it is for this that I have sent for you—make me out a new note for sixteen thousand, which I shall sign. I have no thought of the interest. Make it as large as you will, and make it payable in the next world, when I shall meet you by the fire of the Great Father of all Indians. Then the note will be paid. This I promise you. It is the word of Klakee-Nah."

Porportuk looked perplexed, and loudly the laughter arose and shook the room. Klakee-Nah raised his hands. "Nay," he cried. "It is not a joke. I but speak in fairness. It was for this I sent for you, Porportuk. Make out the note."

"I have no dealings with the next world," Porportuk made answer slowly.

"Have you no thought to meet me before the Great Father!" Klakee-Nah demanded. Then he added, "I shall surely be there."

"I have no dealings with the next world," Porportuk repeated sourly.

The dying man regarded him with frank amazement.

"I know naught of the next world," Porportuk explained. "I do business in this world."

Klakee-Nah's face cleared. "This comes of sleeping cold of nights," he laughed. He pondered for a space, then said, "It is in this world that you must be paid. There remains to me this house. Take it, and burn the debt in the candle there."

"It is an old house and not worth the money," Porportuk made answer.

"There are my mines on the Twisted Salmon."

"They have never paid to work," was the reply.

"There is my share in the steamer Koyokuk. I am half owner."

"She is at the bottom of the Yukon."

234

Klakee-Nah started. "True, I forgot. It was last spring when the ice went out." He mused for a time while the glasses remained untasted, and all the company waited upon his utterance.

"Then it would seem I owe you a sum of money which I cannot pay . . . in this world?" Porportuk nodded and glanced down the table.

"Then it would seem that you, Porportuk, are a poor business man," Klakee-Nah said slyly. And boldly Porportuk made answer, "No; there is security yet untouched."

"What!" cried Klakee-Nah. "Have I still property? Name it, and it is yours, and the debt is no more."

"There it is." Porportuk pointed at El-Soo.

Klakee-Nah could not understand. He peered down the table, brushed his eyes, and peered again.

"Your daughter, El-Soo—her will I take and the debt be no more. I will burn the debt there in the candle."

Klakee-Nah's great chest began to heave. "Ho! ho!—a joke. Ho! ho! ho!" he laughed Homerically. "And with your cold bed and daughters old enough to be the mother of El-Soo! Ho! ho! ho!" He began to cough and strangle, and the old slaves smote him on the back. "Ho! ho!" he began again, and went off into another paroxysm.

Porportuk waited patiently, sipping from his glass and studying the double row of faces down the board. "It is no joke," he said finally. "My speech is well meant."

Klakee-Nah sobered and looked at him, then reached for his glass, but could not touch it. A slave passed it to him, and glass and liquor he flung into the face of Porportuk.

"Turn him out!" Klakee-Nah thundered to the waiting table that strained like a pack of hounds in leash. "And roll him in the snow!"

As the mad riot swept past him and out of doors, he signalled to the slaves, and the four tottering old men supported him on his feet as he met the returning revellers, upright, glass in hand, pledging them a toast to the short night when a man sleeps warm.

It did not take long to settle the estate of Klakee-Nah. Tommy, the little Englishman, clerk at the trading post, was called in by El-Soo to help. There was nothing but debts, notes overdue, mortgaged properties, and properties mortgaged but worthless. Notes and mortgages were held by Porportuk. Tommy called him a robber many times as he pondered the compounding of the interest.

"Is it a debt, Tommy?" El-Soo asked.

"It is a robbery," Tommy answered.

"Nevertheless, it is a debt," she persisted.

The winter wore away, and the early spring, and still the claims of Porportuk remained unpaid. He saw El-Soo often and explained to her at length, as he had explained to her father, the way the debt could be cancelled. Also, he brought with him old medicine-men, who elaborated to her the everlasting damnation of her father if the debt were not paid. One day, after such an elaboration, El-Soo made final announcement to Porportuk.

"I shall tell you two things," she said. "First I shall not be your wife. Will you remember that? Second, you shall be paid the last cent of the sixteen thousand dollars—"

"Fifteen thousand nine hundred and sixty-seven dollars and seventy-five cents," Porportuk corrected.

"My father said sixteen thousand," was her reply. "You shall be paid."

"How?"

"I know not how, but I shall find out how. Now go, and bother me no more. If you do"—she hesitated to find fitting penalty—"if you do, I shall have you rolled in the snow again as soon as the first snow flies."

This was still in the early spring, and a little later El-Soo surprised the country. Word went up and down the Yukon from Chilcoot to the Delta,

236

and was carried from camp to camp to the farthermost camps, that in June, when the first salmon ran, El-Soo, daughter of Klakee-Nah, would sell herself at public auction to satisfy the claims of Porportuk. Vain were the attempts to dissuade her. The missionary at St. George wrestled with her, but she replied—

"Only the debts to God are settled in the next world. The debts of men are of this world, and in this world are they settled."

Akoon wrestled with her, but she replied, "I do love thee, Akoon; but honour is greater than love, and who am I that I should blacken my father?" Sister Alberta journeyed all the way up from Holy Cross on the first steamer, and to no better end.

"My father wanders in the thick and endless forests," said El-Soo. "And there will he wander, with the lost souls crying, till the debt be paid. Then, and not until then, may he go on to the house of the Great Father."

"And you believe this?" Sister Alberta asked.

"I do not know," El-Soo made answer. "It was my father's belief."

Sister Alberta shrugged her shoulders incredulously.

"Who knows but that the things we believe come true?" El-Soo went on. "Why not? The next world to you may be heaven and harps . . . because you have believed heaven and harps; to my father the next world may be a large house where he will sit always at table feasting with God."

"And you?" Sister Alberta asked. "What is your next world?"

El-Soo hesitated but for a moment. "I should like a little of both," she said. "I should like to see your face as well as the face of my father."

The day of the auction came. Tana-naw Station was populous. As was their custom, the tribes had gathered to await the salmon-run, and in the meantime spent the time in dancing and frolicking, trading and gossiping. Then there was the ordinary sprinkling of white adventurers, traders, and prospectors, and, in addition, a large number of white men who had come because of curiosity or interest in the affair.

It had been a backward spring, and the salmon were late in running. This delay but keyed up the interest. Then, on the day of the auction, the situation was made tense by Akoon. He arose and made public and solemn announcement that whosoever bought El-Soo would forthwith and immediately die. He flourished the Winchester in his hand to indicate the manner of the taking-off. El-Soo was angered thereat; but he refused to speak with her, and went to the trading post to lay in extra ammunition.

The first salmon was caught at ten o'clock in the evening, and at midnight the auction began. It took place on top of the high bank alongside the Yukon. The sun was due north just below the horizon, and the sky was lurid red. A great crowd gathered about the table and the two chairs that stood near the edge of the bank. To the fore were many white men and several chiefs. And most prominently to the fore, rifle in hand, stood Akoon. Tommy, at El-Soo's request, served as auctioneer, but she made the opening speech and described the goods about to be sold. She was in native costume, in the dress of a chief's daughter, splendid and barbaric, and she stood on a chair, that she might be seen to advantage.

"Who will buy a wife?" she asked. "Look at me. I am twenty years old and a maid. I will be a good wife to the man who buys me. If he is a white man, I shall dress in the fashion of white women; if he is an Indian, I shall dress as"—she hesitated a moment—"a squaw. I can make my own clothes, and sew, and wash, and mend. I was taught for eight years to do these things at Holy Cross Mission. I can read and write English, and I know how to play the organ. Also I can do arithmetic and some algebra—a little. I shall be sold to the highest bidder, and to him I will make out a bill of sale of myself. I forgot to say that I can sing very well, and that I have never been sick in my life. I weigh one hundred and thirty-two pounds; my father is dead and I have no relatives. Who wants me?"

She looked over the crowd with flaming audacity and stepped down. At Tommy's request she stood upon the chair again, while he mounted the second chair and started the bidding.

Surrounding El-Soo stood the four old slaves of her father. They were age-twisted and palsied, faithful to their meat, a generation out of the past

238

that watched unmoved the antics of younger life. In the front of the crowd were several Eldorado and Bonanza kings from the Upper Yukon, and beside them, on crutches, swollen with scurvy, were two broken prospectors. From the midst of the crowd, thrust out by its own vividness, appeared the face of a wild-eyed squaw from the remote regions of the Upper Tana-naw; a strayed Sitkan from the coast stood side by side with a Stick from Lake Le Barge, and, beyond, a half-dozen French-Canadian voyageurs, grouped by themselves. From afar came the faint cries of myriads of wild-fowl on the nesting-grounds. Swallows were skimming up overhead from the placid surface of the Yukon, and robins were singing. The oblique rays of the hidden sun shot through the smoke, high-dissipated from forest fires a thousand miles away, and turned the heavens to sombre red, while the earth shone red in the reflected glow. This red glow shone in the faces of all, and made everything seem unearthly and unreal.

The bidding began slowly. The Sitkan, who was a stranger in the land and who had arrived only half an hour before, offered one hundred dollars in a confident voice, and was surprised when Akoon turned threateningly upon him with the rifle. The bidding dragged. An Indian from the Tozikakat, a pilot, bid one hundred and fifty, and after some time a gambler, who had been ordered out of the Upper Country, raised the bid to two hundred. El-Soo was saddened; her pride was hurt; but the only effect was that she flamed more audaciously upon the crowd.

There was a disturbance among the onlookers as Porportuk forced his way to the front. "Five hundred dollars!" he bid in a loud voice, then looked about him proudly to note the effect.

He was minded to use his great wealth as a bludgeon with which to stun all competition at the start. But one of the voyageurs, looking on El-Soo with sparkling eyes, raised the bid a hundred.

"Seven hundred!" Porportuk returned promptly.

And with equal promptness came the "Eight hundred" of the voyageur.

Then Porportuk swung his club again.

"Twelve hundred!" he shouted.

With a look of poignant disappointment, the voyageur succumbed. There was no further bidding. Tommy worked hard, but could not elicit a bid.

El-Soo spoke to Porportuk. "It were good, Porportuk, for you to weigh well your bid. Have you forgotten the thing I told you—that I would never marry you!"

"It is a public auction," he retorted. "I shall buy you with a bill of sale. I have offered twelve hundred dollars. You come cheap."

"Too damned cheap!" Tommy cried. "What if I am auctioneer? That does not prevent me from bidding. I'll make it thirteen hundred."

"Fourteen hundred," from Porportuk.

"I'll buy you in to be my—my sister," Tommy whispered to El-Soo, then called aloud, "Fifteen hundred!"

At two thousand one of the Eldorado kings took a hand, and Tommy dropped out.

A third time Porportuk swung the club of his wealth, making a clean raise of five hundred dollars. But the Eldorado king's pride was touched. No man could club him. And he swung back another five hundred.

El-Soo stood at three thousand. Porportuk made it thirty-five hundred, and gasped when the Eldorado king raised it a thousand dollars. Porportuk again raised it five hundred, and again gasped when the king raised a thousand more.

Porportuk became angry. His pride was touched; his strength was challenged, and with him strength took the form of wealth. He would not be ashamed for weakness before the world. El-Soo became incidental. The savings and scrimpings from the cold nights of all his years were ripe to be squandered. El-Soo stood at six thousand. He made it seven thousand. And then, in thousand-dollar bids, as fast as they could be uttered, her price went up. At fourteen thousand the two men stopped for breath.

240

Then the unexpected happened. A still heavier club was swung. In the pause that ensued, the gambler, who had scented a speculation and formed a syndicate with several of his fellows, bid sixteen thousand dollars.

"Seventeen thousand," Porportuk said weakly.

"Eighteen thousand," said the king.

Porportuk gathered his strength. "Twenty thousand."

The syndicate dropped out. The Eldorado king raised a thousand, and Porportuk raised back; and as they bid, Akoon turned from one to the other, half menacingly, half curiously, as though to see what manner of man it was that he would have to kill. When the king prepared to make his next bid, Akoon having pressed closer, the king first loosed the revolver at his hip, then said:

"Twenty-three thousand."

"Twenty-four thousand," said Porportuk. He grinned viciously, for the certitude of his bidding had at last shaken the king. The latter moved over close to El-Soo. He studied her carefully for a long while.

"And five hundred," he said at last.

"Twenty-five thousand," came Porportuk's raise.

The king looked for a long space, and shook his head. He looked again, and said reluctantly, "And five hundred."

"Twenty-six thousand," Porportuk snapped.

The king shook his head and refused to meet Tommy's pleading eye. In the meantime Akoon had edged close to Porportuk. El-Soo's quick eye noted this, and, while Tommy wrestled with the Eldorado king for another bid, she bent, and spoke in a low voice in the ear of a slave. And while Tommy's "Going—going—going—" dominated the air, the slave went up to Akoon and spoke in a low voice in his ear. Akoon made no sign that he had heard, though El-Soo watched him anxiously.

"Gone!" Tommy's voice rang out. "To Porportuk, for twenty-six thousand dollars."

Porportuk glanced uneasily at Akoon. All eyes were centred upon Akoon, but he did nothing.

"Let the scales be brought," said El-Soo.

"I shall make payment at my house," said Porportuk.

"Let the scales be brought," El-Soo repeated. "Payment shall be made here where all can see."

So the gold scales were brought from the trading post, while Porportuk went away and came back with a man at his heels, on whose shoulders was a weight of gold-dust in moose-hide sacks. Also, at Porportuk's back, walked another man with a rifle, who had eyes only for Akoon.

"Here are the notes and mortgages," said Porportuk, "for fifteen thousand nine hundred and sixty-seven dollars and seventy-five cents."

El-Soo received them into her hands and said to Tommy, "Let them be reckoned as sixteen thousand."

"There remains ten thousand dollars to be paid in gold," Tommy said.

Porportuk nodded, and untied the mouths of the sacks. El-Soo, standing at the edge of the bank, tore the papers to shreds and sent them fluttering out over the Yukon. The weighing began, but halted.

"Of course, at seventeen dollars," Porportuk had said to Tommy, as he adjusted the scales.

"At sixteen dollars," El-Soo said sharply.

"It is the custom of all the land to reckon gold at seventeen dollars for each ounce," Porportuk replied. "And this is a business transaction."

El-Soo laughed. "It is a new custom," she said. "It began this spring. Last year, and the years before, it was sixteen dollars an ounce. When my father's debt was made, it was sixteen dollars. When he spent at the store the money he got from you, for one ounce he was given sixteen dollars' worth of flour, not seventeen. Wherefore, shall you pay for me at sixteen, and not at seventeen." Porportuk grunted and allowed the weighing to proceed.

"Weigh it in three piles, Tommy," she said. "A thousand dollars here, three thousand here, and here six thousand."

It was slow work, and, while the weighing went on, Akoon was closely watched by all.

"He but waits till the money is paid," one said; and the word went around and was accepted, and they waited for what Akoon should do when the money was paid. And Porportuk's man with the rifle waited and watched Akoon.

The weighing was finished, and the gold-dust lay on the table in three dark-yellow heaps. "There is a debt of my father to the Company for three thousand dollars," said El-Soo. "Take it, Tommy, for the Company. And here are four old men, Tommy. You know them. And here is one thousand dollars. Take it, and see that the old men are never hungry and never without tobacco."

Tommy scooped the gold into separate sacks. Six thousand dollars remained on the table. El-Soo thrust the scoop into the heap, and with a sudden turn whirled the contents out and down to the Yukon in a golden shower. Porportuk seized her wrist as she thrust the scoop a second time into the heap.

"It is mine," she said calmly. Porportuk released his grip, but he gritted his teeth and scowled darkly as she continued to scoop the gold into the river till none was left.

The crowd had eyes for naught but Akoon, and the rifle of Porportuk's man lay across the hollow of his arm, the muzzle directed at Akoon a yard away, the man's thumb on the hammer. But Akoon did nothing.

"Make out the bill of sale," Porportuk said grimly.

And Tommy made out the till of sale, wherein all right and title in the woman El-Soo was vested in the man Porportuk. El-Soo signed the document, and Porportuk folded it and put it away in his pouch. Suddenly his eyes flashed, and in sudden speech he addressed El-Soo.

"But it was not your father's debt," he said, "What I paid was the price for you. Your sale is business of to-day and not of last year and the years before. The ounces paid for you will buy at the post to-day seventeen dollars of flour, and not sixteen. I have lost a dollar on each ounce. I have lost six hundred and twenty-five dollars."

El-Soo thought for a moment, and saw the error she had made. She smiled, and then she laughed.

"You are right," she laughed, "I made a mistake. But it is too late. You have paid, and the gold is gone. You did not think quick. It is your loss. Your wit is slow these days, Porportuk. You are getting old."

He did not answer. He glanced uneasily at Akoon, and was reassured. His lips tightened, and a hint of cruelty came into his face. "Come," he said, "we will go to my house."

"Do you remember the two things I told you in the spring?" El-Soo asked, making no movement to accompany him.

"My head would be full with the things women say, did I heed them," he answered.

"I told you that you would be paid," El-Soo went on carefully. "And I told you that I would never be your wife."

"But that was before the bill of sale." Porportuk crackled the paper between his fingers inside the pouch. "I have bought you before all the world. You belong to me. You will not deny that you belong to me."

"I belong to you," El-Soo said steadily.

"I own you."

"You own me."

244

Porportuk's voice rose slightly and triumphantly. "As a dog, I own you."

"As a dog you own me," El-Soo continued calmly. "But, Porportuk, you forget the thing I told you. Had any other man bought me, I should have been that man's wife. I should have been a good wife to that man. Such was my will. But my will with you was that I should never be your wife. Wherefore, I am your dog."

Porportuk knew that he played with fire, and he resolved to play firmly. "Then I speak to you, not as El-Soo, but as a dog," he said; "and I tell you to come with me." He half reached to grip her arm, but with a gesture she held him back.

"Not so fast, Porportuk. You buy a dog. The dog runs away. It is your loss. I am your dog. What if I run away?"

"As the owner of the dog, I shall beat you—"

"When you catch me?"

"When I catch you."

"Then catch me."

He reached swiftly for her, but she eluded him. She laughed as she circled around the table. "Catch her!" Porportuk commanded the Indian with the rifle, who stood near to her. But as the Indian stretched forth his arm to her, the Eldorado king felled him with a fist blow under the ear. The rifle clattered to the ground. Then was Akoon's chance. His eyes glittered, but he did nothing.

Porportuk was an old man, but his cold nights retained for him his activity. He did not circle the table. He came across suddenly, over the top of the table. El-Soo was taken off her guard. She sprang back with a sharp cry of alarm, and Porportuk would have caught her had it not been for Tommy. Tommy's leg went out, Porportuk tripped and pitched forward on the ground. El-Soo got her start.

"Then catch me," she laughed over her shoulder, as she fled away.

She ran lightly and easily, but Porportuk ran swiftly and savagely. He outran her. In his youth he had been swiftest of all the young men. But El-Soo dodged in a willowy, elusive way. Being in native dress, her feet were not cluttered with skirts, and her pliant body curved a flight that defied the gripping fingers of Porportuk.

With laughter and tumult, the great crowd scattered out to see the chase. It led through the Indian encampment; and ever dodging, circling, and reversing, El-Soo and Porportuk appeared and disappeared among the tents. El-Soo seemed to balance herself against the air with her arms, now one side, now on the other, and sometimes her body, too, leaned out upon the air far from the perpendicular as she achieved her sharpest curves. And Porportuk, always a leap behind, or a leap this side or that, like a lean hound strained after her.

They crossed the open ground beyond the encampment and disappeared in the forest. Tana-naw Station waited their reappearance, and long and vainly it waited.

In the meantime Akoon ate and slept, and lingered much at the steamboat landing, deaf to the rising resentment of Tana-naw Station in that he did nothing. Twenty-four hours later Porportuk returned. He was tired and savage. He spoke to no one but Akoon, and with him tried to pick a quarrel. But Akoon shrugged his shoulders and walked away. Porportuk did not waste time. He outfitted half a dozen of the young men, selecting the best trackers and travellers, and at their head plunged into the forest.

Next day the steamer *Seattle*, bound up river, pulled in to the shore and wooded up. When the lines were cast off and she churned out from the bank, Akoon was on board in the pilot-house. Not many hours afterward, when it was his turn at the wheel, he saw a small birch-bark canoe put off from the shore. There was only one person in it. He studied it carefully, put the wheel over, and slowed down.

The captain entered the pilot-house. "What's the matter?" he demanded. "The water's good."

Akoon grunted. He saw a larger canoe leaving the bank, and in it were a number of persons. As the *Seattle* lost headway, he put the wheel over some more.

The captain fumed. "It's only a squaw," he protested.

Akoon did not grunt. He was all eyes for the squaw and the pursuing canoe. In the latter six paddles were flashing, while the squaw paddled slowly.

"You'll be aground," the captain protested, seizing the wheel.

But Akoon countered his strength on the wheel and looked him in the eyes. The captain slowly released the spokes.

"Queer beggar," he sniffed to himself.

Akoon held the *Seattle* on the edge of the shoal water and waited till he saw the squaw's fingers clutch the forward rail. Then he signalled for full speed ahead and ground the wheel over. The large canoe was very near, but the gap between it and the steamer was widening.

The squaw laughed and leaned over the rail.

"Then catch me, Porportuk!" she cried.

Akoon left the steamer at Fort Yukon. He outfitted a small poling-boat and went up the Porcupine River. And with him went El-Soo. It was a weary journey, and the way led across the backbone of the world; but Akoon had travelled it before. When they came to the head-waters of the Porcupine, they left the boat and went on foot across the Rocky Mountains.

Akoon greatly liked to walk behind El-Soo and watch the movements of her. There was a music in it that he loved. And especially he loved the well-rounded calves in their sheaths of soft-tanned leather, the slim ankles, and the small moccasined feet that were tireless through the longest days.

"You are light as air," he said, looking up at her. "It is no labour for you to walk. You almost float, so lightly do your feet rise and fall. You are like a deer, El-Soo; you are like a deer, and your eyes are like deer's eyes, sometimes when you look at me, or when you hear a quick sound and wonder if it be danger that stirs. Your eyes are like a deer's eyes now as you look at me."

And El-Soo, luminous and melting, bent and kissed Akoon.

"When we reach the Mackenzie, we will not delay," Akoon said later. "We will go south before the winter catches us. We will go to the sunlands where there is no snow. But we will return. I have seen much of the world, and there is no land like Alaska, no sun like our sun, and the snow is good after the long summer."

"And you will learn to read," said El-Soo.

And Akoon said, "I will surely learn to read." But there was delay when they reached the Mackenzie. They fell in with a band of Mackenzie Indians, and, hunting, Akoon was shot by accident. The rifle was in the hands of a youth. The bullet broke Akoon's right arm and, ranging farther, broke two of his ribs. Akoon knew rough surgery, while El-Soo had learned some refinements at Holy Cross. The bones were finally set, and Akoon lay by the fire for them to knit. Also, he lay by the fire so that the smoke would keep the mosquitoes away.

Then it was that Porportuk, with his six young men, arrived. Akoon groaned in his helplessness and made appeal to the Mackenzies. But Porportuk made demand, and the Mackenzies were perplexed. Porportuk was for seizing upon El-Soo, but this they would not permit. Judgment must be given, and, as it was an affair of man and woman, the council of the old men was called—this that warm judgment might not be given by the young men, who were warm of heart.

The old men sat in a circle about the smudge-fire. Their faces were lean and wrinkled, and they gasped and panted for air. The smoke was not good for them. Occasionally they struck with withered hands at the mosquitoes that braved the smoke. After such exertion they coughed hollowly and painfully. Some spat blood, and one of them sat a bit apart with head bowed forward, and bled slowly and continuously at the mouth; the coughing sickness had gripped them. They were as dead men; their time was short. It was a judgment of the dead.

"And I paid for her a heavy price," Porportuk concluded his complaint. "Such a price you have never seen. Sell all that is yours—sell your spears and arrows and rifles, sell your skins and furs, sell your tents and boats and dogs, sell everything, and you will not have maybe a thousand dollars. Yet did I pay for the woman, El-Soo, twenty-six times the price of all your spears and arrows and rifles, your skins and furs, your tents and boats and dogs. It was a heavy price."

The old men nodded gravely, though their weazened eye-slits widened with wonder that any woman should be worth such a price. The one that bled at the mouth wiped his lips. "Is it true talk?" he asked each of Porportuk's six young men. And each answered that it was true.

"Is it true talk?" he asked El-Soo, and she answered, "It is true."

"But Porportuk has not told that he is an old man," Akoon said, "and that he has daughters older than El-Soo."

"It is true, Porportuk is an old man," said El-Soo.

"It is for Porportuk to measure the strength his age," said he who bled at the mouth. "We be old men. Behold! Age is never so old as youth would measure it."

And the circle of old men champed their gums, and nodded approvingly, and coughed.

"I told him that I would never be his wife," said El-Soo.

"Yet you took from him twenty-six times all that we possess?" asked a one-eyed old man.

El-Soo was silent.

"It is true?" And his one eye burned and bored into her like a fiery gimlet.

"It is true," she said.

"But I will run away again," she broke out passionately, a moment later. "Always will I run away."

"That is for Porportuk to consider," said another of the old men. "It is for us to consider the judgment."

"What price did you pay for her?" was demanded of Akoon.

"No price did I pay for her," he answered. "She was above price. I did not measure her in gold-dust, nor in dogs, and tents, and furs."

The old men debated among themselves and mumbled in undertones. "These old men are ice," Akoon said in English. "I will not listen to their judgment, Porportuk. If you take El-Soo, I will surely kill you."

The old men ceased and regarded him suspiciously. "We do not know the speech you make," one said.

"He but said that he would kill me," Porportuk volunteered. "So it were well to take from him his rifle, and to have some of your young men sit by him, that he may not do me hurt. He is a young man, and what are broken bones to youth!"

Akoon, lying helpless, had rifle and knife taken from him, and to either side of his shoulders sat young men of the Mackenzies. The one-eyed old man arose and stood upright. "We marvel at the price paid for one mere woman," he began; "but the wisdom of the price is no concern of ours. We are here to give judgment, and judgment we give. We have no doubt. It is known to all that Porportuk paid a heavy price for the woman El-Soo. Wherefore does the woman El-Soo belong to Porportuk and none other." He sat down heavily, and coughed. The old men nodded and coughed.

"I will kill you," Akoon cried in English.

Porportuk smiled and stood up. "You have given true judgment," he said to the council, "and my young men will give to you much tobacco. Now let the woman be brought to me."

Akoon gritted his teeth. The young men took El-Soo by the arms. She did not resist, and was led, her face a sullen flame, to Porportuk.

"Sit there at my feet till I have made my talk," he commanded. He paused a moment. "It is true," he said, "I am an old man. Yet can I understand the ways of youth. The fire has not all gone out of me. Yet am I no longer young, nor am I minded to run these old legs of mine through all the years that remain to me. El-Soo can run fast and well. She is a deer. This I know, for I have seen and run after her. It is not good that a wife should run so fast. I paid for her a heavy price, yet does she run away from me. Akoon paid no price at all, yet does she run to him.

"When I came among you people of the Mackenzie, I was of one mind. As I listened in the council and thought of the swift legs of El-Soo, I was of many minds. Now am I of one mind again but it is a different mind from the one I brought to the council. Let me tell you my mind. When a dog runs once away from a master, it will run away again. No matter how many times it is brought back, each time it will run away again. When we have such dogs, we sell them. El-Soo is like a dog that runs away. I will sell her. Is there any man of the council that will buy?"

The old men coughed and remained silent

"Akoon would buy," Porportuk went on, "but he has no money. Wherefore I will give El-Soo to him, as he said, without price. Even now will I give her to him."

Reaching down, he took El-Soo by the hand and led her across the space to where Akoon lay on his back.

"She has a bad habit, Akoon," he said, seating her at Akoon's feet. "As she has run away from me in the past, in the days to come she may run away from you. But there is no need to fear that she will ever run away, Akoon. I shall see to that. Never will she run away from you—this is the word of Porportuk. She has great wit. I know, for often has it bitten into me. Yet am I minded myself to give my wit play for once. And by my wit will I secure her to you, Akoon."

Stooping, Porportuk crossed El-Soo's feet, so that the instep of one lay over that of the other; and then, before his purpose could be divined, he discharged his rifle through the two ankles. As Akoon struggled to rise against the weight of the young men, there was heard the crunch of the broken bone rebroken.

"It is just," said the old men, one to another.

El-Soo made no sound. She sat and looked at her shattered ankles, on which she would never walk again.

"My legs are strong, El-Soo," Akoon said. "But never will they bear me away from you."

El-Soo looked at him, and for the first time in all the time he had known her, Akoon saw tears in her eyes.

"Your eyes are like deer's eyes, El-Soo," he said.

"Is it just?" Porportuk asked, and grinned from the edge of the smoke as he prepared to depart.

"It is just," the old men said. And they sat on in the silence.

About Author

John Griffith London (born **John Griffith Chaney**; January 12, 1876 – November 22, 1916) was an American novelist, journalist, and social activist. A pioneer in the world of commercial magazine fiction, he was one of the first writers to become a worldwide celebrity and earn a large fortune from writing. He was also an innovator in the genre that would later become known as science fiction.

His most famous works include The Call of the Wild and White Fang, both set in the Klondike Gold Rush, as well as the short stories "To Build a Fire", "An Odyssey of the North", and "Love of Life". He also wrote about the South Pacific in stories such as "The Pearls of Parlay", and "The Heathen".

London was part of the radical literary group "The Crowd" in San Francisco and a passionate advocate of unionization, workers' rights, socialism, and eugenics. He wrote several works dealing with these topics, such as his dystopian novel The Iron Heel, his non-fiction exposé The People of the Abyss, The War of the Classes, and Before Adam.

Family

Jack London's mother, Flora Wellman, was the fifth and youngest child of Pennsylvania Canal builder Marshall Wellman and his first wife, Eleanor Garrett Jones. Marshall Wellman was descended from Thomas Wellman, an early Puritan settler in the Massachusetts Bay Colony. Flora left Ohio and moved to the Pacific coast when her father remarried after her mother died. In San Francisco, Flora worked as a music teacher and spiritualist, claiming to channel the spirit of a Sauk chief, Black Hawk.

Biographer Clarice Stasz and others believe London's father was astrologer William Chaney. Flora Wellman was living with Chaney in San Francisco when she became pregnant. Whether Wellman and Chaney were legally married is unknown. Stasz notes that in his memoirs, Chaney refers to London's mother Flora Wellman as having been his "wife"; he also cites an advertisement in which Flora called herself "Florence Wellman Chaney".

According to Flora Wellman's account, as recorded in the San Francisco Chronicle of June 4, 1875, Chaney demanded that she have an abortion. When she refused, he disclaimed responsibility for the child. In desperation, she shot herself. She was not seriously wounded, but she was temporarily deranged. After giving birth, Flora turned the baby over for care to Virginia Prentiss, an African-American woman and former slave. She was a major maternal figure throughout London's life. Late in 1876, Flora Wellman married John London, a partially disabled Civil War veteran, and brought her baby John, later known as Jack, to live with the newly married couple. The family moved around the San Francisco Bay Area before settling in Oakland, where London completed public grade school.

In 1897, when he was 21 and a student at the University of California, Berkeley, London searched for and read the newspaper accounts of his mother's suicide attempt and the name of his biological father. He wrote to William Chaney, then living in Chicago. Chaney responded that he could not be London's father because he was impotent; he casually asserted that London's mother had relations with other men and averred that she had slandered him when she said he insisted on an abortion. Chaney concluded by saying that he was more to be pitied than London. London was devastated by his father's letter; in the months following, he quit school at Berkeley and went to the Klondike during the gold rush boom.

Early life

London was born near Third and Brannan Streets in San Francisco. The house burned down in the fire after the 1906 San Francisco earthquake; the California Historical Society placed a plaque at the site in 1953. Although the family was working class, it was not as impoverished as London's later accounts claimed. London was largely self-educated.

In 1885, London found and read Ouida's long Victorian novel Signa. He credited this as the seed of his literary success. In 1886, he went to the Oakland Public Library and found a sympathetic librarian, Ina Coolbrith, who encouraged his learning. (She later became California's first poet laureate and an important figure in the San Francisco literary community).

In 1889, London began working 12 to 18 hours a day at Hickmott's Cannery. Seeking a way out, he borrowed money from his foster mother Virginia Prentiss, bought the sloop Razzle-Dazzle from an oyster pirate named French Frank, and became an oyster pirate himself. In his memoir, John Barleycorn, he claims also to have stolen French Frank's mistress Mamie. After a few months, his sloop became damaged beyond repair. London hired on as a member of the California Fish Patrol.

In 1893, he signed on to the sealing schooner Sophie Sutherland, bound for the coast of Japan. When he returned, the country was in the grip of the panic of '93 and Oakland was swept by labor unrest. After grueling jobs in a jute mill and a street-railway power plant, London joined Coxey's Army and began his career as a tramp. In 1894, he spent 30 days for vagrancy in the Erie County Penitentiary at Buffalo, New York. In The Road, he wrote:

> Man-handling was merely one of the very minor unprintable horrors of the Erie County Pen. I say 'unprintable'; and in justice I must also say undescribable. They were unthinkable to me until I saw them, and I was no spring chicken in the ways of the world and the awful abysses of human degradation. It would take a deep plummet to reach bottom in the Erie County Pen, and I do but skim lightly and facetiously the surface of things as I there saw them.

> —Jack London, The Road

After many experiences as a hobo and a sailor, he returned to Oakland and attended Oakland High School. He contributed a number of articles to the high school's magazine, The Aegis. His first published work was "Typhoon off the Coast of Japan", an account of his sailing experiences.

As a schoolboy, London often studied at Heinold's First and Last Chance Saloon, a port-side bar in Oakland. At 17, he confessed to the bar's owner, John Heinold, his desire to attend university and pursue a career as a writer. Heinold lent London tuition money to attend college.

London desperately wanted to attend the University of California, located in Berkeley. In 1896, after a summer of intense studying to pass certification exams, he was admitted. Financial circumstances forced him to leave in 1897 and he never graduated. No evidence has surfaced that he ever wrote for student publications while studying at Berkeley.

While at Berkeley, London continued to study and spend time at Heinold's saloon, where he was introduced to the sailors and adventurers who would influence his writing. In his autobiographical novel, John Barleycorn, London mentioned the pub's likeness seventeen times. Heinold's was the place where London met Alexander McLean, a captain known for his cruelty at sea. London based his protagonist Wolf Larsen, in the novel The Sea-Wolf, on McLean.

Heinold's First and Last Chance Saloon is now unofficially named Jack London's Rendezvous in his honor.

Gold rush and first success

On July 12, 1897, London (age 21) and his sister's husband Captain Shepard sailed to join the Klondike Gold Rush. This was the setting for some of his first successful stories. London's time in the harsh Klondike, however, was detrimental to his health. Like so many other men who were malnourished in the goldfields, London developed scurvy. His gums became swollen, leading to the loss of his four front teeth. A constant gnawing pain affected his hip and leg muscles, and his face was stricken with marks that always reminded him of the struggles he faced in the Klondike. Father William Judge, "The Saint of Dawson", had a facility in Dawson that provided shelter, food and any available medicine to London and others. His struggles there inspired London's short story, "To Build a Fire" (1902, revised in 1908), which many critics assess as his best.

His landlords in Dawson were mining engineers Marshall Latham Bond and Louis Whitford Bond, educated at Yale and Stanford, respectively. The brothers' father, Judge Hiram Bond, was a wealthy mining investor. The Bonds, especially Hiram, were active Republicans. Marshall Bond's diary mentions friendly sparring with London on political issues as a camp pastime.

London left Oakland with a social conscience and socialist leanings; he returned to become an activist for socialism. He concluded that his only hope of escaping the work "trap" was to get an education and "sell his brains". He saw his writing as a business, his ticket out of poverty, and, he hoped, a means of beating the wealthy at their own game. On returning to California in 1898, London began working to get published, a struggle described in his novel, Martin Eden (serialized in 1908, published in 1909). His first published story since high school was "To the Man On Trail", which has frequently been collected in anthologies. When The Overland Monthly offered him only five dollars for it—and was slow paying—London came close to abandoning his writing career. In his words, "literally and literarily I was saved" when The Black Cat accepted his story "A Thousand Deaths", and paid him $40—the "first money I ever received for a story".

London began his writing career just as new printing technologies enabled lower-cost production of magazines. This resulted in a boom in popular magazines aimed at a wide public audience and a strong market for short fiction. In 1900, he made $2,500 in writing, about $77,000 in today's currency. Among the works he sold to magazines was a short story known as either "Diable" (1902) or "Bâtard" (1904), two editions of the same basic story; London received $141.25 for this story on May 27, 1902. In the text, a cruel French Canadian brutalizes his dog, and the dog retaliates and kills the man. London told some of his critics that man's actions are the main cause of the behavior of their animals, and he would show this in another story, The Call of the Wild.

In early 1903, London sold The Call of the Wild to The Saturday Evening Post for $750, and the book rights to Macmillan for $2,000. Macmillan's promotional campaign propelled it to swift success.

While living at his rented villa on Lake Merritt in Oakland, California, London met poet George Sterling; in time they became best friends. In 1902, Sterling helped London find a home closer to his own in nearby Piedmont. In his letters London addressed Sterling as "Greek", owing to Sterling's aquiline nose and classical profile, and he signed them as "Wolf". London was later to depict Sterling as Russ Brissenden in his autobiographical novel Martin Eden (1910) and as Mark Hall in The Valley of the Moon (1913).

In later life London indulged his wide-ranging interests by accumulating a personal library of 15,000 volumes. He referred to his books as "the tools of my trade".

First marriage (1900–04)

London married Elizabeth "Bessie" Maddern on April 7, 1900, the same day The Son of the Wolf was published. Bess had been part of his circle of friends for a number of years. She was related to stage actresses Minnie Maddern Fiske and Emily Stevens. Stasz says, "Both acknowledged publicly that they were not marrying out of love, but from friendship and a belief that they would produce sturdy children." Kingman says, "they were comfortable together... Jack had made it clear to Bessie that he did not love her, but that he liked her enough to make a successful marriage."

London met Bessie through his friend at Oakland High School, Fred Jacobs; she was Fred's fiancée. Bessie, who tutored at Anderson's University Academy in Alameda California, tutored Jack in preparation for his entrance exams for the University of California at Berkeley in 1896. Jacobs was killed aboard the USAT Scandia in 1897, but Jack and Bessie continued their friendship, which included taking photos and developing the film together. This was the beginning of Jack's passion for photography.

During the marriage, London continued his friendship with Anna Strunsky, co-authoring The Kempton-Wace Letters, an epistolary novel contrasting two philosophies of love. Anna, writing "Dane Kempton's" letters, arguing for a romantic view of marriage, while London, writing "Herbert Wace's" letters, argued for a scientific view, based on Darwinism and eugenics. In the novel, his fictional character contrasted two women he had known.

London's pet name for Bess was "Mother-Girl" and Bess's for London was "Daddy-Boy". Their first child, Joan, was born on January 15, 1901, and their second, Bessie (later called Becky), on October 20, 1902. Both children were born in Piedmont, California. Here London wrote one of his most celebrated works, The Call of the Wild.

While London had pride in his children, the marriage was strained. Kingman says that by 1903 the couple were close to separation as they were "extremely incompatible". "Jack was still so kind and gentle with Bessie that when Cloudsley Johns was a house guest in February 1903 he didn't suspect a breakup of their marriage."

London reportedly complained to friends Joseph Noel and George Sterling:

> [Bessie] is devoted to purity. When I tell her morality is only evidence of low blood pressure, she hates me. She'd sell me and the children out for her damned purity. It's terrible. Every time I come back after being away from home for a night she won't let me be in the same room with her if she can help it.

Stasz writes that these were "code words for fear that was consorting with prostitutes and might bring home venereal disease."

On July 24, 1903, London told Bessie he was leaving and moved out. During 1904, London and Bess negotiated the terms of a divorce, and the decree was granted on November 11, 1904.

War correspondent (1904)

London accepted an assignment of the San Francisco Examiner to cover the Russo-Japanese War in early 1904, arriving in Yokohama on January 25, 1904. He was arrested by Japanese authorities in Shimonoseki, but released through the intervention of American ambassador Lloyd Griscom. After travelling to Korea, he was again arrested by Japanese authorities for straying too close to the border with Manchuria without official permission, and was sent back to Seoul. Released again, London was permitted to travel with the Imperial Japanese Army to the border, and to observe the Battle of the Yalu.

London asked William Randolph Hearst, the owner of the San Francisco Examiner, to be allowed to transfer to the Imperial Russian Army, where he felt that restrictions on his reporting and his movements would be less severe. However, before this could be arranged, he was arrested for a third time in four months, this time for assaulting his Japanese assistants, whom he accused of stealing the fodder for his horse. Released through the personal intervention of President Theodore Roosevelt, London departed the front in June 1904.

Bohemian Club

On August 18, 1904, London went with his close friend, the poet George Sterling, to "Summer High Jinks" at the Bohemian Grove. London was elected to honorary membership in the Bohemian Club and took part in many activities. Other noted members of the Bohemian Club during this time included Ambrose Bierce, Gelett Burgess, Allan Dunn, John Muir, Frank Norris, and Herman George Scheffauer.

Beginning in December 1914, London worked on The Acorn Planter, A California Forest Play, to be performed as one of the annual Grove Plays, but it was never selected. It was described as too difficult to set to music. London published The Acorn Planter in 1916.

Second marriage

After divorcing Maddern, London married Charmian Kittredge in 1905. London had been introduced to Kittredge in 1900 by her aunt Netta Eames, who was an editor at Overland Monthly magazine in San Francisco. The two met prior to his first marriage but became lovers years later after Jack and Bessie London visited Wake Robin, Netta Eames' Sonoma County resort, in 1903. London was injured when he fell from a buggy, and Netta arranged for Charmian to care for him. The two developed a friendship, as Charmian, Netta, her husband Roscoe, and London were politically aligned with socialist causes. At some point the relationship became romantic, and Jack divorced his wife to marry Charmian, who was five years his senior.

Biographer Russ Kingman called Charmian "Jack's soul-mate, always at his side, and a perfect match." Their time together included numerous trips, including a 1907 cruise on the yacht Snark to Hawaii and Australia. Many of London's stories are based on his visits to Hawaii, the last one for 10 months beginning in December 1915.

The couple also visited Goldfield, Nevada, in 1907, where they were guests of the Bond brothers, London's Dawson City landlords. The Bond brothers were working in Nevada as mining engineers.

London had contrasted the concepts of the "Mother Girl" and the "Mate Woman" in The Kempton-Wace Letters. His pet name for Bess had been "Mother-Girl;" his pet name for Charmian was "Mate-Woman."Charmian's aunt and foster mother, a disciple of Victoria Woodhull, had raised her without prudishness.Every biographer alludes to Charmian's uninhibited sexuality.

Joseph Noel calls the events from 1903 to 1905 "a domestic drama that would have intrigued the pen of an Ibsen.... London's had comedy relief in it and a sort of easy-going romance." In broad outline, London was restless in his first marriage, sought extramarital sexual affairs, and found, in Charmian Kittredge, not only a sexually active and adventurous partner, but his future life-companion. They attempted to have children; one child died at birth, and another pregnancy ended in a miscarriage.

In 1906, London published in Collier's magazine his eye-witness report of the San Francisco earthquake.

Beauty Ranch (1905–16)

In 1905, London purchased a 1,000 acres (4.0 km2) ranch in Glen Ellen, Sonoma County, California, on the eastern slope of Sonoma Mountain.He wrote: "Next to my wife, the ranch is the dearest thing in the world to me." He desperately wanted the ranch to become a successful business enterprise. Writing, always a commercial enterprise with London, now became even more a means to an end: "I write for no other purpose than to add to the beauty that now belongs to me. I write a book for no other reason than to add three or four hundred acres to my magnificent estate."

Stasz writes that London "had taken fully to heart the vision, expressed in his agrarian fiction, of the land as the closest earthly version of Eden ... he educated himself through the study of agricultural manuals and scientific tomes. He conceived of a system of ranching that today would be praised for its ecological wisdom." He was proud to own the first concrete silo in California, a circular piggery that he designed. He hoped to adapt the wisdom of Asian sustainable agriculture to the United States. He hired both Italian and Chinese stonemasons, whose distinctly different styles are obvious.

The ranch was an economic failure. Sympathetic observers such as Stasz treat his projects as potentially feasible, and ascribe their failure to bad luck or to being ahead of their time. Unsympathetic historians such as Kevin Starr suggest that he was a bad manager, distracted by other concerns and impaired by his alcoholism. Starr notes that London was absent from his ranch about six months a year between 1910 and 1916 and says, "He liked the show of managerial power, but not grinding attention to detail .... London's workers laughed at his efforts to play big-time rancher the operation a rich man's hobby."

London spent $80,000 ($2,280,000 in current value) to build a 15,000-square-foot (1,400 m2) stone mansion called Wolf House on the property. Just as the mansion was nearing completion, two weeks before the Londons planned to move in, it was destroyed by fire.

London's last visit to Hawaii, beginning in December 1915, lasted eight months. He met with Duke Kahanamoku, Prince Jonah Kūhiō Kalaniana'ole, Queen Lili'uokalani and many others, before returning to his ranch in July 1916. He was suffering from kidney failure, but he continued to work.

The ranch (abutting stone remnants of Wolf House) is now a National Historic Landmark and is protected in Jack London State Historic Park.

Animal activism

London witnessed animal cruelty in the training of circus animals, and his subsequent novels Jerry of the Islands and Michael, Brother of Jerry included a foreword entreating the public to become more informed about this practice. In 1918, the Massachusetts Society for the Prevention of Cruelty to Animals and the American Humane Education Society teamed up to create the Jack London Club, which sought to inform the public about cruelty to circus animals and encourage them to protest this establishment. Support from Club members led to a temporary cessation of trained animal acts at Ringling-Barnum and Bailey in 1925.

Death

London died November 22, 1916, in a sleeping porch in a cottage on his ranch. London had been a robust man but had suffered several serious illnesses, including scurvy in the Klondike. Additionally, during travels on the Snark, he and Charmian picked up unspecified tropical infections, and diseases, including yaws. At the time of his death, he suffered from dysentery, late-stage alcoholism, and uremia; he was in extreme pain and taking morphine.

London's ashes were buried on his property not far from the Wolf House. London's funeral took place on November 26, 1916, attended only by close friends, relatives, and workers of the property. In accordance with his wishes, he was cremated and buried next to some pioneer children, under a rock that belonged to the Wolf House. After Charmian's death in 1955, she was also cremated and then buried with her husband in the same spot that her husband chose. The grave is marked by a mossy boulder. The buildings and property were later preserved as Jack London State Historic Park, in Glen Ellen, California.

Suicide debate

Because he was using morphine, many older sources describe London's death as a suicide, and some still do. This conjecture appears to be a rumor, or speculation based on incidents in his fiction writings. His death certificate gives the cause as uremia, following acute renal colic.

The biographer Stasz writes, "Following London's death, for a number of reasons, a biographical myth developed in which he has been portrayed as an alcoholic womanizer who committed suicide. Recent scholarship based upon firsthand documents challenges this caricature." Most biographers, including Russ Kingman, now agree he died of uremia aggravated by an accidental morphine overdose.

London's fiction featured several suicides. In his autobiographical memoir John Barleycorn, he claims, as a youth, to have drunkenly stumbled overboard into the San Francisco Bay, "some maundering fancy of going out with the tide suddenly obsessed me". He said he drifted and nearly succeeded in drowning before sobering up and being rescued by fishermen. In the dénouement of The Little Lady of the Big House, the heroine, confronted by the pain of a mortal gunshot wound, undergoes a physician-assisted suicide by morphine. Also, in Martin Eden, the principal protagonist, who shares certain characteristics with London, drowns himself.

Plagiarism accusations

London was vulnerable to accusations of plagiarism, both because he was such a conspicuous, prolific, and successful writer and because of his methods of working. He wrote in a letter to Elwyn Hoffman, "expression, you see—with me—is far easier than invention." He purchased plots and novels from the young Sinclair Lewis and used incidents from newspaper clippings as writing material.

In July 1901, two pieces of fiction appeared within the same month: London's "Moon-Face", in the San Francisco Argonaut, and Frank Norris' "The Passing of Cock-eye Blacklock", in Century Magazine. Newspapers showed the similarities between the stories, which London said were "quite different in manner of treatment, patently the same in foundation and motive." London explained both writers based their stories on the same newspaper account. A year later, it was discovered that Charles Forrest McLean had published a fictional story also based on the same incident.

Egerton Ryerson Young claimed The Call of the Wild (1903) was taken from Young's book My Dogs in the Northland (1902). London acknowledged using it as a source and claimed to have written a letter to Young thanking him.

In 1906, the New York World published "deadly parallel" columns showing eighteen passages from London's short story "Love of Life" side by side with similar passages from a nonfiction article by Augustus Biddle and J. K. Macdonald, titled "Lost in the Land of the Midnight Sun". London noted the World did not accuse him of "plagiarism", but only of "identity of time and situation", to which he defiantly "pled guilty".

The most serious charge of plagiarism was based on London's "The Bishop's Vision", Chapter 7 of his novel The Iron Heel (1908). The chapter is nearly identical to an ironic essay that Frank Harris published in 1901, titled "The Bishop of London and Public Morality". Harris was incensed and suggested he should receive 1/60th of the royalties from The Iron Heel, the disputed material constituting about that fraction of the whole novel. London insisted he had clipped a reprint of the article, which had appeared in an American newspaper, and believed it to be a genuine speech delivered by the Bishop of London.

Views

Atheism

London was an atheist. He is quoted as saying, "I believe that when I am dead, I am dead. I believe that with my death I am just as much obliterated as the last mosquito you and I squashed."

Socialism

London wrote from a socialist viewpoint, which is evident in his novel The Iron Heel. Neither a theorist nor an intellectual socialist, London's socialism grew out of his life experience. As London explained in his essay, "How I Became a Socialist", his views were influenced by his experience with people at the bottom of the social pit. His optimism and individualism faded, and he vowed never to do more hard physical work than necessary. He wrote that his individualism was hammered out of him, and he was politically reborn. He often closed his letters "Yours for the Revolution."

London joined the Socialist Labor Party in April 1896. In the same year, the San Francisco Chronicle published a story about the twenty-year-old London's giving nightly speeches in Oakland's City Hall Park, an activity he was arrested for a year later. In 1901, he left the Socialist Labor Party and joined the new Socialist Party of America. He ran unsuccessfully as the high-profile Socialist candidate for mayor of Oakland in 1901 (receiving 245 votes) and 1905 (improving to 981 votes), toured the country lecturing on socialism in 1906, and published two collections of essays about socialism: The War of the Classes (1905) and Revolution, and other Essays (1906).

Stasz notes that "London regarded the Wobblies as a welcome addition to the Socialist cause, although he never joined them in going so far as to recommend sabotage." Stasz mentions a personal meeting between London and Big Bill Haywood in 1912.

In his late (1913) book The Cruise of the Snark, London writes about appeals to him for membership of the Snark's crew from office workers and other "toilers" who longed for escape from the cities, and of being cheated by workmen.

In his Glen Ellen ranch years, London felt some ambivalence toward socialism and complained about the "inefficient Italian labourers" in his employ. In 1916, he resigned from the Glen Ellen chapter of the Socialist Party, but stated emphatically he did so "because of its lack of fire and fight, and its loss of emphasis on the class struggle." In an unflattering portrait of London's ranch days, California cultural historian Kevin Starr refers to this period as "post-socialist" and says "... by 1911 ... London was more bored by the class struggle than he cared to admit."

Race

London shared common concerns among many European Americans in California about Asian immigration, described as "the yellow peril"; he used the latter term as the title of a 1904 essay. This theme was also the subject of a story he wrote in 1910 called "The Unparalleled Invasion". Presented as an historical essay set in the future, the story narrates events between 1976 and 1987, in which China, with an ever-increasing population, is taking over and colonizing its neighbors with the intention of taking over the entire Earth. The western nations respond with biological warfare and bombard China with dozens of the most infectious diseases. On his fears about China, he admits, "it must be taken into consideration that the above postulate is itself a product of Western race-egotism, urged by our belief in our own righteousness and fostered by a faith in ourselves which may be as erroneous as are most fond race fancies."

268

By contrast, many of London's short stories are notable for their empathetic portrayal of Mexican ("The Mexican"), Asian ("The Chinago"), and Hawaiian ("Koolau the Leper") characters. London's war correspondence from the Russo-Japanese War, as well as his unfinished novel Cherry, show he admired much about Japanese customs and capabilities. London's writings have been popular among the Japanese, who believe he portrayed them positively.

In "Koolau the Leper", London describes Koolau, who is a Hawaiian leper—and thus a very different sort of "superman" than Martin Eden—and who fights off an entire cavalry troop to elude capture, as "indomitable spiritually—a ... magnificent rebel". This character is based on Hawaiian leper Kaluaikoolau, who in 1893 revolted and resisted capture from forces of the Provisional Government of Hawaii in the Kalalau Valley.

An amateur boxer and avid boxing fan, London reported on the 1910 Johnson–Jeffries fight, in which the black boxer Jack Johnson vanquished Jim Jeffries, known as the "Great White Hope". In 1908, London had reported on an earlier fight of Johnson's, contrasting the black boxer's coolness and intellectual style, with the apelike appearance and fighting style of his Canadian opponent, Tommy Burns:

> [What won] on Saturday was bigness, coolness, quickness, cleverness, and vast physical superiority ... Because a white man wishes a white man to win, this should not prevent him from giving absolute credit to the best man, even when that best man was black. All hail to Johnson. ... superb. He was impregnable ... as inaccessible as Mont Blanc.

Those who defend London against charges of racism cite the letter he wrote to the Japanese-American Commercial Weekly in 1913:

> In reply to yours of August 16, 1913. First of all, I should say by stopping the stupid newspaper from always fomenting race prejudice. This of course, being impossible, I would say, next, by educating the people of Japan so that they will be too intelligently tolerant to respond to any call to race prejudice. And, finally, by realizing, in industry and

government, of socialism—which last word is merely a word that stands for the actual application of in the affairs of men of the theory of the Brotherhood of Man.

In the meantime the nations and races are only unruly boys who have not yet grown to the stature of men. So we must expect them to do unruly and boisterous things at times. And, just as boys grow up, so the races of mankind will grow up and laugh when they look back upon their childish quarrels.

In 1996, after the City of Whitehorse, Yukon, renamed a street in honor of London, protests over London's alleged racism forced the city to change the name of "Jack London Boulevard"[failed verification] back to "Two-mile Hill".

Eugenics

London supported eugenics, including forced sterilization of criminals or those deemed feeble minded. His novel Before Adam(1906–07) has been described as having pro-eugenic themes.

London wrote to Frederick H. Robinson of the periodical Medical Review of Reviews, stating, "I believe the future belongs to eugenics, and will be determined by the practice of eugenics."

Works

Short stories

Western writer and historian Dale L. Walker writes:

London's true métier was the short story ... London's true genius lay in the short form, 7,500 words and under, where the flood of images in his teeming brain and the innate power of his narrative gift were at once constrained and freed. His stories that run longer than the magic 7,500 generally—but certainly not always—could have benefited from self-editing.

London's "strength of utterance" is at its height in his stories, and they are painstakingly well-constructed. "To Build a Fire" is the best known of all his stories. Set in the harsh Klondike, it recounts the haphazard trek of a new arrival who has ignored an old-timer's warning about the risks of traveling alone. Falling through the ice into a creek in seventy-five-below weather, the unnamed man is keenly aware that survival depends on his untested skills at quickly building a fire to dry his clothes and warm his extremities. After publishing a tame version of this story—with a sunny outcome—in The Youth's Companion in 1902, London offered a second, more severe take on the man's predicament in The Century Magazine in 1908. Reading both provides an illustration of London's growth and maturation as a writer. As Labor (1994) observes: "To compare the two versions is itself an instructive lesson in what distinguished a great work of literary art from a good children's story."

Other stories from the Klondike period include: "All Gold Canyon", about a battle between a gold prospector and a claim jumper; "The Law of Life", about an aging American Indian man abandoned by his tribe and left to die; "Love of Life", about a trek by a prospector across the Canadian tundra; "To the Man on Trail," which tells the story of a prospector fleeing the Mounted Police in a sled race, and raises the question of the contrast between written law and morality; and "An Odyssey of the North," which raises questions of conditional morality, and paints a sympathetic portrait of a man of mixed White and Aleut ancestry.

London was a boxing fan and an avid amateur boxer. "A Piece of Steak" is a tale about a match between older and younger boxers. It contrasts the differing experiences of youth and age but also raises the social question of the treatment of aging workers. "The Mexican" combines boxing with a social theme, as a young Mexican endures an unfair fight and ethnic prejudice to earn money with which to aid the revolution.

Several of London's stories would today be classified as science fiction. "The Unparalleled Invasion" describes germ warfare against China; "Goliath" is about an irresistible energy weapon; "The Shadow and the Flash" is a tale about two brothers who take different routes to achieving invisibility; "A

Relic of the Pliocene" is a tall tale about an encounter of a modern-day man with a mammoth. "The Red One" is a late story from a period when London was intrigued by the theories of the psychiatrist and writer Jung. It tells of an island tribe held in thrall by an extraterrestrial object.

Some nineteen original collections of short stories were published during London's brief life or shortly after his death. There have been several posthumous anthologies drawn from this pool of stories. Many of these stories were located in the Klondike and the Pacific. A collection of Jack London's San Francisco Stories was published in October 2010 by Sydney Samizdat Press.

Novels

London's most famous novels are The Call of the Wild, White Fang, The Sea-Wolf, The Iron Heel, and Martin Eden.

In a letter dated December 27, 1901, London's Macmillan publisher George Platt Brett, Sr., said "he believed Jack's fiction represented 'the very best kind of work' done in America."

Critic Maxwell Geismar called The Call of the Wild "a beautiful prose poem"; editor Franklin Walker said that it "belongs on a shelf with Walden and Huckleberry Finn"; and novelist E.L. Doctorow called it "a mordant parable ... his masterpiece."

The historian Dale L. Walker commented:

Jack London was an uncomfortable novelist, that form too long for his natural impatience and the quickness of his mind. His novels, even the best of them, are hugely flawed.

Some critics have said that his novels are episodic and resemble linked short stories. Dale L. Walker writes:

The Star Rover, that magnificent experiment, is actually a series of short stories connected by a unifying device ... Smoke Bellew is a series of stories bound together in a novel-like form by their reappearing protagonist, Kit Bellew; and John Barleycorn ... is a synoptic series of short episodes.

Ambrose Bierce said of The Sea-Wolf that "the great thing—and it is among the greatest of things—is that tremendous creation, Wolf Larsen ... the hewing out and setting up of such a figure is enough for a man to do in one lifetime. "However, he noted, "The love element, with its absurd suppressions, and impossible proprieties, is awful."

The Iron Heel is an example of a dystopian novel that anticipates and influenced George Orwell's Nineteen Eighty-Four. London's socialist politics are explicitly on display here. The Iron Heel meets the contemporary definition of soft science fiction. The Star Rover (1915) is also science fiction.

Apocrypha

Jack London Credo

London's literary executor, Irving Shepard, quoted a Jack London Credo in an introduction to a 1956 collection of London stories:

I would rather be ashes than dust!

I would rather that my spark should burn out in a brilliant blaze than it should be stifled by dry-rot.

I would rather be a superb meteor, every atom of me in magnificent glow, than a sleepy and permanent planet.

The function of man is to live, not to exist.

I shall not waste my days in trying to prolong them.

I shall use my time.

The biographer Stasz notes that the passage "has many marks of London's style" but the only line that could be safely attributed to London was the first. The words Shepard quoted were from a story in the San Francisco Bulletin, December 2, 1916, by journalist Ernest J. Hopkins, who visited the ranch just weeks before London's death. Stasz notes, "Even more so than today journalists' quotes were unreliable or even sheer inventions," and says no

273

direct source in London's writings has been found. However, at least one line, according to Stasz, is authentic, being referenced by London and written in his own hand in the autograph book of Australian suffragette Vida Goldstein:

Dear Miss Goldstein:–

Seven years ago I wrote you that I'd rather be ashes than dust. I still subscribe to that sentiment.

Sincerely yours,

Jack London

Jan. 13, 1909

In his short story "By The Turtles of Tasman", a character, defending her "ne'er-do-well grasshopperish father" to her "antlike uncle", says: "... my father has been a king. He has lived .... Have you lived merely to live? Are you afraid to die? I'd rather sing one wild song and burst my heart with it, than live a thousand years watching my digestion and being afraid of the wet. When you are dust, my father will be ashes."

"The Scab"

A short diatribe on "The Scab" is often quoted within the U.S. labor movement and frequently attributed to London. It opens:

After God had finished the rattlesnake, the toad, and the vampire, he had some awful substance left with which he made a scab. A scab is a two-legged animal with a corkscrew soul, a water brain, a combination backbone of jelly and glue. Where others have hearts, he carries a tumor of rotten principles. When a scab comes down the street, men turn their backs and Angels weep in Heaven, and the Devil shuts the gates of hell to keep him out....

In 1913 and 1914, a number of newspapers printed the first three sentences with varying terms used instead of "scab", such as "knocker","stool pigeon"or "scandal monger"

274

This passage as given above was the subject of a 1974 Supreme Court case, Letter Carriers v. Austin, in which Justice Thurgood Marshall referred to it as "a well-known piece of trade union literature, generally attributed to author Jack London". A union newsletter had published a "list of scabs," which was granted to be factual and therefore not libelous, but then went on to quote the passage as the "definition of a scab". The case turned on the question of whether the "definition" was defamatory. The court ruled that "Jack London's... 'definition of a scab' is merely rhetorical hyperbole, a lusty and imaginative expression of the contempt felt by union members towards those who refuse to join", and as such was not libelous and was protected under the First Amendment.

Despite being frequently attributed to London, the passage does not appear at all in the extensive collection of his writings at Sonoma State University's website. However, in his book The War of the Classes he published a 1903 speech entitled "The Scab", which gave a much more balanced view of the topic:

> The laborer who gives more time or strength or skill for the same wage than another, or equal time or strength or skill for a less wage, is a scab. The generousness on his part is hurtful to his fellow-laborers, for it compels them to an equal generousness which is not to their liking, and which gives them less of food and shelter. But a word may be said for the scab. Just as his act makes his rivals compulsorily generous, so do they, by fortune of birth and training, make compulsory his act of generousness.

> [...]

> Nobody desires to scab, to give most for least. The ambition of every individual is quite the opposite, to give least for most; and, as a result, living in a tooth-and-nail society, battle royal is waged by the ambitious individuals. But in its most salient aspect, that of the struggle over the division of the joint product, it is no longer a battle between individuals, but between groups of individuals. Capital and labor apply

themselves to raw material, make something useful out of it, add to its value, and then proceed to quarrel over the division of the added value. Neither cares to give most for least. Each is intent on giving less than the other and on receiving more.

Legacy and honors

Mount London, also known as Boundary Peak 100, on the Alaska-British Columbia boundary, in the Boundary Ranges of the Coast Mountains of British Columbia, is named for him.

Jack London Square on the waterfront of Oakland, California was named for him.

He was honored by the United States Postal Service with a 25¢ Great Americans series postage stamp released on January 11, 1986.

Jack London Lake (Russian), a mountain lake located in the upper reaches of the Kolyma River in Yagodninsky district of Magadan Oblast.

Fictional portrayals of London include Michael O'Shea in the 1943 film Jack London, Jeff East in the 1980 film Klondike Fever, Aaron Ashmore in the Murdoch Mysteries episode "Murdoch of the Klondike" from 2012, and Johnny Simmons in the 2014 miniseries Klondike. (Source: Wikipedia)

NOTABLE WORKS

NOVELS

The Cruise of the Dazzler (1902)

A Daughter of the Snows (1902)

The Call of the Wild (1903)

The Kempton-Wace Letters (1903) (published anonymously, co-authored with Anna Strunsky)

The Sea-Wolf (1904)

The Game (1905)

White Fang (1906)

Before Adam (1907)

The Iron Heel (1908)

Martin Eden (1909)

Burning Daylight (1910)

Adventure (1911)

The Scarlet Plague (1912)

A Son of the Sun (1912)

The Abysmal Brute (1913)

The Valley of the Moon (1913)

The Mutiny of the Elsinore (1914)

The Star Rover (1915) (published in England as The Jacket)

The Little Lady of the Big House (1916)

Jerry of the Islands (1917)

Michael, Brother of Jerry (1917)

Hearts of Three (1920) (novelization of a script by Charles Goddard)

The Assassination Bureau, Ltd (1963) (left half-finished, completed by Robert L. Fish)

SHORT STORIES

"An Old Soldier's Story" (1894)

"Who Believes in Ghosts!" (1895)

"And 'FRISCO Kid Came Back" (1895)

"Night's Swim In Yeddo Bay" (1895)

"One More Unfortunate" (1895)

"Sakaicho, Hona Asi And Hakadaki" (1895)

"A Klondike Christmas" (1897)

"Mahatma's Little Joke" (1897)

"O Haru" (1897)

"Plague Ship" (1897)

"The Strange Experience Of A Misogynist" (1897)

"Two Gold Bricks" (1897)

"The Devil's Dice Box" (1898)

"A Dream Image" (1898)

"The Test: A Clondyke Wooing" (1898)

"To the Man on Trail" (1898)

"In a Far Country" (1899)

"The King of Mazy May" (1899)

"The End Of The Chapter" (1899)

"The Grilling Of Loren Ellery" (1899)

"The Handsome Cabin Boy" (1899)

"In The Time Of Prince Charley" (1899)

"Old Baldy" (1899)

"The Men of Forty Mile" (1899)

"Pluck and Pertinacity" (1899)

"The Rejuvenation of Major Rathbone" (1899)

"The White Silence" (1899)

"A Thousand Deaths" (1899)

"Wisdom of the Trail" (1899)

"An Odyssey of the North" (1900)

"The Son of the Wolf" (1900)

"Even unto Death" (1900)

"The Man with the Gash" (1900)

"A Lesson in Heraldry" (1900)

"A Northland Miracle" (1900)

"Proper "GIRLIE"" (1900)

"Thanksgiving on Slav Creek" (1900)

"Their Alcove" (1900)

"Housekeeping in the Klondike" (1900)

"Dutch Courage" (1900)

"Where the Trail Forks" (1900)

"Hyperborean Brew" (1901)

"A Relic of the Pliocene" (1901)

"The Lost Poacher" (1901)

"The God of His Fathers" (1901)

""FRISCO Kid's" Story" (1901)

"The Law of Life" (1901)

"The Minions of Midas" (1901)

"In the Forests of the North" (1902)

"The "Fuzziness" of Hoockla-Heen" (1902)

"The Story of Keesh" (1902)

"Keesh, Son of Keesh" (1902)

"Nam-Bok, the Unveracious" (1902)

"Li Wan the Fair" (1902)

"Lost Face"

"Master of Mystery" (1902)

"The Sunlanders" (1902)

"The Death of Ligoun" (1902)

"Moon-Face" (1902)

"Diable—A Dog" (1902), renamed Bâtard in 1904

"To Build a Fire" (1902, revised 1908)

"The League of the Old Men" (1902)

"The Dominant Primordial Beast" (1903)

"The One Thousand Dozen" (1903)

"The Marriage of Lit-lit" (1903)

"The Shadow and the Flash" (1903)

"The Leopard Man's Story" (1903)

"Negore the Coward" (1904)

"All Gold Cañon" (1905)

"Love of Life" (1905)

"The Sun-Dog Trail" (1905)

"The Apostate" (1906)

"Up the Slide" (1906)

"Planchette" (1906)

"Brown Wolf" (1906)

"Make Westing" (1907)

"Chased by the Trail" (1907)

"Trust" (1908)

"A Curious Fragment" (1908)

"Aloha Oe" (1908)

"That Spot" (1908)

"The Enemy of All the World" (1908)

"The House of Mapuhi" (1909)

"Good-by, Jack" (1909)

"Samuel" (1909)

"South of the Slot" (1909)

"The Chinago" (1909)

"The Dream of Debs" (1909)

"The Madness of John Harned" (1909)

"The Seed of McCoy" (1909)

"A Piece of Steak" (1909)

"Mauki" (1909)

"The Whale Tooth" (1909)

"Goliath" (1910)

"The Unparalleled Invasion" (1910)

"Told in the Drooling Ward" (1910)

"When the World was Young" (1910)

"The Terrible Solomons" (1910)

"The Inevitable White Man" (1910)

"The Heathen" (1910)

"Yah! Yah! Yah!" (1910)

"By the Turtles of Tasman" (1911)

"The Mexican" (1911)

"War" (1911)

"The Unmasking of the Cad" (1911)

"The Scarlet Plague" (1912)

"The Captain of the Susan Drew" (1912)

"The Sea-Farmer" (1912)

"The Feathers of the Sun" (1912)

"The Prodigal Father" (1912)

"Samuel" (1913)

"The Sea-Gangsters" (1913)

"The Strength of the Strong" (1914)

"Told in the Drooling Ward" (1914)

"The Hussy" (1916)

"Like Argus of the Ancient Times" (1917)

"Jerry of the Islands" (1917)

"The Red One" (1918)

"Shin-Bones" (1918)

"The Bones of Kahekili" (1919)

SHORT STORY COLLECTIONS

Son of the Wolf (1900)

Chris Farrington, Able Seaman (1901)

The God of His Fathers & Other Stories (1901)

Children of the Frost (1902)

The Faith of Men and Other Stories (1904)

Tales of the Fish Patrol (1906)

Moon-Face and Other Stories (1906)

Love of Life and Other Stories (1907)

Lost Face (1910)

South Sea Tales (1911)

When God Laughs and Other Stories (1911)

The House of Pride & Other Tales of Hawaii (1912)

Smoke Bellew (1912)

A Son of the Sun (1912)

The Night Born (1913)

The Strength of the Strong (1914)

The Turtles of Tasman (1916)

The Human Drift (1917)

The Red One (1918)

On the Makaloa Mat (1919)

Dutch Courage and Other Stories (1922)

AUTOBIOGRAPHICAL MEMOIRS

The Road (1907)

The Cruise of the Snark (1911)

John Barleycorn (1913)

NON-FICTION AND ESSAYS

Through the Rapids on the Way to the Klondike (1899)

From Dawson to the Sea (1899)

What Communities Lose by the Competitive System (1900)

The Impossibility of War (1900)

Phenomena of Literary Evolution (1900)

A Letter to Houghton Mifflin Co. (1900)

Husky, Wolf Dog of the North (1900)

Editorial Crimes — A Protest (1901)

Again the Literary Aspirant (1902)

The People of the Abyss (1903)

How I Became a Socialist (1903)

The War of the Classes (1905)

The Story of an Eyewitness (1906)

A Letter to Woman's Home Companion (1906)

Revolution, and other Essays (1910)

Mexico's Army and Ours (1914)

Lawgivers (1914)

Our Adventures in Tampico (1914)

Stalking the Pestilence (1914)

The Red Game of War (1914)

The Trouble Makers of Mexico (1914)

With Funston's Men (1914)

POETRY

A Heart (1899)

Abalone Song (1913)

And Some Night (1914)

Ballade of the False Lover (1914)

Cupid's Deal (1913)

Daybreak (1901)

Effusion (1901)

George Sterling (1913)

Gold (1915)

He Chortled with Glee (1899)

He Never Tried Again (1912)

His Trip to Hades (1913)

Homeland (1914)

Hors de Saison (1913)

If I Were God (1899)

In a Year (1901)

In and Out (1911)

Je Vis en Espoir (1897)

Memory (1913)

Moods (1913)

My Confession (1912)

My Little Palmist (1914)

Of Man of the Future (1915)

Oh You Everybody's Girl (19)

On the Face of the Earth You are the One (1915)

Rainbows End (1914)

Republican Rallying Song (1916)

Sonnet (1901)

The Gift of God (1905)

The Klondyker's Dream (1914)

The Lover's Liturgy (1913)

The Mammon Worshippers (1911)

The Republican Battle-Hymn (1905)

The Return of Ulysses (1915)

The Sea Sprite and the Shooting Star (1916)

The Socialist's Dream (1912)

The Song of the Flames (1903)

The Way of War (1906)

The Worker and the Tramp (1911)

Tick! Tick! Tick! (1915)

Too Late (1912)

Weasel Thieves (1913)

When All the World Shouted my Name (1905)

Where the Rainbow Fell (1902)

Your Kiss (1914)

PLAYS

Theft (1910)

Daughters of the Rich: A One Act Play (1915)

The Acorn Planter: A California Forest Play (1916)